CW01086381

The Trophy Room

Barry Litherland

Published by Barry Litherland, 2021.

THE TROPHY ROOM

First edition. March 31, 2021.

Written by Barry Litherland.

Chapter 1

If you climb off the D75 bus where the main road swings right to bypass Grantley, you will see, on the opposite side of the road, beyond the four lanes of the dual carriageway, a narrow lane rising sharply through trees. The trees are largely ancient oak, beech and elm, although there are more recent plantings, too: rowans and silver birches, near the roadside verge. These huddled trees have some minor significance in the story I'm here to relate, but for the moment it is simply necessary to pass them in order to reach three landmarks which play a major part.

The first of these is the old clifftop castle, a ruin now but once of some importance in the local area. It rises on a vertiginous sea cliff from where an observer can scrutinise a hundred and eighty degrees of sea before finally resting their eyes on the harbour town of Grantley to the north. The older settlement of Leybury lies to the south, now no more than a cluster of cottages set, as if posing for a photograph, around a tiny harbour. Around this defensive line of tightly packed fishermen's dwellings, a sprawl of modern housing gathers like an invading force. The old village is under siege.

The second landmark is the nineteenth century watchtower to the north of Leybury, perched on a grassy cliff, and peering out through narrow windows over the open sea. Beyond it, the horizon hovers, as if suspended; a tightrope for ships to balance on. Over that first horizon, lies nothing but more sea and more horizons, and a distant ocean of snow and ice.

The third landmark is Leybury Grange, an old house with a disturbing history. Secure behind the protective barrier of oaks and sycamores, by which we passed, it has provided sanctuary to a succession of dubious owners who would have served their communities better by never being born. It also provided accommodation of various sorts for a number of poor unfortunates who served or were imprisoned there. It is said to be haunted.

At present, it is owned by Mr Rupert Fitzwilliam, a man in his mid-thirties who retired from public office after a scandal involving the teenage daughter of a minor royal, a footman and a ceremonial carriage.

But more of Rupert Fitzwilliam later.

Nobody else will disembark at your chosen stop. The road is dangerous here, and the traffic unremitting. You will wait for several minutes before a brief opportunity presents itself to scuttle to the central reservation, where you will stand, sandwiched between four streams of traffic. Another heart-stopping foray will bring you to the far verge, from where you can cry sanctuary to the narrow lane.

When you are fully recovered from the crossing and start to walk up the lane, you will notice how quickly the sound of traffic is left behind. You will have the strange sensation that you are walking not only into the quiet of the countryside but also back into the depths of time.

A chill will ripple though you, which will grow to a tremor as you pass beneath the trees which loiter round the ancient Grange like suspicious old men. You will be relieved when you emerge from their gloom, and take a path through fields of dairy cattle, before reaching open moorland. There, the cry of gulls and the freshness of the air will announce the proximity of the sea, the cliffs and the ruined castle.

A mile to your left, tucked discreetly behind low dunes and adjacent to a sandy beach, lies a holiday caravan park. Halfway between the caravan park and Leybury, the watchtower stands guard.

It is mid-October, when the days are shortening and there are fewer people about than in the height of summer. But there are still many visitors willing to take advantage of reduced tariffs and greater solitude. Frank and Janice, and Janice's son, Danny, are among those currently residing in a holiday caravan, enjoying a late season break.

We will hear more of them shortly.

But first...

Chapter 2

A young boy approaches the watchtower along the cliff path. He is alone and intent on some game which absorbs all his attention. He swerves and circles, arms outstretched, and accompanies each move with excited chatter. He is about ten and has a mop of untidy red hair, and a rash of freckles.

So intent is he on his game that he doesn't see the low, wooden door of the watchtower open, and a man step out, at least not until it is too late. When the boy does notice, he pauses, and his hands drop to his side. His shoulders hunch, and he stands there, waiting for the man to approach. The look of fear on the boy's face seems to entertain the newcomer, because he offers an unpleasant smile—close to a sneer—and takes up a position blocking the path. The man is gaunt, with a sickly complexion, and his clothes hang loose, like they were intended for a stockier man. He's in his mid-twenties but has a pinched, shifty look, and a hollow face which makes him look ten years older. There's something cold about him, too, and a glint of malice lingers around his mouth and eyes. He has the air of someone who would pull the wings off a butterfly, just for fun.

The boy senses the danger and looks around for other walkers, but it's early and it's October, and there is nobody else out. They are alone on the cliff.

'Are you following me, Sammy?' The man's voice curls around him like a snake, then it darts a poisoned tongue. 'Because if you are—'

'I'm not. I didn't know you were here. How could I?'

The man eyes him up and down. His stare lingers until the boy trembles, and looks away.

'You know I don't like people knowing my business.' His lips curl, and his eyes are cruel. He's enjoying himself.

'I don't want to know your business.'

'So, what are you doing here, Sammy, if you're not following your Uncle Dominic?'

'Nothing. Just playing.'

'On your own as usual. Got no friends, eh, Sammy?'

'I've got friends.' Sammy's voice is sullen. He looks down and drags a foot across the grass. 'Lots of them. They live in the town.'

'No, you haven't. They think you're weird.'

'Do not.'

'You *are* weird, talking to yourself, playing on your own.'

'There are no other kids in the village, just old people.'

'No wonder they stay away from you, Sammy No-mates.'

Sammy bites his lip, and holds back tears. Dominic scents victory.

'You want to come and see what I've been up to, Sammy? You want to come in the watchtower, and I'll show you? Just you and me, eh?'

Sammy takes a step back, and then another.

'No. I told you, I don't want to know.'

Dominic smiles, like a predator eyeing its prey.

'I'm going home now,' Sammy says.

Dominic steps forward, slowly, casually. Then he darts.

'Boo!'

He laughs as Sammy stumbles back, and falls on the grass and heather.

'You haven't seen me, Sammy. You remember that. If you know what's good for you.'

Sammy scrambles to his feet, and nods.

'I haven't seen you.'

'You know what'll happen if you talk.'

Sammy's face is pale, his lips tremble. He runs a sleeve across his eyes. Dominic watches him: the same narrow smile, the same cold eyes.

'Well, off you go then,' he says, and he shoos Sammy with a wave of his hand, suddenly bored. He points towards the caravan park, away from the village.

Sammy stumbles forward, then runs down the path. Behind him he can hear a cold, grating laugh, like someone crunching gravel.

Chapter 3

Sammy's route takes him down a grassy path towards a shingle and sand beach, where the caravan park nestles behind low dunes. He had planned to weave through the park on a tarmac road between closely packed holiday statics, and pick up the footpath at the other side, but meeting Dominic spoiled that. Now, he wants nothing more than the solitude of the beach, the rigour of a slippery climb over rocks at the base of the cliff, and home. He won't go to the castle today.

I have got friends.

He runs fast over the sand, and throws punches at the air in front of him; solid, heavy punches right in Dominic's face.

Take that, you bastard.

A small victory for a young boy.

I have got lots of friends. More than you've got, because nobody likes you, because you're a bastard.

An uppercut and a hook, and down goes Dominic. Sammy pauses, and looks down at him. Then he levels a sandy kick at him for good measure, before placing a conqueror's foot on his chest.

You can't make me do anything I don't want to. So, go away.

He glances back in case someone heard him, but he has reached the end of the sand, away from the straggle of tourists walking their dogs. He looks ahead to where bedrock gives way to wrinkled, grey ridges of stone. They lie at sharp angles, brittle and scarred, reaching around the headland towards Leybury, and home. Autumn waves roll and heave towards the shore. As they hit the bedrock, they burst and fall all around, throwing white diamonds.

He walks more cautiously now over rocks; mis-shapes of granite, pink and green and grey. He picks up a particularly nice black-and-white pebble, sparkling with tiny specks of silver, and inspects it before putting it in his pocket. Another addition to his collection, displayed on the windowsill in his bedroom.

He reaches a shallow sea cave at the headland, and clambers out along the lines of jagged rock, towards the sea. Further out, it is slippery with green seaweed, so he stops and sits on the rough, barnacled stone.

Far out, a yacht with blue-and-white sails glides, swan-like, without haste. Closer in lies the pink buoy—Dominic's buoy—the place he sails out to every couple of weeks.

Bastard.

Sammy goes with him. He has to because Dominic says it's better to have him along, even though he hates him.

It stops folk prying. Just me and my fake nephew going for a sail, innocent like.

Bastard. Bastard.

His dad doesn't like him going with Dominic, but he lets him go because Dominic makes him.

Sammy picks up a stone and flings it as far as he can. It falls unremarkably, lost beneath the surface of the sea. He has just picked another stone when he hears a sound behind him; shoes scraping on rock, someone clambering out.

A boy, about his own age, but dark haired and thin, balances on the rock, and stares at him.

'Hi,' he calls.

'Hi.' Sammy turns away, and stares out at the sea. He picks up another piece of stone, and throws it.

'I'm Jason,' the boy says.

'I'm Sammy.'

'You live round here?'

Sammy glances again, just briefly, then back to the sea.

'In the village. My dad has a boat. He's a fisherman.'

'Cool. I'm on holiday in the caravan park, with my mum and Frank. Frank's my step-dad. Kind of. My real dad lives in Blackpool.'

'I didn't see you. We're you in the cave?'

'Yeah, just messing. Pretending and things. There was a girl here yester-day. And today, there's you. Were you out there on your dad's boat yesterday?'

'Yes, we were checking the pots.'

'I saw you. The girl said you go out with your dad a lot. She said we should be holiday friends, since we're both on our own.'

'I'm not on my own. I've got lots of friends.' Dominic's words burn into him again like hot needles. 'What did the girl look like? Maybe she's from my school.'

'About nine or ten, with dark hair and brown eyes. She was kind of dis-tant, like she was only half here. I think she must live nearby because she knew a lot about the village.'

'Maybe she's comes on holiday. Some people come every year.'

'She was a bit weird.'

They are quiet for a moment.

'I've got to go.' Sammy says. He hesitates. 'See you around, maybe.'

'Yeah, see you around.'

Chapter 4

'Where's Jason?'

Frank Miller passes a hand over a tousled head, and yawns. He drops on a bench seat beneath the large end-window of the holiday caravan, and picks up a *Daily Mail* from the table top. His dressing gown falls open to reveal a surprisingly muscular stomach which he scratches. 'Is that a pot of tea you've made, pet? I could murder a cup.'

'Our Jason brought me a cup before he went out. He was up early.' Janice Farley pours a mug, and adds three sugars. 'He said he was going exploring. He's a good boy, you know, deep down. He'll come around eventually. You see if he doesn't.'

'He's had nearly a year to come around. I hardly get a word out of him.' Frank drops the paper heavily on the coarse fabric of the bench seat: silver and yellow flecks on a grey base. 'Damn it, I've tried hard enough. Rugby, go-karting, and now this holiday.'

Janice carries the mug across, and sits down beside him. 'Of course you have. Nobody could've tried harder. This holiday will sort him out, just see. A couple of weeks together in the caravan, it's just what we need.'

'I hope you're right. It's a long time, cooped up with a boy who looks like he wants to spit at me all the time.'

'It was hard for him, his dad leaving like that. He worshipped him, you know.'

'He's better off without him.'

'He'll see that soon enough. Vince will let him down once too often, just watch.'

Frank slips an arm round her waist. 'Well, I'll be here when he does. I'll not let him down, nor you neither. You've been through enough.' He pecks her cheek, and then frees his arm to consult his watch. 'I hope he doesn't have us waiting here all day.'

'He'll be back soon. His stomach will bring him, same as ever.' Janice sips from the plain, white mug—a job-lot from the market at Grantley, she'd said, when she first saw them—and laughs to herself. 'That was a good night, wasn't it? Worth a bit of a headache.'

Frank laughs, and rubs his head.

'I'm supposed to stay in trim, what with the job interview and everything. Still, it was worth it. You were on good form with the karaoke, everyone said so, even that old bird with the tweed skirt. She said you could've been a professional.'

Janice smiles, a little wearily. She looks tired. 'You didn't get the chance back then. Soon as I reached sixteen it was out to work. That's how it was, especially where I lived.'

'Never mind, pet, it's not all it's cracked up to be. Fame.'

'I'd have given it a bloody good try.' She pulls away, and pours another cup. 'But I've got Jason, and I've got you, and a nice house. What more could a girl want?'

The door bursts open, and Jason leaps into the van, vaulting the aluminium steps outside. He's breathing heavily, and his face is flushed.

'I ran all the way along the beach, mum. I thought I was late for lunch, so I ran all the way.' He flops on the seat beside Janice. 'I'm the fastest runner in my school. Mr Caine said so.'

'I'll have to have a race with you, won't I?' Frank pats him on the back but snatches back his hand when he feels the boy stiffen against him. 'What do you say, shall we have a race? See if you can beat the best scrum half, and the fastest policeman, in the north?'

Jason shrugs, and doesn't turn around. 'Where are we going for lunch, Mum?'

'What do you fancy? A burger? Fish and chips?'

'Fish and chips would be nice, wouldn't it, Jason?'

Frank stands, and walks across to the table. He picks up a couple of plates and cups, and takes them to the kitchen. Stainless steel sink and a cheap, plastic drainer. First thing Janice did when she arrived: washed all the pots and disinfected the sink and drainer. Just like Janice, that was.

You can't be too careful. Who knows what the last folk were like?

He drops the pots in the sink, and walks back.

'I'll do them after lunch.'

He sits down, and puts his arm round Janice's shoulder.

'I want a burger,' Jason says, without looking at him.

'A takeaway, eh? Good idea. I'll go and get them. You want to come, Jason?' Frank picks up his wallet from the table, and heads to the door.

'Can we eat in the Club House Café, Mum?'

Jason throws a half-glance at Frank, which he tries to ignore.

Janice reaches back to pick up a light coat from the bench seat.

'Why not? Café, it is.'

She glances at Frank, but doesn't speak.

Jason opens the door, and jumps down.

'I'll save you a seat, Mum,' he says, as he disappears, like a tormenting elf, along the roadway.

'If I said black that boy would say white,' Frank says.

'Just give him time.'

'He's had enough bloody time.' Frank pauses to collect himself, feeling like a sheet of paper caught in a sudden squall. 'Yes. I know, I know. I said as long as it takes, and I mean it. I'm here to stay.'

Chapter 5

After he leaves Sammy, Dominic walks back to the village and up a narrow, stone path to a cramped cottage. It is one of many which line the harbour side, each with its gable end to the sea, hunched and braced in readiness for the next storm. It is newly painted and there are flower boxes under the windows, and hanging baskets bracketed to the walls.

The path leads upwards, in uneven steps, towards the top of the village, where newer houses have been constructed for an expanding population looking for a retirement home near the sea.

Dominic pauses by a small window in the cottage, and peers inside.

'In the kitchen, maybe,' he says.

He passes through a gate beside a stone outbuilding, leaving it open behind him, and crosses a paved yard to the kitchen door.

'More flowers,' he says, noting with distaste the colourful pots beside the door. 'He hasn't two coins to rub together, and he buys plants.'

He shakes his head. Something that might be mistaken for a smile escapes his narrow lips.

'Anyone home?'

He opens the door, and steps inside. The smell of freshly baked bread greets him, but it has little effect on Dominic. He brushes it away like a mosquito, and speaks to the woman standing beside a long, oak table, adding the final touches to a number of confectionaries laid out before her.

'Is Richard about?'

The woman looks up, her eyes hostile, her body tense. Her round face, which looks like the natural refuge for a smile, is taut, like a stretched tarpaulin. She hesitates for a moment, and then her plump arms resume their work.

'He's out. Down at the boat, I think. Or maybe at The Harbour Inn. Why do you want him?'

'I need the boat tomorrow.'

'He was going out to the pots, first thing.'

Dominic shakes his head. 'Not any more, Maggie. I'm going out at eight. Sammy's coming with me.'

He reaches a hand across towards some biscuits on a cooling tray, pauses when he sees her expression change, and her body stiffen. He takes one anyway, laughing softly.

'Always a nice welcome here, Maggie.'

He knows his words are like cigarette burns on her skin and it makes him laugh all the more. He watches her like she's an animal in an experiment. What will she do if he keeps pushing and pushing? What can she do? Nothing.

'I don't like you involving the boy. You know that.'

'He doesn't mind. He's got nothing else to do. Besides, it keeps people from prying.'

'You'll push us too far, one day.' Maggie catches him with a sharp look.

'You shouldn't threaten me, Maggie. If it wasn't for me...' He casually waves a hand to indicate the room, and the house.

'We should never have got involved. We didn't know.'

'You guessed, though. Didn't you, Maggie? You still took the money.'

'We didn't know.'

Maggie's hands clench the table. Her eyes flash. For a moment, she and Dominic are locked in a battle of wills. It doesn't last long. Maggie picks up some oven gloves, and turns to the stove, as Dominic heads to the door, a smile of victory on his lips.

'Tell Sammy to be there by eight.'

The door closes behind him. Maggie sets hot loaves on a cooling tray on the table. She stops, picks up the empty glass she uses to cut pastry circles, and throws it against the door, where it explodes. The pieces are caught in the air, and held for a moment like splinters of ice, only to fall and melt to nothing.

'Damn you, Dominic.'

Chapter 6

Richard Trevelyan wipes his hands on an oily, tartan cloth, and looks down into the engine of *The Lovely Maggie*. Richard has a mop of reddish hair and startling blue eyes set in a round, freckled face. He looks like a man whose calm and affectionate nature restrains a lively temper; a racehorse at the starting gate.

'You'll outlast us all,' he says to the boat, and taps the steel engine casing with a look of satisfaction. 'You just need a bit of looking after as you get older, same as the rest of us.'

He shuts the casing with care and climbs out onto the deck, closing the hatch, and padlocking it behind him.

'Twenty years we've been together, me and you and Maggie. Then along comes Sammy and there's three of us, a proper family.' He raises his head, and looks across the harbour to another craft, red and white, with wooden bench seats, and a central wheelhouse. 'And then *Sammy's Pride* came along for the tourists.' A quick look back towards the harbour. 'Not that there's many of those around this morning. Maybe later.'

Someone walks along the harbour towards him. Another fisherman, heading to a boat moored just beyond *The Lovely Maggie*.

'How's the world treating you this morning, Richard?' Unshaven, and with hands as coarse and wrinkled as his face, the newcomer stops for a moment. He runs a sandpapered palm over his greying hair.

'Same as ever, Frederick. Flowers in one hand, and a brick in the other.'

Frederick's laugh is like a low growl.

''And how's *The Lovely Maggie*?'

'Which one? Be precise, Fred.'

Frederick's laugh broadens. 'Both, either.'

14

'Both tip-top. Maggie's at home, baking, so I'm keeping a low profile.'

'Out here with your other woman?'

'Aye, indeed. This one's getting on a bit, though she won't admit it.'

'Needs a bit of attention, eh? I see you've been working.' He nods towards the oily hands and forearms. 'Dominic was looking for you. He was heading for The Harbour Inn. He said if I saw you, I was to tell you.'

He can't restrain a momentary look of distaste, as if he's discovered half a slug on a lettuce leaf.

Richard's face clouds. 'That man's nothing but trouble. I wonder what he wants now.'

'Nothing good. I don't know how you put up with him.'

'No choice. I made a mistake. I trusted the bastard.' He waves a hand towards *The Lovely Maggie* and *Sammy's Pride*, and the harbour-side. 'He's got a hand in everything, him and that other bastard at the Grange. If I'd known then what I knew soon after—'

'Aye, aye.' Frederick pats his arm. 'You weren't to know. Hindsight's a wonderful thing.'

'He's got my balls in a vice and he likes nothing better than to tighten it.'

'Aye, aye...'

'Still, no point in wishing for what I can't have. I'd better see what he wants.'

'And I'll get on. Lots to do this morning. Have you got a trip this afternoon?'

'If I've got customers.' Richard looks towards the harbour side, its row of hunched cottages, its narrow paths, the road leading round a tight corner past the shop and café, out to the bypass, and the rest of the world. A few holiday-makers take advantage of the clearing sky and late-morning sunshine. 'The weather's picking up, so maybe.'

The Harbour Inn is quiet. A few tourists, couples mainly, are seated over sandwiches, cakes, and coffee. Trevor Wales, landlord, leans on the bar. His eyes scan the room but return, as if drawn there, to one figure, seated in a quiet corner. Dominic leans back on his chair, his legs outstretched.

'He's had two already,' Trevor says, as Richard approaches the bar. 'He'd better not think he's in for a session. I'm having none of it. There are few enough tourists about at the moment, as it is.'

'All you need is the other one.'

'Don't even mention it. When the two of them get together... Business is hard enough without them, driving folk away.'

Richard taps the polished surface of the bar.

'I've been summoned. I'd better go and see what he wants. The sooner I see him, the sooner I can get away from him.'

'You want a drink to wash away the taste?'

'Just a half. I'm hoping for a trip this afternoon.'

'Can you be done for being drunk in charge of an inshore vessel?'

'I don't plan on finding out.'

Dominic makes no effort to shift his position as Richard walks over, glass in hand. Only his eyes—grey holes in an empty face—follow him until he sits down.

'Have you not brought me a refill?' he drawls, enjoying the discomfort he inspires, and savouring the power he wields, like something sweet on his tongue. 'I want to get a head start, before Rupert arrives.'

Richard didn't disguise the look of disgust.

'Rupert Fitzwilliam?'

'He'll be wanting his money. Have you got it?'

'It's gone through the bank.'

'You're a month behind. He'll want that in cash.'

Richard's eyes flash, and his lips narrow. Maggie would have known the signs. Dominic, if he knows them, chooses to ignore them. He laughs softly, spitting contempt like poison.

Richard reaches a hand into a deep pocket, and draws out an envelope. 'That's half. The weather's been against us recently. There's not the tourists.'

Dominic takes the envelope, glances, then leaves it on the table top, as if it is beneath his dignity to check it. He looks around. 'This place is dead. Nobody comes here anymore. Grantley takes all the tourist traffic.'

'They'll be here when the sun shines. There's nowhere better, not even Grantley.'

Dominic's sneering laugh is like vinegar on a wound. Richard's hand tightens on his glass. Dominic leans forward and takes a long draft from his own. 'Another here, Trevor,' he calls. 'Richard's paying.'

The look Trevor bestows on his customer is less than convivial, but he reaches for a fresh glass.

Dominic grunts. 'There's another loser. He's spent a fortune on this place. New windows, new carpets, new bar, new kitchen. And for what? He's up to his neck in debt and there are no more customers than there were before.'

'They'll come. The restaurant's busy now, and people like the new windows. You can see out over the harbour.'

'He's a loser,' Dominic says.

Richard finishes his beer and stands up. 'I've got to be going.' He points at the envelope on the table. 'Is that all you wanted?'

'I need the boat tomorrow. Sammy, too.'

'I don't want Sammy involved in any of your dirty business.'

'It's just a quiet sail. Sammy and his Uncle Dom. We'll be back by ten. Besides, you've no choice. Not if you want to keep your boats, and your house. You owe the wrong people.'

'And whose fault is that?' Richard leans forward, his knuckles white on the table.

Dominic leans in to meet him. For a moment, the two men are fixed, face to face, eye to unblinking eye.

'Everything okay?' Trevor pauses and looks over. 'Richard?'

The sound of his name acts like a switch inside Richard. He blinks and steps back, then turns sharply and heads towards the door. He raises a hand towards Trevor, but doesn't stop, not trusting himself to speak.

'Eight o'clock,' Dominic calls after him. 'Tell Sammy to be on time.'

Chapter 7

D o you see that herring gull perched on the harbour rail, its beak wide and its head forward, heckling villagers and tourists alike, and then rising contemptuously away? Watch as it rises to hang in the air on those loose wings? See how its tail rudder turns and flicks, as if a key turns in its ignition; and see how those wings, muscle-driven, sweep once, twice, as the clutch engages and the sleek form eases away. Maybe it's not the Peregrine Falcon sports model or the Gannet Convertible, but it still has all the power it needs in the engine of that broad chest. A four by four, go-anywhere vehicle, perfectly designed for this terrain.

Do you wish you could fly? That you could relax, raise your arms, feel the air lift you, like a baby from a cot, feel yourself soar and circle higher and higher until, below, the coast stretches for miles and the sea casts restless banks of waves onto the shore, like new settlers searching out new lands?

Inland lie green and yellow fields, separated by lines of mottled hedgerows, sometimes bruised with the red of rowan or rose. And trees. Old soldiers dressed in military reds and browns, some hunched in surly groups, others standing proudly, shoulders back; a military bearing. And in the centre of a pasture, a solitary oak, a memorial where walkers pause to remember, and reminisce.

In the distance, the town of Grantley settles on a bank of mist, and rests its head against the cushion of the sea.

There is little movement below you. A few human dust specks scurrying from point to point, a car parking, a van departing. Going somewhere, going nowhere. Everything is trapped, as if painted there, waiting for the sweep of a brush to pass over it, preparing the canvas for something new.

The gull wheels and, with a few pulses from those broad wings, draws away into the distance, while you hover, eyes fixed like a kestrel. And you watch.

You see Richard Trevelyan emerge from The Harbour Inn, and walk across to the harbour. He pauses by the rail, beside the concrete steps which lead down to a tiny beach of sand. He grips the rail, and he stares down at the harbour, deep in thought. He is fixed there, as permanent as stone, as other people, transients with whom this story has no concern, pass by.

Someone calls a greeting. He raises a head and then a hand. Frederick, on his way back to his cottage. Richard says something as he looks out towards Sammy's Pride. Maybe it's about the afternoon's trip along the coast. A brief exchange of words, and Frederick moves on.

A blue sports car passes, and pulls up outside The Harbour Inn and a man—tall, well-dressed, an air of arrogance hanging from him like an ermine cloak—opens the door, and steps out. He pauses, sees Richard, and despatches a surly nod. Richard nods back, unwillingly it seems.

There's a tension which fills the space between them and, through it, something passes like an eddy in the currents of air. The newcomer remains still for a moment, then smiles as if pondering a private joke. He turns, and walks towards the inn. He pauses at the door, where he turns again, and looks back. Richard has looked away; his grip on the rail has tightened. He stares at the harbour, holding his thoughts tight in his skull. Then, without looking back, he walks fifty yards along the road, and turns up the steps beside his cottage.

The man enters the inn.

Richard pauses, leans forward to smell the flowers, strokes a petal and a leaf. His shoulders relax, he practises a smile, and disappears inside the gate.

'Maggie?' you hear him call, as if to another bird on the shore.

It is hard, from up here, to imagine the thoughts which course through him like a wrecking ball.

Drop lower now, settle on the rail, and watch, watch.

Chapter 8

The sash windows of the Trevelyans' cottage look out to the side and front over flower boxes which still carry late blooms. Inside, the cluttered trappings of a home: whorled shells brought up in nets, driftwood pieces in intricate shapes, an old oil lamp, a mirror and a homely sofa and armchairs with moulded hollows to fit familiar shapes.

'It's okay, I'll go.' Sammy sits on the sofa, stroking the brown-and-white terrier which lies across his lap. The dog looks up at him, as if recognising in that voice the fear it tries to hide. 'I'll come straight home soon as we get back.'

'What does he do out there? Every few weeks, it's the same.' Maggie stands up to fetch a magazine from the table: last week's Sunday Supplement.

'We're best not knowing. It's not our business.'

'Sammy is our business.' Maggie leans over the sofa back, and put her arms around Sammy's neck. 'I don't like it.'

'It's okay, Mum. I just sit at the prow where people can see me, and then I go in the wheelhouse when we reach the buoy. I never see what he does.'

He doesn't tell them how he'd been curious once—just once—and peeped out of the door when Dominic was raising something from below the buoy. He didn't see what it was because Dominic saw him, and grabbed him by the throat. He pushed him back into the wheelhouse, and twisted his arm up his back. He pushed him face-down over the console. Then he hurt him, really bad.

'Straight home as soon as you get back, then,' Richard says.

Maggie shakes her head. 'One of these days that man will pay for all this.'

It's always *one of these days* with his mum and dad. They never do anything. They never stand up to Dominic, no matter what he does or says. They just aren't like that. Sammy loves that about them. He hates it, too.

Sammy doesn't see Yapps follow him onto the boat, not until it is too late. Yapps is their brown-and-white terrier. She must have sneaked on when Dominic was at the stern, and Sammy was unfastening the ropes which secure the boat to the harbour. She lies down at the prow, behind a sheet of tarpaulin, and Sammy only notices her when he goes to sit there, same as usual.

This is not good news. They don't like each other, Dominic and Yapps. When she sees him, her lips curl into a warning snarl and so do his. Sometimes he levels a kick at her, and she yelps. But that just makes her worse. Sammy glances back to see if Dominic has noticed.

'What are you doing here?' Sammy whispers, stroking her ears. 'You know what he's like. We'll both be in trouble if he sees you.'

Sammy sits with his back to the prow so he can watch Dominic, and keep Yapps hidden, held down behind the tarpaulin. It isn't her fault. She often goes out on the boat with his dad and him. She goes on the tourist boat, too. The visitors love her, and fuss her. Some regulars bring biscuits, just for her. Everyone loves her; except Dominic.

'He's in a filthy mood, same as ever,' Sammy whispers. 'You've got to stay low and keep quiet, Yapps.'

Easier said than done when you're a restless, young terrier, made up mostly of squirm and wriggle. But everything goes well until they reach the buoy, and Dominic eases the engine. He sticks his head out of the wheelhouse; thin and grey and lined like a month-old turnip. That's what Sammy thinks, but he only tells Yapps.

'Get yourself down here, Sammy,' Dominic says. 'Be quick about it.'

Yapps growls deep in her throat, and her hackles rise like the bristles on a coarse brush.

Sammy calms her, talking gently, and watches as Dominic moves to the stern and fixes his eyes on the buoy.

'Stay,' he tells Yapps, pointing a finger behind the tarpaulin, but he knows it's a futile instruction. Yapps is too excited. Her tail is wagging like a frenzied metronome.

He clambers to his feet and hurries to the wheelhouse. Yapps follows, close at his heels, sharing in the game. He closes the door, and breathes with momentary relief. But now he is caught in a trap. There is no way he can leave the wheelhouse until Dominic comes back and, when Dominic comes back, Yapps is sure to growl and snarl and bark. He looks around. This is urgent. But he knows already there is nowhere to hide her. He'll just have to keep a tight hold and drag her out quickly, get her back to the prow, and away from Dominic. If he's quick and Yapps causes no trouble, they'll be okay. Maybe.

The door opens and Dominic stands there, blocking out the sun, and blocking the way out, too, like some troll on a fairytale bridge. Yapps responds predictably, snarling and barking. She tugs and wriggles; it's like trying to hold a lubricated eel, and it's only a second before she breaks free of Sammy's hold on her.

'I told you never to bring that fucking dog.' Dominic kicks out at Yapps, who jumps at him, snapping at his leg.

'I didn't bring her. She just followed me. I'll take her down the front. She'll be no trouble.'

Dominic levels another kick which Yapps evades, but then he bends forward and grabs her by the scruff of the neck. She yelps and screams and wriggles as he carries her out onto the deck, but his hold is too tight.

'Don't hurt her.' Sammy runs out after him, and grabs his arm. 'I'll keep her out of the way, honest. I'll make sure she never comes again.'

Dominic holds the squirming dog at arm's length. His face breaks into an ugly sneer.

'I've got a better idea,' he says.

He swings his arm back, and flings Yapps into the sea. She disappears beneath the surface and is lost from sight behind a wave. He turns, and strides back to the wheelhouse, dusting his hands. The door closes behind him, and the engine rumbles into life.

Sammy stands looking out, sobbing, his face pale, his mind unable to grasp what has happened.

'Yapps!'

The little dog emerges for a moment between two waves.

'YAPPS!'

She hears him and turns, and paddles towards him. For a moment Sammy feels a warm flicker of hope; but it dies like a gutted candle when the engine roars and white foam churns, and the boat moves towards the harbour. Through the glass of the wheelhouse window, Sammy sees a strange look on Dominic's face. He'll never forget that look, not ever. He seems pleased, proud of himself, like he's shown the world who is in charge. He even smiles.

Sammy turns back, and stares out over the stern, but Yapps is floundering behind them; a small, dark dot disappearing into the watery distance. Inconsequential, lonely. Sammy's tears flow, and he sobs uncontrollably. He can do nothing but watch.

'Yapps...'

Far away on the shore, outside the sea cave, someone else is watching.

Jason. The boy from the caravan park.

Behind him, on the cliff edge, stands a girl. She too is watching. It is as if, even over that distance, their eyes lock.

Chapter 9

'So, who's this girl you're meeting, eh?' Frank winks at Janice, and nods at Jason. 'Looks like Jason's got himself a holiday romance, Janice. What do you say, Jason? Do we get to meet her?'

Jason ignores him.

'Can I go, Mum? I said I'd meet her at the cave.'

'How romantic.' Frank laughs. 'Is he blushing, Jan? I bet he's blushing.'

Jason isn't blushing. The pink glow which suffuses his face has a different cause.

'Leave the boy alone, Frank.' Janice can see what Frank can't. She flashes a warning look but Frank is enjoying himself, and doesn't see.

'When are you meeting her, love?' Janice turns back to Jason.

'She said nine o'clock so we can watch Sammy's boat.'

'Sammy?'

'The boy I met yesterday. I told you. The girl said we're going to be friends.'

'Ooh, a love triangle. Mind he doesn't run off with her, Jason.' Frank laughs, and nudges Jason's shoulder.

It is too much for Jason. He spins around, screaming, his temper gone, his blood pulsing, his heart racing. Tears, too. He hates that. He always cries when he loses his temper.

'Leave me alone. Just go away and leave me alone. I hate you.'

Frank just hasn't seen it coming, and he's bewildered, and shocked. He looks at Janice for support, but she just glares at him.

'What did I say? I was only teasing. Come on, Jason, I was only joking with you.'

'I wish you'd go away and leave us alone. You spoil everything.' Jason raises his clenched fists as if he is about to beat them down on Frank, but then he turns aside, flings himself on the window seat, and buries his head. Muffled sobs cling to the air around him.

Frank looks at Janice again. He is pale, and his hands are trembling. 'I didn't mean any harm,' he tries to explain.

'You and your big mouth.' Janice sits down beside Jason, and lays a calming hand across his shoulder, but he shrugs her away. 'I tried to warn you, Frank.'

Frank's face is ashen. He reaches a hand towards the sobbing boy, and then draws it back. No point asking for more trouble.

'I'm sorry, Jason. I didn't mean to upset you. It'll be nice for you to have a friend or two. It'll make up for... well, you know... at school and all that...'

Jason sits up and turns, his eyes burning, tears flowing, his cheeks glowing red. His temper, not easily restrained, has burst its banks, and floods out across the room.

'I've got friends. I've got lots of friends. You don't know anything about me. I wish you'd die.'

'I just meant it hadn't been easy for you—'

'For God's sake, shut up Frank.' Janice interrupts him. 'Talk about digging a hole for yourself and jumping in it. You know what a temper he's got. Just go out. You're making things worse staying here. Go for a walk for ten minutes 'til I calm him down.'

Frank looks at her, and then at Jason. He's about to speak but thinks better of it, grabs his coat, and heads for the door.

'Whatever it takes,' he says. 'But to say he wants me dead—'

'He doesn't mean it. It's just his temper.'

Frank slams the door behind him.

'I hate him,' Jason says. 'He spoils everything. I want him to go away. I never want to see him again. Not ever.'

He beats his fists against the seat back. Maggie grips him, holding him firm. 'Now, that's enough, Jason. Frank didn't mean any harm. It was just a bit of silly teasing. He should know better. But so should you. Fancy saying you wish he was dead. That's awful.'

'Well, I do. My dad will never come back while he's here.'

Janice pulls him in until he's facing her. His body is tense, uncompliant, his head low. He sniffs and drags a sleeve across his eyes.

'Now, let's get this straight, once and for all. Jason, look at me.' She waits. Her voice grows stern. 'I said, look at me.' Jason looks up slowly, unwillingly. 'What happened between me and your dad was nothing to do with Frank. I didn't even know him then. What happened was our fault, me and your dad. Especially your dad.'

Jason is sullen, silent.

'And don't you dare defend him. You're ten now. You're old enough to face up to the truth. Your dad was too fond of his fists, too fond by half. I put up with it as long as I could but when he started on you—'

'It was my fault. I wound him up. I was bad.'

'No.' Janice shakes her head, and grips him even tighter. 'No, he's a grown man. You're just a boy. It was never your fault. Don't you ever say that. You hear me?'

He nods.

'Look at me and say it. I want to hear it.'

'It wasn't my fault.'

'No, it wasn't. And it wasn't Frank's, either. And don't go thinking your dad doesn't love you, because he does. He just has a temper, see, and he can't keep it under control. He's always sorry, after. But folk can't live like that, Jason.'

'Am I like that? I mean, my temper.'

'No, you're not.'

'But, school. I got suspended and I've no friends, and Mrs Barker says—'

'Mrs Barker!' Janice scoffs. 'What does she know?'

'She says—'

'I don't care what she says. Just wait 'til after the holidays. You'll be with Mr Caine. He'll be better, just you see. He likes you, doesn't he?'

Jason nods. 'Because he's in charge of the cross-country team and the football.'

'There you are, then.'

'I'm good at running. I'm the fastest.'

'I know, love. I know. Now, wipe your face before Frank gets back, eh? He's a good man, you know, and he cares for you.'

Jason nods.

'You'll tell him you're sorry, then?'

He nods again.

'And then you can go and meet your friend. What's her name again?'

'She's called Molly. She's nine.'

'Then you can go and meet Molly. Maybe she's staying on the site, you never know.'

The door opens, and Frank lets himself back in. His head is down, and he looks subdued. Jason looks up.

'I'm sorry,' he says.

'Me, too.' Frank's eyes meet Jason's. 'I shouldn't have teased you. Friends?'

'Yeah, friends.'

Chapter 10

Jason arrives at the cave just before nine. He checks the shoreline and then inside the cave but there is no sign of Molly. He feels a momentary pang of disappointment, but he sits on a flat ridge of bedrock and watches the sea, and waits. A small craft is making its way out towards a pink buoy a few hundred yards off shore.

Sammy.

He stands up, a sudden surge of hope springing like a fountain. Molly said they'd be friends. It was a strange thing to say, but then she was a strange girl. She didn't look different. She was just like other girls he knew: blue jeans, pale green top, longish hair tied back, dark eyes, dark hair. Her accent wasn't local, but then it wasn't anything really; just kind of ordinary, like she could come from anywhere. She was the same height and build as most of the kids her age back at his school: not too thin, not fat, ordinary height, pretty in a sort of girly way.

No, she was just ordinary really, except... well, she had this weird darkness about her, and she stood so still all the time, while inside her there were... forces trying to get out. He could see it in her eyes.

And she spoke like she'd known him forever, like she was his sister or something. It was weird. And she said the strangest things, like how he'd be best friends with Sammy when he didn't even know him, like how he had to be here today at this time, and mustn't be even one minute late.

Make sure you're by the cave at nine o'clock, or I'll go.

And now she hasn't even come.

He turns his attention back to the boat. It is blue-and-white and brown. The brown is rust. As it passes opposite him, he watches to see if Sammy is on board. He sees a movement and then, yes, there's Sammy, sitting near the prow. He waves, but Sammy doesn't see him, and he feels a pang of loneliness, like at school when the other kids play, and he stands by the wall on his own, watching.

He hates those kids, back at school, but he envies them, too. He wants to play, but if they ask him, he swears at them, and he laughs at them and their stupid game. They stop asking, then he gets angry, and he lashes out, hurts people, gets in trouble. Last time, it was Leigh. Leigh said something—he couldn't even remember what it was—but it was like he was holding this volcano deep inside him and it was rumbling and snarling and bubbling and pushing, pushing all the time.

He erupted.

By the time the teachers got there, Leigh was bleeding all over, and Jason was snarling and crying and swearing. Even the teachers couldn't hold him back, until Mr Caine got there and grabbed his arms, and pulled him away. Only Mr Caine could hold him tight enough until he calmed down. Then he saw what he'd done.

The worst thing, though, wasn't the blood, snot and tears on Leigh's face. It was the shock on the faces of the other kids, especially the younger ones. It was how they looked at him. They were scared, like they were gaping at some animal; something not human, something they couldn't understand.

Even now, when he closes his eyes, he can see their faces. They appear in his dreams. They stop him sleeping.

He got suspended of course, and they got some shrink to see him, and talk to him. They even got someone to take him out of class, and work on this thing called *anger management*.

Frank was right. The holiday came just at the right time, before things got even worse.

The boat reaches the buoy, and the engine stops. Jason sees a tall, skinny man come out of the wheelhouse, shoulders hunched, hands trailing at his side. He swings himself down towards the stern. He must shout something over his shoulder, because Sammy clambers to his feet, and stumbles to take up his place in the wheelhouse.

The man roots about near the buoy, turning a handle like he's drawing something up from the sea bed, a lobster pot maybe. He gathers something from it. Not a lobster or a crab, though, because he stuffs it inside his coat before he swings his way back to the wheelhouse. You wouldn't stick a crab or a lobster in your coat.

After that, everything happens quickly. There is a lot of noise. The man shouts and there's another sound, a bit like a dog barking, and Sammy screams and cries out. Jason watches; he daren't move. The man bursts from the wheelhouse; Sammy is behind him, reaching out, grabbing at his arm, trying to hold him back. The man shoves Sammy hard against the door frame, and then he bends his arm, and throws something overboard, something small and dark, something which moves and twists in the air. It hits the water and sinks and then, a moment later, it rises again. Above the cries and angry shouts, Jason hears something else: a terrible, desolate sound. It comes from Sammy. He leans over the side of the boat, his arms stretched out.

Jason scans the sea. Between the waves, the dark object takes shape. It has a head, eyes, ears. A dog! It is trying to reach the boat but there's little hope of that. The man has gone back into the wheelhouse, leaving Sammy howling, and crying out a name, over and over again.

'Yapps!'

The boat moves slowly at first, then accelerates away, back towards the harbour. Jason stands and stares but there is little left to see, just the boat fading into the distance, and the dark, solitary speck of life, swimming and circling helplessly around. And above it all, he still hears Sammy's anguished cry. He thinks he'll hear it forever. And Jason knows, at that moment, that the look on his face is the look he'd seen on the faces of those little children in the playground. It's like he's watching something so far beyond his understanding it terrifies him.

Chapter 11

Frank and Janice walk from the caravan down to the beach. It's a sunny morning and mild despite the late season, and a warm breeze skims the ocean, as if to cool itself before making landfall. They cross a small bank of shingle and head to where low dunes offer softer and warmer sand.

'Here's a nice spot.' Janice inspects the location with the eye of a connoisseur. 'Put the screen up here and it'll be nice and sheltered.'

Frank drops the poles and screen he has carried from the caravan.

Janice nods. 'Near enough to pop back to the van if needs demand.'

While Frank erects the screen, Janice unpacks a beach bag: mats, sunhats, sunglasses, a bottle of wine and two glasses. She looks round, itemising the collection.

'When you go back, you can bring a couple of beach chairs.' She scans the beach. 'Can you see our Jason?'

'No, he must be further on.'

'I hope he's alright. You and your size ten policeman's boots.'

'I'll go and have a look when I've got this thing up. Trust you to choose dry sand. It's like trying to stand a spoon up in gravy.'

'Use stones. There's some back down there.' Janice nods back along the beach.

Frank persists with his spoon and gravy. He scoops away the dry sand until he finds the damp beneath; water in a desert.

'*Eureka.*'

'I what?'

'Wet sand,' he says. 'Be done in minutes now.'

He is about to drop down onto the floral beach mat beside Janice, when they hear someone shouting.

31

'Is that our Jason?' Janice sits up, masking her eyes against the sun, peering towards the headland. 'He sounds upset. Have a look, love.'

Jason is running across the sand, and stumbling as he runs. Even at a distance, Frank knows there's something wrong, something badly wrong.

'You wait there, pet,' he tells Janice. 'I'll sort it.'

He meets Jason halfway back, crying, almost hysterical.

'He threw it off the boat... He just picked it up and threw it... It'll drown...' He grabs Frank's arm, and drags him back towards the headland. 'Quickly, you've got to rescue it.' He bursts into tears.

'Hold up, Jason. Who's thrown what? What's drowning?' Frank holds him back and crouches down beside him; a policeman soothing a distraught witness. Gathering the facts. Calm, methodical. 'Take a deep breath and tell me.'

'Sammy's dog. The man on the boat just threw it in the water. You've got to come.' He wipes a sandy arm across his eyes. 'Please, Frank.'

'Show me.'

'He just sailed away like he'd done nothing. He didn't care. And Sammy was screaming and screaming.'

The headland is empty; just the same diamond spray, the same dark sea and, far out, the pink buoy. The boat has gone. Bare, black rocks, covered here and there with slimy seaweed and fissured with pools, stretch to the edge of a dark sea.

'Careful now, it's slippery.'

Frank edges his way closer to the sea. He pauses and scans the waves.

'Can you see it?' Jason stands beside him, no tears now, but a wild desperation in his eyes.

'No.'

'Has it drowned?'

'I don't know, Jason. How far out was it?'

'By the pink buoy.'

'That's a long way, Jason, even for a good swimmer. A little dog... I don't know. And even if it did...' He points to where the rocks end abruptly, several feet above the water. 'The tide's only just turning. Poor thing would never get up there.'

Jason is sobbing again now. 'Will you go and look?'

Frank eyes the slippery expanse between him and the end of the rock. 'It's like a bloody skating rink.'

'*Please.*'

Frank takes a deep breath. 'If I break my neck, tell your mum it was in a good cause. She'll give me hell if I die and spoil her holiday.' He steps forward, following a fissure in the rock which gives him some purchase, transfers to a barnacled rock, and then back to another fissure. Finally, he gets down on his hands and knees, and crawls over slimy, green seaweed. 'If the guys in the rugby team could see me now...'

He reaches the edge of the rock, and lies down to peer over.

'Nothing,' he shouts back.

'Try further round. Please!'

Frank mutters under his breath as he edges further round, and further round still.

'It's not here, Jason. I'm sorry, son.' He kneels up and looks out. 'My clothes are ruined.' He mumbles something under his breath, best not heard. 'Your mum will have something to say about that when I get back.' He studies the sea, scrutinising the rolling waves. 'Hang on. Wait a minute. What's that?'

'Where? I can't see.'

'Bloody hell.'

'What?'

It's too much for Jason. He speeds across the slippery rocks, following the same route as Frank, arms held wide like a tightrope walker. Frank inches to the edge of the rock. He lies on his stomach, and reaches down.

'I can't reach it,' he gasps. 'It's just too far.'

Beneath them, wild-eyed, barely moving in the swell, the little dog tries, with the dregs of its remaining strength, to clamber to safety. But it has little energy left, and is carried back and forth, helpless in the swell, crashing against the rock.

'I can reach if you hold my legs,' Jason cries. .

'I don't know, Jason. What'd your mum say?' He looks at Jason then down at the dog, and back at Jason, weighing the options. 'Oh, bugger it. Here. And don't bloody drown yourself.'

Jason inches forward, and leans over the rock, the jagged points cutting into him like blunt blades. Frank takes a firm hold on his legs, and allows him to drop lower and lower. Caught on the swell, the dog rises once more towards Jason's hand. He reaches out and grabs at the red collar. There'll be no second chance. The dog has exhausted the very last of its strength.

'I've got it. I've got it, Frank. Help me up.' He is laughing through tears. 'I've got her.'

'Thank bloody Christ for that.' Frank gasps with the effort but, taking a firm hold, on Jason, he drags him back onto the rock where they both sit, panting.

'Is she okay?' Frank wipes an arm across his forehead. 'She'd better be, after all that. Here, she's shivering. Pass her to me and I'll put her under my coat.'

'We've got to tell Sammy.'

'Give me a minute, Jason.'

'He thinks she's drowned.'

'I want to meet the man who threw her off the boat,' Frank says. 'I'll knock his bloody block off.'

'I'll help you.' Jason wipes away the last of his tears. He looks down at his trousers and jumper, and then at Frank's.

'What are we going to tell Mum?' He grins, a fellow conspirator.

'Bloody hell,' says Frank. 'I'd better phone.'

Chapter 12

Frank isn't a man prone to outbursts of temper. Despite the occasional conflict on the field of play—he is a regular on the town rugby team—he is generally considered a disciplined and self-controlled character. It takes a great deal of effort on the part of an opponent to rouse him to any degree of violence and even then, it is short-lived. He prefers to let a remarkable turn of speed for a man of his age, a sharp wit and a cheeky grin do the fighting for him. He is also aware that his profession demands a high level of restraint.

But, as he clambers over the rocks with Jason at his side and the exhausted dog under his coat, the cold water from the poor animal soaks through his clothes to meet the boiling heat of anger surging outwards, and the combination turns to an explosive steam.

They cross the narrow strip of sand and enter the village.

'I think she's getting better.' He holds tight to his coat. 'She's wriggling like a sack of eels. I think she knows she's home.'

'She'll know the smells, won't she?'

'That she will. She's a brave little dog, too. Imagine swimming all that way, and still having enough energy to wriggle.'

'She's tough, isn't she?'

'She is. She's tougher than a front row forward. And prettier, too.'

They leave the beach, and pass between a warehouse and a garage to reach the tiny harbour. The blue-and-red craft, *Lovely Maggie,* is fastened up and deserted.

'Sammy will have gone home.' Jason points to the white cottage at the harbour-side. 'That's his house. The one with the flower baskets.'

'How do you know that? Did he tell you?'

Jason looks confused. 'No, I don't think so. Maybe it was Molly, I don't remember. I know that's his house, though.'

'Aye, well, we'd better get this little wriggler to him as quick as we can. I don't like thinking how upset he must be.'

Evidently, Yapps has the same thought because her wriggling now grows so intense that she forces her way out of the bottom of Frank's coat, slips out of his hands like a wet fish, and drops to the ground. She shakes herself, makes her way on unsteady legs towards the white cottage, and clambers up the stone steps to the side gate.

'There we are.' Frank wipes his wet hands on his coat. 'A happy ending. I think we deserve a coffee and cake, don't you?'

'Can we go and see Sammy?'

Frank looks uncertain. 'No, lad, let them be. There'll be enough emotion in that house without us adding to it.'

'But I want to see Sammy. I have to explain.'

Frank looks past the house towards the far end of the harbour, where a wall projects out to the open sea. A few tourists walk up and down. Some have found benches to sit on, and watch the boats. A man in a blue coat takes a photograph of a woman in green, leaning against the harbour rail. A girl watches them from across the road. She sits on a low, lichen-covered wall beside another narrow path.

Frank's lips and eyes narrow as if he's thinking, or remembering.

'Okay,' he says, turning on a bright smile. 'You go and see you friend-to-be, eh? I'll just take a walk for a bit, maybe even get myself a drink in The Harbour Inn over there.' He winks. 'Our secret.'

'You won't come with me?'

'Meet you back here in half an hour. What do you say?'

Jason nods, and runs over to the cottage. He pauses by the gate, which lies open, and leads to the back of the house through a bare yard with a stone workshop. He glances back at Frank, momentarily uncertain. Frank gives him an encouraging wave, and ushers him inside.

Then the smile on Frank's face slides away, as if wiped with a damp cloth, and his lips grow pale, and his eyes sharp.

'Right. Let's see if we can find you.'

He walks across to where the girl is sitting on her rough, stone perch but before he reaches her, she jumps down from the wall, and points.

'He's in there.'

'Who?' Frank smiles but the girl remains sullen.

'The man you're looking for. The man from the boat.'

Frank hesitates for a moment. 'How do you know...?' he begins, but then he pauses. Long, dark hair. Dark eyes, blue jeans, about nine maybe. 'Are you Molly? My boy, Jason, met someone called Molly out by the cave on the headland.'

'I know,' the girl says. 'I'm Molly, sometimes.' She turns away and walks up the steps beside another cottage, end-on to the sea like all the others. She pauses and looks back. 'My friend says you should be careful.'

'Aye, I will, lass. I know what I have to do.'

Molly shakes her head impatiently. 'No, not only now. Be careful later. Be careful all the time.'

She turns, and skips away between the cottages.

Frank scratches his head, a half-smile on his face. He looks across to the old hotel on the harbour side, and the smile fades. A sign hangs from a wrought iron frame: *The Harbour Inn*. The picture of an old, weather-beaten, bearded fisherman with oilskins stares down.

He strides across to the hotel, pushes open the door, and goes in.

It takes a moment for his eyes to adjust to the dim light, but then, in a glance, he takes in the bar and its occupants. A plush carpet, rich red and blue, dark mahogany tables, windows looking out over the harbour. Everything looks new and old at the same time. Tasteful, expensive. Not many customers, though. Just a handful, tourists mainly, and one skinny, sullen guy in the corner.

Frank walks over to the bar, and leans his elbows on the polished surface.

'Pint, please.' He nods, indicating a particular pump. 'A guy came in a few minutes ago, from the blue-and-red boat in the harbour.'

'That'd be Dominic.' Trevor nods towards the skinny guy, who watches them closely. 'Trouble?' Trevor asks.

Frank grits his teeth. 'Not for you or your hotel.' He indicates the drink Trevor is serving. 'I'll be back for that in a couple of minutes.'

He dusts his hands and walks over to Dominic.

'You called Dominic?'

'Yes, what of it?'

'Got a message for you.'

'Who from?'

'Not in here. Outside. Too many ears.'

He walks over to the door, winking at Trevor as he goes. Dominic eyes him, but follows, a few feet behind.

As he reaches the outside door, and before he has time to react, a powerful hand grabs him by the collar and another lifts him by the belt and marches him across the road.

'What are you doing? Who the hell are you?'

Frank doesn't answer.

'Do you know who you're dealing with here? You're fucking dead, you hear me? Fucking dead.'

Dominic struggles and swears, and tries to kick out, but Frank walks quickly, retaining a tight grip. Dominic struggles to keep on his feet. Under the curious eyes of a handful of tourists, Frank marches him down the end of the harbour.

'Now, let's see how you like it,' Frank whispers in his ear and, without breaking stride, he throws Dominic off the end wall and into the water where he lands with a heavy and undignified splash. Dominic flounders in the water, spluttering and coughing. 'The dog got out okay,' Frank calls down. 'Let's see how you manage.'

And he turns and walks back, a grim smile on his lips.

'Lovely day,' he nods at a bemused couple.

Trevor stands at the door of The Harbour Inn, watching. There's a smile on his lips as wide as the harbour entrance.

Frank grins. 'I'll have that pint now, I think.'

'It's on the house,' Trevor says.

Chapter 13

Yapps sits on the step, waiting for Sammy to open the door. She's shivering but manages a weak bark as Jason approaches.

The door opens.

'Oh, hello, I was only expecting to see a dog. Who are you?' The round-faced woman manages a smile but can't hide the anxious look which lies beneath it. She glances behind her, preoccupied with something inside and, as if by way of a distraction, pushes her sleeves up over plump arms.

'Is Sammy in?' Jason asks. 'I'm Jason. I'm kind of a friend.'

'Well, hello Jason,' Maggie looked down at him. 'I'm Maggie and I'm Sammy's Mum. He's in his room. He came in twenty minutes ago, ran upstairs, and locked his door. I can hear him crying, but I can't get him to answer. Do you know what's happened, because I'm blessed if I do?'

She looks down at the kitchen floor, where pools of water form a trail, and stifles a scream. 'And now Yapps comes running in, and she's dripping water everywhere. I bet any money she's lying on the couch in the lounge now, dead to the world, and soaking the fabric. I don't know what's going on, I'm up to my elbows in flour and Richard, that's Sammy's dad, he isn't back yet, and I don't know what to do. If it's anything to do with that Dominic, I'll—'

She doesn't have time to complete her threat. Sammy appears in the doorway, his eyes red and swollen, his body trembling.

'I heard a bark.' He sees Jason, and stifles a sob.

'I found Yapps,' Jason explains. 'I brought her back.' He can't mask a feeling of pride and excitement.

'Aye, she's in the lounge, ruining the furniture,' Maggie grumbles. 'There'll be no sitting on that sofa for the rest of the afternoon.' She pulls out a pine kitchen chair. 'Now, sit down here, Sammy, and you and your friend can tell me what the hell is going on.'

But there'll be no immediate answers. Sammy has already disappeared into the lounge, from where Jason can hear a mixture of laughter and tears.

'You'd better go through.' The woman shakes her head, and frowns. 'I'll catch up on everything later.' She eyes Jason up and down, suddenly aware of his less than sanitary appearance. 'What's happened to you? You're as wet as the dog, and covered in muck and slime.'

Jason grins. 'Yapps went for a swim, and I rescued him.'

'You make no more sense than Sammy.' Maggie grabs a tea towel. 'Here.' She hands it to him. 'That's not to wipe yourself with, it's to sit on, and take those shoes off before you go through. Tell Sammy I'll give you ten minutes to get your stories straight, and then I want an explanation.'

Jason slips off his shoes, and goes through to the tiny cottage lounge, where he finds Sammy, with Yapps on his knee. He's smiling now, but his whole body still shakes.

'She swam to shore. Me and Frank, my step-dad, got her out of the water.'

'You saw what happened?'

'Yeah, everything.'

'You can't tell Mum or Dad. Say she fell in the harbour, and I thought she was drowned. Tell them you stayed for a minute, after I'd gone, and you saw her by the boat. Say you called her, and she came to the edge of the water, and you brought her back.'

'But that man threw her in the sea. He wanted her to drown.'

'You can't tell them. You don't understand. There's not just Dominic. There's others.'

'Who?'

'I can't tell you. But promise you'll stick to my story. Please?'

'Okay.'

A door opens at the back of the house, and a man's voice calls out. 'Come and look at this, you two. I wouldn't believe it if I hadn't seen it. Come on now, quick before it's all over. Come on. Sammy, Maggie, shake a leg.'

'That's my dad.' Sammy lies Yapps back on the sofa, and heads to the door. Jason only has a moment to take in the interior of this fisherman's cottage—glass floats, shells, driftwood animals with painted eyes, photographs and round mirrors—before he has to run after him.

'Neat!' he says to himself.

'You'll never believe what's just happened,' Richard says, as he opens the gate, and hurries them down to the harbour. 'Dominic picked on the wrong person this time. I didn't see everything but Fred says that this chap marched him out of the inn, and carted him by the seat of his pants right to the end of the harbour. You'll never guess what happened then. It made my day, I can tell you.'

'Well, go on, tell me.' Maggie reaches the rail by the harbour side. She stops and looks up at Richard, choking back a giggle. 'He never did, did he?'

'Aye, he did. He didn't break stride. He just flung him into the harbour. I got there just in time to see it. Look, he's just reached the rail, and he's dragging his miserable self out. I'd like to shake the hand of the man who did that. I wonder who he was.'

Jason reckons he has a pretty good idea who it was, and, if he's right, the guilty party is walking towards them past a number of tourists, who have gathered to watch the spectacle; a good story to tell when they get home. Something for social media. Frank ignores the looks that follow him. He holds out a hand to Richard.

'I'm Frank,' he says. 'Jason's step-dad. You must be Sammy's mum and dad.'

Richard and Maggie join the dots.

'Was that you?' says Maggie.

She points back to where Dominic is dragging himself the top of the iron steps. He clambers onto the harbourside, and glares at anyone who has the audacity to glance in his direction.

'I thought he should have a taste of his own medicine, after what he did. Has our Jason told you?'

'No, but I think the pair of them had better start now.' He turns a severe parental look on his son. 'Sammy?'

'Don't lose your temper, Dad.'

Richard is flushed red, with angry eyes and clenched fists. 'Come on,' Maggie says. 'Let's go back in the house, eh? They can explain over a cup of tea and some sandwiches. What do you say, love?' She holds his arm in a firm grip. Richard doesn't move.

'Sammy, you tell me right now what that bastard's been up to. Right now, you hear me?'

'Yapps sneaked on the boat. I didn't know. Then, when we got out to the buoy, she fell off—'

'You mean, he threw her off.' He turns back towards the harbour. 'I'll kill him. I'll bloody kill him.'

'No,' Sammy pulls at his arm. 'No, she just fell. That's right, isn't it, Jason?'

Jason nods quickly, fearing an outbreak of hostilities. 'She just fell.'

'And he sailed off and left her there? Is this true?' He turns to Frank. 'We're you there? Did you see?'

'No, but I know what happened alright. Jason told me. Come on, back to the house. We can explain everything there. He's got his reward, look.'

Dominic is slouching along the harbourside, leaving a trail of seawater in his wake, his lank hair hanging like shredded cloth down the side of his face. He pushes a couple of people out of his path, and swears at them. At the end of the harbour he pauses, and turns to stare at Frank and Richard. He mouths something which could only be a threat, and stumbles away to his lair at the end of the village.

Richard tries to wrest his arm free so he can follow, but Maggie's hold, both physical and mental, is limpet-firm. 'Come on, Richard. We need to get these boys inside. They've been through enough today.'

'Aye, come on,' Frank says. He is becoming aware that his actions could prove expensive; he's got a promotion in the pipeline.

Richard relaxes his shoulders, and looks at Sammy and Jason, whose eyes are brighter and more excited than he reckons their situation warrants.

'Dominic can wait,' he says, ominously. He frowns at the boys. 'But we'll have the truth from you two.' He looks at Frank, and manages a smile. 'There's one good piece of news. Neither of these two could tell a lie if their lives depended on it. That's reassuring. We've bred honest children.'

Outside The Harbour Inn, someone else takes a keen interest in the spectacle. He watches from the driver's seat of a low-slung sports car. He's in his mid-thirties, casually but expensively dressed, and he stares from a pallid face, impassive. His grey eyes follow Dominic as he slouches away. Then he glances back to where Maggie is leading the little group back to her cottage. Something like a snarl passes across his lips.

The window closes, and the car eases away.

Chapter 14

That evening, the driver of the sports car, Rupert Fitzwilliam, entertains guests at Leybury Grange and, as usual, he is bored. Dinner is over and the guests pass through the great hall towards the drawing room. Portraits of solemn ancestors and their horses stare down.

'Jocelyn, if you didn't remind me constantly how we need their society, I'd pay to see them all shot.'

Jocelyn, his sister and a year or two his junior, smiles without looking at him. She is tall, fair-haired and slender, and a picture of elegance. There's a certain sadness about her blue eyes, which escapes only during moments of solitary reflection, when her guard is down. Tonight, it is carefully hidden behind a mask of sophisticated reserve.

'Force yourself, brother of mine. They are important investors in our way of life. Just imagine money and influence cascading from their wallets into ours. It'll see you through the tedium.'

She turns and exchanges a few words with an ageing gentleman in a dinner jacket. Rupert forces a smile, and nods.

'He's as tight as the proverbial,' he says, as the old man trots towards the brandy. 'He'll eat and drink us out of house and home, and then leave. Full of promises but no return. He's a parasite.'

'Just smile,' Jocelyn says. 'Plead business, and escape to your study for a while. Leave them to me.' She allows a frown to crease her forehead. 'Though why you had to invite *him*, I simply don't know.' She waves a long wrist in the direction of a hunched, sour-looking individual perched beside a display cabinet. 'He's like a blood-clot on an illuminated manuscript. He always looks like he's about to steal the silver.'

'A quaint turn of phrase, Jocelyn, but Zachary Blight is the only person here in whom I have the slightest interest. The fact that he's quite obnoxious is his most redeeming feature.'

'He makes my flesh creep, and if he draws on that inhaler one more time, I shall simply scream.'

'Did you see the expression on the face of her ladyship when she found herself seated beside him at dinner? I could barely restrain my laughter. If you'd place her beside a lecherous six-foot slug she couldn't have looked more uncomfortable. It was a delight to watch.'

'You're incorrigible, Rupert, but do take him with you to the study. He's has a terribly depressing effect on the atmosphere. Banquo's ghost could do no worse.'

'We have some business dealings. You won't see him again tonight.'

As the guests disappear into the drawing room under the sociable eye of Jocelyn, Rupert draws Zachary Blight to one side.

'Let's escape these vultures, shall we?'

Zachary casts a contemptuous look at the departing figures. His creviced brow tightens into a frown. Beneath a receding hairline, his face is as grey as what remains of his hair.

'Sooner the better. Another few minutes, I'd have slapped her ladyship.'

The study door closes behind them.

'Peace at last.' Rupert drops heavily on a Chesterfield sofa beneath an arched window. 'One has to do these things, but really, it's too much. One can have a richer conversation at the bar of The Harbour Inn.'

'I don't know why you have to invite me.'

'I do it to punish you, Zachary. And to punish them. It's my only entertainment. My ancestors were better served in that respect. They could always fall back on torture.'

Zachary sits in an armchair, breathing heavily. 'That sense of humour of yours will be the death of you.'

'Or of others.' Rupert's practised smile could frost the windows. 'My family has a reputation to maintain.'

'Let's get down to business.' Zachary pulls a blue inhaler from his pocket, and draws on it. Rupert studies his guest closely, like an exhibit in a glass case:

overweight, pale, in poor health, the skin sagging on his cheeks and neck. Only the eyes are firm, like they're wired in place by a suspicious mind.

Rupert's look turns to contempt. 'I was in the village this morning to meet our man.'

'Dominic?' Zachary looks up. 'Why?'

Rupert smiles. 'I like to keep the reins tight. Besides, he makes me laugh. He's such a weasel, don't you think?'

'We don't socialise. It's purely business for me. I don't have your sense of humour.'

Rupert stands up, and walks over to large mahogany desk. A computer sits at one side, angled towards the red leather chair. He reaches for an intricately carved cigar box, and opens it. He withdraws a thick cigar, and clips the end.

'One has to maintain one's standards, don't you think? One's peers expect it.' He lights it slowly, and exhales a volume of grey smoke. 'I hope this doesn't affect your lungs.'

'You know it does.'

'Yes, I suppose I do.' Rupert walks back and assumes his seat on the Chesterfield. 'He's becoming a liability.'

'Who?'

'Our friend Dominic. I may need to take action.'

'What do you mean?'

Rupert shrugs. 'Imagination was never your strong point, was it, Zachary?' He exhales a cloud of smoke towards his visitor.

'He brought in a shipment today.' Zachary waves away the toxic fumes, and his face wrinkles with distaste.

'He also brought a lot of attention. I was at the harbour front. Did you know he threw the boy's dog in the sea?'

'He never did like dogs.'

'Then along came this muscle-bound, he-man type who dragged him out of The Harbour Inn and deposited him off the end of the harbour.'

Something close to a laugh emerges from Zachary. It sounds like rusty chains, and is drowned by a rasping cough.

'That must have entertained the tourists.'

'The tourists and the locals alike. Our friend's one claim to fame is that he's insignificant, and unremarkable in every way. He has the sort of face that one turns away from. But suddenly, he's a local celebrity. Now, everyone will notice him, and watch where he's going. *Look. There goes that chap who got thrown off the harbour wall. I wonder what he's up to?*'

'I see what you mean.'

'We've got another shipment coming in this week. I won't act before then, but those with whom we deal will need to know. In the meantime, have a little word. See if you can plant the seeds of understanding in his Neanderthal brain.'

'Yeah, okay, I'll have a word.'

'And find out who the great hero of the hour is, will you? We can't have some winged avenger cruising round the neighbourhood, fighting the good fight. It's disrespectful. He was with that other upstanding citizen, Trevelyan. We wouldn't want *him* getting ideas, and becoming heroic, would we?'

'No, I'll look into it.'

'See you do. Maybe put someone on them for a while. Now, if there's nothing else, you can piss off. I'm going to stay in here, and finish my cigar before I re-join the corpses in the drawing room.'

Zachary walks to the door, and opens it. A blast of conversation and low laughter flees towards him from the drawing room. He pauses, as if remembering something.

'Who's the kid?' he asks. 'I don't recall seeing her before.'

'What kid?'

'She was standing on the stairs when I came in here. About nine or ten. Dark hair, long. Quite skinny. She looked kind of out of place, like she was lost or something.'

The moment of silence is a little too long. Zachary turns, and Rupert disposes of a look of anxiety, replacing it with a sardonic smile.

'There are no kids here. You must be mistaken.'

'No mistake, I assure you. She was there, plain as day.'

Rupert waves a dismissive hand. Like the silence, it is just too lingering, too casual. Zachary's eyes sharpen, and focus on every nuance.

'Perhaps she came with one of the guests.' Rupert brushes an imaginary speck of dust from the polished desk. 'We all have our idiosyncrasies. At least they had the decency to keep them away from the dinner table. I cannot abide children at dinner, unless they're on the menu, of course.'

Zachary forces a smile, and closes the door behind him.

The smile drops away. He looks back, his mouth distorted by a look of contempt and hatred.

'I know what you did,' he says. 'I know you, Rupert Fitzwilliam.'

Chapter 15

'Is that the last of them?'

Rupert strolls through to the drawing room where Jocelyn sits back on a plush, floral sofa, resting her head against damask cushions, her eyes half closed. A glass of white wine lies on a table beside her.

'Sebastian Sands clung like a slug to a drainpipe. I had to prise him off my arm but, yes, they're gone.'

Rupert pours a brandy, swirls it, and inspects it like a connoisseur. 'The first is always a great pleasure,' he sighs, 'but by this time of the evening the palate has become rather jaded. Did they miss me?'

'I think they were relieved. You can be sharp, you know, and opinionated. Even when the opinions aren't your own.'

'Oh, I rarely divulge my own opinions. I wouldn't want to scare our dear guests.'

'They find it difficult to converse with you. Haven't you noticed?'

'I take pride in it. I don't suffer fools, my dear, and they are, to a man and a woman, the biggest fools in Christendom.'

'But they're influential fools, and important to your business interests. How did your meeting go? I saw Mr Blight creeping out. He was frowning like he'd eaten something unpleasant. Not at all a nice sight. When he saw me watching, he turned on that ugly smile of his.'

'Mr Blight means to cause us trouble, Jocelyn. People of his sort always do. It's just a matter of time.' He pauses. 'Do you mind if I smoke?'

'Light one for me, I think I've earned it.'

He sits down beside her, and hands over a cigarette.

'Tell me, did any of our odious guests bring a child with them?'

'The Morris's, perhaps. They have a daughter, though I wasn't aware of her presence tonight. I always ask that children be relegated to the kitchen.'

His long fingers curl around a monogrammed lighter.

'I'm afraid our Mr Blight saw one on the stairs. A girl, about nine or ten, dark hair.'

Jocelyn stands and walks across to the window, dark behind heavy, velvet curtains. When she speaks again, her voice is tremulous.

'It wasn't her, Rupert. You mustn't think that.'

Rupert inhales, and rests the cigarette on the corner of an ash tray. He leans back, and yawns.

'I'm tired, Jocelyn. Tired of everything. If it wasn't for you...'

Jocelyn's expression turns to one of anxiety as she turns to him. 'I'm here, aren't I? I'm not leaving.' She hesitates, softens her voice. 'It wasn't her.'

'He may enquire.' Rupert continues, brooding now, monotone. 'It's what people like Blight do, you see. They enquire. They make connections, they find angles to exploit.'

'But, there's nothing to find. We were careful.'

'There are always traces, my dear, you know that.' He stands up. 'It's time for bed, I think.'

Jocelyn holds his arm.

'I told you, I won't leave you, not ever.'

'Everyone leaves, eventually.'

'You're frightening me, Rupert. You mustn't do anything foolish.'

Rupert moves towards the door. 'He's a moth, Jocelyn. Just a moth flying perilously close to a flame. He flutters helplessly around, staring at the flame, thinking it may do him some good to approach it. But we both know well enough what happens to moths when they get too close to a flame. Leave Mr Blight to flutter a little longer. I have plans for him.'

'Like you had plans for...' She hesitates, aware of the sharp glance and the cold and dangerous eyes which now pin her.

'That was you, my dear, not me. Just remember that. I wasn't even in the house that evening. It was all you.'

'But I didn't know what I was doing. You tricked me.'

'I'll look after Mr Blight, Jocelyn. You needn't fear. Your secret is safe, just as long as you stay here with me.'

As Rupert leaves the room, and closes the door behind him, Jocelyn stumbles across to the cabinet, and pours a drink with trembling hands. It's a whisky this time.

Chapter 16

'I'm sure he's following us.'

'Who?'

'That man over there in the pale jeans and dark coat. He's too old to be wearing jeans, especially with lace-up shoes and a shirt and tie. That's why I noticed him. He's pretending to look in the window of the fancy goods shop.'

Janice pauses by the pedestrian crossing on the busy road which runs through Grantley. Behind her, people bustle past to force entry into crowded seaside shops. Across the road: grass parkland, a walkway beside the sea defences and, beyond them, a beach. The constant flow of traffic pauses for an impatient moment as she crosses, Frank and Jason behind her.

Frank glances back. 'He's not following us. He's just standing there looking in the window.'

'He keeps watching me when he thinks I'm not looking. Then he looks away quickly.'

'Maybe he fancies you.' Frank grins at Jason and winks.

'Yuk!' Jason mouths. 'People don't fancy Mum. That's horrible.'

'Mind your manners, you. I was a good-looking woman in my day, I'll have you know.'

'And still are, my petal.' Frank soothes her.

'Ugh!' Jason puts his finger in his mouth, and mimes vomiting, then runs ahead, and calls back. 'Let's find somewhere to sit so we can watch him. Maybe he's a spy or a secret agent.'

'Well, I could do with a sit down. My feet are killing me. And it's so warm.' Janice fans herself with the palm of her hand.

'We've been lucky this week, right enough. It's been lovely weather, considering the time of year. A real Indian summer.'

They cross the grass towards a cast iron bench, painted purple with a coat of arms and set in a concrete rectangle, surrounded by grass. The bench is fastened down. Sign of the times. Twenty metres away, the sea wall. Frank looks over his shoulder towards the road, the traffic and the crowds.

'Nobody's watching us now. He's gone.'

Jason runs across to the sea wall, and leans over it, his feet off the ground, his stomach resting on smooth concrete. The tide is coming in; people are packing up, and wandering away. The beach is emptying. Far out, a blue yacht with billowing white sails drifts close to the horizon.

'Look at the yacht, Mum,' Jason calls back. 'Can you see it, Frank?'

Frank looks up, a fleeting look of surprise turning to one of pleasure.

'I think you may be winning him over,' Janice whispers. 'Although throwing someone in the sea isn't the best way to do it. Hardly setting a good example. And you a policeman, too.'

'He had it coming. Everyone said so.' Frank wanders across, and leans on the sea wall beside Jason. 'I've never been on a yacht. I'd love to learn how to sail.'

'Sammy's been on a yacht. He went with his dad. He told me he wants to get a yacht of his own when he's older. Do you think it's difficult to sail a yacht? It *looks* difficult.'

'You need someone to teach you, that's all. Like everything else.'

Jason rests his back against the concrete wall. His mum, on the bench, pulls a packet of sherbet lemons from her bag.

'Want one?' she calls.

They shake their heads. Jason points. 'Look, Frank, there's that man Mum thought was watching her. He's at the end of the wall where the path goes over to the marina. He's staring at us.'

The man makes no pretence of looking elsewhere. His eyes are pinned firmly on Frank and Jason. Even when he takes an inhaler from his pocket and draws on it, his eyes don't shift.

'Ignore him.' Frank returns the stare, and the man turns casually, and leans on the sea wall. 'He's probably wondering why your mum and I brought our pet monkey on holiday.' He laughs but his eyes are still fixed on Zachary. There is something unsettling about the casual way he stares at them, like he wants Frank to know he's watching.

'You're the monkey, not me. A big, hairy gorilla.'

Frank adopts his knuckle-trailing gorilla pose, and jumps around Jason, pawing at him, and grunting.

'You're mad, you are.' Jason laughs, half-delighted, half-embarrassed. 'People are looking at you.'

Zachary isn't. His eyes are fixed on the sea, where the yacht tacks and turns. People smile as they pass or exchange a joke with Frank. Holiday folk maybe, or locals walking their dogs, taking the air.

'Come on,' Frank says at last, 'let's go back to your mum. See if she's got a banana for my favourite monkey.'

He puts an arm round Jason's shoulder, tentatively at first, then more firmly as he meets no resistance, and they walk back to the bench. Jason doesn't pull away as he might have done once; maybe he thinks it's kind of nice having someone like Frank about. For his part, Frank can't hide his pleasure.

'What are you grinning at?' Janice opens a carrier bag, and removes a lunch box.

'Just thinking,' Frank says.

It's only when they sit down with a salad roll—Janice is on another diet, apart from the sherbet lemons—that they see the man again. He walks along the path, and pauses to lean on the sea wall, directly facing them.

'He's staring at me again,' Janice says. 'The cheeky sod is staring right at me. I'm going to have a word.' She starts to get to her feet, but Frank holds her back.

'No, let me,' he says. 'There's no need to make a fuss.'

He strolls casually over, and stands by the sea wall.

'Do I know you?' he asks. 'Only you seem to be taking an interest in us.'

The man doesn't look at him. 'No, I don't think so.' Something which might pass for a smile squats on his lips.

'Why the interest, then?'

'No interest.' He pauses for a moment, as if weighing his words. 'Though I have seen you before.'

'Oh?'

'Yesterday at the harbour at Leybury. I was there.' Again, a silence. Frank glances at the man, who continues to stare at Janice and Jason. He feels a surge of temper but represses it.

'You're upsetting the missus,' he says. 'Maybe you should find someone else to stare at.'

The man turns an icy gaze on him.

'If I were you, I'd be more concerned about *him*.' He flicks a glance, a mere movement of the eye, across the open grass towards the road. A thin, wiry figure, in shorts and a T-shirt, leans against a lamp-post. He has a newspaper folded under his arm, and wears earphones. 'And *him*.' He nods towards another figure, sitting on a bench beside a children's playground; beside him, on the bench, he has a flask, and a steaming cup. He too has earphones.

'They're just people. You could've picked them at random. They're not doing anything.'

'Don't make an enemy of Dominic Sheedy. He has dangerous friends.'

'You know him?'

The man smiles. 'Well enough. He's a bitter, resentful, little man. He won't forget what you did.'

He turns back to the sea wall and, as his coat slips open, Frank sees the unmistakable black leather of a shoulder holster, and the bulge of a handgun. 'Enjoy your holiday, Mr Miller. But look after your family. Look after Janice and Jason. Make sure they come to no harm.'

His words sound like a warning, or perhaps a threat. Frank holds him by the lapel. 'How do you know our names? What's going on?'

The man eases Frank's fingers from his coat, and dusts himself down as if smoothing out a crease. His grey face is cold and impassive. A couple, walking past, eye them nervously.

'Have you heard the name Rupert Fitzwilliam, Mr Miller?'

'No. Should I have?'

The man doesn't answer. He turns to walk away. Then he hesitates. 'Keep your family close, Mr Miller. For now, you're safe enough, but you have no idea who you are dealing with. You would be well advised to leave it that way.'

He strolls casually away; just a portly man in his late middle age, taking a stroll in the autumn sunshine. He pauses, and looks back.

'I'm not your enemy, Mr Miller. You would do well to remember that.'

'What are you, then?' Frank calls after him. The man walks on, waving a hand back over his shoulder.

Frank checks the road, and the children's playground. The two men have gone.

'What was that all about?' Janice asks as he rejoins her. 'You're as white as a sheet.'

'It's nothing.'

'Who was he? What did he want with us?'

'He says he saw me throw that guy off the harbour, that's all.' He forces a smile. 'I think he wanted an autograph.'

At the end of the path, Zachary has stopped. He turns and watches them but only Frank notices, and he says nothing.

'So, no harm after all?' Janice says. 'And no mystery?'

'No, none at all.'

Chapter 17

*Z*achary Blight strolls along the shore path to join the throng of tourists who mill round the cluster of shops and amusement arcades.

He is not a well man, that much is clear. He breathes heavily even on the slightest incline, and stops frequently, as if to inspect a shop display, although the hand he rests on the window frame to support himself tells another story. There is a determination in those eyes and in the tightness of the lips and teeth, which suggests he is a man who will not give up easily. There is something, too, in the manner with which he draws himself upright and strides forward which suggests he is driven by some burning mission.

Intrigued, you follow him.

The road curls inland from here as it arches past more shops, away through growths of new housing to the countryside, and the bypass beyond. But Zachary turns to follow a narrow road towards the harbour and marina. He leaves the ice cream sellers, the fish and chips cafes, the pizza parlours, the litter, the noise, and the gaudy tourist shops to pass between old warehouses, now converted into smart holiday accommodation. Just before he reaches the bustle of the harbour with its boat trips and yachts, he opens the door of a café, and slips inside.

You follow him, take up a seat in a quiet corner and mask your face behind a laminated menu. From there, you watch and listen.

'Ah, there you are,' you hear him say.

A young man, mid-twenties, is sitting at a window seat. He has a can open in front of him, a glass beside it. He drinks from the can.

'Not partaking of the cakes and pastries?' Zachary asks.

The young man looks round at the clientele with an ironic eye. 'Perhaps in another twenty years,' he says.

Zachary shakes his head, sadly. 'I like Jessie's Tea Room,' you hear him say. 'There's something reassuringly civilised about it. It's like something I'd forgotten existed. I come here to remind myself.'

The young man seems unconvinced.

'Well, Adam,' Zachary continues, 'I think we can consider that a job well done. I think Mr Miller is sufficiently confused. He doesn't know if I'm an enemy or a guardian angel, and he's equally uncertain whether you and your colleague are hit men or figments of my imagination. Or perhaps a red herring, introduced to divert attention from some nefarious plots. He is, however, aware now of the name Rupert Fitwilliam, and of a connection with Dominic. I doubt he's anything more than he appears. Just a copper from the city on holiday with his family. But he could be useful, nonetheless.'

'Is he in any danger, do you think?'

'I doubt it. He's only here a few more days, with his family. It might be useful if his presence here acts as a distraction. Now, to the other matter. Have you anything for me?'

Adam shakes his head. 'Just some talk about Rupert's sister. There was a child, I believe.'

'Jocelyn? You surprise me.'

'Not Jocelyn. The other one.'

'Ah, yes. Louise.'

Adam nods.

From where you sit, you are free to study Zachary's expression, to read what others, even Adam, may not see. You notice how his eyes divert momentarily, and then flicker back, and how they relay something which his words cannot articulate. Perhaps he already knows about Louise, you think.

They pause for a moment as a waitress appears at the table: black aproned, white bloused and carrying a small notebook, and a smile. Young, too; the only signs of youth in the room. She has a pleasant face, and bright eyes. Very attractive.

Zachary sighs. Nostalgia. Feeling old, you think.

'I'll have a pot of tea and a plate of cakes. No nuts, please, and only fresh cream. None of your synthetic stuff.'

'All our cakes have fresh cream, sir.' The girl's tone is humorous, and only mildly disapproving.

'*Of course.*' *He returns her smile as best he can.*

Poor Zachary. You can see what he's thinking. Bloodshot eyes, and rotting teeth, and every breath like it's his last. When did he become so old? When did it happen? Where did his life go?

He turns his attention back to Adam, who is studying the waitress with the eye of a connoisseur. A faint blush suffuses her cheeks, but she jots his order and leaves.

'*Now, about Louise?*'

'*She died last year. She drove into a concrete barrier on a motorway. Quite intentionally, it seems. No suspicion of foul play. She was a few years older than Rupert.*'

'*And the child? It was a girl, I believe. What happened to the girl after her mother's death?*'

'*I don't know yet. I'll check the schools.*'

Zachary turns, and stares out of the window. You see how he watches the middle-aged tourists roll past, sweating and muttering about the heat. You see his eyes follow the zig-zag of impatient children.

You note too how Adam watches him: a look not without concern, not without affection for the older man. They have known each other a while, these two. Work colleagues, perhaps.

'*You look ill, Zachary. Maybe it's time to withdraw from all of this, while you still can.*'

Zachary shifts his gaze back from the window. His hands shake; his skin seems even paler and greyer.

'*Soon,*' *he says.* '*Just a few days longer. We're nearing the end. After that, it doesn't matter.*'

'*Are you sure? Why don't we stop now, and take what we've got? It should be enough.*'

Zachary's eyes harden, and seem to sparkle with an unnatural fervour. '*It's not enough,*' *he says,* '*not yet.*'

Adam looks away, and then back again. He seems tempted to reach out a hand to the older man, but draws back.

'*But why?*' *he asks.* '*What's so important that you'd risk your health?*'

'*Ghosts, Adam.*' *Zachary smiles.* '*Just ghosts pulling at my sleeve.*'

He takes an inhaler from his pocket, and draws on it.

'Shall I continue to enquire?' Adam asks.

'Check the schools. After that, you've done enough. I'll call you if I need any-thing more, but I have to finish this alone. That's how it has to be.'

'Be careful, Zachary. You're walking very close to quicksand. If Rupert knew we were enquiring into his family business—'

'Yes, indeed. Rupert Fitzwilliam is a psychopath, you know, like so many of his family.'

Adam smiles. 'I didn't know psychopathy was inherited.'

'It is in his case. He makes a virtue of it. He enjoys nothing more that ex-tolling the murderous virtues of his ancestors.'

'You'll need to be careful.'

Zachary cracks a weary smile. 'Don't be concerned for me. I know what I'm doing. Besides, Rupert is clearly of the opinion that everyone in his employ is also under his control. Arrogance is his fatal flaw. Ah, cakes!' He smiles as the wait-ress appears at his elbow. 'Are you sure you won't, Adam? You really should, you know. They are excellent cakes. A memorable experience.'

Adam relents. 'An éclair, then.' He smiles at the waitress.

'And for me, a Bavarian Slice.'

The waitress serves them, and glides away through a door into the kitchen, without a backward glance.

'This is a dangerous game you're playing, Zachary.'

The waitress re-enters, and carries her smile, as if on her floral tray, across to where you sit listening.

'Are you ready to order?' she asks, disturbing your concentration.

You hear no more.

Chapter 18

'You're pre-occupied tonight, Frank. What are you thinking about?'

Janice, Jason and Frank sit at a table in the club house of the caravan site; corner seats on cushioned chairs, near a window. There's a bustle of noise, but it's early, and the room is still half empty. A long bar—a confusion of wipe-down laminate and brass—stretches half the length of a wall. The barman leans on it, talking to a retired couple, taking a few minutes before the rush.

'They're in the van next to us,' Janice nods. 'The people talking to the barman, over there. They own it, too. Not hired for a couple of weeks like ours.'

'Must be nice. A real home from home.'

Janice inspects the room with satisfaction. 'Best seats in the house,' she announces, 'close enough to the bar, and a good view of the band. Not too noisy, either.'

The speakers stand like large, black monoliths on either side of a temporary stage on the dance floor.

Frank leans across the table towards her. 'I was thinking maybe a boat trip would be nice for tomorrow. What do you think?'

Jason looks up. 'Can we go on Sammy's boat? They do trips down the coast. That'd be ace.'

'What do you think, Janice?'

'I'm not sure. Boats make me all queasy. It's all that water, and no land. It makes me uncomfortable.'

'Well, what about just me and Jason?' Frank says. 'Your mum could stay in the village, Jason. Go to the shops or something. It's going to be another nice day.'

'I could see Sammy again. Go on, Mum, please?'

Janice looks from one to the other.

'I'm outnumbered,' she says, laughing. 'I suppose I'll have to come along to keep an eye on you. Who'd have bloody thought it? Me on a boat.'

'Yes!' Jason and Frank punch knuckles.

'It's filling up,' Frank says, looking round the room. The bar is busier now; the barman has moved away from the couple, and is pouring drinks with comfortable expertise. The stage is filling with equipment for the band: guitars, drums, microphones. On the ceiling above it, there are revolving disco lights, 1980s style.

'You can watch the band until the end of the first set, and then it's back to bed for you, Jason.' Janice raises her voice, and leans forward to make herself heard. 'Ten o'clock is late enough.'

Jason pulls a face but he knows he has his victory for tonight and, if he goes back early, he can phone Sammy and tell him they'll be going on the boat trip.

'I'll walk back with you,' Frank says.

'He's big enough to take himself back.' Janice looks at him, surprised. 'You don't want to miss the second half of the show.'

'I'll feel happier knowing he's safe in the van.'

The meeting with the man at Grantley has unsettled Frank and he scans the faces at the bar with a professional eye. Just tourists: rosy, sunburnt, laughing too much, drinking even more. Ready for the cabaret. Nothing to worry about here.

The ceiling lights dim, and the disco lights begin to roll.

'Here they come.' Frank nudges Jason. 'The group. They're good, you'll like them.'

An hour later, after he has walked Jason back to the caravan, Frank stands outside the club house. He takes out his phone, and calls a number. Then he waits. A drowsy voice eventually speaks.

'Frank? Bloody hell, man, do you know what time it is?'

'Yeah. Sorry, Guy. It's urgent.'

'I only finished an hour ago. Domestic on the Mill Estate. A nasty one. The feller's on the run with a kitchen knife, and a baseball bat. Doped up to the eyeballs, too. I'll be back in if they find him.'

'I won't keep you. I need you to check out a couple of names for me. Have you got a pen?'

'Yeah, go on.'

'Rupert Fitzwilliam.'

'Got an address?'

'No, but he's from round here somewhere, some big house. The second's a local called Dominic Sheedy, from Leybury. That's near Grantley.'

'Am I looking for anything in particular?'

'I had a bit of a run-in with Dominic. I'm afraid I upended him into the harbour. I want to know if I should expect repercussions.'

'You mean a complaint? You'll be in deep shit if he does that. Goodbye, promotion, nice to have met you.'

'No, I don't think he's the complaining type. It's more direct action I'm worried about. There are some weird vibes around him. Warning signs. I've got Janice and Jason to think about. You can put my mind at rest if it turns out he's just your everyday, mouthy thug.'

'And this Rupert Fitzwilliam?'

'That's an interesting one. I may have stumbled into something. I'll fill you in if anything comes of it. Just check him out for me.'

'Yeah, okay. It'll be tomorrow, though.'

'Tomorrow's fine. Cheers, Guy. I owe you one. Get back to sleep.'

'You, too. See you, Frank. Be careful.'

Frank frowns.

A lot of people have been telling me that recently: Richard, Maggie, the landlord at The Harbour Inn, the guy in Grantley, and now Guy.

He closes the phone, and takes one last look around. Lights are on in the caravan windows now, and the tarmac roadways shine under street lights. An elderly man walks with an ageing Labrador, partners in their declining years.

'Goodnight.' He nods to Frank. 'Another good day, tomorrow.' The man glances at the sky as if the darkness tells the future. A nest of stars on black branches.

Frank stirs from his thoughts. 'Goodnight.'

He opens the club house door, and is immediately struck by a blast of noise, fists of sound beating him about the head.

Straight from the bowels of hell, he thinks. *I'm getting too old for this.*

But he knows he's not.

He takes a deep breath, and disappears inside.

Chapter 19

Jason can't tell what wakes him. All he knows is that he's asleep one minute, and wide awake the next. The caravan is eerily dark but a pale glow penetrates from the streetlights outside, a gradual dawn on waking eyes.

'Mum?' he calls.

There is no reply so he leans up on his elbow and checks his watch, the new one with an illuminated face. Quarter to twelve. His mum and Frank will be back soon. Maybe someone walking past has knocked into a bin or dropped a bottle. He lies back, his head forming a warm hollow in the pillow, wide awake now, and listens through the silence.

It is in that silence that he hears her.

A young voice, hushed, calls his name.

'Jason, Jason.'

He turns to kneel on his bed, wipes the condensation from the window and squints out.

At first, he doesn't see her, but then, as his eyes adjust, she materialises from the shadows, and stares up at him.

'Molly?'

He unfastens the window catch, pushes the window open, and leans on the sill.

'What are you doing here?'

She doesn't answer, just stares. She is pale, as if her face carries its own white light, and her dark hair curls down to her shoulders like a strange frame.

'What do you want?'

A single tear trickles down her cheek.

'What's the matter?'

Her face is impassive, expressionless. A second tear follows, and then a third.

'Wait there. I'm coming out.'

Jason grabs a coat, and heads to the door. In the distance he hears his mum's voice, then he sees her, holding on to Frank for support, as they round the distant corner, heading back to the van. They're laughing; slightly drunk, he thinks.

'Molly?' he calls quietly. 'Molly, where are you?'

There's no sign of her.

'Jason?' he hears Frank call out. 'Is that you? What are you doing outside?'

Frank runs towards him.

'Molly!' Jason calls again.

As Frank reaches him, and encloses him in his arms, he hears her, somewhere out towards the sea; a voice carried on the breeze, with no more substance than the hush of the distant waves.

'Save yourself,' she calls, on the salty breath of the sea. '*Save yourself.*'

Chapter 20

He tells them he's been dreaming. He says it was a nightmare. He says he woke up, and found himself out there, in the half-light behind the van.

'Sleepwalking.' Janice hugs him close while Frank prepares a milky drink. 'He used to sleepwalk when he was little, when his dad... you know.'

'I dreamt that Molly was outside. The girl I met at the cave.' Jason wants to tell them the truth, that he was awake, that it wasn't a dream, that it was as real as the hot, milky drink he takes from Frank and holds in both hands. But he can't. He only half-believes it himself. 'She was outside my window, and she was crying. I went out to see what she wanted.'

'Well, you're safe now.' Janice strokes his head. 'It was just a dream, and it's all over now.'

'She said something strange just before she...' He hesitates. 'Just before I woke up. She said, *save yourself.* I was frightened.'

'No wonder.' Janice pretends to shudder, and then laughs gently. She glances at Frank. 'I'd have been terrified. They'd have come running from the clubhouse to see what I was screaming about.'

She laughs again, nervously.

'We'll go on that boat trip tomorrow.' Frank sits down beside him, and Janice. 'That'll be good, won't it? Sammy will be there.'

Jason's face breaks into a tired smile. He yawns. 'I haven't been on a boat trip before.'

'Well then,' Frank grins, 'something to look forward to, eh?'

Jason nods.

'I'm okay,' he says. 'I think I'll go back to bed now.'

'Good lad. I'm beat. Time we were all asleep.'

Sammy is dreaming, too.

He is walking down a long, narrow corridor. There are old paintings on the wall, set between wooden panels, small portraits and sea scenes, and pictures of an old house with a long, pale drive, and lawns and trees. Here and there, a ship, a storm flashing lightning bolts from a sky cannon. He is in a hurry but the corridor seems to go on for ever and ever. He checks his watch because he has to be somewhere. He has to meet someone, and he's late. But the corridor is unrelenting. Sometimes he thinks he's reaching the end but then it's further away again. And all the time, he's looking for something familiar, something to show him where he is. Something to show him which way he has to go; a door he recognises, a picture he's seen before.

Everything is vaguely familiar but nothing is clear, and he has such a long way to go.

Then the corridor is a hall; a huge hall, wide and long with chandeliers and dark paintings of old, unpleasant men leering down at him, and at the end, someone waits. He hurries on, past a dining table with silver cutlery, and silver candlesticks, but it's like walking through syrup. His legs are heavy and move slowly, and ahead of him, the room and the table stretch as if he's viewing them through the wrong end of a telescope. He tries to run but no matter how hard he tries he doesn't seem to get anywhere.

Then, just as quickly, the scene changes again, like a movie set, and he is in a library. Leather-backed books climb the walls, stacked on shelves which stretch forever towards a distant ceiling which he cannot see. There isn't a space on any wall which isn't covered in shelves full of unread, dusty tomes - except for the doorway through which he has entered the room, and another in the far corner, and two small, deep-silled windows.

He pauses, suddenly still. A clock ticks from somewhere; he can't tell where, perhaps tucked deep in a row of books. And there, on one deep sill, a boy sits, facing the window, looking out. He doesn't turn but his voice creeps over the wooden floor.

'You're late,' he says. 'I thought you might not come.'

'Of course I came.' Sammy hears himself say. 'I promised, didn't I?'

'People don't always keep their promises.'

He is next to the boy now. He can hear him crying; a desolate, heart-wrenching sound. He reaches a hand to his shoulder. It feels strangely soft and weak, and a cold dread slips though him as he pulls the boy round to look at him. The body slumps and falls on its back, and a round, red-cheeked face with glazed eyes stares at him.

A doll. A life-sized, round-eyed, staring doll. It laughs, and the laughter spins around him like mist or smoke, making him choke. He turns to find a door but the room is consumed with black, toxic fumes. He gasps and struggles, and he wakes.

Sammy stares at the ceiling of his bedroom, his eyes wide open, and his heart beating. For a moment, the dream lingers but then it slips away, and he is in his bed in his home, and his mum and dad are in the room close by. He lies still for a moment, then turns on his side, and switches on his bedside lamp.

Something stands there in the corner of the room, half hidden in the shadow. It turns its head slowly, to catch and fix him like a butterfly on a pin. A rosy-cheeked doll with glassy eyes.

The mouth moves. 'Tell nobody,' it says. Then again. 'Tell nobody.'

The next he knows, his mum is sitting beside him on the bed and his dad is behind her, leaning forward, reaching a hand to him. Sammy shouts and screams, and his mum makes soothing sounds, and strokes his forehead.

And he wakes up for a second time.

'Just a dream,' his mum says. 'It's just a dream.'

'A nightmare.' His dad's voice is anxious and concerned. 'It's just a horrible nightmare. You're alright now, Sammy. Mum and Dad are here.'

He looks from one to the other, wild-eyed.

'I can't tell you,' he repeats to his mum, and again to his dad. 'I can never tell.'

Chapter 21

'Look at those two. You'd think they'd been friends forever.'

Maggie sits on a bench seat, just outside the wheelhouse of *Sammy's Pride*, with Janice beside her. She holds an old chrome microphone, through which she speaks occasionally, to share her love of the coast, and her knowledge of its history and wildlife.

To your right you can see...

The boat is half-full; plenty of bare boards between the scattered passengers, room for children to dart from one space to another, tugging on the anxious reins of their parents' eyes. They lean over the side, to watch the water curl, to feel the spray, to taste salt on their lips.

'Don't lean too far, Carly.'

'Bottom on the seat, Simon.'

'Don't run, Erin. You might trip.'

To no avail.

Sammy and Jason sit on slatted, wooden seats at the prow of the boat with Yapps between them. They talk and gesticulate, and every now and then fill the air around them with peals of careless laughter.

'It's nice to see our Jason so happy.' Janice takes a packet of lemon sherbets from her pocket, and offers one. 'He's not had an easy time of late.'

Maggie declines, indicating the microphone. Sucking a sweet, she obviously feels, is not compatible with her professional duties.

'Poor Jason' she says, then quickly adds, 'I'm not prying. There's no need to explain.'

'It's alright. I'm well past it now, though our Jason has taken it all very badly. Me and his dad split up about a year ago, you see. He was a charmer, his dad, and Jason loved him to bits. But he was a bit too handy with his fists, and when the drink was on him... well, you can imagine.'

'I can indeed. How long did you put up with it?'

'Too long. I might still be putting up with it, but one night he turned on our Jason, and that was that.'

'Good for you.'

'Jason blamed himself, kept saying over and over that if he'd behaved better, his dad wouldn't have left. Not a word of truth in it, of course, but you know how kids can be. Everything is black-and-white. Then Frank appeared on the scene. He's a police detective, you know. He came to see me about everything with Bernard, that's my husband, and we hit it off pretty much straight away, though it was a few months before we really got together. We had to wait. It's what they call a clash of interests, what with his job and all. He's a good man, but it's taken time for Jason. It was all too much for him.'

'I can imagine. It can't have been easy for any of you.'

'No, Jason's been in all sorts of trouble at school. Angry, resentful, lashing out. But I think we've turned a corner this holiday.'

'I hope so.'

'It took throwing someone in the harbour to finally convince him. Hardly the best example to set.'

'Oh, I can think of worse.'

'What about your Sammy? He's such a nice boy.'

'He's a bit of a loner. He likes his own company. His teacher says he's the same at school. Reserved, like. Doesn't make friends. Meeting your Jason has done him the world of good. I mean, look at the pair of them.'

Aware that they are being watched, the boys wave cheekily before looking back towards the shore. The boat passes the caravan park. Jason whispers something, and they stand up and wave.

'Who are you waving to?' Maggie calls across.

'Jason says we're to wave at him, as if he's on the beach, even though he's here, and not there at all.' Sammy yells.

'Look,' Jason points towards the beach. 'You're with me. Wave to yourself.'

Sammy turns, and waves frantically with both arms.

'We're waving back. Look!' They break into howls of laughter. A few passengers share smiles with Maggie and Janice. Oh, to be young, and carefree.

'You're mad as a sack full of ferrets, the pair of you.' Maggie shakes her head, then lowers her voice. 'Lovely to see them, though, isn't it? Even if it looks like we've hired them as a cabaret.'

At the stern of the boat, Frank leans against the rail, and watches the white wake trailing behind them. Gulls wheel and black-and-white darts of guillemots fly before the boat, the remnants of the hordes which lined the cliffs not many weeks ago. He opens his phone, and checks his messages. Nothing. He checks for missed calls. Still nothing.

What's keeping you, Guy?

He stumbles across to the wheelhouse—a landlubber with no sealegs—and stands with Richard, who opens a small window.

'Come on, Maggie,' Richard says, 'we're near the castle and the seals. Get your skates on.' He glances at Frank, and raises his eyes. 'Once they start talking, there's no stopping them.'

The speakers crackle, and Maggie's voice emerges.

'It's ghost story time.' Richard chuckles. 'The tourists love a good ghost story, and that castle has its share. Fitzwilliam property for hundreds of years, since 1066 probably. Eventually, they moved over to the Grange, and filled that place with ghosts, too.'

'Rupert Fitzwilliam?' Frank asks.

'He's the current owner. That family has more skeletons than the parish graveyard. They've been a nasty bunch to a man. The latest is no better, as we know to our cost.'

'Oh?'

'Maybe later.' Richard slows the engine to a stop. They are close to the castle, which rises from a vertical slab of rock, like it's welded there. 'I've got to reverse in now to get close to the rocks. I can't go too close or I get hell to pay from Maggie. We've to be careful not to disturb the seals. We get nice and close but not close enough to scare them. The white ones are babies, and not fully waterproof yet. There are still a few, though not as many as in September.'

'I'll go and take a look.' Frank drifts away, and stands with the other passengers near the stern. Janice joins him, and slips her arm through his.

'Maggie's such a nice person,' she whispers. 'We're to go for tea, and spend an evening with them when they get back. That's alright, isn't it? I said yes. I didn't think you'd mind.'

'That'd be nice.'

'Have you seen those two? I wish our Jason had friends like Sammy back home.'

The two boys lean over the side rail, their eyes wandering to the bedrock and the seals, and then to the high battlements of the ruined castle. Frank follows their eyes. The castle rises so sheer that it's hard to see where the rock ends and the building begins. From the single remaining tower, a couple watch them. The man raises a camera to take a photograph of the boat. Sammy and Jason wave. Photo taken, the couple wave back.

'It's nice to see him happy.'

Frank slips an arm round Janice's waist and holds her close, staring up at the towering cliff, and the gaunt skeleton of the old castle. The Fitzwilliam lair. Already, that name affects him, as if a cold breeze has passed over wet flesh.

Chapter 22

It's after four when they get back to the harbour, and there's still no phone call from Guy.

If I don't hear by nine, maybe I'll give him a ring. I'll just have to be patient.

Only, patience isn't a virtue for which Frank is noted.

Fortunately, the evening passes easily. Good company and lively conversation, and an inexcusable amount of alcohol. The hours pass.

'You'll stay over, won't you?' Richard asks as darkness gathers outside, and the village snuggles down beneath a blanket of sky, lulled by the soft wash of the sea. 'There's no point going back at this time, not unless you have to. We've a spare room, and Jason can have a camp bed in with Sammy.'

'I think they'd like that.' Janice can see the excitement on the two young faces. 'If it's no trouble.'

'None at all. That way, you don't have to rush off.'

'Which means we can open another beer.' Richard rises unsteadily from his chair, and collects two bottles from the sideboard. He opens them, and hands one to Frank, who eases back in his chair.

'You were going to tell me about Rupert Fitzwilliam and Leybury Grange,' Frank says. 'If it won't spoil the evening.'

Richard grimaces. 'A nasty piece of work. He's got us by the—'

'Richard!' Maggie interrupts sharply. 'There's children.'

'Aye, okay, not in front of the children.' He nods, slurring his words. 'But he's a *b word* in a long line of *b words*.' Jason and Sammy laugh. 'There hasn't been a good one among them. Ask Maggie, she knows the history.'

'No,' Maggie shakes her head. 'Not now, and not here.'

'Rupert Fitzwilliam and Dominic are great pals, I heard.'

'Aye, indeed they are, and I wouldn't trust either of them as far as I could spit a roast chicken.' He winks at Jason and Sammy. 'They're both *b words.*' He covers his mouth with his hand as if he has spoken in error.

'But you trusted Dominic once?' Frank hesitates. Perhaps this isn't the time for that, either.

'It's no secret,' Richard says. 'People warned us, but we were in desperate straits. The bank wouldn't lend us money and we were going to lose the boats, and the house. *Rupert Fitzwilliam knows people in the banking world,* Dominic told us. *Genuine businessmen, all above board.* But we'd have to sign over part shares to Rupert. *Just on paper,* he said. *He'll just take a small percentage to keep things straight between us, but he won't interfere in the running of the business. Sleeping partner,* he said. *He wants to give something back to the community,* he said, *A charitable gesture,* he called it. Well, it was no such bloody thing and now the pair of them have got their feet under our table and we can't get rid of them.'

There's a moment's silence and Frank regrets asking about Rupert Fitzwilliam at all. Janice swings one of her looks at him, like a pebble in a sock.

'I'm sorry,' he says. 'I should never—'

'Nay,' Richard brightens, and takes a deep draught. 'We'll not let those beggars spoil our evening. Let's have one of your ghost stories, Maggie. What do you say, eh?'

'Oh, yes,' Janice says. 'I love a good ghost story.'

It's Maggie's turn to swing the sock at Richard. 'Maybe it's not such a good idea,' she says, 'after last night.' She turns to Frank and Janice, and explains in a low voice. 'Sammy was having nightmares.'

'Well, there's a coincidence,' Frank says. 'When we got back from the club last night, Jason was outside the van, in his pyjamas, sleepwalking no less.'

'Well, I never.' Maggie gasps. 'Maybe no ghost story then.'

Howls of protest from Sammy and Jason.

'I'm not scared of ghost stories,' Sammy says. 'I've heard loads of them.'

'Me, too,' says Jason, even though he hasn't.

Maggie steals a glance at Janice, who nods.

'Well,' Maggie says, 'let's turn the lights off, and, Richard, maybe you can light a candle or two to get the atmosphere right. What do you say?'

She stands up and walks to the chimney breast, resting her hands on the lintel, as if to prepare herself. The lights go out and, a moment later, candles flicker to life, as they gather round a table. The candlelight cast a low, yellow glow, throwing into ghostly relief the driftwood creatures gathered around them on the windowsill, and dresser. Maggie lays her hands on the table, and clears her throat.

'St Michael's Church stands just beyond the village. It's an old church, dating from the Middle Ages, with a tower, and an arched doorway. It's surrounded by a very old graveyard full of stones which date back many, many centuries. There are ancient trees, too, and, in the spring, daffodils and crocuses grow in an abundance. It can be a beautiful place to sit on a warm spring day with the flowers and the birds and the insects. But at night, or on a late autumn evening, or, as in the case of this particular story, Halloween itself, it can be an unnerving, even terrifying place. Few people can walk though that graveyard, or pass the ancient graves, without feeling a chill pass through their flesh and gnaw deep into their bones. It is a chill which is at its deepest and most penetrating as you pass the grotesque statues of the Fitzwilliam mausoleum.'

Maggie's voice has fallen to a hush. Even the darkness outside the windows seems to hold its breath. Driftwood eyes glisten. The figures round the table lean forward towards the flame, until their faces are caught in half-light, and their eyes too shine strangely.

'Well,' Maggie continues, *'that Halloween, two girls, two very foolish village girls returning from a party, decided to take a short cut through the graveyard. It was a dare, a silly prank, nothing more. As they rounded the corner of the ancient church the cold gathered round them, and they clung to each other, uncertain whether to continue towards the lane or to turn, and run for their lives.*

The door of the church creaked open, and a warm, orange light shone out, casting a glow on the porch. An elderly man backed out and closed the door behind him. You can imagine the relief those girls felt when they saw him. They could follow him now, down the path and onto the lane. Once safely back on the village streets, they could boast to their friends that they had accomplished the challenge and had passed safely through the graveyard on Halloween night.

The man saw them, huddled together in the shadows, and he smiled a strange smile as he walked over.

"It's a frightening place at the dead of night," he said. "Shall we walk down to the path together, through the ancient gate and onto the street?" He seemed a friendly old man, and had a warm smile on his grey face, so the girls nodded gratefully. He looked around at the graves, and at the church. He had a wistful look on his bearded face. "Yes," he said, "I remember how terrifying this place could be, even years ago." He turned a grey-eyed stare on them, and bent his head forward, his voice a hushed whisper. "When I was still alive."

There's a gasp from around the table, and then a moment's silence.

'What did the girls do?' asks Jason.

'They ran down the path as if their silly feet were on fire. They didn't stop running until they were back home.'

'And the man? The ghost?'

Frank tries hard to hold back his laughter. It's Richard who speaks.

'Oh, Francis Dunwoody just strolled back, chuckling to himself. He was the caretaker of the parish church, and a man with a wicked sense of humour. He dined off that story for years.'

'You mean...' Janice begins. Then she sees a sly smile on Maggie's face. 'Well,' she says, breaking out in a pealing laugh. 'You rotten sod. I fell for that. Hook, line and sinker.'

Sammy isn't laughing. He stares at the mirror on the wall opposite the fireplace, as it catches the flickering glow of the candles. Frank falls silent, watching him.

'What's the matter, Sammy?'

Sammy continues to stare at the mirror. His mouth opens and then closes, but he cannot speak. He raises a hand and points.

'There's a face in the mirror,' he cries, 'and it's watching us.'

Chapter 23

Maggie is the first to recover. She bustles across and turns on the light. 'There's nothing there,' she says to Sammy. 'See? It's just your imagination and my silly story.'

Sammy turns and stares at her, wild-eyed, scared, his face pale and drawn. 'It was there, Mum. I saw it.'

Jason looks at the mirror and then at his friend.

'There's nothing there now,' he says. 'What was it like?'

Sammy doesn't speak, just shivers.

Maggie walks across to the mirror and brushes a sleeve across it. 'Condensation,' she says. 'The mirror was misted up with all of us here, and the room so warm. Look, it's gone now.'

'You just saw what looked like a face made up of candlelight and a misted mirror.' Richard kneels beside him, holding his hands. 'Nothing to worry about. There are no ghosts in our house.' He rubs Sammy's hair and grins at him. 'Ghosts wouldn't dare, would they? Not with your Mum here.'

Sammy returns his smile.

'It wasn't a ghost,' he says.

'Of course not.'

Frank stands up, and walks across to sit between Sammy and Jason. He puts an arm round Jason's shoulder, something he wouldn't have risked just a few short days ago. 'That was the best ghost story ever, wasn't it?' he says. 'I hope you'll sleep okay.'

'Now then,' Richard claps his hands together, 'a nice hot drink for you two and then off to bed. Hot chocolate?' He glances at Frank. 'Maybe a nightcap for the adults? Will you do the honours, Frank, while Maggie and I make the chocolate? Put the TV on, too, eh? Get us all back to normal.'

'I'll have a brandy,' Janice says, and laughs, 'for my nerves.'

'See what's on TV, Sammy,' Frank jokes, glancing at Jason. 'See if there's a good detective series, so I can get some tips.'

Sammy is smiling now; nervous, but smiling. In a moment, he'll be laughing at himself.

Gradually the atmosphere relaxes, and the laughter and conversation resume. They watch the television for a while and then the boys are despatched to their beds.

Janice holds Frank's arm. 'I'm glad we're staying here tonight. It's good the boys being together.'

'They'd never sleep, otherwise,' Frank says.

Chapter 24

Jason lies on his bed, staring at the ceiling. Thin cracks weave webs in the plaster, creating shapes, faces.

'Are you asleep, Sammy?' A quiet voice for sharing secrets.

'No.'

'What was the face like, that you saw in the mirror?'

Sammy hesitates for a moment.

'Horrible,' he says. 'Like a nightmare.'

Another silence, and a darkness full of thoughts.

'Sammy?'

'Yeah?'

'Was it a ghost?'

The silence hangs above them like an un-rung bell.

'No.'

'Who then?'

A longer silence, then a hushed, frightened voice.

'It was Dominic.'

Through the silence, Jason hears a strange sound. Sammy is sobbing. He is hiding his head in a pillow to mask the sound but he's sobbing.

'What's the matter, Sammy?' Jason stumbles across and kneels at his bedside.

'I can't tell you.'

'Yeah, you can. Friends forever, remember?'

'I can't. It's awful.'

'Course you can.'

Sammy turns his head away, and then, for the first time, he slowly starts to tell.

'Dominic...'

He begins, and, once he starts his story it is like a wave unfurling, flowing and crashing on the shore, and only when he finishes does the sea settle.

'You won't tell anyone?'

'Not if you don't want.'

His sobbing subsides, and he sleeps.

Jason lies awake for a long time, staring at the ceiling, before he too finally sleeps.

Chapter 25

It's late evening of the same day, in the summer house on the lawn at Leybury Grange. Rupert leans back on a cane chair and flicks cigarette ash on the wooden floor. He hasn't allowed Dominic to sit, not yet. It's important, he thinks, that anything he gives Dominic should feel like a concession, a gift, an indulgence. Authority has to be imposed, maintained. It is lord to serf; it is master to servant; it is slave-owner to slave. It is tradition.

'I don't know why you have to call me at this time of night.' Dominic looks down at his shoes, and trouser legs. Mud splatters reach up to the knee. 'Or why I had to walk here.'

Rupert's smile is venomous.

'Slip those shoes off, there's a good chap. My cleaner, you know, is a difficult, tiresome woman. In the good old days, she'd have been burnt as a witch. Personally, I would've had her flayed first, just for being so horribly ugly. Perhaps you know her. Libby something or other. All you villagers are related somewhere, I believe.'

Dominic looks uncertainly at him as if can't tell whether he speaks in jest or means every word.

'Perhaps you should stand on a sheet of newspaper,' Rupert continues, turning the screw on Dominic's anxiety, grinding him down. 'But perhaps not. Let her work for her pittance.'

'Why have you brought me here. I've better things to do than walk all this way for a meeting.'

He glances at the curtained windows where darkness peers; black eyes in a dark face. Rupert watches him, and smiles. He knows what Dominic is thinking; he can see the doubt on his face. They are cocooned here, on a lawn cut between the trees, invisible except from the old hall, with its gothic towers and crow-step gables.

'How am I going to get back? It's pitch-black out there now.'

'Sit down, Dominic.' Rupert allows the leash to slip, just a little. 'We need to talk, you and I.'

Dominic sits on the edge of the chair, his stockinged feet tucked beneath him. He looks uncomfortable, ill at ease.

'What do you want? Why the secrecy? Why couldn't we meet at The Harbour Inn, as usual? We could have had a few drinks.'

'I would have thought that was obvious, even to someone as intellectually challenged as you. You're the talk of the town, Dominic. The centre of attention. A local celebrity. *There goes the guy who threw a kid's dogs off a boat, and left it to drown. There's the guy who got dumped in the harbour by an irate tourist.* An irate tourist, I might add, who happens to be a city detective with a reputation for being something of a bastard for people like you and me.'

Dominic's face grows pale. 'He's what?'

'I think you heard me, Dominic but, for clarity, he's a detective from the city, and he's taking rather too much of an interest in you and, consequently, me. He's been asking questions.'

Rupert slams a fist on the table, and leans sharply forward.

'Shit,' Dominic murmurs.

'Shit, indeed.' Rupert allows his hand to unclench, permits his body to relax, impels his face to soften a touch, and his body to lean back. Urbane once more, sophisticated, restrained. Even his eyes are back in control, smiling again.

'We have a shipment coming, I believe?'

Dominic nods, and drags his mind from where it had lingered, like an anchor in a swamp. 'A big one. You want the stuff brought here, same as usual, just after dark?'

Rupert wags a long, artistic finger. 'I think not. There's no point drawing attention. Take it to the old place. Zachary can collect. Do it in daytime. Nobody will suspect.'

'You'll tell Zachary?'

Rupert looks towards the door. He leans forward, like a conspirator, drawing Dominic in, a member now of the inner circle. 'I have a little job for you. I can trust you, can't I, Dominic? You're a man who wouldn't betray a confidence? You see...' He glances theatrically left and right, and leans even closer. 'I don't trust Zachary Blight. He's been asking questions, too. Once a policeman, always a policeman. And he's been speaking out of turn. He even had the audacity to question your loyalty. Can you believe the arrogance of the man?'

He sees Dominic's body tremble, and his eyes widen. He sees him swallow from a dry mouth. He sees his nervous hand slip into his right pocket.

'You can trust me, Rupert, you know you can.'

'That's what I said. I said, Dominic is my colleague, my friend, my trusted boon companion. Why, I would no more suspect my dear sister Jocelyn than I would Dominic. Besides...' His eyes pin Dominic. 'Were Dominic to move even the tip of a single finger out of place, I would rip out his fucking heart, and feed it to him. I would flay his skin, and lay him out for the crows. I would break every bone, one by one, and amputate every limb. And I would do it slowly. That's what I told him.'

Rupert leans back, the smile once more on his lips. He studies Dominic, who sits, pale faced, nodding, mumbling, nicely scared. Rupert's mind turns to squawking chickens just before their throats are cut.

'Besides, we have a secret, you and I. It wouldn't do to share it.'

'What do you want me to do?'

That artistic hand waves once more. 'Oh, just listen to what he has to say. Engage in conversation. Perhaps you should hint at some discontent, give him sufficient space and sufficient rope to throw himself from the cliff, and hang himself.'

'Then what?'

'Well, then, Dominic, I may have another job for you.'

'You mean—'

Rupert raises a hand.

'All in good time. If it comes to pass, you can be sure you'll be well rewarded. Now, perhaps you could remove your hand from the weapon you have in your right pocket, and place both hands on the table. Just as an indication of trust.'

Dominic blanches but he lays his hands on the table. His eyes flicker towards Rupert.

'It was only—'

Again, the hand waves.

'There's no need to explain. A dusk meeting, a secret rendezvous, alone, after all that's happened. I understand your concern.' He laughs a long, slow laugh. 'In fact, I took a similar precaution myself.'

He draws a gun from beneath the table, and levels it at Dominic, moving it forward until the muzzle touches his forehead. 'You're sweating, Dominic.'

'You've got a gun pointing at my head. Of course I'm sweating.'

Rupert withdraws the weapon.

'It's time I went back. I need a nightcap before bed.' He stands up, and walks towards the door. 'Turn the lights off on your way out.' He pauses, as a gust of cold air penetrates the room. 'Make final arrangements for the pick-up, and see what our friend Zachary has to say.'

'Shall I phone you?'

'I'll phone you.'

The door closes. The chill breeze slips round Dominic, and grips him in a dead embrace. He shivers. He can hear Rupert's low laugh as he walks back across the lawn.

Chapter 26

I t is half past ten the following morning before Frank's phone finally rings. He takes the call in the yard outside the Trevelyan's house, resting his back against the stone wall, standing beside the assorted bins: recycled this, recycled that, unrecyclable other. An old Madonna number plays on the kitchen radio. Radio 2. BBC. Was that Janice, singing along? Probably. She can't resist a good tune. Maggie's face hovers in the lace-fringed window, as she washes the breakfast pots. Janice appears beside her, tea towel at the ready.

'It's been bedlam here.' Guy sounds tired, like he's been working all night. 'That domestic turned into a hostage situation. It took all day. Then there was a burglary. A nasty case. An old guy living on his own. He's in hospital. He looked like he'd been hit by a truck.'

'A bad day.'

'Yeah, one of those where you start to lose the last of what little faith you have in the human race.'

'We've got some weird shit going on here, too. Did you find anything on Dominic or this Fitzwilliam guy?'

The subdued laugh from Guy carries a heavy weight of irony.

'You could say that.'

'Go on.'

'You know those old war films where a group of sappers tunnel towards the enemy lines? They're usually lugging dynamite in wooden crates. Claustrophobic, dangerous work.'

'Yeah.'

'In one film I saw, can't remember what it was now but it was old, maybe sixties or seventies, this group of guys stopped because they heard a noise coming towards them. It took a few minutes to figure what it was, then they realised the enemy were digging directly towards them. Any minute and the wall of rock and earth would collapse, and they'd be face to face.'

'Scary.'

'Yeah, scary indeed. Anyway, there was a quick fumbling for guns and knives and people whispering, then they heard exactly the same sounds on the other side of that narrow wall between them, and nobody knew whether they were more scared of the enemy or of the roof collapse that might bury them if they fired those guns.'

'A nasty situation.'

'Very. But let me get to the point.'

'That'd be nice.' Frank checks his watch. 'I've got a hangover.'

'I found out about Dominic easily enough. A few misdemeanours, petty stuff generally. He's an unpleasant guy with a penchant for violence, but he's no master criminal. Anything more complicated than swinging a fist at someone a lot weaker than himself, and he's out of his depth. If he's involved in anything, you can be pretty sure someone else is pulling the strings.'

'And Rupert Fitzwilliam?'

'Yeah, well that's where the sapper analogy comes in. I hadn't been digging into Rupert very far when I got the distinct impression that someone was digging in the opposite direction. The person or persons digging towards me were gathering information, too. I got the definite feeling they were heavily armed, and didn't welcome my intrusion. I beat a hasty retreat. It may be my imagination but I'm also getting a feeling that whoever it was, knows it was me down there, digging.'

'Any idea who?'

'None, but too many more questions from your truly, and I might find myself eye to eye.'

'Time for a dignified withdrawal then.'

'Yeah, I've got enough on my plate. I can tell you one thing, though. Mr Rupert Fitzwilliam is a nasty and dangerous piece of work. He wears his sophistication and wealth like a mask, to hide something truly rotten underneath. There's nothing on him, of course. But there's a lot going on around him. Getting down to the real Rupert Fitzwilliam is like swatting flies to reach a turd.'

'Nicely put.'

'And apt. There have been a couple of nasty assault accusations, later withdrawn, a few non-disclosure agreements, and a lot of unpleasant rumours about his preferences and his habits. If I had time, and hadn't felt the warm breath of conspiracy on my cheeks, I'd have looked into his financial dealings, too. There's something distinctly dodgy about your Mr Fitzwilliam.'

'At least I've got some idea what I'm dealing with.'

'If I were you, and I say this knowing what a stubborn son-of-a-bitch you can be, I'd get on with my holiday, steer well clear of everyone involved, and then get back to the nice, safe city, and the day-to-day grind of sordid urban crime.'

'Yeah, I think you're right. I've got Jason and Janice to think about. Cheers, Guy.'

'Look after yourself.'

Frank slips his phone back in his pocket. Behind him, Maggie and Janice are still in the kitchen, and the radio pulses out a song by The Pogues. Richard is already out, down at the boat; he's obviously a man with a cast iron constitution. Jason is in the lounge on a computer game, and Sammy is snoring away in bed.

Everything is as it should be, he tells himself.

Only it isn't.

Something deep inside him is churning. He has this feeling, something he can't shift, like indigestion, like a knot in his intestines. He drives away the sensation with a shake of the head. This is their holiday, for God's sake, and for two weeks they're supposed to be bonding over crazy golf, beach games and pub lunches, not getting embroiled in ghostly happenings, and village villainies.

This isn't the way normal people bond.

He manages a rueful smile.

It's working, though.

Frank walks back into the kitchen to find Maggie.

'We should be setting off back.' He opens the hall door and calls through to the lounge. 'Come on, Jason, it's time we were going.'

'You'll come again?' Maggie asks.

'We'd love to.' Janice's face brightens in a wide smile. 'We've a few more days yet.'

Chapter 27

Jason lies on his bed in the caravan, his head sinking into the pillow, his book unread on the table beside him. He closes his eyes. He has a lot to think about, like how he ought to tell Frank what Sammy has told him, like how he's promised Sammy he won't tell, like how Frank is a policeman, and policemen have rules to obey, and how he's pretty sure that one of those rules will require Frank to pass on what he knows, and get Dominic arrested.

That would be good.

That would be really good.

He forces his eyes tight shut.

It wouldn't be good for Sammy's mum and dad, though.

Sammy said that if Dominic was locked away, Rupert would want all his money back, and his mum and dad would have to sell the house and the boats, and go and live somewhere else.

'You could come and live near me,' Jason had said hopefully.

'That'd be cool,' Sammy had said, 'but Mum and Dad wouldn't like the town. This is where they live. It wouldn't be the same. You've got to promise not to tell.'

And Jason had promised.

You keep promises you make to your friends. Otherwise, you aren't a proper friend at all. You're like those sneaks at school who pass on secrets to everybody, and laugh at you for telling them in the first place. He doesn't want to be like them.

But it worries him. An annoying voice deep inside keeps asking the same question, chewing on his conscience.

A really good friend would do what was right, and what was best, even if it meant breaking a promise, wouldn't he? A true friend would rescue Sammy, no matter what. A true friend would tell Frank, and face the consequences.

But Jason isn't ready for that.

Not yet.

'You're quiet.' Frank looks up from the sports' pages. It's early afternoon now and the family are lounging on the caravan's bench seats. The sun breaks through the windows and casts long shadows of cups and cans across the table.

'Still tired after last night,' Maggie says. 'It was good fun, though, wasn't it?'

Jason allows his eyes to settle momentarily on each of them—Frank with his newspaper on his lap and his feet on the table, his mum sipping a cup of tea and checking photographs on her phone—and he feels a warmth inside him, slipping out to meet the warmth of the sun. But he feels guilty, too. Like he doesn't deserve it.

'I love holiday photos,' his mum says. 'I've got lots from the boat. Some of you and Sammy. Look.'

She holds the phone for him to see, and there he is, leaning over the side of the boat, reaching down to catch the spray, with Sammy beside him, watching.

'You look really happy, the pair of you. Just think what lovely memories we'll have of our holiday.'

Conscience chews at his flesh; nipping, tearing.

If it was me, Mum and Frank would want to know. They'd make it stop. They'd help me.

Then he remembers what Sammy said.

If my dad finds out, he'll kill Dominic.

He glances at Frank, the same question lurking like a monster in the cupboard of his mind. Frank threw Dominic in the harbour because of Yapps. What would he do if Dominic hurt him like he hurt Sammy? Would he act like a policeman, or would he go looking for Dominic?

He'd kill him. Jason's brow tightens. *He would. He'd kill him. And then where would we be? Mum? Me?*

He is saved from having to think any more by a knock at the door.

'Who on earth can that be?' His mum looks across at Frank. 'Be a pet, Frank, I've barely sat down since we got back.'

'I've a feeling I already know,' Frank says. 'I'll bet it's Sammy.'

He's right. Sammy stands on the step, breathing hard, his eyes bright and excited.

'It's nice to see you've woken up at last.' Frank looks him up and down. 'You were out for the count when we set off home. Come on in, lad. You look shattered.'

Sammy grins a particularly wide grin. 'I ran all the way. Can Jason come up to the old castle with me? The one we saw from the boat. It's not far. We can take a phone so you know we're safe.'

'Ooh, I don't know, Frank,' Janice says. 'It looked dangerous and they'd have to walk along the cliff path an' all.'

Frank looks from Janice to the boys, sitting together now on the bench seat, eyes hopeful, waiting.

'Are you planning to throw yourselves off the cliff?' he asks. 'A straight answer now. No messing about. And the castle. Do you intend to fall off the wall, and crash onto the rocks?'

They shake their heads, wide-grinning faces.

'Of course, it's up to your mum, Jason, but I'm inclined to offer a compromise. I'll walk with you half way, and when we can see the castle, I'll leave you. I fancy a walk of my own, and I know your mum would rather stay here this afternoon. You can phone me when you're on your way back, and I'll join you.'

Janice still looks uncertain.

'I've been lots of times,' Sammy says. 'I know which bits to keep away from.'

'We'll be careful, Mum. Go on, say yes.'

'Jason is ten, Janice. You can't mollycoddle him. He's got to learn to look after himself.'

'You'll keep an eye on them?'

'Scout's honour,' he says.

'You were never in the bloody scouts.' Janice's face breaks, and light floods through the fissures. 'Alright, go on then. But you be careful, you hear me?'

'I'll just finish my cup of tea, and grab a sandwich,' Frank says. 'Do you want something while you wait, Sammy?'

Sammy nods, and the two boys grin at each other.

Fifteen minutes later, they set off across the beach, and onto the steep incline of the cliff path. Frank sets the pace. He hasn't said anything to Janice but he plans to keep an eye on the boys for as long as he can. He also wants to take a look somewhere else. He reckons if he cuts across the moorland, he can reach the path inland, and cut through the woods to Leybury Grange.

I just want to see the place. Take a look, nothing more. Nice walk. Idle curiosity.

Then he remembers.

I never was a good liar, not even to myself.

Chapter 28

Frank leaves Jason and Sammy at the top of the first, long cliff. He checks his watch. Plenty of time. It is no more than half an hour to the road and, from there, another ten minutes to the woodland surrounding the hall. Two and a half hours max, there and back. He'll be able to keep a check on the boys, too, off and on, as they come into sight on the cliff path, and then on the battlements and towers of the castle itself.

He sets off walking across the grass and heather and then, the ground being mostly even and easy, he breaks into a jog. When he finds a sheep path leading towards the track, he allows his pace to increase.

Just what I needed. There are some big matches when I get back. Can't be letting the side down.

He pauses when the sheep path reaches the track, and looks back for Jason and Sammy. At first, he doesn't see them and then... there they are. Rounding a rocky bluff and running towards a bay, just before the final rise to the castle. He hears a cry, carried on the wind; a laugh, a shout. Jason.

Oh, to be that age again.

Or maybe not.

Childhood isn't always easy. Look at Jason. He's spent his share of tears. Sammy is a lonely kid too. His heart flies across the moorland, and circles the two boys, protecting them. He's always been like that. Hardened as he is to the seedier side of life, it's the harm done to kids that always get to him.

He recalls some of the cases he's worked on and, over the distance of the grey moor, and against the restless sea, he gathers Jason and Sammy, and holds them close.

Looks like they've met another friend.

Behind the two boys, arms held wide for balance, another child tries to catch them. He watches as she slows, her arms now at her side.

A wave of sadness ripples the moor grasses, and circles round him like a warning.

There's nothing more desolate than a lonely child.

He watches as she turns back, and disappears around the cliff, then he walks along the track until it joins the road at an open gate. Another five minutes brings him under the cover of oaks and sycamores, where he pauses to watch the flickering light breaking through the foliage, brightening leaves and casting rippling shadows, like sunlight on water.

A path, narrow and leaf-strewn, curls through the trees to his left. He checks all around, and then slips into the deeper shade. Out of the sun, the chill autumn air takes a firm hold.

It is necessary to move carefully now. The path, although recently trodden—he can see footprints in damp patches and muddy pools—is overgrown, and branches hang perilously low. Frank takes in the footprints as he passes them. A professional eye tells him they're size ten or eleven and from a training shoe with a worn tread. He's tempted to guess the weight of the man but laughs the idea away.

Sherlock Holmes, I'm not.

He is certain though that the prints were made in poor light. Why else do they pursue a line through muddy pools which he, Frank, sidesteps? Either this guy was in a hurry or he couldn't see clearly.

His imagination starts to play games. Why was someone walking along this path in the late evening or after dark?

It could be entirely innocent, of course. Perhaps Rupert Fitzwilliam enjoys an evening walk. Perhaps he has a pair of trainers specifically for the purpose. Curious though, that the footprints only go one way, towards the house.

A circular walk? Down the drive and back through the trees - or a midnight visitor? Nefarious intent, or a meeting?

Frank decides it's fruitless to speculate, and wipes the slate of his mind clean. Ahead, the sky brightens, and there's hope of a release from the oppression of the trees. He steps forward, ducking below branches until the path opens on a lawn partly circled by trees. In the centre stands a summer house:

octagonal, half wood and half window and a roof rising from eight sides to a point where a weather vane stands. A witch with a pointed hat.

Beyond the summer house, perhaps seventy metres away, the gothic façade of a country house stands in splendid isolation, surrounded by lawns and sandy driveways. Its turrets rise darkly and the front, with false battlements and small windows, has all the qualities of a Victorian melodrama. Ugly French windows have been gashed into the walls; the only sign of the modern world.

Frank waits for a moment and watches. It won't do to approach openly across the wide lawns, but neither will it be sensible to skulk in the undergrowth like some sort of thief.

A stroll along the edge of the trees, like someone who thought he was on a footpath, and only recently lost it. Looking for a way out, keeping a discreet distance. Dark against the trees but not hiding.

He is about to step forward when he sees a movement in the summer house. He slips back into the shadows, and watches a young woman emerge through the single door. She is tall and elegant, and holds her hands clasped in front of her. She walks with a casual gait and there is a certain nonchalance in her movements and manner. She is at home here. Everything about her oozes elegance and good taste, from the dark hair—shoulder length and curling gracefully across her forehead and cheek—to her expensive pastel blouse and flesh-tight jeans. There's an attractive vulnerability about her.

The man who follows her is younger, perhaps in his mid-twenties and he seems ill at ease, as if nervous to be found in such a place and in such company. He glances back at the house, and ahead towards the trees.

'Can we not go back inside?' Frank hears him say. 'We're too conspicuous. He might see us.'

The woman flicks an irritable look at him, like ash from a cigarette. She turns aside, and walks towards the trees. Frank slips down behind the trunk of an oak, and listens. They are only a few metres away.

'How did you find him, Mr Carver?' Her voice is quiet and her words, like her gaze, slip away from her, and disappear among the trees.

'How do you mean?'

'Did you find him...' She hesitates, fumbling for the words like gloved fingers at a lock. 'Did you find him his usual self or... perhaps more anxious, more distracted?'

'He spoke about ghosts, but that's nothing new. Then, for a moment, it was as if he thought they were listening. It was creepy. But it lasted only a moment and then he was okay again. His usual self, whatever that is.'

'How do you mean?'

'It's like he flicks a switch in his head. One minute he's cold, sarcastic, distant and the next... well, you know how scary he can be. Paranoid, angry.'

Her voice is fainter, as she turns and faces Carver.

'What news did you bring him?'

'He had me follow Zachary Blight, keep an eye, report back.'

'And what did you report, Mr Carver?'

'Nothing much. There was nothing much to tell.'

'Then you can tell *me*. Leave nothing out.'

'I followed him to Grantley. He spent a lot of time on the green beside the harbour.'

'Doing what?'

'Watching the cop and his family, like he wanted them to know he was there. He made no secret of it. I think he wanted to provoke a reaction.'

'And did her succeed, Carver?'

'The guy walked across. There was an exchange.'

'What did they say?'

'I was too far away. They talked, that's all, then the cop went back to his family, and Blight walked away. He went to a café down near the harbour, and met a guy I've not seen before. They sat there for half an hour and then Blight left.'

'You told my brother all this?'

'Yes.'

Jocelyn's voice becomes faint. Frank strains to hear it. It's as if she has to have an answer but dreads to know. He kneels down, and risks a glance round the bole of the tree. Her back is towards him. Carver is blocked from view.

'How did he respond?'

Carver looks across the lawn as if Rupert Fitzwilliam might be listening.

'Not well. He sees conspiracies everywhere. He scares me, sometimes.'

'He's ill. Poor Rupert. If you knew, you'd understand.' She stops, seemingly fearful to say more.

'I don't want to understand. I'm getting out of here. I told him tonight.' Jocelyn's voice has a hair-line fracture, a sliver of pain breaking.

'He feels so alone. He thinks we all leave him.'

There's a moment of silence. Frank begins to think the meeting is at an end, that the figures will part and go their way. But Carver speaks again.

'There was something else,' he says. 'Something I wish I hadn't told him.'

Carver's voice drops to a whisper, as if the blades of grass might absorb his words, recording them to be played back later, incriminating him.

'After Blight left the café near the marina, he walked through the town to the local library.'

Jocelyn laughs softly.

'I didn't have Zachary Blight down as a literary man. More of your *Sun* or *Daily Mail* sort. I always imagined his lips would move if he had to read anything with more than two syllables. What could he possibly want in a library?'

'I couldn't get close, not without drawing attention but I know he found what he was looking for. After an hour, he called the librarian, and had him print out a page. Then he headed back to the car park, and drove away.'

'I assume you made conversation with the librarian.' There is a tremor in Jocelyn's voice which she tries hard to repress. She kneels down and plucks a flower, then rolls the stem round and round in her fingers, slowly, casually, like therapy.

'He was a miserable jobsworth of a guy. A retired type with a suspicious mind, and a red face, swollen with self-importance. He wouldn't tell you the time without authorisation. But I got into conversation with a younger man who was sitting close to Blight. He said he didn't pay much attention but he caught an occasional glimpse of what he was reading. He was definitely interested in Leybury Grange and its recent history. And...'

He pauses, as if unsure whether to continue.

'And?'

'At one point, Zachary leaned back sharply, and the guy saw what he mouthed, remembered what he said.'

Jocelyn is breathing quickly. She turns aside, the flower forgotten, its therapy failing. She drops it, broken, onto the grass.

'It was a name. Melissa.'

Jocelyn gasps, and her hand rises to her mouth. 'You told Rupert that?'

'Yes.'

For a moment Jocelyn looks like she might fall, but she regains control, draws herself up, and turns back.

'Thank you,' she says, without a tremor, her eyes firm once more. Only the rapid palpitation of her breast gives any indication of the turmoil within. 'You've done well. I won't forget what you've done for me. Now, go. Leave me alone.'

Frank ducks down and hugs the shadows, as Carver slips away through the trees. Jocelyn remains for a few minutes more, deep in thought. A strangled sob breaks from her, but she subdues it, and raises her eyes to follow the charcoal line of the trees.

'Then it's time to act,' she says, and her voice is firm, and her eyes determined. 'It can wait no longer.'

Frank watches as she walks away. His gaze flies ahead to settle on the old, gothic hall. At first, he sees nothing, but then a curtain moves, and behind it a figure.

Has Rupert Fitzwilliam been watching? For how long? What has he seen?

Frank slips back among the trees. He checks his watch. It's time he got back to Jason and Sammy. He's stayed far longer than he intended, but at least he's learned something.

Chapter 29

*C*lose your eyes.

From your vantage point beside the summer house, you can see Jocelyn and Carver and, beyond them, crouched among the trees, peering round the cratered trunk of an old oak, Frank Miller. He, like you, is watching, listening, questioning.

Is there someone else, too, watching them from the distant Grange? You look closely. Yes, there it is again, the movement of a curtain, a change in the field of darkness, a face perhaps.

Move closer.

Rupert Fitzwilliam holds the skein of curtain between finger and thumb, and eases it from his face. He stares, impassive. His eyes are motionless and there is no more expression than on a topiary gnome. But beneath that exterior, something stirs.

For reasons you cannot quite comprehend, he makes you shudder.

Back at the summer house, Jocelyn shudders, too, though that is more likely the consequence of the chill breeze which flits through her light clothes as she talks to Carver. She too betrays little emotion. Her hand, on occasion, drifts through her hair or reaches across her shoulder in a half hug. She holds the reins of her emotions tight, and betrays nothing, while her mind works like a gnawing jaw on the bones of information Carver feeds her. Then he names the child, and oh, how she struggles to master her emotions, and how powerfully they surge.

What does she fear? That Zachary Blight tip-toes close to something she would keep concealed? If he stamps his foot, what worms will come crawling? If he speaks to Rupert, what then?

You wonder too about her sudden resolve and those words, those strange words.

'Then it's time to act. It can wait no longer.'

You feel a creeping dread encroach, like a poison filling your veins, slow and relentless.

You watch Jocelyn as she fades across the lawn and disappears like summer mist into the Grange and, as her slender form fades, you feel the feather touch of compassion. What, you wonder, is the burden she carries? It is a burden whose gravity drags at her core.

It is time now for you to slip away, like a coiled snake circling the ancient trunk into the treetops, to transform and leap like a squirrel from tree to tree, to break from the shadows, whence you sail like a bird through an ocean of sky.

As you fly, you pass over the old castle and your attention is caught by the sound of young voices.

Sammy and Jason are down there, temporary shadows scratched on the earth, then moving across the courtyard, over the walls and down passageways.

You cannot help but smile.

And weep.

Chapter 30

There is little left of the old castle. Much of the stonework was torn down in earlier centuries to build field walls, byres, and farmhouses. One tower rises high and misshapen above a stretch of battlement. Below lies the cliff and the restless sea. The tower and battlement, too close to the cliff to be removed safely, have escaped destruction. Below, doorways lead from a cobbled courtyard through shattered arches into the draughty shells of rooms, and through the crippled remnants of a gatehouse. Pathways wind around and down to a dark, round-arched cellar.

Jason pauses by the broken archway, and allows his eyes to follow the broken walls.

'This is brilliant.'

'There's a board which tells you about the castle.' Sammy balances on one low, uneven stretch of wall, arms outstretched. 'You went right past it.' He walks along to the end, and jumps down.

'We can read it later. I want to explore.'

'You want to go up to the tower?'

'Yeah, and the battlements where those people took our photograph.'

'Come on, then. Through that arch, and up the steps. Careful, though. They're all broken and worn down.'

'Hundreds and hundreds of feet walking round and round and up and up.'

'Knights and earls and dukes....'

'And servants.'

'Maybe even a king or queen...'

'And soldiers with swords, fighting back the enemy.'

Jason turns around on the narrow stair, and attacks. Sammy fights back valiantly.

'It's hard fighting upwards,' he pants, and concedes defeat.

From the battlements they gaze out over the sea.

'Look at that yacht.' Jason points to a blue-and-white vessel far out.

'I've seen it before,' Sammy says. 'I think they're on holiday.'

Jason raises a pretend camera to his eye and focusses.

'What are you doing?'

'I'm taking a photograph of me and you on your boat. We're out there waving back at us up here. Can't you see us-them?'

'You're mad.' Sammy raises a hand, and waves. 'I'm waving at us waving at us.'

'You're mad, too.'

'I know. We're mad together.'

'Imagine if we had guns. We could sink ships like on a fairground game.' Sammy takes a shot at the blue-and-white yacht. 'Got it!' he cries. 'Lost with all hands.'

'Someone's coming.' Jason points inland, where a car approaches along the track, raising a wake of dust.

'A tourist, probably.' Sammy takes another shot at the fairground boat, and sinks it for a second time. 'Or maybe someone with a dog. Not many people come here. There's only enough space for a couple of cars.'

'Maybe they're spies or secret agents.'

'We'd better hide.'

'Quick! The cellar.'

They flit down the uneven stairs, and into the courtyard.

'This way.' Sammy calls in a low voice. 'Keep down, don't let them see.'

They slip around walls and down a narrow passageway beneath the arched roof of the cellar, which supports, it seems, the entire weight of the tower. There they stop, in the damp shadows, and they wait.

Nothing. Not a sound.

'Let's sneak back.' Jason's voice is low and conspiratorial, the voice of a secret agent on a dangerous mission. 'Let's hear what they're saying. We can stay hidden behind the wall.'

They retrace their steps to a point where they can see the courtyard without much danger of being seen. A man stands beside a metal grille which covers a deep well. He draws on a blue inhaler.

'I know him,' Jason whispers. 'He's the guy who was watching us when we went to the town. My dad went to speak to him. What's he doing here?'

'He's talking to someone. Can you hear what he's saying?'

'No.'

'Shall we creep closer?'

'He'd see us.'

'Who's he talking to? Can you see?'

Jason creeps forward, hidden by the crumbling stone, and then drops down, his back set against the wall, his legs outstretched. He waits a moment until he feels courage fill him like fuel, then he turns to the wall, and slowly raises his head. He drops back down, and scurries back to Sammy on his hands and knees.

'Who is it?'

Jason is breathing hard, and trembling. The dial measuring courage had dropped to empty.

'Dominic,' he manages to mouth.

Sammy looks back the way they came, towards the tower, the battlements, the sea.

''We've got to run away. If he sees us, he'll—'

Jason, as pale as his friend, his eyes glazed, shakes his head. 'He's coming this way.'

The two boys draw in behind the wall and sit, their knees tucked, their arms wrapped round their legs. They draw deeper into the shadows as if, with luck, they might disappear, sucked into the world of ghosts and stone.

They listen.

Above the beating of their hearts and the aching of their lungs, they hear voices. The men have stopped. Jason hears the striking of a match, and a deep intake of breath. They're sitting on a wall, not far away; the same wall which Jason recently deserted. Their voices are low, difficult to hear. Sammy's arms are wrapped around his head now, which is drawn low over his knees, as if invisibility lies there, and the tighter he closes his eyes, the less chance there is of discovery.

'There's one more consignment,' Zachary says, his voice grating like a knife sharpened on the rock.

'Yeah.'

'Just you and the kid, same as usual, then it's over. Finished. For us, anyway.'

His voice carries a strange menace, certainly a warning.

Dominic yawns, nonchalant. 'He'll be planning something else for us. He always has plans.'

'One step ahead, same as ever. You're right, but be careful.'

'Why?' A fleeting tremor in his voice.

'You've become a liability, Dominic. The dog, the kid, the guy at the harbour. You're drawing attention. He doesn't like that.'

Dominic risks a nervous laugh. 'I'm safe enough. He needs me. Worry about yourself.'

It isn't hard to imagine a smile slip over Zachary's face, like a sheet over a corpse.

'I'm not worried. I've got plans. You could be part of them.'

'Yeah?'

More definite. 'Yeah.' A pause. 'You know things.'

It's Dominic's turn to laugh.

'He'd kill you if he thought you were making plans.'

'He'll kill us both, if he thinks there's a risk. He doesn't take chances.'

A silence. Dominic is thinking, weighing words, grains of sand.

'What's your plan?'

A smile from Zachary, giving nothing away.

'Get the consignment first. Then we'll talk.'

'I could tell him you plan to betray him. Make myself safe, trusted.'

A deep, low laugh, stretched tight and long.

'Safe? You think you can ever be safe from him? You've seen what he's like, how he's become. He's unstable, dangerous.' A longer laugh, like a private joke, not very funny. 'I'm offering you a way out. Take it or leave it. I don't give a shit.' He stands up, ready to leave. 'If you're in, you're in. If you're out, you're dead. Trust me, I know. Your choice.'

'And if I'm in?'

Another low growl of a laugh.

'There's something I need from you. Something you know. You tell me, and I'll finish him, and make you safe.'

'And if I go straight back, and tell him what you've said?'

A heavy silence.

'You underestimate me, Dominic. A lot of people do that. It's a mistake.'

Zachary walks away,

'What do you want to know?' Dominic calls after him.

'Later, not now. I need to be sure of you.'

Dominic must follow him because their voices are distant now. Jason slips round to the wall, and raises his head to watch. The two men are side by side, walking between the crumbling towers. He creeps back.

'Come on, Sammy. It's time to go. Come on.'

He drags Sammy by the arm, and they slip from their hiding place, and run, crouched, towards the gate, where they stop and check the way ahead. Dominic walks towards the cliff path, Zachary towards his car. They stay hidden as he reverses, turns and drives away, raising a cloud of dust from the track across the field.

In the distance, Frank is making his way across the moorland towards the cliff top.

'Come on, let's head that way.' Jason points a line inland to cut in front of Frank. 'We'll be safe with Frank.'

They slip out and run. Only as they get close do they shout. Frank turns towards them and waves.

On the clifftop, Dominic hears their call. He pauses and watches as they reach Frank, and his arms circle round their shoulders. He hears their distant laughter. An ugly sneer curls his lips, resentful, angry. Something burns deep inside him, something he can't extinguish, seeing them now, down there, heading across the heather, together.

After a moment, his eyes slip their envious leash, and he turns to look back at the ruined castle. Then he looks at the boys. He's working something out. Could they have? Did they?

He frowns, and turns to pace over the cliff top, down towards the caravan park, and the village. His head is down, his brow furrowed.

He's thinking.

Chapter 31

Frank wakes early next morning to the sound of an ambulance, its siren blazing, heading towards their van. It pulls up outside, the siren cuts, the engine turns off. Doors open and close, and there are voices: urgent, hurried voices, asking questions, giving answers. Someone sobs. Someone groans.

Frank leans up on his elbows, and reaches for the curtain, but their window overlooks the dunes, and the beach. The noise is coming from the other side of the van, nearer to Jason's window, maybe at the van next to theirs.

'What's going on?' Janice, drowsy, hair in her half-closed eyes, leans up now. 'What's all that noise?'

Then Jason flings back the door, his eyes excited.

'There's an ambulance and a police car outside. Come and look.'

Then he's gone, pulling on a shoe as he opens the door, impatient to be outside.

'Wait,' Frank calls after him. 'Don't get in the way.' He drags on his trousers and shoes, and grabs a shirt.

'Tell Jason to come back in at once.' Janice clambers from her bed, and reaches for a dressing gown. 'There'll be enough ghouls out there with their bloody camera phones.'

A uniformed policeman is cordoning off the area around the neighbouring van. Another is in a police car, door open, talking on his radio. Lights flash. The ambulance reverses to the van, and its rear doors open. Jason stands beside a small cluster of people, near the cordon, peering round them, and looking for a gap where he can get to the front.

'Your mum says you're to go inside and watch from the window. It's not nice, gawping at other people's misfortunes.'

He gets a sharp look for that, from a middle-aged, overweight guy in a rock band T-shirt, but stares him out.

'Go on, Jason. I'm going to talk to the detective over there, the guy talking to the site manager.'

Jason disappears into the van. The detective is a young guy, clean shaven, neat, blue suit a bit worn on the collar and pockets, a shirt on the grubby side of white; two days wear, Frank reckons. He knows the signs. When he closes his notebook, Frank raises a hand and beckons him over.

'DI Frank Miller. I'm a city cop on holiday. We're in the van next door. Anything I can do to help?'

'DS Templeton.' He holds out a hand, bitten nails cut to hide ragged edges. He has a tight grip, though, and clear, enquiring eyes, weighing and measuring. 'Did you hear anything last night? Anything out of the ordinary? Anyone wandering around late on, probably well after midnight?'

Frank shakes his head. 'Out like a light. I'll ask Janice and Jason, though. They might have.'

'Wife and kid?'

'Sort of, yeah. Good as.'

'I'll come and talk when I've finished here. You'll be in the van?'

'Yeah.'

The door to the neighbours' caravan opens, and a paramedic backs out, holding the end of a stretcher. An old woman's face above a blanket, eyes closed, blistered lips, stone white complexion. Like a photograph of a corpse.

'Jesus,' Frank says.

'Yeah. She'll be lucky to make it.'

'What happened?'

'Not sure yet. We'll get the experts in to take a look. It looks to me like some kind of poisoning, with those blisters round the mouth. Maybe she mistook a bottle, drank the wrong thing or maybe it's something else. It's bad, though.'

An old man, as pale as his wife—eyes blotched red, mouth trembling—steps into the ambulance. A paramedic climbs in and closes the door behind her. The ambulance reverses and turns and, as it makes its way along the roadway between caravans, and reaches the clubhouse, the siren rises to a crescendo once more. It speeds, lights flashing, alarm screaming, into the distance.

'There's a strong smell in there,' Templeton says. 'It gets in your eyes, burns. I've had to keep the guys out.'

'Any ideas what?'

'Ammonia maybe, or bleach. I've got to go. I've got lots of questions and, so far, not many answers. You know how it is. I'll call over. Half an hour maybe?'

'I'll have the kettle on.'

'Good man.'

Frank opens the kitchen cupboards.

'What's happened out there?' Janice calls through. 'Jason says the old woman next door is ill.'

'Looks like she mistook one bottle for another, and drank something nasty.'

'Ugh.'

'Have we got any cleaning materials in here, Janice?'

'In the tall cupboard behind you, with the mops and brushes. What are you looking for?'

'Bleach or ammonia. Something like that.'

'The bleach is on the shelf facing you. It's bright yellow plastic with one of those funny locking tops. You can't miss it.'

Frank picks up the bottle, turns it in his hand, presses and twists the lid, takes a sniff, recoils.

He closes the cupboard, and goes back to the end lounge.

'Did you hear anything last night?' he asks. 'Anyone wandering about?'

'Not a thing. I slept like a dormouse. I didn't wake until the racket from that ambulance. Why? It's just an accident, isn't it?'

'Maybe. What about you, Jason? Did you hear anything?'

'No.'

Janice shakes her head. 'If it wasn't an accident—'

'They've got to cover every base. It's just good police work.'

'Well, I suppose you'd know.'

Half an hour later, there's a knock at the door.

DS Templeton steps inside and extends a hand.

This is Janice,' Frank says. 'and the funny-looking one over there is Jason.'
Jason sticks out a tongue in reply.

'I'm DS Templeton,' Templeton says. 'Keith.'

'Would you like a coffee, Keith?' Janice asks. 'Sit yourself down.'

'Is the woman dead?' Jason asks. 'She looked dead.'

'For goodness sake, Jason, what sort of a question is that?' Janice snaps, but Templeton laughs.

'Kids,' he says. 'She's gone to the hospital. They'll look after her there.'

Templeton pauses over his coffee. He looks across at Frank.

'No harm telling you, I suppose,' he says. 'It looks to me like there was some chemical in the water tank. Unfortunately, the water was low so it was quite concentrated, and the old woman has no sense of smell. Her age, I suppose. But why? I mean...' He shrugs. 'An elderly couple on holiday. It doesn't make sense. They've been coming here for years apparently. They've got a couple of grown -up kids back home and three grandchildren.'

'Will she be alright?' Janice says.

'It's too soon to tell. She's got bad chemical burns around her mouth.'

'What a horrible thing to happen.'

'Maybe they...' Frank hesitates, holds his tongue.

Maybe the old couple weren't the target.

Chapter 32

'I worry about that boy.' Maggie is at the kitchen table, pastry rolled, potatoes cubed, carrots sliced, onion and mince simmering nicely on the stove. 'Sometimes, it's like he's carrying the weight of the world. And the hours he spends in his room, with never a friend in sight. And now, just when everything seemed to be getting better...'

Richard is at the sink, making a preliminary foray against the washing-up, which has gathered its forces on the worktop and table. He scrubs and rinses a baking dish.

'Maybe you should ring Frank, see if he can cast any light, see if anything happened at the castle? He won't mind. He knows what it's like worrying about family. Ask him if Jason said anything. Maybe him or Janice noticed something, some change between them, when they came back from the castle. Sammy was so looking forward to taking Jason up there. He was like a normal, happy boy again. It was lovely to see. Then he comes back and locks himself in his room, and we can hardly get a word out of him.'

Richard keeps his head down. He looks like there's something on his mind.

'He says they had a nice time,' Maggie continues. 'and that they're still good friends. So, I don't know what—' Maggie rolls the pastry with more aggression than is necessary, lifts it, places it over a large plate, and trims the edge. 'But listen to him now.' Music beats through the floor, vibrating the glassware. 'He's played that bloody tune ten times now. It's not natural.'

Richard throws the washing-up cloth down and turns around.

'I phoned earlier,' he says. 'I'd have told you earlier but...'

'What?' Maggie wipes her hands on a floral tea towel, and drops onto a wooden-backed kitchen chair. Beads of sweat form on her brown. 'Is it our Sammy? Tell me.'

'No, nothing like that. Frank says he'll talk to Jason, and he'll phone back as soon as he can. No, it's something else. I didn't want to worry you. The old woman in the van next to them. She drank bleach or ammonia or some chemical cleaner, apparently. She's in hospital and in a bad way.'

'How the hell do you drink ammonia? Was she, you know, not quite right upstairs?'

'Dementia, you mean? I suppose that would explain it. I don't know. Frank says the police officer told him they think someone put it in the water supply. It's their own van, and it isn't plumbed into the mains. There's just a tank outside. Frank thinks someone tampered with it.'

'Why would someone do an awful thing like that?'

'Frank thinks...' He hesitates. 'He wonders if it might not have been intended for them, someone daft enough to think it was *their* tank.'

Maggie stares at him, her eyes catching his and locking on to them. He tries to look away but is drawn back, caught by the magnet of her fear.

'Dominic,' she says. She stands, gets back to her baking, brushing her fear aside like flour from the table top. 'No, even Dominic isn't that stupid. It sounds like Frank is adding two and two and making forty-seven. It'll be an accident. There'll be an explanation.'

'But if Dominic is capable of something like that, then—'

'No!' Maggie slams the ball of pastry heavily on the table. A flock of flour birds rise up, scatter in the air, and settle further away. 'It'll be an accident.'

'But if it isn't an accident, we can't let it carry on, Maggie. We've got to tell the police what we know.'

'We don't know anything. We've never known, not for sure.'

'We can tell them what we suspect, then.'

'We've no proof, not a shred of it. Just a few boat trips, some suspicions, the way he takes Sammy with him. It's not enough. He'd be free in hours, and then what? Tell me that! Then what?'

'The police could stake him out, do whatever police do.' Richard raises his hands, a gesture of futility. Even his voice betrays him. Maggie beats the dough: angry, destructive pounding. She stops, and stares at nothing, her hands gripping tight.

'We'll lose everything. The boats, our home. We'll have to sell up, and move away. Besides, Rupert Fitzwilliam...' She shudders. 'Think what he might do. We've got Sammy to think of.' She brushes tears from her eyes with a dusty sleeve.

Richard is beside her in a few steps. He holds her close, with her cheek on his chest, her powdery hands leaving dusty prints on his back.

'I'll find a way,' he says. 'I promise.'

The back door flies open.

Dominic.

'Get yourselves a room,' he sneers.

Maggie feels Richard's body tense beside her. His muscles tighten, his mood darkens. Powder keg. She holds him closer, speaking to him, mind to mind, body to body.

He hears her, feels her warning him, and relaxes, forces himself to breathe slowly, to drag a smile from somewhere, and make a joke of it.

'I need the boat tomorrow, and Sammy, too.' Dominic raises a hand to quell the protest. 'It's the last time.'

Richard eyes him. 'The last time?'

'For a few months, maybe longer. Maybe forever. Who knows?'

Richard knows better than to ask. Long ago, they'd agreed he wouldn't ask, and he wouldn't know. That was okay by him and Maggie. They didn't want to be involved.

'He just borrows the boat, that's all. We keep our eyes, ears and mouths closed.'

'But he's got Sammy involved.'

'Sammy doesn't see anything. He doesn't know anything. I don't like it, but there it is. And we get to keep the boats, and our home. That's good for all of us. Sammy, too.'

'I still don't like it.'

'Me neither, but he's got us, hasn't he? There's nothing we can do.'

'I know. If it was only us... but Sammy?'

'He won't come to any harm.'

The kitchen door opens behind them. Sammy stands there, his eyes red, his cheeks blotched.

'I'm not going with you,' he says, straight at Dominic. His fists are clenched, and he's shaking.

Dominic eyes him slowly up and down, like a predator surveying his next meal. A smile drags itself over his lips.

'Someone's in a bad mood.'

'I'm not going with you.'

Dominic turns to the door. His hand on the handle, he turns back. If eyes could snarl...

'Eight o'clock, Sammy. Last trip. Don't let me down.'

The door closes behind him.

'I'm not going,' Sammy screams. 'I'm not.'

Richard's arm is round his shoulder, holding him tight, and his mum is in front of him, kneeling, stroking his cheeks.

'No,' Richard says. 'You're bloody not.'

'Over my dead body.' His mum glares back, as if Dominic is still in the doorway; a look that could staple him to the wall.

'We won't be here at eight o'clock. We'll go for a walk tomorrow morning,' Richard says, and the line of his jaw is as hard as the rocks below the castle walls. 'Me and you. We'll go and see Jason and his family. What do you say?'

Sammy nods. A watery smile breaks, and flickers like sunlight on water; a momentary glimmer, nothing more.

'I'm coming, too.' His Mum hugs him close, all three now together, backs facing outwards like defensive walls, buttressed against the world.

The telephone rings.

Chapter 33

'Richard was on the phone earlier,' Frank picks up a spoon and stirs sugar into a cup of coffee. 'He was asking if anything happened when the boys were at the castle. He says Sammy's acting strangely.'

Janice looks up. 'Jason seemed alright when he came back, until the drama next door. Did you notice anything when you met them?'

'They were kind of clingy, didn't move far from me. I thought they were just tired. Has Jason said anything to you?'

'He's been in his bedroom reading his holiday book, the one he bought in Grantley. I've hardly seen him.'

'Maybe a bit quiet? Kind of pale?'

'Hardly surprising after an ambulance visit, and a poor old lady poisoned. I wish we'd kept him away.'

'We weren't to know.'

'I wish he wouldn't keep his feelings boxed up like he does. It's not healthy.'

'Most kids are like that, boys especially. I was the same. I had to deal with everything myself. Nobody was allowed to help.'

The door opens, and Jason appears.

'What's up?'

'Richard phoned. Was everything okay at the castle? Sammy seems a bit strange, upset like. You didn't fall out, did you?'

'No, nothing. It was fun.'

'You're still friends?' Janice asks.

'Course we are. Can I have a biscuit? I'm hungry.'

'You've no idea what's bothering Sammy?'

Jason has his head in the cupboard. He doesn't look up. 'No.'

It's clear from his voice, his posture, the momentary pause, that Jason is hiding something. When he emerges, cream biscuit in hand, he avoids their eyes and his words flutter like an injured bird.

'We had a great time, climbed the tower and everything.'

He returns to his room, and the door closes. A moment later, music fills the caravan; a barrier of sound cutting him off, shutting them out. It's as if they can hear his voice, caught and carried in the waves of sound.

Help me.

'There's something wrong.' Frank stares through the window, towards the sand and the sea, as if the answer lies out there somewhere. 'I'm sure there is.'

'Maybe a man-to-man talk would help,' Janice says.

Frank hesitates. They've made a lot of progress, him and Jason; they're almost close. But the bond is like brittle plastic. It could fracture as quickly as it has formed.

'I'll sound like a policeman. He might not like it.'

'Then I'll do it. I'll let him know we're here for him, and he can tell us anything, and that we'll help him, no matter what.' She stands up. 'I'll go and have a chat, see how things go.'

Chapter 34

It is a short conversation. It's clear to Janice from the moment she enters the room that Jason has nothing to say.

'You know you can tell me anything,' she says.

He frowns, looks irritable. 'There's nothing to tell. I'm fine. Why don't you listen to me?'

'Richard is worried about Sammy, you know. And we're worried about you.'

Jason groans, and throws himself on the bed, back turned.

'There's nothing to worry about. I'm fine. Will you go away and leave me alone? I want to read my book, and listen to my music.'

'And Sammy?'

'He's fine, too. Go away.'

'So long as you know we're here if you ever want to talk.'

'Whatever. Just let me read, will you?'

Janice reverses out of the room.

'Are you enjoying your holiday?' she ventures, and then regrets asking. It's such a foolish thing to say, almost like an accusation, like a plea, an invitation to lie.

A deep sigh. 'Yes. Now leave me alone.'

She closes the door, more worried than ever.

'No good?'

She shakes her head.

Frank sighs. 'Maybe I'll take him for a walk along the beach later. You never know.'

It's nearly an hour before Jason emerges. Frank reaches for his coat.

'I'm going for a walk out to the sea. I need a breath of air.'

He turns when he reaches the door, as if acting on an afterthought.

'Want to come?' he asks Jason. 'Twenty minutes, there and back. Give your mum some peace.'

Jason is about to shake his head, then seems to think about it.

'Yeah, okay.'

He picks up a coat, and they head down the narrow path to the shingle, from where they cross to the wide expanse of beach. There are just a few dog walkers along the shoreline. Jason doesn't speak, and Frank doesn't try to make him; they just walk, breathing the sea air, taking in the sky and the clouds.

'I wish I could fly,' Jason watches gulls circle and fall, and rise again.

'Me, too.' Frank holds his arms wide. 'Come on.'

'You're daft, you are.' Jason glances along the beach for anyone watching, stands still for a moment, then unfurls his arms, and flies after Frank, gathering speed. Take off. And, circling wide and wild they run until they reach the edge of the sea, breathless, and breathing hard.

'When you're playing for a team,' Frank says, as they gaze out towards the slender curve of the horizon, 'you can't let the opposition know you're tired. You have to breathe through your teeth so they can't tell. Like this.' He demonstrates. 'Go on, you try.'

Jason copies him.

'That's it. You've got to hide how tired you really feel, keep it secret, like.'

Secret. The word seems to impact on Jason. He turns and strolls slowly along the shore, kicking the seawater pools.

'If someone shares a secret, you have to keep it, don't you?' Jason doesn't look back, just down, like he's talking to the sand, and the sea. 'If you promised not to tell.'

'You do.' Frank puts an arm on his shoulder. 'What kind of a friend would you be if you broke a promise?' He hesitates, sensing Jason has something to share, something he needs to tell. It is so close he can feel it. But he also knows that it can disappear just as quickly, behind a wall of stony, hunched silence. Better to stay casual, conversational, nothing heavy.

He wishes Janice was there so he could walk ahead, and leave her and Jason together. They can talk to each other, those two. He used to feel left out, like it was a weapon Jason used against him. Now he's here, him and Jason, and he's the one he wants to talk to.

'Only...' he starts to say.

Jason looks up.

'Only sometimes, just sometimes, there are things more important than keeping a promise.'

'Like what?'

This is deep water; difficult, especially for him. He isn't used to children.

'Imagine you kept a secret, and someone got hurt because of it, maybe even the person you promised. How would you feel then?'

Jason miskicks a pebble. He picks it up and skims it across the flat calm beyond the waves.

'That was five,' he says. 'Bet you can't beat it.'

'I need a flat stone.' Frank searches, and finds a solitary flat pebble. He sends it skipping over the water until it crashes into a wave.

'Eight. You're looking at a champion skimmer, Jason. Don't forget that.'

'What if telling is very dangerous?'

Frank's heart beats harder.

'Like what?'

'Like lose their house or get beaten or killed or something. What if telling the secret might make everything worse?'

'Then it depends who you tell, whether you trust them. Maybe it should be someone who could offer advice, help even.'

A distant gull calls, the shrieks of children further along the shore, a wisp of breeze through his hair.

'You're a policeman,' Jason says. He looks up again, stands still. 'What if I shared a secret with you? Someone else's secret. Would you tell?'

A deep breath.

'I can't always promise to keep secrets, not if there's a crime or someone's in danger,' he says. Textbook reply. 'But I can promise to do everything in my power to make sure everyone is safe. I'm good at that.' He flexes an arm muscle. 'Tough guy, see.'

Jason grins. 'Mum's tougher.'

'That's true.' A moment's silence while Frank weighs his words. 'There comes a point where you have no choice, Jason. You know that point when you reach it. Deep down, it's clear. You have to tell, and you have to trust.'

'Sammy won't be my friend any more, not if I tell. He made me promise.'

'Is Sammy in danger?'

Jason thinks for a moment, nods.

'Then he might want you to tell. Deep down, he might want you to help him. You're his friend. You've got to make the right choice, decide what's best for him.'

Another stone, another wave, skimming slow then fast.

'Twelve.'

'Looks like you've got me beat. Damn, just a two. The wave got me.'

They're getting close to the end of the beach now, and the rocks and the cave lie ahead. Out on the bedrock, facing out towards the sea, a solitary figure, a girl, turns, and stares.

Molly.

Frank sees her, and draws in his breath, as if there are ripples in the air, unsteadying him. She turns, and walks towards the cave.

'Dominic was at the castle,' Jason says. 'He met someone. He's going to take the boat out, and Sammy has to go with him. He collects something from the pink buoy, and brings it back. Sammy doesn't want to go with him because Dominic hits him and things. He's really cruel to him.'

Quiet voice. Caring. 'Why couldn't you tell me?'

'Sammy wouldn't let me. He said, if you knew, you'd have to do something, and it would be bad for his mum and dad. He said that Dominic would talk his way out of everything, and then he'd come looking for him, and...'

The dam is breached and at first the words flow like floodwater. Then he grows quiet and more hesitant, as if he's holding something back.

'Is that everything, Jason?' Frank asks.

Jason nods, but his eyes flicker away.

Frank reads the signs. 'Are you sure?'

'Yes,' Jason says. 'What will you do?'

'Firstly,' Frank says, 'we make damned sure Sammy doesn't get on that boat, and secondly, I'll get the evidence we need.'

'Promise?'

Frank steps in front of him, and kneels down. He holds his shoulders and looks straight at him, eye to eye.

'I promise.' Then, repeating words he's used before... 'As long as it takes.'

Chapter 35

The phone in Dominic's first floor flat rings at ten that evening. It takes a few moments for him to find it, in the pocket of some old jeans on the floor beside the solitary chair. Dominic drops back into the worn sofa and raises one socked foot onto the table between him and the gas fire. He pushes aside a couple of beer cans and a plate, to make room.

'Hm?' More of a grunt than a greeting.

'A change of plan for tomorrow,' Zachary says. 'Rupert's nervous. He says you've drawn too much attention, and it's a big shipment. We can't be too careful.'

''What's the plan?'

'Take the kid, go out as normal, only there'll be nothing to collect. Just act the same as usual, go out to the buoy and then back to the harbour.'

'Who's picking up the shipment?'

'He's made arrangements.' Zachary pauses a moment, just long enough to make Dominic nervous. 'You've messed up. What the hell were you think-ing, poisoning some old lady in a caravan?'

Dominic grows pale. He sits down, and breathes quickly.

'It wasn't meant for her. How did he find out?'

'It didn't take Einstein to figure it. It only took Rupert ten seconds to guess it was you. I took a little longer. The full half minute. You can be pretty sure the cop has worked it out.'

'They can't prove anything. I was careful.'

'There's always proof, somewhere. I get the impression Frank Miller will be a limpet when it comes to finding out who tried to kill his family. He won't be prised off easily.'

'I didn't want to kill them.' Dominic is almost apologetic.

121

'Just poison them?' Zachary's voice has a sarcastic edge. 'It's a subtle distinction under the circumstances. He threw you in the harbour for trying to drown a dog. You think he won't come after you for trying to murder his family?'

'I told you, I didn't try to murder them.'

'That's not how he'll see it. More to the point, it's not how Rupert sees it. He thinks Miller will start digging. He doesn't like the idea of some cop on a mission, getting too close to him. And there are police all over the place.'

'What did Rupert say?' Dominic's voice tremors.

Zachary pauses. 'He doesn't trust you. You're a liability, he says. His exact words.'

Dominic's breath catches in his throat. He feels beads of perspiration carve escape routes down his cheeks. He knows what happens to people Rupert doesn't trust. Hell, Rupert only had to take against you because of your hair colour, your eyes, your way of looking at him. People disappear, and they stayed disappeared. That's what Rupert tells him, what he tells everyone who works for him.

It's my hobby, he says, with that look he has, like a sadistic kid with a sharp knife and a frog. *Making people disappear.*

When Rupert speaks, his eyes burn into yours. Dominic saw something in those eyes once, something he doesn't want to see again; something beyond cruel, a madness. He remembered it clearly. Rupert's lips fractured into a sneer, he allowed his eyes to break from Dominic's like a splinter of rock, and he waved a gracious hand around the elegant drawing room where they were standing.

People think there are ghosts in this house, but they're wrong. Do you want to know where the ghosts are?

Dominic didn't, but he nodded nonetheless.

Rupert brought his face close. His eyes widened, frenzied. He tapped his temple repeatedly.

Here. They're all in here, generations of them. And one day, one day I'll let them loose.

Dominic remembers that moment. How can he not? It is inked into his flesh like a living, quivering tattoo.

Fear doesn't describe his feelings towards Rupert. Nothing does.

'He can't touch me. I know things.'

'Like what?'

'Like things he wouldn't want me to share. Bad things.' He hesitates. 'I know things even *he* doesn't know.'

He stops, the words choking in his throat, as a memory surges like a shock wave.

If Rupert knew... If he ever found out.

Jocelyn...

Zachary hears the turmoil in Dominic's voice. 'Intriguing. But not much help if you're dead. When this consignment is in, he doesn't need you. You know what that means.'

Dominic knows what it means. 'What am I going to do?' he repeats.

Another pause. Zachary weighs his words like gold dust.

'I've got something on him, something big. Only...'

'Only what?'

'There's a piece missing. I need to know what he keeps in his Trophy Room.'

The Trophy Room, the room at the top of the east tower, top of the spiral stair which passes each floor, leading to a straight, stone stair to a narrow, oak door. He'd been to the top of those stairs once, with Rupert. He remembered Rupert's words.

This is our Trophy Room. All my family's nasty little secrets lie beyond that door. I love the place. It echoes with the screams of its victims.

Dominic scurried down those steps with Rupert's hysterical laughter ringing behind him. He heard something else, too, something from beyond that door: an echo of a scream, a cry, a wail, as if it were resounding through the centuries, and reaching out to him on a dying breath.

A child's voice.

'I'm not going in there,' Dominic says.

'It's the only way. He's got things in there, I know he has. Things which he doesn't want anyone to know about. I've seen him sneak int there when he thinks everyone is asleep. I've heard him pacing up and down, for hours. It's still a Trophy Room, same as it's been for everyone in his twisted family. He told me once he could hear the history of the human race in there. What did he call it? *A long, agonised scream stretching into eternity.*'

'He's insane.'

'Yes, he is.'

'I'm not going in that room. No way. Not ever.'

'Then I suggest you perform the task required of you tomorrow, as indeed you must, and then you flee the country.'

'What about you?'

There's a moment's silence, a dry laugh, and the phone goes dead.

Chapter 36

Rupert is in the lounge of Leybury Grange with Jocelyn when he hears the phone ring. It is on the top of a low display cabinet elegantly stocked with antique pottery, miniatures of distant ancestors, and crystal glassware. Above it, a large gilt mirror. He looks up and measures the distance from where he is lying on a sofa, his legs stretched across its length, his hand supporting a brandy glass.

'Pass me that, my dear,' he says, yawning.

He lays down a glossy magazine over which he has been casting a bored eye.

Jocelyn eases herself from an arm chair, and glides over to the phone. 'Who could be phoning at this time of night? Hello?'

She holds the phone between finger and thumb, and proffers it to Rupert.

'It's that ghastly little man you insist on inviting to dinner.'

'Zachary Blight? How entertaining.' He takes the phone, and holds it away from his face, as he speaks to his sister. 'Thank you, Jocelyn. Perhaps you'd like to take a little walk, powder something, prepare a potion?'

The look on Jocelyn's face is not accommodating.

'You really are an utter pig, Rupert. I love you dearly, but sometimes you test me to the limit.' She slides gracefully from the room, drawing the door shut behind her, closing out all sound.

Rupert swings his feet onto the carpet, and snaps questions at Zachary.

'Are we set for tomorrow? Is Dominic aware of my displeasure? Does he know his role in the game we must play?'

The questions are short, precise.

'Good,' Rupert says. 'Then tomorrow night we can celebrate. You'll come for dinner? Just a few guests. The usual utterly tedious bores.'

Zachary emits a groan.

'Seven o'clock, then.' Rupert allows himself a cold laugh. He closes the phone and a rumble deep in his chest breaks out like a lava flow, and he laughs louder, with relish.

The door opens and Jocelyn enters.

'We're you listening?' he asks, choking back the laughter.

'Of course. Are you really inviting that toad to dinner again?'

'Business, my dear. But don't concern yourself. After tomorrow night, you will never need to see him again. Everything is coming to a most satisfactory conclusion.'

Chapter 37

Even before he sails into the harbour, Dominic can see the police waiting for him. It's like a scene from a TV drama: a yellow cordon across the street, two cars parked at an angle at the end of the harbour, as if to block a runaway vehicle, three uniformed officers, arms folded, legs slightly apart, like improvisation at a urinal, and a couple of detectives.

No sign of Frank Miller.

Pity. He'd enjoy watching his face when they find nothing. Say what you like, Rupert is a clever bastard.

Another thought passes like a shadow, and his smile turns to poison. Sammy wasn't at the boat at eight o'clock, and the house was locked up when he called. Nobody answered the phone either. It could only mean one thing. They knew the police would be waiting. A surge, like acid reflux, rises to his throat. He spits a globule of phlegm overboard.

They can wait till later. Nobody crosses him and gets away with it.

He licks his lips in anticipation.

Sammy can pay the price.

The police officer introduces himself. DS Templeton. He waves a piece of paper, and marches a couple of burly PCs on board.

'Help yourselves,' Dominic says, sneering. 'I've nothing to hide.'

They search everywhere: unbolt panels; check over, under, between; pull back fittings; unscrew controls. If anything's there, they'll find it. Only there isn't, and they won't. The policemen emerge, shake their heads to DS Templeton, and retreat to their car.

'Is that it? Can I go now? I'm a busy man.'

Templeton eyes him up and down as only a trained detective can: slowly, professionally, and with deep contempt. Dominic bristles, his triumph feels short-lived.

'We need you to come to the station with us.' Templeton's voice is dry, and cold. 'Just a few questions.'

'About what?'

'Just to help us with our enquiries. If you don't mind.' Dominic does mind. He minds a lot. But the outstretched arm, the smile, the open door of the car... 'If you come voluntarily, it'll save me arresting you.'

'Fucking persecution.' Dominic flings himself in the back seat, the door closes, and the car draws away.

As he passes the end of the harbour, Dominic's mood improves. Frank Miller stands at the roadside, his eyes fixed on the car. Dominic feels a resurging sense of elation. He raises a hand, and waves it up and down, like a child.

Yeah.

He looks down at his thin knees, and dusts them with a bony hand. A secret smile flickers.

'What are you grinning at?' The policeman in the passenger seat looks back.

'Just telling myself a funny story.'

Dominic lets his head fall back and chuckles. He pictures his revenge.

Templeton walks along the harbour to where Frank is standing.

'Nothing,' he says, 'not a damned thing. We'll talk to him, maybe scare him a little, grill him about the poisoning at the caravan site, rip into him about the smuggling and so on. But he'll be free by the end of the day.'

Frank swears under his breath. 'Someone knew what we'd do, or guessed.'

'And the stuff he was supposed to collect from the buoy?'

'Long gone. Probably someone else, and early this morning, maybe not even from the buoy.'

'Where then?'

'There's been a blue-and-white yacht hanging around for the last couple of days.'

'There are always yachts round here. It's that sort of place.'

Frank glances towards the harbour where *The Lovely Maggie* and *Sammy's Pride* roll on a gentle swell.

'I'll have to tell the Trevelyans,' he says.

Templeton's frown deepens. 'Dominic may guess they had a part in this.'

'I'll keep an eye on them. I guess I've no choice. This is my fault. Maybe you could spare someone to watch the boats? They're easy targets. Shit, what a mess.'

'Are you going to see them now?'

'Yeah, everyone's at the caravan. They'll be waiting for news. Let me know if you get anything from Dominic, will you?'

'No problem. I'll have the forensics guys go over the boat, just in case, but I'm not hopeful.'

There's nothing Frank can do but walk back to the caravan. Maggie and Richard will be there, with Sammy. And what can he tell them? That he's broken all his promises? That Dominic is still free? That they're no safer than they were before?

He sits on a heather bank near the cliff top, his feet below him in a sandy hollow. It's a nice spot, on a sheltered slope above the tumbling flight of cliff, with a vertiginous drop to the sea. It's the sort of place where you can sit and stare, watch birds on the sea or admire the late flowers. There's barely a breeze today; just a shiver ruffling his hair. A perfect place to think, to let the updraft lift away the clouds.

A line of gannets passes, banking and moving south to richer grounds. One lingers a moment, circles, and then dives; an arrow straight to the heart of the sea. It emerges to shake itself, and sits, looking around, as if surprised at its own audacity. A minute later, not without an effort, it rises and follows the disappearing line of birds.

Far out, loitering on the horizon, there's a bank of mist, rising in thin, fading wisps, like thoughts; pale plumes dissolving in the sunlight.

There's no blue-and-white yacht. It is long gone, probably early that morning; no surprise there. Maybe Templeton will contact the coastguard, try and pin it down, apply a little pressure. If nothing else it will let them know the police have figured it out. It's what he would do in their place. He'd call to see Rupert Fitzwilliam, too. Just a courtesy call, all smiles and handshakes, to let him know they've searched the boat, of which, after all, he was part owner. It's always good to keep the target of your enquiries guessing.

Is Rupert a target? There's nothing tangible to link him to anything. It's just Frank Miller's legendary sixth sense. Dominic and Rupert; the names seem to occur together too much for coincidence. Still, it's nothing to do with him; not him the Detective Inspector, anyway. He's just a participant, an observer, a witness, someone on holiday caught up in a local crime.

He feels a pang of irritation, and a rush of envy. This is the sort of job he likes to get his teeth into. *The limpet.* They call him that behind his back, the officers he works with. *Because I never let go. Once I latch onto something, I stay latched.* Makes him kind of proud, though he doesn't tell them that.

Sitting here isn't going to help matters. He has a job to do, and not a particularly pleasant one. At least he can reassure Richard and Maggie that they'll be safe from Dominic. He can imagine the warnings Templeton will be screwing into Dominic's head.

He gets to his feet, takes a final look around, thinking for a moment of Janice and Jason. Who'd have thought it, just twelve months ago?

I wouldn't change it, though. Not one bit.

He sees Jason and Sammy as he drops down towards the caravan site. They're down on the beach, not far from the tideline, kicking a ball Jason bought in Grantley. It's a flimsy, colourful thing, more balloon than ball, but fun for two kids on a beach.

He increases his pace. It would be better not to have to explain in front of them; Sammy is scared enough. He wonders what he would do if Jason was that scared, if someone, some adult, bullied him, and threatened him. His fists clench, and a knot rises in his stomach.

I'd rub his bastard face along the barnacled rock like it was a cheese grater.

He wouldn't, of course, but it was nice to think about.

Richard has seen him approaching along the inside of the dunes, and ducks out to meet him. Maybe it's something about Frank's body language, his hunched look, his despondency, but Richard knows even before he asks.

'Bad news?'

'Yeah.'

'I knew it. I've had this feeling all morning.'

'The police had the harbour sealed off as soon as he sailed out to the buoy – they had coppers waiting, cars blocking the road end – everything. When he came back, they searched every corner of the boat.'

'And?'

'Nothing – not a thing. Just Dominic with a smug, self-satisfied smile waving at me as the police car drove past. Someone was a step ahead of us. It's the only explanation.'

'Rupert Fitzwilliam.'

'That's my guess. No proof, of course.'

'And Dominic?'

'They'll keep him in custody as long as they can, but they've got no reason to hold him, unless they come up with some forensic evidence. He'll be out within a few hours.'

'And then what?'

'He won't bother you. Templeton will scare the shit out of him. He won't come within a mile.'

'And Rupert Fitzwilliam?'

Frank hesitates. Something about Rupert Fitzwilliam weighs on his stomach, like a heavy meal.

'As far as he's concerned, everything has gone swimmingly. His little plan worked a treat.'

Richard runs a hand through his fiery hair, as if to dampen flames of doubt. 'He's a nasty piece of work.'

'You can stay with us for a day or two, if you like. There's not much room, but we can manage.'

Richard stares out across the beach. He shakes his head fiercely.

'If they think they can keep me from my own home, they've got another think coming.'

'Well, maybe let Sammy stay over, just for a night. Him and Jason would like that. Let things get back to normal.'

'Things will never settle down while that bastard is alive. He'll never let us go. But yes, that'd be kind. Thank you. Sammy has enough on his mind without this.'

His eyes still focus out towards the sea, where Jason and Sammy stand, silhouetted against the waves. There is something in Richard's tone, something desperate, like the last cry of a man backed so deep into a corner he has only one way out.

'You won't do anything foolish?'

Richard grunts a bitter laugh. 'I've done all the foolish things I'll ever do. I let Dominic and Rupert Fitzwilliam into our lives. They haunt us. Whatever we do, wherever we go, they are there, in our heads, gnawing at us. I have to think about Sammy and Maggie now, nothing else.'

Chapter 38

'You seem nervous.'

Rupert Fitzwilliam and Zachary Blight sit in the study at Leybury Grange, having once again escaped the dinner guests.

'I'm not at ease with these people, Rupert. You know that. They look at me as if I've been living on the streets.'

'You do have something of the charity shop about you, Zachary. Besides, you hardly go out of your way to ingratiate yourself. The major seemed to be trying hard to engage you in conversation.'

'He asked me if I'd been to Epsom and then talked about the evils of socialism, and the glory days of Thatcher.'

'Ah, red rag and all that. You were diplomatic, I assume? Didn't share your political credentials, and social background?'

'I didn't wipe my nose on my sleeve, if that's what you mean. I did suggest that dementia was a fitting end for the dragon queen.'

'That wouldn't have gone down well. The major met her socially, you know. They were on friendly terms.'

Zachary glances round the room as if the scent of affluence offends him. The leather chairs, the mahogany desk, the curtains and the cut-glass, the mirrors and clocks and paintings. Rupert watches with amusement.

'You're a typically envious, bitter socialist, Zachary. You wouldn't reject our wealth if it was offered to you.'

'They're parasites.' Zachary speaks like a man poisoned by his own phlegm. 'And, for the record, yes I would. There are more important things than money.'

'You worry me, Zachary. Our relationship is built on what I perceived to be a rock-solid foundation. I have money, and power. You want money, and are willing to play the subservient drone in order to acquire it.'

Zachary's smile conveys as much humour as a bee sting.

'We are all slaves. Even you, Rupert. All prey to powerful parasites.'

'Perhaps.' Rupert swirls his drink, and yawns. He rests a casual arm across the chair back. 'Personally, I prefer to think of myself as a predator. I look down on mere parasites. They can get little pleasure from their lifestyle, don't you think? I positively relish my own little predatorial forays.' He ventures a smile. 'Which brings me to my village yokel friend. He was arrested, I believe?'

'I think you knew he might.'

'Of course. He said nothing, I assume.'

'He hardly had time to give his name and address. Besides, he was trembling with fear after Jonas Smythe had a word in his ear.'

'Ah, dear Jonas. He has been our family solicitor for years, as was his father before him. He has dealt with numerous crises. I think he looks forward to them. Where is Dominic now?'

'He's planning on skipping town, hiding himself away in some suburban sewer until he thinks he's safe.'

'Poor Dominic. He could never be safe, not unless I want him to be. For the moment, we'll let the rat scurry about in his filth. The yacht has gone?'

'Of course.'

'And the consignment?'

'I took a boat out early, like you said. The consignment is locked in my car. What do you want me to do with it?'

'Wait until we're all in the drawing room, and then go and fetch it.' Rupert reaches in his pocket, removes a small key on a silver chain, and throws it to Zachary. 'Just leave it in the box in the bottom left-hand drawer of the desk. Then you can piss off.'

'And the key?'

'In the waste paper bin. I'll retrieve it later.'

Rupert stands up, and dusts down the legs of his trousers.

'It's time you left, Zachary. That damp, second-hand smell you carry is starting to bother my senses. I'm surprised you can tolerate it, with your condition.'

'And my money?'

'It's waiting for you, same as ever.'

'How about Dominic?'

Rupert drums his long fingers on the desk. Cat's claws.

'I'll deal with Dominic. I hate delegating these matters to other people. Why should they have all the fun?'

He walks to the door, and holds it open.

'I doubt we'll meet again,' he says, holding out a pale hand.

Zachary looks at Rupert's cold, pale face, and empty eyes.

'I won't be sorry,' he says.

He turns his back, and walks away.

Chapter 39

Zachary doesn't go far; he pauses outside the doorway in the entrance hall and waits. As soon as he hears the drawing room door close, he turns back and, with an agility which belies his physical condition, he flits silently into the study. He crosses to the desk, and slides open the top drawer.

There you are.

He lifts a large key: old, with a strange pattern carved around an oval handle. A mouth maybe, and eyes.

Like everything else in this bloody house.

He pauses at the doorway, checks each way, hears the murmur of voices from the drawing room; a sudden rising laughter, a deep baritone.

Her ladyship and the major. Bloody parasites.

Then he shudders as he remembers Rupert's words.

Personally, I prefer to think of myself as a predator. I look down on mere parasites. They can get little pleasure from their lifestyle, don't you think? I positively relish my own little predatorial forays.

No time to dwell on that now, though. He slips across the hallway, and up the stairs.

Bloody stairs could be the death of me.

On the first floor, he follows a portrait-lined corridor, breathing hard, and finds his way to the tower. The tower rooms are rarely used by Rupert and Jocelyn; maintaining them is too great an expense. He continues up the stairs, past arched windows which look out over the lawns towards the trees and the summer house. The walls on the second-floor support dusty portraits of the long-dead. Zachary shudders again.

Bloody place. Full of ghosts.

There's something of the long-dead about everything in this wing of the house. He feels a connection, like a wire momentarily touched.

He turns towards a narrow, cheaply carpeted staircase which leads to the third floor and pauses before a final flight of narrow steps: worn granite, carrying the footprints of generations towards the heavy, oak door. Zachary pauses, his breath escaping in heavy gasps, his heart beating faster and faster. Sweat forms on his forehead and he wipes clammy hands on his trousers.

The sooner I'm out of here...

His foot finds the first step, and then the second.

Voices echo in his head.

Jesus Christ, what am I doing here? I'm not cut out for this.

('You're here because you had to be. Because you have to know.')

And then what?

('You get away, you run, you hide. Like Dominic.')

And then?

('And then you act, you finish this, and you move on. Leave it to the police, go away and forget.')

Do you think I can forget? Ever?

('Maybe. Maybe not.')

At the door, he holds out a trembling hand, touches the catch, finds the lock, inserts the skull key, and then...

He listens, his ear close to the door. It's as if his hands, on the lock and key, amplify sounds he has not heard before. They come at him in waves, rising and falling, rolling onto the shores of his mind. Soft moans, cries, a distant scream, then muttered words, spoken quickly. Mumblings, like someone old talking to themselves, lost in the past. Wrapped around it all, the medium through which the sounds travel, he hears the hush of waves, and the whisper of a seaborn wind.

He turns the key, braces himself against the door, and opens it. A cold, musty air pushes past him, and flies down the stairs, escaping this insanity He steps inside.

A deep intake of breath, a low, restrained cry, a moan of pain, words caught in his throat.

'No. Please, God. Let it not be.'

In the corner of the room: a trestle bed, a soiled sheet, dust and, perhaps, the imprint of a body.

The door closes behind him.

Chapter 40

The next morning, Jason and Sammy are out by the edge of the sea. Their conversation takes a serious turn. In a silent moment, the waves draw in their breath, and the breeze pauses.

'You should tell your dad.'

'About what?'

'About Dominic. What you told me.'

Sammy bends down, and scoops a handful of wet sand. He scatters it in one throw across the waves.

'I can't. My dad would kill him.'

'Then tell Frank. He's a police inspector. He'd know what to do. You can't just do nothing.'

'I'm going to draw my name in the sand. Come on. You do the same.'

He walks across the wet sand, dragging his foot in a huge letter *S*. Then an *A* and *M*, *M*, *Y*. Jason finds another smooth patch, and does the same for his own name.

'Let's write *FRIENDS*,' he says.

They stand back, and admire their work.

'I bet you can see that from space,' Jason says.

'From the clifftop anyway. Look, that seagull is flying round and round. I think it's reading it.'

'It'll be there forever.'

'Till the sea comes in, and washes it away.'

'Yeah, but it'll be here forever, in my head. I'll remember it.'

'Me, too.'

Sammy steps towards the edge of the waves, which scurry towards his feet, fret around them, and withdraw.

'I'll be safe if Dominic is locked up.'

'He should be locked up forever.' Jason thinks for a moment. 'Your dad can't kill him if he's in prison.'

'Maybe.'

'You should tell Frank. He'll get him locked up, and then he'll tell your dad, and keep you safe. You've got to tell. You've just got to.'

'It's not easy to tell. You know why.'

'I'll help you.'

Sammy trails a foot in the sand, tracing the outline of a face.

'I don't know. Maybe everything will be okay now. There's no more trips in the boat, and my dad won't let him in the house.'

'What if he comes out of prison, and hurts someone else?'

Sammy scars a sad mouth on the sand face, and two big eyes with tears.

'Will you tell Frank first, and then I'll tell?'

'Yes.'

'And he'll help me? And he'll help Mum and Dad. You promise.'

There are tears on his cheeks now. He sobs, and wipes a sandy hand across his eyes.

'Yes.'

'When will you tell?'

'Now, if you like. He's in the caravan.'

Sammy sniffs, and fights back the tears. He nods.

They run back, and Jason leaves him sitting on the sandy dune, among the razor-leaved marram grasses, while he runs to the caravan. His mum and Frank are lounging on the bench seats by the back window, coffee and biscuits on the table, a folded newspaper, and a couple of leaflets promoting tourist attractions in Grantley.

They look up.

'Hello, love.' His mum has a smile as wide and warm as a tropical sea.

'Hi, Champ.' Frank sits up, yawning. 'Where's Sammy?'

Jason nods back towards the beach.

'In the dunes. Can I talk to you, Frank?'

'Course you can. What's up?'

'Outside, with Sammy?'

Frank glances at Janice, and shrugs his shoulders. 'Lead the way.'

Frank follows him outside.

When they're beyond sight of the van, Jason stops and turns.

'Sammy says I can share his secret with you. Only, you've got to help him, Frank. I promised you would.'

'And you always keep a promise.'

Jason nods. 'He says I've to tell you everything and then you'll know, and he'll be able to talk to you.'

'Then I promise you that I'll keep him safe.'

'And his mum and dad? He's worried what his dad will do.'

A surge of dread turns in Frank's stomach.

'And his mum and dad, too. I promise.'

Jason takes a deep breath. It isn't easy for him either, not a subject like this; it's not the sort of thing you talk to anyone about. But he has to. His voice tremulous, his eyes fixed anywhere except on Frank, he begins and the words pour like tears until he has finished. Then he cries and Frank holds him close.

'I'm proud of you,' he says quietly. 'I'm really proud of you, Jason. Now, where's Sammy?'

A lonely, tear-stained face rises from behind a low dune.

Chapter 41

Rupert Fitzwilliam looks up from his breakfast as Jocelyn glides into the dining room. She pours herself a coffee, and sits down.

'These kippers are superb,' he says. 'You should try them.'

'I've no appetite.'

'You look tired. Did you not sleep well?'

'I never sleep well. This house is full of noises, like old bones creaking. Sometimes, they sound like voices. They never stop.'

'I think of it as the house talking to me, and the voices of our ancestors. But I only hear them if I choose to.'

'In the Trophy Room, you mean? I don't know how you can stand to be in that room, knowing what we do. You know it isn't good for you.'

He looks up, an expression of mild amusement flickering. 'On the contrary, I find it reassuring, like a tradition. It's our very own echo chamber, resonating with the past. Does it not make you feel proud to be part of a family with such a fine reputation?'

'A reputation for what? Savagery, and insanity. I'm scared for you. Have you forgotten what happened there?'

She looks up, waiting, but he doesn't look at her, and he doesn't speak. Her eyes, having risen like an otter's head, sink back into a pool of darkness. Rupert pretends not to notice, closes his eyes to savour a mouthful of food.

'I never forget anything, my dear,' he sighs.

Jocelyn takes a breath, and tries again.

'The voices were loud, last night. Louder than I've ever heard, as if they were rumbling with some deep discontent. They scare me, Rupert. It's like they're trying to break out. What will happen if they do? You must stop them. You must get help.'

Rupert dabs his mouth, and pushes his chair back.

'I shouldn't, I know, but I really must have another of these kippers. Are you sure you won't?'

'For goodness sake, Rupert, this is serious. You've got to stop. They're getting inside my head. I can't sleep, I can't think... Every night is the same. If I don't numb my mind with alcohol, I can't get a moment's rest.' She pauses, glances at him, looks down again. 'I've made up my mind. I'm going to leave.'

Rupert pauses by the silver plate on which the kippers are laid out.

'You can't. Nobody can ever leave this house again.'

'I've packed a suitcase. I'm leaving this morning.'

Rupert's hand hovers over the plate, and his face hardens.

'You know it's impossible to leave us. You carry us in your DNA. You have embraced your heritage, as I have done.'

'I'm not like you, you know that. And everything is getting worse. Sometimes, now, I imagine meeting figures on the stairs, in the bedrooms, everywhere. And I hear voices, cries and screams. Even words. Terrible words. I can't bear it. It's every time you're in the Trophy Room. And you're in there for hours now.'

'I'm listening to my family's music.' He gives a sudden laugh, like something savage escaping, like an infection; a rabid expulsion from a foaming jaw. 'Sometimes I talk to Melissa. She sends her love.'

Jocelyn's voice breaks. Her face is pale, and her body trembles. She sobs, and then stifles the sound.

'You know I love you, no matter what. Unconditionally.'

Rupert continues eating. 'Will you come back?'

'Of course. I would never leave you.'

'Because you can't leave me, can you?' His laugh is strangely triumphant. 'You should feel proud, darling sister. The first female member of our family to add a trophy. Although you *did* require a little help. Call it encouragement.'

'You tricked me. You and that monster, Dominic Sheedy.'

'It was for your own good. Besides, you were only too aware of our guilty little secrets. You could never have reconciled yourself to them if you didn't become, as it were, a member of our club. A few drops of a particularly virulent potion, and your initiation was complete.'

Jocelyn picks up her coffee cup and throws it against the wall where it fractures, and explodes. She grips the table, and her eyes fire shells of anger. They miss their target. Rupert, amused, continues to eat. He sips his coffee, dabs his lips again, leans back. He watches his sister with curiosity.

She sighs, and drops back onto her seat.

'I didn't know what I was doing.'

'But it was your hand which fed the poor innocent, wasn't it? It was you who prepared her customary supper. I wasn't even in the house. I can call on a Knight of the Realm, an Honourable Member, and a High Court Judge to provide my alibi. Dominic is equally equipped with a garbage collector, a fisherman, and a white van man. It was you, my dear, you alone who served the meal that killed her.'

Jocelyn stares at him. 'You can be a monster, Rupert. Sometimes, I think you are evil through and through.'

'Why, thank you, my dear.'

Jocelyn turns away. There's no point trying to fight; better to just fly. 'I'm leaving in five minutes. The taxi is outside.'

'Where will you go?'

'Away. Anywhere. I'm booked on a flight to Paris. I'll stay there for a few days, with friends. Then I'll move on. I don't know where.'

'And if you did, you wouldn't tell me.'

'No.'

'You seem to have thought this through carefully, meticulously planned every detail. I congratulate you. I assume that loathsome youth who works for us made all the necessary arrangements. What was his name now? Carver? Yes, that was it. A detestable fellow. I do hate betrayal, don't you? It is one crime that simply cannot go unpunished.'

Jocelyn's face pales even more.

'What have you done to him?'

Rupert leans forward, suddenly cold.

'I've added a trophy.'

He snarls. It's beyond savagery, out of control, wild.

Jocelyn gasps, sobs. She stands up, and runs, half-stumbling towards the door.

'If you're lucky, you may meet him on the stairs.' Rupert's laughter echoes after her, like hounds let loose on a chase. 'I've unlocked the Trophy Room door, dear sister. It's time I gave them the freedom to wander the house, don't you think? It's theirs, after all.'

His laughter turns into a howl, following her through the entrance hall to the front door. She flings it open, and staggers, gasping, onto the steps.

'Are you alright, love?'

The taxi driver opens the door of his cab and climbs out.

'I'm fine,' Jocelyn says. She opens the rear door and climbs in. 'Just get me out of here.'

'No luggage?'

Jocelyn grasps a handbag close.

'I have everything I need. I'll send for the rest. Just drive. Please, just drive.'

Chapter 42

F *rom the picnic site in the modern area of Leybury you look down over the harbour. It's a favourite spot and I understand why. Sitting on that bench seat with a coffee in front of you, looking down past the sunny rooftops, framed by bubbling clouds, the harbour shines like it's been newly polished. Even the boats have a pristine look, as if waiting for a festival or a wedding. The air is warm, but not so warm that you feel sluggish and tired. No, it's just right. Perfect. You lay your sunglasses beside the coffee cup, and take in the postcard scene before you.*

Below you, two men walk across the road towards the wrought iron bench by the harbour. They catch your attention. There's nothing particularly notable about them. One is tall and has the solid build of someone who keeps in shape. The second has flaming red hair, made even more distinctive by the angle of the sun, which seems to catch and accentuate it, like an aurora.

They talk casually, a to-and-fro of everyday conversation. They look like friends, at ease with each other. As they reach the bench, they fall silent, and the taller figure pauses while the redhead sits.

Five minutes pass.

The atmosphere has changed now. The standing figure looks tense. He taps the back of the bench as if priming himself to say something that may not be well received. You can see him thinking, weighing words, but it's clear that no amount of planning can prepare him for what he has to say. He swings round the side of the bench and sits down, and then he begins.

You lean forward, curiosity piqued, your coffee growing cold on the table. You replace your sunglasses to help you gain a clearer view.

The tall man speaks. His words seem precise, like forces marshalled for a battle. He leans forward, and places a calming hand on his colleague's shoulder. The words come faster now, until they are both talking at once, forces colliding; one is calm, controlled and strategic, the other a flurry of falling arrows.

The red-haired one pulls away, and stands, grasping the iron bars of the harbour rail, his head lowered. His grip seems tight, as if he would fracture the bars, and cast them in the sea if only his emotions could be translated into energy. He spins around, and fires questions. One. Two. Three. Four. He awaits a measured response, fires more questions, then turns again, and beats the rail with his fist.

The other man stands, rests his hands on the rail beside his friend. He looks out at the harbour and the distant horizon, and its bank of cloud. It's been a feature out there for the last two days, you recall. A sign of changes to come. The redhead stares down at his feet. His back is hunched, and he moves as if racked with sobs.

You lean forward, your emotions linked by ropes of empathy. You watch the tall man rest an arm on his friend's shoulder. He talks again, to comfort perhaps, or to explain, or reassure. For a moment it seems that all may be well. The shorter man rises, rubs a sleeve across his eyes, stands firm. He doesn't look at his friend, but out at that line of cloud, where skies and seas meet. A distant harmony, unattainable.

He pulls away, and stumbles across the harbour road. A car slows and a horn blasts, but it means nothing to him. The other man runs, grabs his arm, holds him back, only to be repulsed again, and then again. Eventually they are still, and the car accelerates past.

The redhead listens now. He hears what is said, nods, wipes a hand across his mouth, nods again. He dusts himself down, and steps forward.

His friend follows, then walks beside him.

They are going to that pretty cottage, gable end-on to the harbour, the one with the flower baskets that you've admired so much, and the shells and floats, and bottled ships glimpsed through the lace-curtained window. Quaint, old-fashioned. You always liked its old-world homeliness. You passed comment to your friends.

What a lovely cottage, you said.

Now, you have glimpsed something of the life within.

You fabricate, you speculate, and weave tendrils of imagination into a coarse tapestry. But, in reality, you are merely crafting shadows. They are two fighters, perhaps, facing an invisible foe. You copy the moves, how they duck and weave, feint and strike, but you cannot feel the blows.

Those are for them alone.

Chapter 43

'I'll kill him! I'll kill him!'

It's late evening. Through the failing light, Richard strides up the cliff path, away from the village. Ahead, the outline of the old lookout station; behind him the streetlights, glowing on the furrowed sea. Frank follows behind, struggling to keep up on the uneven ground.

'What's worst is I feel like it's my fault, like I let it happen. I failed him. I wasn't there.' He stops and turns to face Frank. 'What the hell was I doing that I didn't see what was happening? What sort of a parent am I?'

'It wasn't your fault. There's only one person to blame here, and that's Dominic.'

Frank tries to be calm; he has to, for Richard, for Sammy, for Maggie, and for Jason. He's the professional, the man who's seen it all before, who deals with the tragedy, supports victims, and investigates villains. But this is close to home. He knows too that no matter how much he's exposed to callous brutality, he never gets used to it. It's his complete incomprehension that scares him, his inability to get into the head of a criminal, to gain even the slightest purchase on the mind that can do such things. The petty thief who beats an elderly woman half to death for a few trinkets, the traffickers, the abusers. The guy on the train who knifes someone for the way they look at him, or for the colour of their skin. The person who screams threats and abuse because of their sexuality, religion, dress, accent, football team. It belongs to a world he meets only at the boundaries, of which he catches sordid glimpses, into which he ventures a toe, a foot and, maybe, on occasion, his entire body.

But never his mind, not fully.

And this.

Sammy.

His emotions resonate, they hum to the same electric charge, they burn with the same heat. Richard's grief and anger raise an empathetic echo which will not be silenced. Only for Richard, this is not an echo but the roar of unbearable truth.

When the call comes from Maggie that Richard has grabbed a coat, and stormed out of the house, Frank runs out at once and drives down to find him. He steers him away from the village with all its police activity, and towards the cliff. He hopes a strenuous walk will cool the fury, allow the fire to burn itself out, the outrage to find voice.

'The police will have him soon, if they haven't already.'

'I want to see him first. I want to make him see what he's done. I want him to know that I know, and that I'll rip him apart.'

'I know, I know. But that won't help Sammy, or Maggie. They need you. Going off half-cocked, and kicking the hell out of Dominic won't solve anything. It'll make things worse.'

'I'd feel better.'

'Would you?'

Richard doesn't answer. He stops by the watchtower, and leans against its wooden door. Frank rests his hands on the wall beside him.

'What can I do?' Richard groans. 'I can't even think. If I stop moving, it all catches up with me, and fills my head. I need to walk, and keep walking. I feel so useless. I feel... such a complete failure. I just want to get on board my boat, sail out to sea, and never come back. I can't face them.' He buries his head in his hands, and sobs. 'It shouldn't have happened. I should have looked after him.'

Frank risks a hand on his shoulder.

'They need you.'

'How can I look at our Sammy after what he told me? I feel so ashamed.'

'You're not the villain here. It's Dominic, not you. You've got to be strong, and face up to things, make it better again. That's your job now.'

'I don't think I'm up to it.'

'Course you are.'

Out on the sea the lights of a passing cruise ship shimmer, and beyond that a rig. Darkness has set around them, and a few stars glisten, ice crystals shivering in the cooling air. Frank checks his watch. Why hasn't Templeton called him? Richard needs to know that Dominic has been arrested, and locked away. Urgently.

'Come on,' he says. 'Let's head back. Maybe in time for last orders at The Harbour Inn, eh? What do you say?'

Richard nods, and they stumble towards the lights of the village. In the harbour a small yacht is berthed by the wall. Ropes tap against the tall mast. *Tick, tick, tick, tick.*

A police car cruises down the main street, and pulls up. Frank walks across as the window slides down.

'Any news? Have you got him?'

A shake of the head.

'Shit.' Frank glances back at Richard. 'This isn't what Richard needs to hear.'

'He won't get far.'

The familiar reassuring line, like they're talking to a victim, not to a city DI. He knows better than that. They don't have the personnel, not nowadays. Bloody politicians. Even murder goes unpunished. Not like the old days.

'We'll pick him up skulking in a hideaway somewhere, or on one of the main roads, or on a train or bus.'

'Maybe,' Frank says. 'I hope you find him soon. The family need reassurance.'

'We'll get him, don't worry.'

The window closes, the car pulls away, and Frank turns back to the harbour rail.

Richard has gone. In his place, a girl sits on the top rail, with her feet on the bar below. It's the girl he met once before in the village, the girl he saw on the beach.

'Molly?' he asks.

'He's gone hunting,' she says. She jumps down from the rail. 'I warned you to be careful.'

She turns, and runs across the street to the narrow path beside Richard's house, disappearing like a shadow in darkness; there for a moment, then gone.

'Molly!' Frank shouts after her.

Silence. Just the hush and sweep of sea and air, and the eternally rolling waves.

Chapter 44

Dominic hears the police car draw up outside. He knows it's a police car even before he eases back the curtain to see. He's been expecting it, dreading it, knowing it would only take a word from Sammy. You do something, out of anger, out of envy, for God knows what reason, and it's there forever like a livid scar. A moment's folly, and a life sentence. He's been thinking about that a lot recently.

It's all Sammy's fault. The little shit has been talking to the cops.

He shrinks back and hides in the shadows, thinking quickly, trying to focus through the haze of drugs. A hurriedly packed rucksack lies beside him, ready, just in case. Especially after what Zachary Blight said, especially after Richard Trevelyan slipped his leash.

The car door closes. Footsteps on the tarmac. A heavy hand knocks on the downstairs door.

What do they want? Is it Sammy? Or the shipments?

A surge of guilt, a sudden fear which grips his stomach. No drug can hold back that surge. God knows, he's tried them all.

Sammy?

Rupert?

What?

Everything is coming apart.

He has to get out. Too many people after him, wanting him in gaol or wanting him dead.

There's no point using the back door. Some burly cop will be standing there, ready for him. No, there's only one way: his well-rehearsed secret exit, out the back window, down onto next door's garage roof, into their yard, hop a few walls then out into the maze of lanes and alleyways.

His car is parked down a side street ready for him. He never parks near the house, hasn't done for months. It's his quick getaway. No tax, no insurance, no link to him. He'll leave it somewhere in the city, and then lose himself in the crowd. He'll find work; there are always people on the lookout for someone with his skills. If not, he'll thieve. He's a master of that craft, too. Untouchable.

He promises himself he'll come back. Through the blur of his drugged eyes, he knows who to blame.

In a few months, dead of night, creep through a window. Grim fucking reaper. A spot of revenge.

He lists his enemies.

The Trevelyans, all of them. Save Sammy for last. Something special. Or maybe in front of them.

That policeman and his kid, and the woman with him.

Rupert Fitzwilliam. Yes, even him. He might think he holds all the cards, but he doesn't. I've got the aces, every one of them. I have a secret.

He smiles as he imagines their faces, especially Rupert's.

Then they'll know. Then they'll show me respect.

It's a secret to keep him warm at night, to keep him going when things get tough, something to look forward to.

For now, he turns off the lights, hurries to the landing window, and opens it. The catch is loose. He clambers out, and drops down onto the flat roof of the garage. Nobody sees him. He jumps, soft-footed into the neighbour's yard then hoists himself over their wall, skips across another yard, over another wall. Two more then into an alleyway. Silent running up the narrow paths, and out onto another road, full of newer houses, their curtains closed; keeping things out, keeping things in.

On the corner, there's an old woman with a sullen-looking dog as old as herself. Dominic doesn't speak, strolls past her, head down, then rounds a corner and runs. Ahead of him, the car. There's nobody near it, the street is empty. He unlocks it from a distance, flings himself in the driver's seat, and starts the engine. The cold air has cleared his mind a little, but not enough. He's had quite a cocktail tonight, he recalls. He checks the mirror, half-expecting to see a face in the back seat: Rupert, Zachary, even Richard or the cop. He laughs under his breath.

Been watching too many horror films.

Still, he looks again, then turns to check behind the seats, just in case. No nasty shocks. He's edgy enough. He eases the car from its parking place, and along the road, just wide enough between parked cars. They weren't built for cars, these streets. Different times.

He's nervous. It's funny how things always go wrong at the last minute, or maybe that's just in films. Real life is easier, or maybe it's harder. Slower, or faster.

Ten minutes and I'll be clear. Half an hour and the motorway, an hour and a half, the city.

He takes a final glimpse in the mirror.

A girl's face stares back.

A pale face, dark hair, dark wide eyes. A strange smile breaking to reveal small, white teeth, shining in the darkness of the mirror.

Dominic slams on the brakes, and his eyes return to the road.

God help me, he cries. *Hallucinogens. What was I thinking?*

A second child, a boy, maybe nine or ten, stands in front of the car. Dominic glances in the mirror. No girl now. Just the empty space, and darkness. He looks back, but the boy has gone. There's just the empty road, and a streetlight, twenty yards away, casting a subdued glow.

He's sweating now, breathing hard, and his hands grip the wheel to stop them shaking.

It's the drugs. Just the drugs.

A boy emerges from a doorway, and then a girl from an alleyway, both watching him, both motionless, just staring. Ahead of him another boy, about twelve; he is limping, and supported by a girl maybe fourteen or fifteen, with long, wavy hair, and barefoot. Behind them, more, rounding the corner, all shapes and sizes, colours, nationalities, even a sickly girl in a wheelchair, all moving slowly towards him. He fumbles with the car door, throws it open, and steps out.

Everything is still, as the village holds its breath.

'What do you want?'

The silence is broken like a twig, and a hush of wind stirs him. Then another sound, low at first then growing; a gentle sobbing, and those still, young faces with lines of tears channelling down their cheeks. Dominic clings to the car door. He doesn't dare move, can't move.

'What do you want from me?'

The sobbing is in the air around him; it is everywhere, and yet the faces are motionless, as if their cries, locked so long in silence, have broken free and fly to occupy every corner of the sleeping village. Tears roll down silent cheeks; cries flit like midnight cats, around houses, over fences and walls, through gardens, and yards.

The crying grows louder, more insistent, more intense, until Dominic drops to the ground beside the car.

A girl steps forward; she moves through the others until she stands separate, at their head. Dominic scrambles back, pulling himself along the ground. He cries out to her to stop.

She raises a hand, points at him, stares at him, sees though him, and strips him bare.

No more, he hears her cry.

And behind her, they echo. First one and then another, until every voice cries as one.

NO MORE!

NO MORE!!

NO MORE!!!

And, as slowly as they appeared, they turn and drift like smoke, drawn into the darkness, curling and spiralling into the emptiness. Until only the girl is left. Then she turns, and skips away.

Ahead of him, emerging from the darkness another figure rises, like the devil drawn from hell.

The figure steps forward, reaches the streetlight, pauses. Dominic clambers to his feet.

Richard's voice, but unearthly and chill.

'I know everything, Dominic. Sammy told me.'

Like a thrown switch, Dominic springs to life, casts off the shadows, the ghostly visitations, the drugs. He turns, and stumbles towards the street end, conscious of Richard's relentless steps behind him, drawing in like the inevitability of death. He increases his speed, running now.

Ahead of him, rounding a corner and taking up a position in the middle of the road, blocking his path, he sees another figure.

The cop. Frank Miller.

Dominic hesitates, glances left and right, looking for a way to escape. He sees a narrow path between houses, and turns into it, flies up the ascending steps, his breath coming heavily, his heart beating in his chest so loud he can hear it.

Left into another lane, right along a path, left again, and then again. He pauses, allows a semblance of a plan to form through the haze. He is going to double back, cut through the yards and gardens, find his way to the car. It's the only way. He knows the place well, so he can plot a route, take himself around and back, and down.

He clambers over the nearest fence, then runs along a line of gardens. A dog barks, a cat accelerates into the darkness, a light comes on at a window, and a voice shouts out. He keeps going. Ten minutes later he is back on the street, back by his car. He clambers in; the key is still in the ignition. He turns it, fires the engine, and pulls away.

Then he glances in the rear-view mirror.

'Oh shit.'

Chapter 45

D riving out of the village, Dominic glances again through the rear-view mirror. A face caught in passing lights, half-dark, half-light, transient movements of glistening eyes.

'What do you want?'

'Just drive.'

'Where?'

'North. I'll tell you when to turn.'

Silence now except for his thoughts.

After two miles...

'Turn left here.'

'The Grange?' His stomach lurches, like a shipwreck. 'For God's sake, not there.'

His passenger doesn't speak, but they pass the oaks and sycamores, and the entrance to Leybury Grange. At the road end he slows at a narrow junction where a lane turns sharply left. In a mile it will disappear under the by-pass to emerge reinvigorated on the outskirts of Grantley. A track leads forward through an open gate to the ruined castle on its clifftop perch.

'Down the track.'

'Grantley Castle?'

'To the car park.'

A sudden beating of his heart, a sweating in his palms; an image of the clifftop, the rocky tower, a body falling on the rocks below, caught by the tide, and washed up and down on the swell. Fear grips him. He presses the brake, and draws to a halt.

'I'm going nowhere.' He sits still, and stares at the track ahead, breathing hard. 'You want to kill me, do it here.'

A restrained laugh. 'If I wanted you dead, I'd have killed you already.'

Dominic glances in the mirror once more. The face is closer now, right behind him. He can smell the sour breath, like something dead.

'Jesus, what happened to you?'

Grey hair clings across a gaunt skull, glassy eyes stare, pale white skin stretches like a film over the hand holding a narrow-bladed knife at his neck; everything about his passenger is bloodless, ghostly, ghastly.

Dominic shudders as the point of the knife touches his throat.

'What do you want?'

There's a pause, and a silence so full it might burst. The face comes closer, the dry lips move and a voice whispers in his ear.

'Revenge.' The knife blade presses. He feels a ruby of blood. 'Now drive.'

Two hundred yards along the dusty track, he draws up facing a wire fence, and cuts the engine. They sit there, in silence.

'What now?'

The face is close to his ear.

'Now we talk.'

Chapter 46

'What do you want from me?'

Zachary Blight, or the shell of him, leans back. He takes out an inhaler, and draws on it. He shakes it.

'Empty,' he says.

He takes out a packet of cigarettes, offers one to Dominic. 'Talk about Melissa Fitzwilliam.'

Dominic takes a cigarette, and holds it trembling towards the flame of Zachary's match.

'Who?'

'Louise's daughter. Rupert's niece. She was nine years old. A pretty little girl with soft brown hair, and dark eyes. Remember her?'

'I've never heard the name. Rupert didn't talk about his family.'

'He needed help to deal with the problems she caused. You were the obvious choice.'

He lights a cigarette for himself, inhales and coughs, then opens the window, and drops the cigarette outside.

'I shouldn't touch these things, not with my asthma. I've got emphysema, you know. Doc said so. You should give up before they kill you, he told me.' A strangled laugh turns to another cough, momentarily choking him. His voice comes in gasps, as he slowly recovers. 'Only, in our case, maybe that's not so much of a problem.'

Zachary opens the door and steps out. 'Let's take a walk,' he says. 'It's a nice night.'

Dominic steps out. He glances back towards the track, disappearing into the mouth of darkness, and then towards the silhouette of the ruin: black on grey, with charcoal clouds.

'There's always light on the sea.' Zachary's voice emerges in gasped phrases, every few words separated by a breath. 'I've never understood that. No matter how dark the land, even on a moonless night, the sea always seems to stand out, like it carries a soft fluorescence. Of course, there's no such things as true darkness, not above the ground, no matter what people think. There's always a bit of light, especially nowadays with town and streetlights. I mean, look along the coast there. See that glow? That's Grantley. Looks like it's on fire, and lighting the clouds. No, there's no such thing as true darkness on the surface of the earth. Got to go deep in a cave, deep down, to find real darkness. Or bury yourself in a coffin, I suppose.' He turns to Dominic. 'Have you ever thought about that? No?'

They walk towards the castle, nearing the ruins of the guard towers. Dominic looks back, resisting the hand on his shoulder, slowing down ready to dart away, and run.

Zachary pauses.

'It would be a big mistake to try to escape,' he whispers, as if the darkness can hear him. It's a theatrical whisper, like a secret shared. 'I've got a gun, you see. In my pocket.'

Dominic turns. He sees sleek, black steel, a polished barrel, leather strap round the grip.

'You'd never use it.'

Zachary shrugs. 'I've nothing to lose,' he says. He steps back, opens his jacket as if to reveal his soul beneath. 'Look at me. I've lost everything. I've nothing left. Even my health has deserted me. I can feel the rats clawing their way out, chewing through timbers of flesh. I'll be breathing oxygen from a cylinder before long. Whereas you...'

'What about me?'

'I can let you live. I can even help you escape. I've got friends, contacts.'

'I've told you. I won't go in the Trophy Room.' He shudders. 'I'd rather take my chances here and now, with you and your gun.'

He turns, braced, ready to attack.

Zachary shakes his head. His voice is hoarse, and carries in its faltering rhythms a strange resonance. He glances from side to side as if something is emerging from the night around him. Dark shadows in a dark sky. Thoughts. Memories. The Trophy Room.

His whole body shakes.

Dominic looks on, appalled. The grey hair, the tight, grey skin, the fear and terror in those eyes.

'I saw her. I saw Melissa.'

'What?' Suddenly shocked. 'You've been in there? In the Trophy Room?' His voice, awed and hushed. A ghost-white face confronting another, a ghostly battle between them. 'You couldn't have seen her. We—'

'What? Buried her? Laid her helpless little body under the ground, in the estate, at dead of night? Without a tear, with nobody to mourn for her?'

His hands steady on the gun.

'No, I... we...'

'You threw her aside like waste meat from a butcher's shop. Fit for nothing.'

'I never—'

'Yes, you did, Dominic. I've suspected for a long time. But now I know.'

'I can't tell you what I know. He'd kill me. The secret we share, it's all I have to protect me.'

'What? What do you know?'

Dominic runs a hand through his hair as if he would tear it from his head. He shakes his head, eyes closed to shut out a nightmare.

'I can't say. I can never say. You don't understand.'

Zachary waves the barrel of the gun.

'The battlement,' his voice rasps. 'You have one chance to save yourself. You tell me everything. I have to know, before I die.'

For a moment, he is overcome by a fit of coughing, and gasps for breath. He reaches in his pocket and fumbles for his inhaler, takes a deep breath.

'Even this bloody thing doesn't work anymore.'

Dominic looks for his chance to escape, but the gun, and the eyes, are steady. No chance yet.

Zachary indicates the steps to the battlements.

'Go on, move.'

Dominic calculates the value of his information as if it's money, working out how much to spend, how much to save, what to invest.

'He said Jocelyn would leave him. He was always saying it, like he was obsessed. He said she'd never be truly part of his family unless—'

'Unless what?'

'Unless she killed the girl.'

Zachary holds tight to the rough stone of the wall.

'Melissa?'

'Yes.' Dominic's voice grows louder, faster. 'You know what he's like. Always talking like the ghosts of his ancestors are right there, like they fill the walls around him. It's creepy. I hear him talk to them, just like they're in the room beside him.'

'Poor Jocelyn,' Zachary says. 'Poor Melissa.' Silence. Zachary gasps, draws his breath like he has emptied the air of oxygen. 'How was she killed?'

'It wasn't my fault. I just got the stuff. And Jocelyn never knew what he'd planned, not until I told her. She wouldn't have. She wasn't like him.'

A pause. Zachary speaks in a quiet voice like a sullen schoolboy caught in a lie, sorry he's been caught.

'How was she killed?'

'Poison.'

'You got it for him?'

'No, I... You don't understand... I promised...'

'Don't lie to me, Dominic. Whatever else, don't lie.'

'I'm not. It wasn't me. It was Rupert. Rupert and Jocelyn. I had to do what he said.' A note of desperation in his voice now. 'You know him. He'd have killed me. He went on and on about how he had to make Jocelyn stay, make her part of the house, one of the family. Like him.'

Zachary's lips curl with distaste.

'You were the same, you and him. You shared... interests.'

'You don't know anything. He had a hold over me.' He looks around, desperately, his mind ticking like a metronome, thinking, thinking. 'Listen, I'll tell you. Just don't shoot, okay.'

Zachary's voice is a mere whisper now, air dragged like the ragged remnants of flesh on a corpse.

'Melissa... I need to know... did you—'

'No, no. Nothing like that.' As Zachary's voice fades towards silence, Dominic's becomes strong and cold, searching for the explanation that will save him, the words that will explain, the pleas that might gain his freedom. 'I never hurt her. It was all Rupert.'

'Melissa,' Zachary sinks to the ground, his hand on the floor beside him, the gun held loosely in the palm. 'My poor Molly.'

Dominic inches forward.

'What was she to you?'

Zachary lifts his eyes like weights in his skull.

'Louise was as soft as a foal in sunshine. I thought I was too old, that I'd never love again. Then, Louise.'

'You knew her?' He inches closer, step by careful step, his eyes on the hand, on the gun.

'For a while we were close. Later, we drifted apart.'

'And Melissa?'

A soft smile.

'She was my daughter. I didn't know, not until later, not until after Louise died.'

His eyes close. Tears fall from a motionless face.

Dominic steps forward, kneels down, slips the gun from the helpless fingers. He stands up, steps back, and raises the muzzle. An unpleasant smile creases his face, and his tongue licks dry lips. In the distance, a car turns by the end of the track; its lights pass over the field like a searchlight, then fade down the lane towards Grantley.

Dominic lowers the gun.

'You're dead already,' he sneers.

He turns and walks back to the car and, a moment later, the vehicle falls into the pillow of darkness, like a disturbed mind surrendering to sleep.

Chapter 47

The police station interview room is like any other: bare walls, laminate floor, a table—bolted to the floor—four chairs and, inevitably, the window through which observers can view the proceedings. No viewers today, though. This is just a chat; a detective from the city on holiday, caught up in a local crime wave, helping out his rural colleagues. They are doing this properly, though, in case his testimony turns out to be evidence in a prosecution.

Frank looks around with a practised eye, and checks his watch. It looks like he won't be back at the caravan any time soon. The only ray of hope lies in the way DI Harold Sparks keeps checking the clock on the wall. Perhaps he wants to finish up and get home, too.

'Lots of things to talk about.' Sparks smiles, professionally. 'But we can talk fast.' He's an older officer, solid, seen it all before.

Templeton, sitting beside him, quells a smile.

'Good of you to help us,' Sparks continues. 'We found a body at eleven o'clock. Some old lady, walking her dog, phoned in to say she'd seen something washed up in on the beach, just outside the village.'

'Who was it?'

Sparks doesn't answer; he's keeping his cards close.

'You had a run-in with Dominic Sheedy, I believe.'

'Yeah, you could say that.'

'Enlighten me.'

Frank knows the drill; he also knows that the truth is the best bet. It won't do him or Richard any good if he distorts the facts.

'I took exception to how he treated a little lad and his dog and took it upon myself to show him the error of his ways.'

A flicker of a smile crosses Templeton's face again but he subdues it.

'Tell me, how precisely did you do that?' Sparks asks.

'Dominic threw this lad's dog off his boat and left it there to drown while the boy watched.'

'And?' Sparks remains impassive and focused.

'I gave him a taste of his own medicine.' Frank breathed a deep sigh. 'I threw him in the harbour?'

'You did *what*?'

Frank scratches his head and does his best to sound apologetic. 'I slung him off the end of the harbour.'

'And the dog?'

'Jason and I fished it from the sea and reunited it with its owner – Sammy Trevelyan.'

'Happy ending then?'

Frank risks a smile.

'I'd like to think so.'

Sparks looks diplomatically at the table top before he resumes. 'Okay,' he says. 'Let's move on to last night. You say you set off after Richard Trevelyan because you were worried what he might do if he met Dominic.'

'Yes.'

'What did you think he would do?'

'I knew what he would have liked to have done. I'd have felt the same. But there are not many people who have a stomach for murder, no matter what they might think.'

'You lost sight of him, you say, down by the harbour. How did that happen?'

'I was talking to a couple of your guys, and turned my back for a minute. When I looked back, there was just this kid there. Molly's her name. I've seen her before around the village.'

'And then?'

'I went looking.'

'Worried what he might do.'

'Let's say I just wanted to be around, make sure things didn't get out of control. Dominic's the provocative sort, likes to wind people up.'

'Did you find him?'

'I saw them once, briefly, as the end of a street, about halfway up the village.'

'Trevelyan at one end, you at the other and Dominic in between. Kind of like a good western film.'

'Yeah, just like, only Dominic spots an alleyway and he's gone and Richard's after him, and they both know the village better than I do so they've lost me before I've gone fifty yards.'

He wants to ask about the body, but he knows there's no point. Sparks will tell him when he wants to, no sooner. It's understandable. He knows that Frank's family and Richard's are friendly, and he probably wonders how far that friendship goes.

Frank's mind leaps ahead, though, wondering. If the body is Dominic's, Richard has no alibi. But then, neither does he.

'What were your feelings towards Dominic at that time? I mean, you'd just heard this harrowing tale from Sammy, you'd contacted us, you'd heard that Dominic had slipped through the net, you'd seen how the family had suffered, and now you were wandering the streets in the early hours. You can't have been in the best of moods.'

'You can be assured that I was in a filthy mood. I was worried for Richard, I was longing to get my hands on Dominic and arrest him, and I wanted to go home to Janice and Jason, and my bed.'

'Pretty messed up.'

'Oh yes, but I've seen enough to know how to deal with it. And I've seen enough to know Richard couldn't kill anyone. Kick seven colours of shit out of them, maybe, but kill? No.'

'What about you?' The brightness of the smile is like sunshine on a polished blade.

'I could kill a cup of coffee right now.'

Templeton restrains a smile. Sparks leans back, and sighs.

'Me, too. Sorry about all this, but I've got to ask. You know the form.' He waved towards a camera in the top corner of the room. 'Three coffees,' he mouths, then he turns back. 'You say you never found Richard Trevelyan.'

'Never saw him again after he hared off up the alleyway after Dominic.'

'He could have found him then?'

'I guess so.'

'What did you do?'

'I wandered the harbour, did a tour of the village a second time, called at his house, and then gave up.'

'But you didn't go back to the caravan.'

'No, I've carried enough bad news lately. Besides, they'd have been asleep and I was too pepped up to think about closing my eyes. I settled myself on a bench and failed to sleep. I walked back over about six, after I'd checked the house again.'

'Did you meet anyone else?'

'Like who?'

'Like Zachary Blight.'

'The guy I met by the harbour at Grantley? Why would I have met him?'

The door opened and a uniformed officer appears with three coffees on a tray, a sugar bag and carton of milk beside it.

'I bet there are coffee grains in the coffee.' Frank opens the bag. 'Why do I get the canteen sugar, and not the nice bowl you have for visitors?'

'Because you're one of us, Frank.' Sparks nods. He glances at the clock again, then double-checks with his watch. 'Mrs Sparks has a WI meeting.'

'So, you don't have me down as a murderer? I've no alibi, plenty of motive, definite opportunity. It could even have been a conspiracy, me and Richard Trevelyan together. Come on, guys, give me a hard time.'

He's inclined to laugh but resists. Sparks and Templeton look tired. It's been a long day.

'No,' Sparks says. 'You see, there's something you don't know, something you would surely have known if you were the killer.'

'Oh yes, what's that?'

Sparks leans back, waves a hand casually to Templeton. 'You tell him.'

'The identity of the victim,' Templeton says. 'It wasn't Dominic. It was Zachary Blight and, just for the record, he was one of us, too. Detective Chief Inspector Zachary Blight, to be precise. Recently retired. Left the Met through ill-health.'

Frank leans forward.

'What the hell was his connection with Rupert Fitzwilliam and Dominic?'

Sparks rubs his head, then fixes him with a stare. 'That is a very good question, Frank. Any ideas?'

Chapter 48

To approach the study window of Leybury Grange you must cross the lawns from the summer house, and then take the gravelled path which leads around the left side of the building. You will pass the corner tower, at the top of which lies the Trophy Room. Three quarters of the way along the side of the building, having passed the window of the long drawing room, you will find yourself outside the study. If you approach at night, which you must, you will note that the heavy curtains are closed but the sash window has been raised, just an inch or two, to allow air to enter, or escape. If Rupert Fitzwilliam is within, you may hear him pacing the room—something he does often since Jocelyn left—mumbling words you cannot discern. You may hear the clink of bottle on glass as he takes one drink, and then another, and another.

On this particular night, not long after Jocelyn's departure, you must approach with particular care. You must steal yourself and calm the inevitable tremors in your heart, quell your rasping breath. Approach the window with care. Settle yourself beneath the stone sill, rest your back against the coarse stone, your legs on the sandy gravel, breathe deep, and listen.

At first you will hear nothing. But you are aware there is someone within. A dull light pulls at the curtain, slips through a crack, holds a finger to its lips—shh!—and dissolves into the darkness. You hear a sigh, perhaps a soft footfall, a muttered oath.

Then, emerging as if from the stony darkness of a deep well, a voice from within creeps closer, becoming clearer as it nears you. Rupert Fitzwilliam is talking to someone.

'She can't leave me. She's my family, one of us, loyal to the family.'

You hear another voice, cold and, rasping, like a harsh tongue scraping the walls.

'You were too soft, too kind. You allowed her weakness to grow.'

'I excused her, I pampered her. I was kind, too kind. I suffered her weakness because I loved her, and I believed she loved me.'

'You did, you did.'

'I should have known she would desert me, eventually. Everyone leaves me.'

'Your love for her made you blind.'

'Yes, yes it did. It did. I loved her and I forgave her. I was too willing to ignore those many signs of gentleness. I could not quell her kindness, her loving spirit.'

There's another voice, a woman's, as old and shrivelled as the body of its owner. Its words are grated from a solid block of bitterness.

'You should have stamped them out, ground them under your heel, smashed them to dust, and scattered them, and buried them.'

'Mama!' You hear a child's cry, somewhere far away, beyond the room, somewhere high above, flying like a bat from the darkness. 'Mama, I'm scared!'

The old woman's voice rises in a querulous scream. 'Be quiet, you simpering brat, or you'll feel the back of my hand.'

'Mama! Mama, I'm scared!'

You raise a hand involuntarily towards the voice. It is a desolate cry which tears at your soul.

'Be quiet, brat!'

You hear Rupert pour a drink. He drinks it quickly, and pours another.

'Will she come back, do you think?'

The old woman cackles. 'Oh yes, fear will drive her back.'

'Not love?' he asks.

'Don't be a fool, boy.'

'And then?'

'We shall welcome her, and make her one with us. The house is ours now. You have set us free.'

There are other voices, one after another: some deep, some low, some mean and grasping, some sophisticated and proud.

'My family, welcome,' Rupert cries. You hear him tap a glass, an aristocratic voice, a welcome. 'My friends, my family, upholders of our great tradition. You are truly welcome home.'

You hear answering voices cheer. There is laughter, conversation, and music: Vivaldi, Mozart. Someone approaches the window, eases back the curtain. You daren't look; you don't want to look, for fear of what you might see. Someone sniffs the air.

'A foul smell,' a voice above your head whispers. A cold chill descends, like a corpse's breath. It's time to slip away, sideways, back to the wall, no sound. 'I smell it,' the voice hisses. 'It smells of life.'

You reach the corner, slip around the high tower, turn and sprint across the lawn, grateful for the flat grass, and the darkness. You want to be as far from here as you can get. If you escape this place, you know with absolute certainty, you will never return.

Ahead, you see the summer house, and the safety of the woods. A hundred yards more, and you will reach the road. By the summer house, you turn. There is nobody following you. Only your footprints glisten on the damp grass. A mist rises gently, ghostly white, and moves as if scenting the earth. It rises at the corner of the tower, reaches tendrils up and around, and your eyes are drawn involuntarily to the arched window of the Trophy Room.

There's a face at the window, a child's face.

'Melissa,' you cry, although you don't know why.

Then the face is gone, and you know it is time for you too to go.

And there, behind you, stands a boy, ghostly white, as if he were drawn from the mist, and made solid, as pale as a shadow, his blue eyes pinned to yours.

His mouth opens.

'Go!' he cries, and his voices rises louder, and ever louder. 'GO! GO!!!'

You turn on your heels, and flee as if all the devils in hell were behind you, and you don't stop until you reach home. You close the door behind you, and settle down, a glass of wine before you, your hands trembling.

Time passes.

What a fool you are, you say, to let your imagination run such riot. Imagine someone saw you, running for your life like a child on a dark street. You chuckle and sip your wine, polished deep red, and winking at you from a bright, amused glass. Rupert Fitzwilliam, alone now since Jocelyn left him, probably drunk, talking to himself, talking to a radio like it was a living person. Nothing that can't be explained. You laugh out loud. To be overwhelmed by the reputation of the place, the gruesome history of the family, the reputation cut by Rupert

Fitzwilliam as if from living flesh. To clothe and breathe life into a few strange sounds, a few indistinguishable voices, a few drunken threats.

With the curtains drawn, the lights bright, a glass in your hand, and your family safe in bed, you feel the folly of your hysteria.

But you glance towards the door, and listen, nonetheless. Are they still there, your husband, your daughter? The holiday house you rent is suddenly silent. A secret dread approaches like a cloud over the sea, carrying darkness, rolling it out like a shroud.

Chapter 49

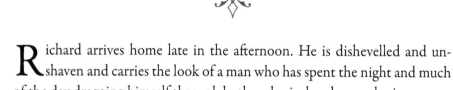

Richard arrives home late in the afternoon. He is dishevelled and un-shaven and carries the look of a man who has spent the night and much of the day dragging himself through both a physical and mental mire.

When he opens the door, Maggie runs through from the lounge. A cry breaks from her lips and she flings her arms round his neck, and hugs him.

'I'm sorry, Maggie.'

'Where've you been, you daft sod?' she asks, pulling back, and looking at him. 'We've been so worried.' She raises her two fists, and brings them down on his chest again and again. 'How could you do that, Richard? How could you? And Sammy up there, thinking it's all his fault, and that if he'd never told...'

He stifles her sobs with his arms, and holds her close.

'There's nothing I can say, so I won't. I won't let you down again, not ever.'

Maggie pulls herself away. She wipes her eyes.

'If you ever do, I'll ding you with those glass floats you're so fond of.' She laughs through her tears. 'See which breaks first, the floats or that thick head of yours.'

The kitchen door opens.

Sammy.

'I'm sorry, Dad,' he cries.

'Not half as sorry as I am. And you have no need. You've done nothing wrong. It's just your silly old dad went for a drink or two with Frank, and ended up a bit worse for wear.' He glances at Maggie. 'Now, come here and give your foolish dad a hug, eh?'

Together, the three of them, weathering another storm.

'I've got to go to the police station,' he says. 'I'll phone them.'
They sit down at the table.

'What will you tell them?' Maggie asks.

Their eyes meet.

'Everything. I'll tell them every damned thing they want to know. There's no more running away now.' He ruffles Sammy's hair. 'My son has shown me what it means to be truly brave. I couldn't be prouder, not in a million years.'

His voice trembles, but he forces back the tears.

'I'll go over there straight away, and get this sorry business finished. I won't run away, not any more, will I, Sammy? Your old dad is going to do what's right, even if it has taken him a bloody long time to get around to it.'

Maggie stands up, hands on hips.

'Well, you're not going looking like a tramp. You can get up those stairs and take a shower. You smell like a blocked drain. Throw your clothes out, and I'll get you some fresh. Imagine what they'd think if they saw you now.'

She ushers him through the door, and drives him upstairs. A smile breaks from Sammy's face. 'I'm glad you're back, Dad,' he shouts.

'Aye, me too, Sammy. I'm going nowhere, not again.'

Late that afternoon, he enters Grantley Police Station, dressed in his only suit, with a clean, white shirt and a red tie. Straight-backed and firm-jawed, he has the look of a man who has made a decision, and intends to stick by it.

'Detective Sergeant Templeton,' he says to the officer at the desk. 'Tell him Richard Trevelyan is here to see him.'

He waits, his eyes fixed on the wall until the door opens, and Frank Miller walks through.

'Hello, Frank. My, I'm glad to see you. What are you doing here?'

'First off, I was interviewed, and then, half an hour ago, I was seconded for a couple of weeks to join the Grantley force. It seems a good idea since I'm on the spot, and already involved. Come on through, Richard. DS Templeton and DI Sparks are waiting.' He pauses. 'I'm really glad to see you. You had me worried for a while.'

'I worried everybody. I've no excuse. It was just selfish.'

Frank raises a smile from somewhere. 'Interview time. I'll show you in, and then I'll go and brew up. Just tell them the truth, and it'll be over in no time.'

'Aye, that I will. Every bloody word.'

When Frank enters the interview room five minutes later, laden with a tray and four cups, Templeton and Sparks are already seated. Opposite them, Richard sits with his hands on his knees, a look of resolve on his face.

'For the tape, Detective Inspector Miller has entered the room. Mr Trevelyan has declined to be represented by a solicitor.' He rests his hands on the table. 'Now, Mr Trevelyan, to begin with, let's reconstruct, if we can, your movements of last night, after you left DI Miller at the harbour.'

'Well, I don't rightly know all the ins and outs. I wandered about the streets, looking for Dominic.'

'Did you find him?'

'Just once, briefly, on Mid Lane. Frank, DI Miller, was there, too, at the other end of the road. Dominic took off, and I set off after him.'

'You didn't wait for DI Miller?'

Richard scratches his head ruefully. He glances across at Frank.

'I'm sorry, Frank. But you being a policeman and all... I wanted to face him myself.'

'What did you have in mind, if you found him?'

'I don't know, really. You've no idea the things that go through your head. Savage things you could no more do than make the seas stop their movements, things that even in your imagination make you recoil.'

'You wanted to kill him?'

'Sometimes, yes, up there in my head. I'd have beaten him within an inch of it, given the chance. Or so I thought. But thinking and doing are different, aren't they? I thought about that a lot during the night, wandering the cliff path, and the streets. I cursed myself for knowing I wasn't man enough to carry it through, even if I caught up with him.'

'But you still wanted to find him?'

Head raised, eyes straight at Sparks. 'Oh yes. I'd have given him a pasting, no doubt about that. But mostly I wanted him to know...'

Sparks, softer now. A quick glance at the clock. 'To know what?'

'To know that I knew everything, to know that we were free of him forever, to know that he was the most contemptible creature on God's earth, and that I'd make sure everyone knew it.' He pauses for a moment. 'There was something else, though. I wanted him to know that we were better than him, and that we'd always be together as a family, and we'd crush his memory like a beetle under the heel of a shoe. I wanted him to know we'd won.' He looks at Frank. 'You understand?'

Frank smiles, nods.

'Did you see anyone else?'

Richard shakes his head.

'Think carefully. Anyone at all?'

'The Harbour Inn was closed. There were lights in windows here and there but mostly, folks were away to their beds. Leybury is that kind of place. Even the dog walkers had given up by that time.'

'Did you see anything unusual? Again, think carefully.'

'Like what?'

'Anything that struck you as unusual.'

Richard frowns. 'Nothing,' he says, then pauses. 'Except, well...'

'What?'

'I reached the bypass once, during my ramblings. It's quiet at that time of night, or as quiet as it ever is nowadays. I was just standing there, wondering where I could go next, when I saw her.'

'Who?'

'Jocelyn Fitzwilliam. She was in the back of a car. White as a ghost, she looked.'

'Which way was she heading?'

'South.'

'Have you heard the name Zachary Blight?'

Richard shakes his head. 'Can't say I have. Who is he?'

Templeton pushes a photograph across the table.

'I might have seen him about. I don't rightly know. He has a familiar look about him.'

'Look carefully. Be sure.'

Richard studies the photograph, then shakes his head.

'No, I'm sorry. Who is he?'

'He was found dead this morning, possibly murdered.'

'And you think I—'

'He was working for Rupert Fitzwilliam,' Templeton says.

'An unsavoury type, then?'

Sparks raises an ironic smile but says nothing.

'What was your involvement with Rupert Fitzwilliam?'

Richard looks round the table, and his eyes fixed on Frank, as if searching for something. He seems lost momentarily.

'Remember, you can have a solicitor at any time, Richard. It's your right.'

Richard, as if drawn back sharply, re-focusses and shakes his head.

'No, I don't want to be here any longer than I need to. I've Maggie and Sammy to think about.' He sits upright, his arms folded across his chest, his feet wide, like a buttress. 'The truth will have to suffice, whatever it might bring. But I want you to know, before I start, that Maggie had no hand in this. Whatever I knew or suspected was nothing to do with Maggie. You're to leave her alone. She's enough to think about with our Sammy.'

He takes a deep breath.

'We were near bankrupt. The fishing didn't bring in much and the summer trips weren't doing as well as we hoped. We had debts with the bank. There was nobody to help us. Then Dominic came along. We'd known him a while, and didn't particularly like him, but you clutch at straws don't you, when you're desperate? I saw him down at The Harbour Inn one night and we got talking, like you do. He said he had this friend who could raise cash, solve our problems. His friend liked a bit of sea fishing, he said, and might like to go out regular during the season. He was a philanthropist, a wealthy local guy who wanted to do his bit for the community. He said we were a worthy cause. Local people who'd been here for generations, still fishing, helping the tourist economy. He said we were just the sort of people his friend wanted to help.

'Well, long story short, his friend was Rupert Fitzwilliam, and he had no more interest in sea fishing than I do in clog dancing, and his only concern for the local community was to get out of it whatever he could to serve himself. They had plans for *The Lovely Maggie.*'

He looks up.

'I swear to you, I had no idea what he was up to. Fool that I am, I believed Dominic. And then later, when I started to suspect, when he dragged Sammy out with him to make it look all innocent, well, by then he'd got his claws into me, and he wasn't going to let go. I turned a blind eye. To this day, I don't know precisely what they're up to. But you can bet your last fiver it's no good.'

He draws a large handkerchief from his pocket, stained with oil and grease, and finds a clean corner. He wipes his eyes where tears have formed.

'Worst thing is, I let them down. Maggie, and...' The tears roll. 'Poor Sammy. That bastard...'

His palms grasp the back of his head. He stifles a deep groan.

'Interview terminated.' Templeton checks his watch and gives the time.

'Thank you, Mr Trevelyan. We'll get your statement typed up and you can sign it. Then you're free to go.'

'You're not charging me?'

Sparks shakes his head. 'I doubt you've anything to worry about.'

He and Templeton stand up, and leave the room.

'Is it over?' he asks Frank.

'Pretty much. You did well.'

'Thank God.'

Richard's eyes darken, and he looks suddenly older, weighed down with the gravity of life. He leans forward, resting his arms on the table.

'We'll have to sell up.' He looks at Frank, suddenly desperate. 'We can't keep the money, not now. I'll have to pay it back, every penny. We'll have to sell the boats and the house, just to clear our debts. How can I tell Maggie and Sammy, after all they've been through? What can I do, Frank?'

Chapter 50

*C*ity streets are unforgiving places. Look at that guy on the park bench, legs stretched inside a ragged sleeping bag. It was probably red once, that bag, but not now; just grime and grey, like his hands and his face and his half-closed eyes. He's wearing a heavy jacket and fingerless gloves because, although it's autumn and although the sun is shining, the nights are chill.

The people who walk past him see him but they don't let on. They move past, momentarily uncomfortable. He pays no attention. His eyes are empty. Maybe it's alcohol, maybe drugs, or maybe he's just given up. He's not even begging.

It's not that they don't care, all those people walking past. Okay, so some of them blame him for what he is, say he should sort himself out, get a job, stop scrounging. Thief, beggar, druggy, junkie. Not human. Not like them. But, see that woman hesitate, check to see if there's somewhere to drop a coin. She wonders if she could buy him a coffee or a sandwich.

God, in this day and age, with all this money, there are still food shelters, and homeless people. Makes you think, doesn't it?

But she walks on. What can she do, just one person? A drop of love in an ocean of despair.

You should check out another guy before you leave: the suspicious-looking guy coming out of the mini-mart. He looks like he slept in that coat, and in that face. Unshaven, grey cheeks. Jeans that could've spent a few hours lying in a gutter. T-shirt not much better, under an open coat.

He looks up and down, then drags a packet of biscuits and a cold pie from under the coat, and searches out a bench. He sees the homeless guy alone on his bench, and turns away to a different seat. Even the damned mix in different circles of hell. He unwraps the stolen pie, and eats it aggressively. He's not eaten since yesterday. When was it? Morning? Can't remember.

He's about thirty, pinched looking, with coal-black eyes which won't stay still. He glances around like he's watching for someone, leaning forward all the time, on the balls of his feet, ready for a quick escape. He drops the packaging from the pie on the ground, and makes a start on the biscuits. And finishes them.

He's got a can in his jacket pocket—looks like Coke—and opens it with that familiar hiss, then holds it out as the liquid froths over, and down onto the sidewalk. Takes a deep swig. Sits back, and belches loudly.

He's more relaxed now, having quelled the pangs of hunger. He stretches his arms along the back of the bench, claiming it as his own, and looks around, studying the people and the street. His eyes have a cunning, cynical look, like he's weighing up his options. A woman with a shopping basket approaches the empty space beside him, pauses, reflects, and moves to a bench some yards away.

It's hard to imagine but, even if it was only for a moment, you were the same as him once. I mean, he was born, same as you, wiped down and handed to his mother, a bare, gurgling blank sheet for the world to scrawl on. The same as you. Five seconds later your paths diverged. His mother looked down at him and, right there and then, decided she didn't like him, didn't want him. Ugly, squirming thing, already demanding her attention. Shitting and crying.

A clean, white nurse in a clean, white coat said it'd be better when they got home.

What did she know?

Things got worse, not better.

You went home to your nice semi with Mum and Dad, didn't you? Newly painted nursery with a mobile over your cot, lots of soft toys, and pretty stencils on the walls. Smiles and cuddles, food and warmth, love. Lots of people coming to aah and ooh and how sweet and he's got his dad's eyes over you.

She got a flat, and her mum and dad bought a cot, and a few things she'd need, nappies and stuff. She looked around and yawned, opened a packet, and took out a cigarette. She left him in the cot, and went through to the lounge. Threw herself back on the sofa, and turned on the television. Loud, so she couldn't hear his bawling.

After a month, social work got involved. Mum and Dad were interfering again. They wanted her to go back to their house—home, they called it—so they could help her. Well, there was no way she was going back there, with her mum looking over her shoulder all the time, telling her how to be a good mother.

They could take the kid if they wanted. She told them that, all the do-good-ers. The social worker thought that'd be good. So, they agreed, and a day later, he was gone. She sat back, feet up, and turned on the television, loud.

Thank God.

She saw him sometimes, maybe once every couple of weeks. Six months later, she fell out with her mum, and took him back, just to teach her who was in charge. That only lasted a month or so, then Les was on the scene, and he hated kids as much as she did. Sometimes he slapped the boy so she took him back to her mum and dad.

Until Les walked out.

And Mal walked in.

When he was six, she took him back for good. She'd grown up, got her act together, and was getting on with her mum and dad. She decided it was time to be a family. He started a new school, near to Nan and Grandpa, and Mum got a council house.

School was bad, though. He couldn't settle to it, hated the teachers, hated the other kids, hated everyone. He had a temper too. The other kids didn't like him; they called him Monkey Boy. He lashed out. Some of the other kids hit him so he lashed out again and again.

The head teacher got some shrink to see him.

Attention deficit hyperactivity disorder. ADHD. Attachment disorder, too.

Every teacher's nightmare.

And his own.

He just couldn't make friends, no matter how; he didn't know how to be liked. Eventually he didn't even want to be liked.

It went on, year upon year. He got by, hating everyone.

His name?

Did I not mention it?

I should have mentioned it.

He's called Dominic. Erstwhile, Monkey Boy. Brat. Scum. Creep. Bastard. Shit. Weirdo.

Look down at him now: paedophile, thief, murderer maybe, and lots of oth-er things, too. You should try to remember that bundle of bawling, pink flesh. It's difficult, isn't it?

And that blank sheet? Look what they drew on it.

He stands up. Tonight, he'll have to find a doorway to sleep in. He daren't go back to sleep in the car. The police will be on the lookout.

And tomorrow?

He's got plans for tomorrow.

Chapter 51

Frank eases the car to a halt as they emerge from the tree-lined drive of Leybury Grange, where it opens onto lawns with scattered trees and, nearer the house, wide flower beds.

'Why have you stopped?' Templeton asks.

Beneath the tyres, the sandy-grey gravel forms a wide arc to the front of the house.

'It's a beautiful building. I just wanted to look. I came here a few days ago, sneaked in through the trees over by the summer house. I wanted to get a feel for the place.'

Templeton's eyebrows rise. 'Oh? And what were your conclusions?'

'Jocelyn Fitzwilliam was by the summer house.' He points away towards the building, an octagonal ship in a sea of green set against a black cloud of trees in a blue sky. 'She was talking to a guy. Carver, I think his name was.'

'Not Harry Carver?'

'I didn't get his first name. Youngish guy, maybe late twenties or early thirties. Casual dress, shortish hair, had a tidy look about him. He was maybe five-ten, eleven or twelve stone. Not a big guy but obviously kept in trim.'

'It could be Harry Carver.'

'Why the interest?'

'He didn't come back to work after his holiday. He was due back a couple of days ago, but didn't show. His wife phoned me.'

'One of yours?'

'No, the Met. I knew him from years back.'

'Undercover?'

'You could never tell with Harry. I think he was caught up in the dark arts down there in the big city.'

'He mentioned a name that Zachary Blight was interested in. *Melissa*. It might be worth checking.'

'Any surname?'

'No, but it'll worth trying Fitzwilliam. I got the feeling she was related.'

Templeton relays the message back to the desk sergeant at Grantley, then asks, 'Are we going to drive on?'

'Yes, I'd like to think he's seen us by now, and wonders why we're here.'

The wheels grind against the drive, and the car accelerates round a wide curve to the front of the house. The ornate front door opens as they turn off the engine.

Rupert Fitzwilliam emerges, a brandy in one hand, and a newspaper under his arm. His clothing radiates pastel simplicity, cool in the warm sun, like he's just changed after tennis.

'DS Templeton and DI Miller, I presume.' He looks as if he's about to extend a hand, and then thinks better, and withdraws it. 'I'm intrigued. Your sergeant is a man of very few words, and most of them monosyllabic. Asking him questions was like prising concrete from a toothpaste tube. Do come in, or shall we walk the gardens? They're really lovely at this time of year. Or so my sister tells me. I find them rather tedious myself.'

'Inside would be fine.' Frank smiles: practised and professional. 'Where is Jocelyn, by the way? I heard she'd left.'

An ugly look flashes across Rupert's face.

'She had to leave. Some tedious business matters in Europe. I couldn't tell you what, and I couldn't tell you where. She'll be back in a few weeks.'

They walk through the wide entrance hall past a staircase which rises from the ground floor, before spreading left and right like elegant wings; an eagle of wood and bronze. Portraits at the top of the stairs, on the facing wall. Rupert, Jocelyn, older faces, and a landscape of the park, and the house.

'Nice,' Frank says, pausing for a moment.

'Indeed. The house has many treasures, and many secrets.' Rupert yawns. 'But I don't suppose you've come here to discuss art. Shall we go to the drawing room, and get on?'

There's a note of impatience in his voice.

They sink into a plush, fabric sofa with cushions floating on its surface, while Rupert eases himself into a soft armchair, and raises one foot into a space on a small table housing magazines and newspapers.

'I won't offer you a drink. You're on duty, and the servants aren't here to provide non-alcoholic refreshments. I have them all on zero hours contracts.' He waves a hand, and laughs at his own joke. 'Not because I need to, but because it entertains me. Life can be so boring, don't you think? And the news...' He flicks a hand towards the newspapers. 'It's so utterly tedious.'

There is a brittleness about Rupert today, like a hard veneer on rotten wood.

'You know Dominic Sheedy, I believe,' Frank says. 'A friend of yours, I was told.'

A quick movement of the eyes, a sudden harshness of tone.

'Hardly a friend. The man has barely risen above the primeval.'

'But you meet up, go for a drink or two at The Harbour Inn. I've heard the stories.'

'He entertains me, rather like a pet rat.'

'Does he work for you?'

'Of course not. I wouldn't trust Dominic to clean drains.'

'So, he's never been inside this house.'

'No. I mean...' Again, that flick of the wrist, that sharpness of the eyes. 'What would the neighbours say?'

'Indeed.'

Frank leans back and, synchronously, Templeton eases forward. Like they're taking turns. Rupert watches with feigned amusement, like he's enjoying a sideshow in a fairground.

'What about Zachary Blight? Do you know him?'

'Zachary? Yes, he's an odious little man, but he visits the house once in a while. Security matters, usually. I invite him to dinner to annoy all the other odious people.'

'When was he last here?'

Rupert shrugs.

'I don't keep a track of time. It's merely the ether in which I exist, nothing more. A week, maybe two...'

'Before your sister left?'

A tick in the cheek, a tightening of the jaw. *A tell*, the poker players call it.

'Yes. It's one of the joys of her departure, however temporary it might be, that I don't need to invite people to the house.'

'Lonely, I would have thought.' Templeton looks around the room, at the portraits, the antique furniture, the deep carpet and heavy curtains. 'Just ghosts of the past for company. It must be strange here on your own.'

Rupert's veneer cracks; the rotten wood is momentarily revealed below, crawling with fungal life. He leans forward, eyes staring and intense.

'I like my ghosts.' He looks at Templeton as if he would willingly strike him. 'And I like my solitude.'

Templeton chooses not to flinch, as Frank watches the bitterness on Rupert's face with not a little alarm.

Eventually, Rupert relaxes, and an ugly sneer passes across his face like a shadow.

'Old houses like Leybury Grange are full of ghosts. It's part of their charm. We're particularly blessed in that respect. We have quite a collection.'

Frank smiles. 'I've read a bit about your family history.'

A long, slow, humourless laugh emerges from Rupert, so smooth it could slide under doors.

'We have something of a reputation, I confess. Not all of my ancestors were respectable citizens. Some of them had... unusual tastes.'

'I'm surprised you've never opened your house to the public.' Templeton's suggestion draws a frown from Rupert. 'Ghostly tales, and a history like that of your family would have an appeal. You'd be fighting them off.'

'Ghouls and voyeurs? No, thank you. Besides...' His voice adopts a more intense tone. 'My ghosts wouldn't emerge for the general public. They would sink deeper into the walls, absorbed into the very fabric of the building. They would be resentful. They might even blame me for the impertinence of intrusion.'

He stares at Templeton again, and then that long, slow laugh unfolds like a roll of velvet.

'I am comfortable with my ghosts. I would hate to lose their company.'

His eyes travel the walls, pausing occasionally, as if catching sight of figures trapped there. A flicker of a smile hesitates on his lips, and moves on.

'You haven't had an addition to your ghostly ranks recently, have you?'
Frank's mouth smiles. His eyes don't.

'How do you mean?'

'Zachary Blight is dead. He was found washed up on the shore at Leybury, near the harbour.'

Rupert looks from on to the other then fixes his eyes on Frank.

'Washed up seems a particularly appropriate phrase, if a little cruel. But
no, my ghostly ancestors are very particular about who they admit to their
ranks. I can assure you that Zachary Blight would find no place here.

'Oh, excuse me.' He sits forward, suddenly earnest. 'I really should ask
how he died. How very discourteous of me. It was his asthma, I assume? A
sudden attack, futile moments fumbling for his ghostly inhaler, a realisation
that he had left it somewhere. A gasping, grasping struggle for breath and a
final stumble from the cliff, dropping down on the rocks below? *Aaaargghh*!'

He pauses, as if for dramatic effect, enjoying the appalled silence from his
listeners. He raises a hand to his ear.

'Do you hear them?'

'Who?'

'My ghosts. They're laughing.'

Frank struggles to restrain his feelings. Templeton, beside him, is pale.

'We suspect he was murdered.'

'Oh, how thrilling.' Rupert claps his hands like an excited child. 'How
fascinating, and ironic, that such a tedious bore, someone so easily forgotten,
should have such a dramatic ending. It's almost worthy of a place in my
ghostly gallery, don't you think? I'll convene a meeting, a family conference.
We'll take a vote.'

'Jesus Christ.' The words emerge as a whisper from Templeton, whose
pallor has intensified. Rupert raises a hand to his lips.

'Oh, you think me insensitive. I'm so sorry. I'll concentrate now, and try
to improve my manners. Is there anything else I can help you with?'

Frank smiles. 'You could make my investigation easier.'

'Oh? How?'

'You could always confess to his murder.'

He allows the smile to crack for a moment, to make room for a sardonic
chuckle.

Rupert too laughs.

'I wish I could help you. I've read about the plight of our overworked police force. But sadly, I didn't kill him.'

'You have an alibi?'

Rupert thinks for a moment. 'No, indeed I haven't. Unless I can call up one of my ghosts to vouch for me.' A cold smile now. 'But I have no motive. I mean, what could I possibly have to gain from the death of someone like Zachary Blight?'

'That's a very good question,' Frank says. 'I met Mr Blight, you know, in Grantley a few days ago. He warned me about you. He seemed anxious our paths shouldn't cross.' That tick in Rupert's cheek pulses again, his teeth and lips glue tight, holding something in. 'Have you any idea why that should be? He seemed to think my run-in with Dominic had angered you.'

A shrug and a sigh. 'People are such a disappointment. You welcome them in your home, you offer them the pleasure of your company, you give them a glimpse of a better life, and the moment you turn away, they come at you with knives.' Another sigh, long and theatrical. 'I prefer my ghosts. At least you can rely on family.'

A moment's silence.

'Well,' Rupert rises to his feet. 'If there's nothing more...'

Templeton stands up; Frank remains seated.

'Does the name Melissa mean anything to you?'

Rupert looks at him sharply, then wipes the look away, and replaces it with one of idle curiosity.

'No,' he says. 'Why?'

'Oh, just a piece in a jigsaw.'

'How about Harry Carver?' Templeton asks.

Rupert frowns, raising his finger to his chin, half-closing his eyes, as if digging deeply into the muddy pools of his mind. He finds something, raises it in his hands, and flourishes it.

'Ah, one of my sister's waifs. She brought him here, gave him some job or another. A gardener, perhaps. I'm afraid I dismissed him.'

'Could I ask why?'

'He seemed over-familiar with Jocelyn. Ideas above his station, you know. We can't have that sort of thing.' He raises a smile, bubbling from the mud pool. 'The ghosts wouldn't approve.'

'Thank you.' Frank stands up, and holds out a hand.

'Do call again.' Rupert shakes hands with Templeton, enjoying the look of distaste on the officer's face. 'This has been a most enjoyable meeting. It has enlivened my day.'

When the oak door closes behind them, and they stand in the refreshing sunshine, Templeton turns to Frank.

'That man is quite mad.'

'Oh yes,' Frank says, 'and, unless I'm mistaken, capable of anything.'

'Even murder?'

Frank walks down the steps to the car.

'Especially murder.'

Chapter 52

The path which leads south of Leybury rises up the cliff at a civilised angle towards a bench, set beautifully above the sea. It's a lovely spot from where you can see, in one direction, across a wide gully to where the cliff is twisted and bent like iron bars by a circus strongman. In the other direction, the old village and its harbour lie undisturbed. It's a favourite spot for visitors, even on a day when the wind hunts the headlands like a peregrine falcon. People come here just to sit and watch.

Today, you see a girl hop down from the last step beside that pretty little floral cottage where the Trevelyan family lives. She pauses by the side of the road, and glances around, looking for friends. She sees two boys and takes a step forward, then pauses, and watches.

The two boys, Sammy and Jason, are running beside the harbour rail to where steps lead down to a narrow beach. Sammy has a ball at his feet, which he controls carefully, his eyes focused downwards.

The girl takes another step, raises a hand to wave, but then lets it fall to her side. They haven't seen her. She turns aside as if to speak to someone standing beside her on the first stone step. Even at this distance it is clear from the movement of her shoulders, and the way she raises and lowers her arms, that she is talking and so real is her conversation that you believe for a moment that you can see her companion. She has a pale look, shadowy, as if a breeze or a cloud passing the sun would see her fade and disappear. You shake away the feeling, and smile to yourself. You recall how, as a child, you too had an imaginary friend.

From up here, the village is all rooftops, chimneys, and satellite dishes. Such an array of shades; reds and greys, mostly. The cottage walls below show more variety. There are whites and pinks, as well as the traditional greys. Here and there you spy an experimental blue or tasteless green.

191

This is a good vantage point, though, from where you can look down to the harbour and beyond. In the distance you can see the watchtower built by herring fishermen. The old castle—you must visit it again one day —is out of sight where the coast curves beyond the cliff.

You watch the girl, curious to see if she will run across to join the boys. They are down on the narrow beach now, passing the ball back and forth, diving occasionally in a dramatic fashion, as boys will. The ball flies a few yards into the sea. Sammy runs in for it, the water tumbling and spitting as he stumbles through, heavy-legged.

Kids. They don't care how wet they get. They've got better things to think about. Not like you, you think; you'd be too concerned about appearances, and about the long, wet walk back to the holiday cottage.

You feel an ache of nostalgia, and a subdued pain, carried on waves of regret. Where have they gone, those days?

Ah, now the girl makes up her mind. She runs over to the rail, slowing only as she nears it. She stands for a moment, waiting to be noticed. It's a lonely sight, to see her pause, and speak to the shadow at her heels. Does your heart not reach out to her? Do you not slip into her mind, and, for a fleeting moment, feel as she feels?

'Molly!'

One of the boys has seen her. It's the boy called Jason, the one from the holiday park. He waves, and a smile brightens her face like sunshine. Sammy, the other boy, looks up. A flicker of recognition. Maybe she used to be at his school. Maybe she went away. A private school, wealthy parents.

You weave a story.

Weave a story too around her shadow, the imaginary friend who lingers now by the rail, just watching.

A cloud passes over the sun.

Chapter 53

'You never came to the cave like you promised.'

Jason kicks the ball towards Molly, and she kicks it on to Sammy.

'I couldn't. Mum wouldn't let me.'

'Didn't you used to go to Grantley Primary?' Sammy pauses, his foot on the ball.

'Yes.' Molly sits down beside the bottom step, and stretches her legs out. Her hands grasp and release fists of sand. She flicks her hair from her face with a quick twist of her head.

'Did you move a different school?'

'Kind of. I live there sometimes. They help me.'

'Help you with what?'

Molly shrugs. 'Just things.' She springs to her feet, kicks off her loose sandals, and runs into the shallow water until it rises above her knees. She stands still, and peers into the water.

'Sometimes there are shoals of little fish,' she says, 'if you stand still, and wait. Once, a fish came out from under the sand. It wriggled between my toes, and made me scream.'

'There are crabs further out,' Sammy tells her. 'When it's still, and you look down in the water, you can see them scuttling about.'

They run into the water and stand beside her, leaning forward, waiting for the water and sand to settle, and the flickering patina of sunlight to become still.

'Look.' She points where a shoal of tiny silver darts flicker and turn; a momentary pulse of movement. Then, as they fall under the shadow of the children, they flee. Several bodies, one mind.

'The water's warm near the edge.' Jason kicks his foot. 'It's cold further out.' He reaches his hands into the water and weaves them from side to side, fish tails flickering. A moment later he lets out a cry. Water is cascading round him, falling from his head and down his face.

Molly laughs with delight. 'I couldn't resist.'

Sammy laughs, too.

Jason looks from one to the other. 'I'll get you back,' he shouts, and he scoops water and throws it, Molly first, then Sammy.

Then the battle rages.

A couple, in their sixties—retired folk taking a holiday break—pause and watch.

'Oh, to be young.' The man turns and smiles at his companion.

The woman sighs. 'Brings back memories. I couldn't do it now, not with my arthritis.'

They walk on but not before the woman shivers violently.

'What's the matter?'

'I don't know. I just went cold. I'm fine now.'

'Someone walking on your grave.'

She looks back, as if searching for the shadow which fell over her. 'Something like that.'

'Let's get a coffee, and warm you up.' They turn towards The Harbour Inn.

On the beach, the children tire of their game, and lie back on the sand, the warm grains clinging to their skin.

'Do your mum or dad still live here?' Sammy asks Molly.

'Only in the summer, and sometimes at weekends. They live in the city the rest of the year. They don't like driving a long way to work in the winter. That's why they bought a flat in the city. That, and to be near me.'

'I live in a city,' Jason says. 'I just come here for holidays.'

'I know. You said.'

'Is your school in the city?'

'I told you, it's not a school. It's kind of like a hospital.'

'Are you sick? You don't look sick.' Sammy sits up, and brushes an insect from his face. 'Ugh, I got a mouthful of sand.' He spits, and wipes his mouth with the back of his hand. 'Disgusting.'

Molly stands up. She turns towards the steps, and then pauses to look up towards the protective rail along the harbour front. Her eyes fix, as if she sees someone standing there; pale, like a mist in darkness.

'What's the matter?' Jason follows where she's staring.

'Nothing.' She hesitates. 'Only... I feel sad sometimes. Like everything changes.'

Sammy stands beside her, anxious. She turns, a strange look on her face, like fear.

'I don't know. I sense things sometimes, and sometimes...' Another hesitation. 'Sometimes my friend tells me things.' She turns to the steps and springs up them. 'I've got to go.' She pauses at the top. 'She's called Melissa. Only she doesn't like that name. She likes the name her mum called her, when she was little.'

'What was that?'

She gives them a strange smile.

'Molly,' she says. 'Like me.'

Chapter 54

F rank crosses a car park and runs, two at a time, up the granite steps of a steel and glass building, which constitutes Grantley's upgraded police station. Holiday over, he's at work now. He pauses at the automatic door before entering and heading to the incident room, where he finds Templeton.

'Any news on Melissa Fitzwilliam?' He hangs a light jacket over his chair, and drops down in front of a computer screen. He switches it on out of habit, and clicks on his emails.

Templeton raises a head, then a chest. He leans back and yawns. 'Melissa Fitzwilliam, born May 2010, to one Louise Fitzwilliam, sister to Rupert. Louise died by suicide in 2018, when Melissa was eight years old. Melissa spent a term here in Grantley Primary School before being shipped off to relatives abroad, I'm trying to trace them but it's proving difficult. I'll be on to South America and Antarctica soon.'

'Rupert was lying to us, then, when he said he had never heard the name. His niece, eh? I assume, if she was at the local school, she was living at Leybury Grange.'

'I checked with the school. Apparently, Rupert didn't want to have her in the house. As soon as he could get rid of her, she was lodged with a family in Leybury, who had a girl in the same class. I guess he found some family member abroad, and then got rid of her as quickly as possible.'

'He's all heart, isn't he, our Rupert? We need to find her, so keep searching. I'll feel happier when I know she's out there, and alive. Even if it is Antarctica.'

'Poor kid. Bad enough your mother dying without having Uncle Rupert as a temporary guardian.'

For some reason, Frank's mind turns to Sammy.

'Yes, indeed.' He glances at his screen. There's a message from Guy, his colleague in the city, bewailing his absence, and the workload left in his wake. There's nothing else of interest. He sends a sarcastic reply: *LOL*.

'What about the mother? Louise Fitzwilliam. Is there anything there we need to know?'

'I'll check. I know she lived here at the Grange before she left to go to university as a mature student. She turned into something of a wild child, despite being rather older than most of her fellow students. Probably the consequence of escaping from Leybury Grange. There was some police involvement, minor misdemeanours, nothing that couldn't be put down to high spirits.'

'Getting away from Brother Rupert would be enough to raise your spirits, I suppose.'

'To the rafters.'

'See what more you can find. Who was Melissa's father?'

'None registered. As I say, a bit of a wild child.'

'I'm going to take a trip out to Leybury Grange. I'll be interested to hear what Rupert has to say about his memory loss regarding his niece. If he's lying about that, there must be a reason.'

'Are you going alone?'

'There's nobody else. Sparks is at a meeting and you're busy.'

'Brave man.'

Templeton turns back to his computer. Frank finishes with his emails and heads to the door.

Half an hour later, he pulls up outside the stone steps of Leybury Grange. He glances up at the tower, and then across the dark frontage of the house. To his right, just before the corner: the French windows of the lounge, like a blister on skin.

He walks up the steps. There's no bell or speaker, just a grotesque door knocker, shaped like a skull. The tongue lolls outwards, and the eyes protrude.

A hanged man.

He beats heavily on the door; the sound echoes through the house.

Loud enough to wake the dead, he thinks, and then wishes he hadn't.

There's no answer so he tries again.

Still nothing.

He looks along the house front, then walks towards the plate glass of the French windows. He peers inside. Nothing. Time for a walk round, check the gardens, peer in a few more windows. He retraces his steps, and rounds the stone tower. If he remembers rightly, the drawing room is on this wall.

He hasn't walked much further when he pauses. There is music, light classical music like you might hear at a late eighteenth-century *soirée*. A bit Jane Austen. He can imagine the tinkling of sophisticated laughter, and the conspiracy of perfect manners. Maybe men talking politics, and being hushed by the ladies. A card table; whist perhaps or rummy.

Too many period dramas on television. Janice fancies herself as the lady of a big house.

He strides up to the window, hesitates.

A voice, or maybe voices.

No cars outside, so maybe Jocelyn is back; that'd be good. Two birds with one stone.

He reaches the window and looks inside, and immediately recoils.

Jesus Christ.

He looks again, drawn like a scared child observing some television horror, peeping through spread fingers, repelled but unable to draw away. Rupert paces wildly across the room, unshaven, hair hanging like oiled string across his cheeks and neck. He is muttering, and waving his arms. Every now and then, he stops and points a warning finger towards the empty sofa, and rants vociferously. Turning, he steps towards the large gilt mirror, levelling blows at the air around him, as if to drive it out of his path. He pauses in front of the mirror, suddenly aware of himself, or of some stranger facing him, a face half-recognised yet alien, frightening. He remains frozen, just staring, and strangled laughter bursts from him like a flood; outrageous, wide-mouthed laughter, almost hysterical. He tilts his head to one side, and reaches out a hand to the face in the mirror. He touches its cheek and hair, and murmurs something.

Then he turns away.

In the background, music plays. Vivaldi.

Frank watches, appalled. But he's come this far; he has no choice but to intrude on this strange pantomime. He raps on the glass, and Rupert spins round. He sees Frank, and his face fumbles for the correct expression, eventually contorting itself into a refined smile. He brushes a hand through his hair and steps to the window, indicating the front entrance. Frank nods, and makes his way round.

He waits fifteen impatient minutes before the door creaks open, and Rupert waves him inside. He's obviously made good use of the intervening time. His hair is combed back, and he is clean shaven. He seems calm, and a smile of smug superiority has assumed its usual position on his face.

'How very nice. I wasn't expecting company.' 'I was entertaining myself listening to music, and getting cross with the lodgers.'

'The lodgers?' Frank asks.

Rupert laughs. 'Just my little joke. Ignore me. Do come through to the lounge.' He turns and leads the way. 'The sun should be in there now; at least, that's what I paid for when I had the doors put in. I'm sure the builder promised me eternal sunshine. I may have to sue him.'

In the lounge, he lowers himself onto an armchair, and spreads gracefully across it.

'Do sit.' The flick of a wrist indicates an adjacent chair.

As Frank sits down, he notices how Rupert's eyes follow him, and how his lips tighten into a sneer of contempt. Then the smile reappears.

'How can I help you?'

'When I was here last, I asked if the name Melissa meant anything to you.'

'Ye-es.' Smug and elongated.

'I recall you said no.'

'Ye-es.' A shrug of the shoulders.

Frank feels his temper surging into his chest. A sudden urge to grab Rupert by the throat assails him. He drives it back. Rupert is playing games. He is adopting this caricature of the landed aristocrat, this Eton-Oxbridge-spoiled-brat-turned-lord-of-the-manor pose. It's like he's playing a part in some old English comedy of manners. He is acting and he knows he's acting and, much to his apparent delight, he is well aware of the effect his performance has on his audience.

Frank withdraws behind his professional defences, and studies him carefully. Rupert's eyes can't keep still. They dart like black flies, back and forth, side to side, never still. The lips tremble, the shoulders twitch. He taps his foot and then, suddenly aware he is being closely observed, crosses his legs to subdue the tremor.

'Melissa is the name of your niece.'

'Really?'

'You didn't know?'

'Louise and I were never close.' Something very sharp in the tone now, like he's spitting razor blades. 'She was a slut, a tart, a whore, a disgrace to the family. We despised her.'

'But you must have known you had a niece.'

'Why? Why should I?' He lurches forward now, his eyes firing dark darts. 'Louise left me. She betrayed me. She preferred the gutter.'

Frank refuses to react. He pauses, tries to catch and hold those darting eyes, fails, calms his breathing. Remaining still, not reacting, is everything now. He feels as if everything he says is like stabbing a bull with spears.

'Jocelyn left you, too.'

Rupert's voice rises in barely controlled anger.

'Jocelyn hasn't left us. She'll come back because she has to. They know she will. They told me.'

He is shaking all over now, his hands on the chair arms, gripping so hard his knuckles are white.

'Who told you?'

Rupert waves an arm wildly around the room.

'THEM!' He screams. 'THEM!'

He stumbles over to where half-empty bottles lie scattered across a polished surface. He grabs one, and pours with shaking hands. He drinks, then pours and drinks again. He grips the wood, his back hunched, breathing heavily, calming himself, slowly regaining control.

'I'm sorry if my questions have caused you distress,' Frank too is controlling strong emotions—fear, shock, horror—though for very different reasons.

Rupert spins on his feet, and rests his back against the cabinet. The smile has returned. He waves a hand, as if to dismiss Frank's words.

'It distresses me to talk about Louise,' he sighs. 'She committed suicide, you know. Jocelyn and I thought it was the shame she felt at deserting her family. But who knows? I'd like to think she felt some regret before the end. Perhaps, as she sat on her lonely bed with the tablets in one hand, and the car keys in her other, the words, *I'm sorry,* were on her lips.'

Frank shudders.

Dear God, what the hell is going through this guy's head?

'Melissa came to stay here.' Frank continues to speak coolly, in a matter-of-fact manner, although it's hard to hide the disgust in his voice.

Rupert carries a full glass back to his chair. He sits, and once more casts an elegant arm casually across its back.

'Did she? I have no recollection.'

'She went to the local school. She was fostered by a family in the village. You made the arrangements.'

'Did I?'

He shakes his head, looks puzzled, shrugs. He leans forward—a moment of animation—and raises a finger.

'Yes, I remember. You mean little Melissa – a ghastly child. I detest children, you know. They are so horribly unrefined, always under your feet, wailing, shouting, running about, wanting things. I had nothing to do with her. Jocelyn took charge, until we could get rid of her.'

Frank can barely restrain his contempt.

'She'd just lost her mother, for God's sake.'

Rupert looks puzzled again; a rehearsed, cultivated look.

'Louise? Hardly a great loss, I'd have thought.'

'Didn't you feel anything for her?'

'Of course, I felt something. She kept me from my work with her wailing and crying, even at night-time. How would you feel?'

'I'd want to care for her, offer her comfort and support. I'd want to make her feel better, and I'd want her to know she had a family who loved her.'

'*Loved her?*' Rupert scoffs. He takes a deep draft from his glass. 'Odious little brat.'

'She seems to have made quite an impression for a child you could barely remember a moment ago.'

Rupert's look is vicious, but Frank ignores it, and presses on.

'I thought family mattered to you. Did you not feel any responsibility?'

Rupert leans forward, fury behind his eyes. His hand grips the glass; as tight as his dry lips, as white as his clenched teeth.

'We didn't recognise her as family. She wasn't one of us.'

Their eyes lock in battle, forces lined up, row on row.

'Where is she now?'

Rupert shrugs. 'Jocelyn found some relative on the continent willing to take her. I had nothing to do with it.'

'Do you have an address?'

'Of course not.'

'What about Jocelyn? Would she have kept an address?'

'Whatever for?'

'Perhaps because she cared about her niece a little more than you did?'

'You'd have to ask her. I had no dealings with the matter. Now...' He eases towards the door. 'I thought you might be entertaining when you arrived at my door, but I've been very disappointed. You've been quite odious. It's time for you to leave.'

Frank forces his own tight-lipped smile.

'There's just one thing, Mr Fitzwilliam,' he says. 'I want you to understand that I have no intention of letting these matters drop. You are in my sights now, and you will remain there until I find Melissa and Jocelyn. And I will find out about your relationship with Zachary Blight and Dominic Sheedy, and I will pursue you if I have to. I assure you, I will not let go.'

Rupert maintains his urbane composure.

'How very melodramatic.' He smiles. 'I wish you luck.'

He closes the door, leaving his visitor on the steps. Frank turns and walks down to his car. For some reason, his legs feel unsteady, as if he's been exposed to something barely comprehensible, something terrifying. He fights back a desire to shudder. When he reaches the car, and opens the door, he pauses and looks back.

From inside the house there is the distant but unmistakable sound of laughter; voices gathering in a cacophony of sound, drifting and turning like bats, then fading into nothing.

Chapter 55

Follow Rupert back into the lounge. Watch him pour another glass, even larger, even deeper than the previous. Study him as he paces the room, then drops into the armchair. He picks up a glossy magazine, a supplement from a national Sunday, and tries to focus his eyes on it. He scans the print, the pictures, but you can see from the glazed look that he cannot distinguish the words. His mind is engrossed in different things. After a few moments he drops it on the floor, and leans back, his eyes half closed.

Even that doesn't work. He stands up, and paces the room, downcast. He pauses at the mirror.

'What must I do?' he asks his image.

You hear a voice, a woman's voice; brittle, as if the words are grated through her teeth.

'Zachary is dead.'

'Yes, yes. That's good. He failed me. He wasn't to be trusted. I was right about him. He's gone, forgotten.'

'Yes, you were right this time. But what about the policeman? He's persistent. Not a man to give in easily. Are you safe?'

'No, not while Dominic lives. He could betray me. Miller might search him out, and draw from him what he knows.'

Another voice, a man's, old, deep and dark, and as rough as a barnacled rock.

'Has he not been found and dealt with?'

'No. I have allied myself with fools.'

'Then you're not safe. You cannot be safe. He knows too much.'

'Molly! He knows where we put her!'

'She must be moved. Dead of night. Alone. Somewhere she will never be found.'

'Yes, yes.'

'And Jocelyn. Have we news?'

'None. But she will return. She promised to be with me, always.'

'They all leave. Louise left you. Now Jocelyn. They cannot bear to be with you.'

'She loves me.'

'Ha! She despises you. Louise despised you. We despise you. Everyone despises you.'

'No, not yet. Not everyone. Jocelyn...'

'Pah! You're a fool. You were always a fool.'

'I dealt with her spy. I followed him, struck him down, watched his blood slide over the rocks like a living thing. I rolled him into an ocean grave.'

The woman's sharp voice, like crushed shells.

'You did well to destroy him. We can't bear spies. Kill them. Kill them all. Torture and kill them. Treason! Treason!'

The man's deep voice rises again. 'Beware the policeman. He's sharp, that one, and he has friends. They are out there. I can feel them in the darkness all around us. An insect swarm. Locusts stripping us bare.'

'I'll face that darkness and I'll destroy that swarm.'

'Ha! You're too weak. You've always been too weak. Even as a child you were a pathetic little squab, with your bawling and shrieking. You were always a disappointment.'

'It's a matter of honour.'

'You have to promise. You must swear on the ghosts of your ancestors. You must swear on the rotting corpse of little Melissa.'

'I swear! I swear on them all.'

'Swear to us all.'

'I swear! I swear!'

It comes again: the child's cry, something distant, drawn as if through a tightened throat. So lonely, so lost. You are filled with a terrible dread.

'Mama! Mama!'

'Shut up the brat! Shut up the brat!'

'Mama! Mama!'

'Kill him! Kill him!'

'Papa!'

The phone rings in the corner of the room, and all is suddenly hushed, silent. Rupert picks it up, opens it, listens.

'Negotiate? What on earth could you mean?' He laughs, softly. 'What could you possibly have to threaten me?' A tell-tale pulse ticks in his cheek. 'Well, if we must. Yes, yes. I'll be waiting.'

He closes the phone, and looks across at the mirror, that whiplash smile curled across his face. 'We'll all be waiting for you.'

You back away, step upon stumbling step, your body trembling, your skin racked by waves of fear. God help me, you think. This is no place for the sane.

Chapter 56

It is late afternoon at Grantley Police Station, almost time to go home after a long day. The sun slants between the blinds, mottling the wall. A light breeze ripples from the open window and the blinds tap, tap arrhythmically.

Frank sits at a desk beside the window. He leans back, and runs his hands through his hair, yawns. 'Best guess then is he fell from the castle wall late at night, and got washed up nearer the village. There's a strong current out there apparently.'

Sparks, sitting opposite, nods. He checks his phone for messages. 'The missus. It's our wedding anniversary. Eight o'clock at the Italian. Can't be late home tonight.' He glances at his watch for reassurance.

Templeton, sleeves rolled, coat slung on the chair back, picks up a report, and scans it.

'He suffered from a chronic asthma condition which deteriorated fast. That was why he retired. He was only in his late forties, you know. Poor sod. The walk to the top of the wall was probably too much for him, especially since he didn't have his rescue meds. Probably got taken by an attack, stumbled and fell. The battlement is low in places. It wouldn't take much.'

Frank stands up, and stares between the slats of the blinds. People everywhere, even this late in the afternoon. He breathes the cool air, and looks over the housetops towards the sea.

'I don't get it. What the hell was he doing up there at night? His car was in Leybury, in the car park at the top of the village, nowhere near the castle.'

Sparks taps a pencil on the pine surface. 'He didn't walk, that's for sure, not in his condition.'

'We've got two questions, then. Who drove him there, because someone sure as hell did. And why? I mean, he wasn't sightseeing, was he? He must have had a reason.'

'Maybe he went there to meet someone,' Templeton says. 'Took a taxi.'

'Check it, just in case. We've sod-all else at the moment.' Sparks gathers the papers on the desk into a neat pile, and logs off the computer. 'There are only two taxi companies in Grantley. If one of them got a call to take someone to the castle at that time of night, they're going to remember it.'

Templeton turns, and picks up the phone.

'It still doesn't answer the question why he was there.' Frank leans across for the autopsy report. 'He clambers to the highest point of the battlements, beyond the protective barrier, has an attack and, with an empty inhaler in his pocket and his rescue meds back in the car, he collapses and falls. Is that really what we're saying?'

'There's no evidence he was struck or pushed, Frank.' Sparks checks his watch again. 'I've got to go. The missus will give me hell if I'm late.'

'I'd still like to know why he was there,' Frank says.

Templeton turns on his chair. 'Nothing from the taxi companies. As far as they're concerned it was a typical boring night.'

Sparks checks his watch for the third time, and yawns. Templeton catches the yawn and amplifies it with one of his own. Sympathetic resonance.

'I wish you two would stop yawning.' Frank draws up the blind enough to draw on the cool air spiriting through the open window. 'Have we any news on Dominic?'

'We've got a possible sighting in the city centre, yesterday. A half-baked description of a thief, and a street camera image which bears some resemblance.' Templeton spins the chair in a half circle, then back again, repeating the movement like therapy. 'There's no evidence to suggest he was anywhere near the castle.'

'Have they found his car?' Frank stares out at the rooftops, sloping away towards the shore, the distant sea. A gull perched on a lamp-post calls out, as if offended by the impertinence of the visitors below. He imagines the taste of salt, the smell of the sea.

'Not yet,' Sparks says. 'They're still looking.'

'He could have met Zachary, driven him to the castle...'

'And left him there? Drove away to the city, to go on a petty crime spree? To raise funds for the next stage of his epic adventure?'

Frank turns around, and rests his back against the sill. He scans the autopsy report again. 'There's nothing here to rule out the possibility that our friend Dominic helped him on his way. I mean, Zachary Blight could have been overcome by an asthma attack, and leaned on the wall while he fumbled to find his medication...'

'Which he hadn't brought...'

'Giving Dominic....

'Or someone else...'

'The opportunity to upend him, and drop him over the wall into the sea.'

Sparks sighs. 'Hypothetical, Frank. This is pure hypothesis. So far, we haven't placed Dominic at the scene. Nor have we a clear motive, other than their shared involvement in the shady world of Rupert Fitzwilliam.'

'Maybe if we find the car?' Templeton says. 'If we could place Zachary Blight in the car, or the car at the scene, it would be a start.'

Sparks has his coat on now, and heads to the door. 'It's time to go home. Wait for tomorrow, and see if the car turns up. We'll find it eventually. Dominic, too. He can't hide forever, not even in the city. Any further news on Jocelyn or Melissa?'

'None. We're waiting.'

'Right, then I'm out of here. Time to call it a day. Get some rest while we can.'

He opens the swing door, and disappears. Templeton yawns and rises to his feet.

'He's right, Frank. There's nothing more we can do today.'

Frank releases his hold on the table, and sighs.

'Yes, yes. You're right. Time to go.'

When Frank clambers from his car in Leybury, he notices a youngish man leaning against the harbour rail, a foot raised on an adjacent bench, checking his phone. He sees Frank, stands up and walks across.

'Adam Calder,' he says, raising a hand which Frank shakes. 'I worked with Zachary Blight. Can we talk?'

Frank motions towards the stone cottage where he, Janice and Jason are in temporary residence, courtesy of the local police department.

'We can talk there. Better than out on the street. I can even offer coffee.'

Adam looks up and down the harbour, checking, double checking, obviously anxious.

'Lead the way,' he says.

Janice is in the tiny lounge, watching the television news. She looks up as they enter, then stands up, dusting herself down to remove popcorn crumbs from her lap.

'This is Adam Calder. He's—'

'A work colleague.' Adam smiles, and holds out a hand.

Frank flings his coat over the back an old faux leather sofa, and settles himself onto it. 'We've got a bit of business. You wouldn't mind doing the honours, would you, pet? I'm parched.'

As Janice closes the door behind her, Frank leans forward. 'Sit yourself down, Adam. How can I help you?'

Adam reaches in his pocket, and draws out a brown leather wallet from which he extracts a card. Frank glances at it. He hands it back.

'Fraud, eh?'

Adam nods.

'And DCI Blight?'

'He was retired. More ill than he ever let on.'

'Yes, I know, but...?'

Adam sighs. 'He came to us with an offer. He'd ingratiated himself with Rupert Fitzwilliam, got the inside track on his dealings. He was feeding stuff back to us.'

'And you were his contact?'

'Yes.'

'If he was so unwell, why would he get involved in the shady dealings of someone like Rupert Fitzwilliam?'

'He had his own agenda, but he was very closed about it.'

'Melissa, you think?'

'Yes. He'd only recently found out about her. It hit him hard, I don't know why. Last time we spoke, I tried to persuade him to get out while he could. It was clear that he wasn't safe anymore.'

'He refused?'

'He was a stubborn old sod. He said there was something he had to finish, and for Zachary that was a red line. If there was something to finish, he'd
bloody well finish it or—'

'Die in the attempt?'

'Exactly. He said he needed just one more item of proof. He seemed to
think he'd have it within days.'

'Do you know what it was?'

'He said it was better I didn't know. He did say one thing, though, just
before he left. It didn't make sense to me. He said that Fitzwilliam was "trophy hunting".'

Frank is struck with the image of Rupert as a macho hunter with a gun,
his foot perched heroically on the back of an animal worth ten of him.

'What do you know about Melissa?' He draws his mind back. Questions.
Facts. Evidence. The tangible, and comprehendible. His world.

'I've checked every database, every known link to the Fitzwilliam family
I can find. Records, bank transactions, social media, all the usual sources.
There's nothing to tell us where she might be or with whom. You?'

'Only just started. Nothing so far.' He pauses. 'You think she's dead?'

Adam nods. 'She could be tucked away in South America, I suppose, but
I'm sure Zachary thought she was dead. I think that was the proof he was
looking for, that one more item.'

'Any ideas what precisely?'

Adam takes a deep breath. 'I think he was looking for the location of her
body.'

Chapter 57

'The estate agent will be here later today.'

Maggie tenses, then turns a page in her book, and continues reading. 'That's good. The sooner it's done, the sooner we can move on.'

A moment's silence.

'Fred says he might take over the coastal cruises. Says he'll go and see the bank, try and get a loan. He'll make a fair offer, will Fred.'

'Yes, he's an honest man.' Maggie continues reading, and turns another page.

Richard stares down at a patch of worn carpet.

'No point in putting it off.'

'No, no point at all.'

Richard's eyes scan the room, taking in the glass floats and model sailing vessels, the strange shells collected from nets, the photographs of the sea and the harbour, old pictures of men and women long dead, his family, his neighbours. He sighs. Above the fireplace, far too big for the space it occupies, hangs a painting he saw in a local shop, of his boat in the harbour; the sea shimmering with light, and those clouds, so real he could touch them. He saw it and bought it, in one breath. Couldn't resist. He remembers taking it home.

'Maggie, look at this. Look what I've bought.'

'Is that our Sammy on the deck?'

'Aye, it is.'

Then Maggie saw the price sticker, a small red circle on the frame.

'Lord almighty. You never did, did you?'

'I just had to. It was a whim.'

'It's beautiful. It'll look nice on the chimney breast. Pride of place.'

As she walked away, she tapped his arm. 'But no more whims, pet. We can't afford them.'

There are so many things like that, scattered about. Memories, all of them; all with a story to tell. It's their story: his, Maggie's, Sammy's, even Yapp's. Maggie complains that the room looks like a car boot sale, but she likes it nonetheless. Memories everywhere. He sighs again.

Maggie looks up. 'For goodness sake, what are you sighing about now? There's no time to sit moping, we've things to do. We've made our bed.'

Richard clambers to his feet.

Sit! Stand! Do this, do that! That's Maggie for you. Just her way.

'Where's Sammy?' he asks.

'Down at the harbour with Jason.' She pauses. 'He'll miss Jason when they go home.'

'He will that. Those two misfits have been good for each other.'

'I like Janice and Frank, too. Good friends, the pair of them.'

She sighs.

'For goodness sake.' Richard mimics her. 'What are you sighing about now?'

He heads for the door, laughter bubbling like sparkling wine. 'That's one to me, I think,' he calls, blocking Maggie's response behind the closed door.

Molly kneels on the chair by the window. This was her home once, but now it's the house they use as a holiday retreat. Her new home is in the city, in a dull cul-de-sac, when she isn't in the residential school. She leans on the sill, and looks down over cottage rooftops towards the harbour.

'Sammy and Jason are sitting on the steps above the sand,' she says, as if to someone behind her, on the bed. 'They're skimming stones over the water. Shall we go down and play with them?'

A girl's voice from behind her, or maybe from within her, from the girl sitting on the edge of her thoughts.

Soon. They've got lots to talk about.

Molly Toodle, that's what Mrs MacKenzie called her friend, when she arrived at the school. Her real name was Melissa Fitzwilliam but she liked to be called Molly, because that's what her mum called her. Her mum died, and she came to live at Leybury Grange with her Uncle Rupert and her Aunt Jocelyn. Her uncle didn't like her. He was cruel.

She was Molly Wondle because she'd been at the school longest. Melissa was Molly Toodle. That's what Mrs MacKenzie said when she joked with the class. Mrs. MacKenzie was their teacher and she was nice. She was especially nice to Molly Toodle because she knew she was unhappy.

'They're standing up, and walking along the harbour,' she tells Molly Toodle. 'I think they're going to climb down onto the boat.'

To say goodbye. Goodbye, house. Goodbye, boat. Goodbye, village. Everything changes. Nothing stays still.

'Are they sad, do you think?'

Are you sad?

'I think they're sad because they're saying goodbye to the village. I was sad when you left. And I was sad when Mum and Dad said we had to leave too.'

They'll say goodbye to each other soon.

'Like you and me.'

Like you and me.

'Let's go and play then, while we can.'

She flings the door open, and runs down the stairs to the lounge.

'I'm going down to the harbour, Mum. Jason and Sammy are there.'

Her mum looks tired. She often looks tired nowadays. Ever since Rupert Fitzwilliam took Molly Toodle away, sent her to Europe or Africa or somewhere, to live with some rich relative. Molly Toodle said she'd write, but she never did. Mum was upset about that.

Molly knows the truth. She tried to tell them.

Molly Toodle is dead.

'That's an awful thing to say,' her mum had cried. 'She's just busy with her new life. She must be very, very happy.'

But Molly knows the truth.

Molly Toodle is dead. Rupert Fitzwilliam killed her. He pretended he'd sent her away, but he never did. If she was alive, she would have sent a message.

Her father was patient with her.

'You can't say things like that, Molly. I know you're upset because she hasn't contacted you, but she's starting a new life. Maybe her relatives want her to forget the past. especially her mother's death and everything.'

'Her Facebook Page has gone. So has her Instagram. It's like she never existed. She's dead and her uncle killed her. He hated her. She told me.'

It made her mum cry sometimes, and then she felt guilty.

'I'm sorry, Mum.'

'I know, love. We all miss her.'

Then one night, Molly Toodle came back to her. She was just there, in her bedroom, sitting on the end of the bed, just like she used to. Molly wasn't even scared. They were friends again, like before, only different, sadder somehow. There was a pain inside her all the time now, and it wouldn't go away. It was like she was being eaten, inside. She cried a lot, especially when Molly Toodle told her what happened, how she'd died, how it was Rupert who killed her, how she was lonely, and how she'd managed to escape, and come back to be with her very best friend.

'*Molly Wondle and Molly Toodle,*' she said.

Just like it was.

Just like it ought to be.

Jason and Sammy sit on the deck of *Sammy's Pride.*

'Perhaps we could steal *The Lovely Maggie* and sail away and never come back until we're rich and famous. I'd like to be rich and famous.'

'I could catch us lots fish and crabs to eat.' Sammy leans back, resting his elbows on the wooden planks. He half closes his eyes against the bright sun, slivers of flickering light colouring his vision, changing from red to yellow to green and blue. 'But we'd need fruit and vegetables,' he says. 'We might catch scurvy if we don't have vitamins, and our gums would rot and go black, and our teeth would fall out. We learned about it in a project at school.'

'We could sneak into gardens at night and dig up vegetables, and we could eat scurvy grass. That gives you vitamins. But only in spring and summer. For the rest of the year we could become pirates, and steal fruit from market stalls.'

'I don't want to be a thief. Dominic is a thief. And my dad grows vegetables.'

'We'd only take what we needed, and we could leave a crab or a fish as a swap. Like Robin Hood.'

'I don't think Robin Hood caught fish and crabs.' Sammy leans forward, and blinks the water from his eyes. A green and blue blind spot gradually fades. 'He killed deer and ate berries and things.'

Jason looks doubtful. 'I don't think I could kill a deer. I saw one once in the countryside. It just stared at us, and then jumped over a fence and ran away. It was nice.'

'Rabbits, then.'

Yeah, maybe.' Jason lies back, and closes his eyes. 'Sometimes, at night, we could find a quiet beach, light a fire, and sleep under the stars.'

'We'd have to anchor the boat, and get a dinghy to row to shore.'

For a moment, they are quiet, before Jason speaks. 'Frank says they'll catch Dominic. He says he's not clever enough to stay hidden. Sooner or later they'll catch him, and then they'll lock him away for ever.'

Sammy's voice is hushed. 'I don't want them to catch him. I'd have to go to court and tell them everything. And Dominic would be there.'

'Frank says it's not like that now. You don't have to be in the court. You're in a different room, on television or something, and there are people to help you.'

'I wish Dominic was dead.'

'Me, too. Perhaps, when we're pirates, we can hunt him down, and kill him with our knives.'

'Make him walk the plank.'

'Yeah, or keelhaul him.'

'What's that?'

'I don't know, but it's really, really bad.'

'We'll do that then.'

Another silence, as they lean back into the sun, catching the warmth in the finely meshed net of their faces.

'My dad says Dominic is a bad man, and that once this is over, we won't talk about him ever again. We'll forget him. He says if we keep thinking about him, it's like letting him win. He says we should imagine we're out on *The Lovely Maggie,* and we should find a desert island and leave him there, and never think about him again because he's not worth it, and he's not going to beat us.'

'What does your mum say?'

'She says we should cut his balls off with a rusty knife.'

Their giggles turn to howls of laughter.

'Did she really say that?'

'Yeah.'

'I like your mum. She's funny.'

'Yeah.'

A voice comes from behind them.

'What are you laughing at?'

Sammy leans his head back. An upside-down Molly stands on the harbour side. He rolls onto his front. Jason kneels up.

'We're making pretend plans.'

Molly climbs aboard, and walks towards the stern of the boat. She raises a hand to wave at someone by the bench opposite The Harbour Inn.

'Who are you waving to? There's nobody there.'

Molly sighs. 'I've got to go back next week. Mum says I'm not right yet. She says it's coming back here that does it.'

'Does what? Makes you ill?'

Molly nods. 'I don't want to go back. I want to stay here.'

'We're leaving soon because our house is for sale.' Sammy stands beside her. 'I don't want to go either. I've always lived here.'

'I want to live here, too,' says Jason, not wanting to be left out.

For a moment, they're quiet, then Jason speaks. 'Who were you waving to?'

Melissa's eyes turn towards The Harbour Inn. 'Melissa. She's my friend. She used to live with me in my house, and she was my very best friend. But she's not there anymore.'

'What happened?' Jason asks.

Molly lowers her voice. 'My mum and dad say she went to live in Europe, but she didn't. I know she didn't.' She bends her head towards them, conspiratorial. 'They say I won't be better until she goes away, and I stop making up stories about her.' Her voice fades to the shadow of a whisper. 'But she can't go away, because she was murdered.'

Sammy hesitates, then glances towards the inn. 'Perhaps she'll be our friend, too,' he says, glancing at Jason. 'Do you think she will?'

'Close your eyes, and keep them closed. Promise?'

'Promise.'

A movement in the air, a sudden chill, something carried to them, something fragile, and trembling like a leaf on a thin branch. And there, behind them, a new voice.

I'm Melissa, but call me Molly.

Jason reacts first. 'Was it you, outside my caravan that night?' His voice is hushed, awed.

A response, like the echo of a whisper in darkness.

I came to warn you.

Now Sammy speaks. Hushed, eyes tight shut.

'Are you really dead?'

'Yes. I've come to warn all of you. You have to be ready.'

'Ready for what?'

The boys feel her kneel beside them.

Do you trust me?

'Of course we trust you.' Jason's words carry the sanctity of an inviolable oath.

Do you believe in me?

Two awed voices in solemn unison. 'Yes.'

Will you be my friend?

'Yes.' Sammy's words are as hushed as a wave. 'We'll be friends. All of us, forever.'

Jason nods. 'Yes, friends forever.'

And he pictures a smile widening across her face, and continuing to widen as she drifts apart like so much mist, fading and evaporating in the warmth of the sun, because when he opens his eyes, she's gone.

Chapter 58

The bar of *The Harbour Inn is a pleasant place to spend an evening. From a window seat overlooking the harbour, you have sufficient elevation to see the setting sun weave sparkling threads of silver, red and gold in a shimmering tapestry on the water. Photographs just cannot capture it. It is there for the eyes and the mind alone.*

Sammy's Pride *lies berthed beside the harbour wall. It hasn't moved today. The small number of tourists who waited, in the hope they might join a cruise along the coast, were disappointed.* Lovely Maggie *hasn't moved either. A couple of yachts shimmer listlessly. There's a restlessness about the sea tonight, as if it has been calm too long, as if it longs to pull and stretch, and tear itself free from restraint. It grumbles and tugs at its mooring, heaves a shoulder restlessly, stamps a foot, looks around for something to relieve the stillness. Miserly ripples and peevish waves will not suffice. It wants excitement, release, a gale, a storm.*

You turn back to the interior of the inn which is, you think, much improved in recent times. As a regular visitor, you have seen its transformation. The windows, the internal décor—so elegant, and yet so warm and tasteful—have changed the weathered old place into somewhere modern and yet traditional, where it is a pleasure to be. Here, in an evening, as the sky grows dark and night settles on the sea, you sit with a glass of wine, and mull over the happenings of the day. The few other customers present are at ease, the conversation is light, and you hear the pleasant ring of laughter from beside the bar.

Frank Miller is there, talking to Trevor, the landlord. He has, perhaps, escaped for an hour in order to relax after the pressures of his day.

But let me draw you away from the warmth of your observations. I have a chilling question for you.

What happened to the package Zachary Blight brought from the yacht? The one he secreted in his car.

If you recall, Rupert sent him out to fetch it, to place it in the drawer of his office desk. He gave him the key. Do you recall if he returned to the house with the package? I don't. Thinking back, I'm certain he didn't.

Is it in the car, waiting for someone to find it? Another nail in the coffin of Rupert's conspiracies? Does Rupert even know that it is missing? He hasn't mentioned it.

So many questions.

Here's another.

Where is Zachary's car?

Ah, yes. The police found it in the top car park at Leybury. They towed it away, searched it for evidence, found nothing.

No package.

Perhaps it was carefully secreted in some place even the police couldn't locate it, like in a good Hollywood movie, just waiting to be discovered. Or not.

I find it difficult to believe that Zachary, despite his failing health, wasn't acutely aware of its presence in his car. Smuggled goods must weigh on the mind. They're like dirt on the hands, that needs to be washed away. You can't wander around for hours smelling of it, or forget about it and pretend it's not there.

But, do you recall Zachary's frame of mind when he fled that house? Do you remember his horror at what he encountered in the Trophy Room? (What DID he encounter in the Trophy Room?). Surely in such a state of fear and desolation he could be forgiven for forgetting the package. If you or I had seen what he saw, we too might have forgotten.

Perhaps, perhaps.

But later, when his mind had settled, and he had regained composure, before he set out to find Dominic, he would surely have recalled something of such importance, something which would buffer him against the danger posed by Rupert. A weapon with which to defend himself. Insurance. Something with which to bargain, to buy his freedom, his safety.

Or something to present, as if on a golden cushion, to Adam Calder and his colleagues in London. But of course, not yet. Remember Melissa? Her grave. One more item of proof.

No, I am adamant that he had that package with him when he kidnapped Dominic and forced him to that cliff-top perch. I am sure too that he had that package when they clambered towards the battlement, when he collapsed. Tucked under his coat, in his belt, at the back, out of sight. A small package, no bigger than a padded A4 envelope.

It wasn't on the body when it was recovered. We would have heard. Was it lost in the sea, torn from his dead body and carried out, dropping its contents beneath the waves, to be lost forever?

I cannot say. Not yet.

What was in it?

I leave you to speculate. Perhaps you think you know.

There's are more questions beating on the door, craving answers.

What happened after Dominic fled the castle, carrying Zachary's gun? Did Zachary climb the battlements? Why, in his condition, would he do such a thing? What happened?

Ah, I see a light shine into your darkness, an answer emerging like a swimmer from the sea. (Remember that swimmer in the movie, emerging from the sea?)

He hid the package there. That's why he made that perilous ascent. It is there, waiting like a guilty secret, a time bomb ticking.

Yes, that's it.

You could be right. But I'd ask you to remember something else. Do you recall the car which passed along the road, turning at the corner where the track began, and continuing towards Grantley? Its headlights cast a beam, like a searchlight across the moorland towards you.

Do you remember?

Imagine now, that the car parked some two hundred metres along that road, waiting for a designated time, and a meeting. Imagine how, a few minutes after Dominic fled the scene, leaving Zachary—dying, he assumed—by the castle walls, that car comes to sudden life, its eyes opening, casting bright beams on the road. Imagine it turns in a narrow gateway, returns, and swings down towards the castle.

It pulls up where Dominic's car had been just a few moments ago. A figure climbs from it, walks between the gate towers, into the castle bailey. The figure pauses, sees the motionless body, and hurries forward, kneels down beside it.

Zachary offers a weak smile of recognition.

'Hello, Jocelyn,' he says.

'Hello, Zachary,' she replies. She kneels down beside him, takes his hand. There is a look of tenderness in her eyes, like she is gazing for the last time on an old friend.

'I am glad you came,' he says, gasping. 'I have something for you.' He pats her hand, then he taps his coat as if something is hidden underneath. 'It is up to you now. You must decide how to act.'

'I'm so sorry,' she says. 'Had I known...'

He waves away her apology. 'There's no time for that now. The past is past. It is too late for recriminations, or for regrets. We must finish this.' He struggles to his feet. 'Help me,' he says. 'You must tell me everything.'

'I will. But first...'

As Zachary drags himself, step by step, towards the battlement, she turns, and walks back to her car. She opens the door and waits.

Someone steps out.

Chapter 59

The weather is changing. After a period of steady calm, of refreshing sunshine and bubbling clouds, the wind veers to the southwest and the isobars close. Just off the coast of Ireland, lurking over the grey Atlantic like a predator, a deep, low pressure area inches slowly forward, stretching one curling limb and then another, swimming the skies like a pulsing, aerial cephalopod.

A pale moon, a mere sliver of light, throws miserly shadows across the lawns of Leybury Grange. Dominic stands under the trees from where he can see the driveway, curls in front of the distant house. The building lies in darkness.

2am.

He'll be awake. He never sleeps.

His thoughts break the silence like the cracking of branches.

He rehearses what he has to say, the bargain he has to strike, the offer he must make, and how he will free himself. It sounds weaker now than it did back in the town, like the last bet of a desperate man, but he has a couple of cards to play; not a perfect hand but better perhaps than Rupert's. It might be enough.

It has to be enough.

He steps forward, a surge of resolution carrying him like a wind at his back.

As he approaches the door, he sees a light in the entrance hall and, in its glow, a trail leading up the steps to the door. It's something dark, like it has been carried on muddy feet. He looks closely and sees that's it's soil from the garden, a trail leading back towards the lawn and the trees, and forward into the house.

He thinks about leaving, but the door gasps open, and he is caught like a dancer in a spotlight. A shadow falls over him and Rupert runs down the steps, casts an arm round his shoulder, and pulls him towards the house.

His eyes dart like fireflies as he turns his head from side to side. 'I knew you would come. I hoped it would be earlier, but no matter. Quickly, come inside. There may be prying eyes. The detective is everywhere I turn. He knows too much and what he doesn't know, he surmises.' He pauses, looks back along the drive, and then out towards the summer house. 'Come in, close the door, lock them out.'

Dominic looks at him, aghast. Rupert's face is covered in soil, and his eyes burn unnaturally bright. His hands are covered, too. His arms, his clothes. Mud and soil.

'Jesus,' Dominic says.

Rupert draws him into the entrance hall, and shuts the door. Behind it sits a huge mahogany table. God knows how he's moved it from the wall. 'Help me,' he says.

Together, they push the table, inch by inch until it blocks the doorway.

'What in God's name...?' Dominic looks across the floor; the same trail of mud and soil weaves towards the staircase, and then, step by step, to the top. Dominic grows pale. He knows where the trail leads.

'I could have done with your help, old friend.' Rupert grabs his hand, and shakes it hard. 'But, no matter. You're here now, and that is all that matters. I've had a wearying night, Dominic, a difficult and tiring time. And I still have much to do.'

'This's not why I came.' Dominic looks back towards the door, the mahogany table effectively imprisoning him.

Rupert waves away his words with a dark hand.

'We must begin with the floors, and the stairs. There are still a few hours before the dawn makes our actions visible. Until then, we can skulk in the darkness, unseen. Come. There are brushes, cloths, buckets. I've readied them in the library.'

Dominic stands back, riding waves of dread. He opens his mouth as if to cry out but no sound comes.

Then... 'What have you done?' Soft, quiet.

Rupert looks up, as if surprised at the question.

'She cannot harm you. Only the living can do you harm.'

'Where have you put the body?'

'You know where.'

The waves are all around him now, a tidal surge billowing and crashing. He can't breathe. He is suffocating. He raises his hand to his throat, gasps, and grabs at the corner of the table to steady himself.

A hand crashes across his face.

'You killed her as much as I did,' Rupert screams. 'You share the responsibility. You share the guilt. You, me, Jocelyn. We are one.'

'I just supplied the poison, nothing more.'

'And Jocelyn just fed it to her.'

'I'll say I didn't know. That it was for rats, vermin, infestations... I've done nothing, *nothing*.'

'And I'll say you're lying to protect yourself. And Jocelyn will say what is necessary to save me. Family is strong in Jocelyn, whatever you may think. We'll say you abused the child, killed her and buried her, and we knew nothing. We'll say your fear brought you back here tonight, to remove her rotting corpse and I found you, and we fought.'

'They'll never believe you. I know the truth. All I have to do is tell them. I've done nothing.'

Rupert doesn't hear him. He raises a hand to his forehead, feigning tears, rehearsing his lines. 'We trusted Dominic. We believed what he told us. We thought he had taken her to the airport for us. We should have known better. Oh, God. God...' He laughs wildly. 'What will they say? That I was selfish, and indifferent to her childish needs? That I never enquired about her safe arrival? That I was glad to be rid of her? What do I care? I have built a reputation for cold indifference. They will censure me, nothing more.'

His hand falls to his side and he laughs. Then his face grows cold, his eyes sharp, his jaw tense.

'But there's no need for any of that,' he says. 'Let's get to work. I've filled the grave, replaced the turf, scattered leaves and branches and stones. There's nothing to find. You see how I look after you.'

He turns and walks towards the library, then pauses and turns back.

'When this is finished,' he says, his voice frighteningly calm, his manner suddenly rational and cold. 'I will ensure you escape. You will have a new identity, a new home. You will never be found unless you choose to be. This I promise you.' He raises a hand, and places it where a heart should reside. 'On the ghosts of my ancestors. That is an oath I will not break.'

In his pocket, Dominic caresses the handle of the gun he took from Zachary. He grips it tight, as he weighs his options.

After a moment, his hand relaxes. He will hold the gun in reserve, and see how things go. A few hours and all trace of what has been done will be gone, and he can spare the time.

'Hurry.' Rupert's voice, calm now. 'We have only a few hours.'

Dominic takes a breath, and walks through to the library.

Chapter 60

The sun rises blind behind darkening clouds; the branches on the distant trees twist in the chill wind, groaning like arthritic old men. Within the house, the windows open to cleanse the putrid air. Dominic can hear their distant discontent. Freshly showered, he lies back on the sofa, his eyes falling shut. Somewhere deep inside him, something moves and turns, as the memory of the last few hours settles. A strange dream. A nightmare. Something unreal. If he can dispose of the memory, as surely as Rupert will soon dispose of the rotting remnants in the Trophy Room, he can move on, start the new life Rupert has promised.

He wears an old dressing gown of Rupert's, because his clothes are bathing in a hot, soapy wash, the final evidence of their night's toil draining away. As the nightmare recedes, a fleeting sense of elation ripples through him. They've done it; they've disposed of all the evidence. In another hour or so they will be free of any danger. Rupert has a solution for the final remains. He said so, a white smile breaking through the dirt and sweat, like a caricature.

Dominic can escape without risk and without revealing what he knows. There's no need to tell Rupert, no need to threaten him.

The door to the lounge opens silently over the thick carpet.

'Breakfast.' Rupert smiles, backing in, drawing a trolley behind him. 'Eggs, bacon, toast, coffee. It's the best I could do. I'm famished. I think we can indulge ourselves with breakfast in the lounge. just for once. He draws the trolley up beside them, and hands Dominic a plate. 'Help yourself,' he says, falling back on the sofa beside him. He reaches out a scrubbed hand, and serves himself.

'Have we time?' Dominic reaches for a slice of toast and drops an egg, and a rasher of bacon, onto it. He takes a deep bite, pauses to savour, and then swallows. 'God, I need this.' His voice is approving, and appreciative. 'I mean, we need to dispose of the remains. It would be bad luck if the police arrived now, after we've done so well.'

Rupert's smile matches the urbanity of his posture and the casual refinery of his dress. He wipes a hand across his lips. 'This feels strangely decadent for such a simple meal.' He laughs. 'We can indulge ourselves for a few minutes. A little reward, a pat on the back, a round of applause for a job well done.'

'Where will you take it?'

Rupert shakes his head, and emits a slow sequence of tutting noises.

'How soon a *her* becomes an *it*. Terribly sad, but much easier to deal with. If you allow your mind to linger on the *her*-ness of *it*, you are taking a step into a minefield. Was Sammy a *him* or an *it* when you attacked him? I ask without criticism, without judgement. The girl was always *it* to me.'

It's crying again, Jocelyn. It won't shut up.

She's sad, upset, be patient.

Get rid of it or I will. It repels me.

'Everyone is an *it* to me, Dominic. That makes my life so much simpler, so much easier to manage.'

'Even me?'

Rupert laughs, his eyes scrutinising Dominic like a specimen in a jar. 'You wouldn't want me to lie to you now, would you? But fear not. We are useful to each other, you and I, and there is a balance of power between us. I have no desire to stamp you underfoot, not at present. And you, my friend, need me if you are to escape unscathed.'

He leans back and checks his watch; an elegant design on a narrow, artistic wrist. He holds a hand over his mouth and belches.

'An excellent breakfast but we must make tracks. There are still things to do. I'll fetch the car round. Go and collect it, will you? It's all stashed in a bin liner and sealed just as you left it. There's nothing to fear. It's just a bag of old bones and rotting, dead flesh.'

Dominic grows pale.

'I'm not going up there.'

'Of course you are. You've nothing to fear from it or from them. They will keep to the darkness and, even if their curiosity brings them out to watch, to study, they have no evil intent towards you.'

Dominic steps back and his hand, instinctively, drops to his side, to his pocket where the gun lies.

Rupert's face hardens.

'Don't be tedious, Dominic. Even if your hand reaches that gun, you will be face-down in a pool of your own blood before you have time to press the trigger.' His smile is fleeting, replaced in an instant by a look of menace. Dominic's eyes flicker, his hand relaxes. He steps back.

'I hate that room. It gives me the creeps.'

'I repeat, there's nothing to fear. The ghosts are all tidied away, sucked back into the walls, slumbering. Open the door, grab the bag, and bring it to the front of the house. Use the French windows. I'll be waiting.'

He turns his back, and walks away, whistling tunelessly. Dominic turns, and makes his way towards the Trophy Room, halting to gather strength and courage at the bottom of the narrow steps. He looks up. That door, slightly ajar, looms like a nightmare. He takes a deep breath and counts. On three!

One... two... three... and he strides up the steps, opens the door, and steps inside, where just the distant light from a small arched window penetrates the gloom.

Behind him, the door slides eerily shut and, before him, the black bag lies on the bed.

There's a tear at one side and a hand, a skeletal hand, protrudes. My God! *It! It!*

How could that be? Not possible. Not...

And beside it, a girl, her back to him, kneeling at the bedside, her pale hand outstretched, holding in her palm the skeletal fingers of the dead hand, like a mother with her child.

A strange sound, a stifled sobbing. Slowly she turns.

He can't move. His whole body shakes.

'No, you can't be... I saw what we did... I was there!'

But before the words leave his lips, she is gone.

Only the black bag remains, sealed, its contents secure.

Chapter 61

*I*f you were to stand in the corner of that room, an unwilling witness, your eyes held as if by taut wires, what would you see? Would you see the dead girl, Melissa, holding her own dead hand, and her tears roll in a silent stream down her cheeks?

What thoughts would pass through those closed fingers? What might have been. What ought to have been. What can never be.

Or would you see... nothing? Just an empty bed and a flimsy mattress, old and stained; a black bag, misshapen, offering no clue to its deadly contents. Just garbage ready for disposal. And Dominic, wild-eyed, and staring at God knows what hideous apparition.

The Trophy Room is full of echoes. Dominic hears them and, if you listen closely, you can hear them, too. And if you close your eyes, you see faces emerge, grey and lifeless, like monochrome portraits: young, old, male, female, hundreds of them. They are in the walls, framed trophies in their stone cabinets.

Dominic stands still, his hands hanging at his sides, his eyes wide open, transfixed. For a moment, he cannot draw them away. He is paralysed. His eyes move slowly, and fix themselves, like anchors, to the sordid bag on the soiled bed.

It, he is reminding himself, over and over, It... It... It...

'I know what you are. Even this room and this house cannot change that.'

You see his eyes flicker as the spell breaks. The faces have gone, the walls are bare, grey stone, and the trophies are locked away. The bag lies sealed on the bed, a plastic tie around its neck and a knot of string for good measure, just as he left it two years ago, buried deep in the soil, forgotten.

'It's the same,' you hear him murmur. 'It hasn't changed. There is nothing to fear. There has never been anything to fear.'

Yes, Dominic is made of sterner stuff. He shuts and locks the cold, steel vault of his heart, and backs away. The bag is surprisingly light, the secret remains within of no more substance than cracked shells, and seaweed. He drags it along the ground, and bump, bump, *down the staircase, then slings it over his back, and hurries down the refined, carpeted steps to the entrance hall.*

You run to the arched window, and look out. Down below, in the grim morning light, the trunk of the car lies open. He heaves the bag into it, then runs to the passenger side, clambers in, and shuts the sleek door with a satisfying click. The car eases away.

But you linger in the Trophy Room, staring at the bed, at the walls, as if everything has changed, as if nothing will ever change again.

Chapter 62

Daniel Urquhart, Molly's father, looks ill at ease. When he speaks, his hands move constantly. His eyes flicker and shift like lights on a screen, especially when he speaks about Molly, describing her 'illness' and her failure to cope with the sudden departure of her friend, her 'sister' Melissa, Molly Toodle.

Frank watches him closely. Daniel is a professional man, a city solicitor, more at ease behind a large desk. He finds talking about Melissa and Molly difficult; unless there's a more sinister reason for his nervousness. Frank knows that it's safer to rule nothing out.

'Molly was upset when she didn't hear from Melissa. We tried to explain to Molly how she would be settling into her new home, and far too busy to think of us, but she was convinced something bad had happened.'

Sandra Urquhart sits beside him on the white leather sofa. A few years younger than her husband, she has a shrewd, incisive look. Frank can also sense a ready humour, a sharp wit and an outgoing nature, which stands in sharp contrast to her husband's anxious reserve.

'We had our own views,' she says. 'We thought she was glad to get away, and wanted nothing more than to forget Leybury Grange and Rupert Fitzwilliam.'

Frank sinks deeper into the cushioned armchair, and sips tea from a china cup. Templeton sits opposite, looking ill at ease. He doesn't move his feet, as if fearful he's brought in something unpleasant from the streets.

'This is a lovely room.' Frank regards the light curtains and pale walls. Everything is bright and airy, and artworks splash colour from a meticulous palette on every surface.

'Sandra works in interior design.'

Daniel squeezes Sandra's hand and smiles. It isn't difficult to imagine his eyes watering with devotion. Does she feel the same, Frank wonders? There is more than a hint of irritation in her look.

'You were living here full-time during Melissa's stay, I believe?'

Sandra frees her hand from Daniel's grip. 'After Melissa left, we moved back to the city. Molly was already becoming obsessed by Melissa's silence, and there was more support for her there.'

'Tell me about Melissa.'

'She and Molly hit it off at once. She was such a sweet, sensitive girl and her mother's death had hit her very hard. She needed a lot of support from different agencies. Bereavement counselling and that sort of thing. Mostly organised through the school and social services. The last thing a girl like Melissa needed was a surrogate parent like Rupert Fitzwilliam. He offered her no support, no sympathy, no understanding, nothing. He was a monster. If it wasn't for Jocelyn, that poor child would have been utterly alone.'

Templeton leans forward to settle his teacup on the table. He looks relieved to be rid of it, his hands having been conditioned over the years to the solid security of police station mugs.

'So, Jocelyn helped her?' he asks.

'As much as she could,' Sandra's hand rests now on her husband's arm. 'It wasn't easy for her, with Rupert watching.'

'She did her best,' Daniel adds. 'She was a strong lady, despite appearances.'

Sandra nods. 'She kept Melissa out of Rupert's way, and gave her what affection she dared. She knew that Leybury Grange was not the place for a young girl.'

'Did she contact you through the school?'

'Melissa talked to Jocelyn about our Molly. She said she wished she could live with her new friend. Then one evening the doorbell rang and there she stood. Jocelyn Fitzwilliam, with Melissa beside her. We spent the evening together, talking.'

'And that was that.'

'Pretty much.'

'How long was Melissa with you?'

'Just three months. She was such a lovely girl. We were very fond of her.'

'And Rupert Fitzwilliam?' Templeton asks. 'Was he happy with the arrangement?'

'We never saw him, not once. Every two weeks, always on a Friday, a taxi would arrive to take Melissa to the Grange for an evening. Once a fortnight, she stopped there overnight. I'm convinced it was Rupert's idea. I think he wanted to show us, and Melissa, that he was in control, and that we could do nothing without his say-so. He makes my flesh creep.'

'Was it always the same taxi which came for her?' Templeton asks.

'Twice, it was a private car. A man called Sheedy, Dominic Sheedy.'

Templeton exchanges a look with Frank then turns away. Frank rescues a smile from the quicksand of his mind.

'What did Melissa say about those evenings at the Grange?'

'Nothing. Not one word. But she was pale when she came back, and very quiet.'

'Did she say anything to Molly, perhaps?'

'We don't want Molly involved in this.' Sandra's voice is firm, not to be argued with. 'She's been through a lot. We don't want her upset.'

Frank smiles, reassuring. No point stirring muddy waters, not yet. But he will need to speak to Molly, that much is clear. Two young girls sharing a room will talk, especially two girls who are as close as these two. Molly may well hold the answer to a number of disturbing questions.

Templeton's mind has stalled at the mention of Dominic, and hasn't moved since.

'Have either of you had any dealings with Dominic Sheedy?' he asks.

'No, definitely not.' Sandra's response is immediate and fierce.

'Mr Urquhart?'

Daniel's eyes flicker from Frank to Sandra, and back again.

'My partner, Mr Grayling, has represented him, I believe. I may have passed him in the waiting room.'

'What offences?'

Daniel shrugs. 'I don't know the details. Petty crime, minor violence, drunken behaviour. There may have been other offences which didn't reach the court.'

'Like what?' Templeton asks. He glances at Frank, clearly anticipating the reply.

'As I said, I don't know the details. He was Mr Grayling's client.'

'Perhaps he mentioned something?' Templeton says.

'To the best of my knowledge, there were certain accusations of... inappropriate behaviour. Exposure, lewd actions...'

'Crimes of a sexual nature,' Templeton says. 'Towards children?'

Sandra springs to her feet.

'What? You let a monster like that take a vulnerable girl like Melissa in his car, alone?'

Daniel's hands reach out, palms down, placating, reassuring. 'The accusations were withdrawn. There was no evidence. And Mr Grayling said—'

'Mr Grayling? You spoke to Mr Grayling? Why didn't you speak to me? What has Grayling got to do with any of this?'

Daniel's eyes plead for an intervention.

'Business...' he stammers. 'Rupert Fitzwilliam... Grayling knows Mr Fitzwilliam... I thought, a quiet word... to keep Melissa safe.'

'A quiet word? From Grayling? Are you seriously telling me you put the safety of our child in the hands of that ineffectual sycophant? And since when has your practice had clients like Sheedy and Fitzwilliam?'

'Grayling...'

'Never mind what *bloody Grayling* said! What about *you*?'

Frank raises a calming hand and simultaneously represses an impish smile. He doesn't look at Templeton. It'd only make it worse.

'Please, I know this is a difficult conversation for both of you. We understand that. But if we could focus on my questions for the moment, I'd be grateful.'

Sandra continues to glare, then sits down, arms folded, legs crossed. Daniel switches on a professional smile which carries a token of gratitude. It's a temporary ceasefire, not a truce.

'Rupert Fitzwilliam is Mr Grayling Senior's one remaining client,' Daniel explains. 'Mr Grayling Senior has all but retired.'

'Another crook,' Sandra says, but there is no time to pursue her comment because the door flies open, and Molly stands there.

'What are you shouting about? I heard you even over my music.'

She sees Frank and Templeton, and her eyes make a quick calculation.

'You're Jason's dad, aren't you?'

'Yep, that's me.' Frank raises another smile.

'He says you're cool. Did you really throw Dominic off the harbour wall?' Templeton's face breaks into a grin. Frank holds up his hands, palm outwards.

'Guilty.'

'Good.' Molly's voice is emphatic. She turns to Daniel. 'Why was Mum shouting?'

'Just adult stuff.' Daniel makes room for her to sit beside him. She lifts his arm, and places it round her shoulders, to snuggle in close. 'Nothing for you to worry about.'

'Are you here about Melissa?' Molly's eyes are dark and sharp, and have the penetrating quality of her mother's. Another strong female in the Urquhart household. Frank feels almost sorry for Daniel.

'I think you should leave the grown-ups to finish their conversation, my girl.' Sandra stands up, and walks towards the door. She beckons with a finger, but Molly doesn't move.

'She was murdered,' Molly says. 'Rupert Fitzwilliam killed her.'

'Oh, Molly, don't start that again. These gentlemen don't want to hear your theories.'

She opens the door, but Molly remains seated.

'I've waited for ages to tell someone and now I'm going to.' She folds her arms across her chest, an immovable object.

There's a momentary mother-daughter stand-off before Sandra, conscious perhaps of the unseemly image of a further family conflict, sighs, and sits on the chair arm beside her.

Molly turns to Frank, her eyes unwavering.

'She told me he wanted to kill her. Jocelyn knew about it. That's why she wanted her to stay with us, so she'd be safe. Only, she wasn't, because Rupert made her go back, and then he said horrid things to her. Really horrid.'

She hesitates, and glances at her mother.

'Go on, sweetie, now you've started.' Sandra strokes her hair.

'He asked if she knew what it was like to choke, to feel your lungs filling up with froth until you drowned in it.'

'Dear God,' Templeton says.

'He described to her what happens when someone was burnt to death or hung. She had awful nightmares. She used to wake up sweating and crying. Then she'd come into my bed so she'd feel safe.'

'I didn't know any of that.' There's a tremor in Sandra's voice. Daniel is as pale as the walls.

'She wouldn't let me tell. She was scared Rupert might make her go back to live at Leybury Grange if we caused trouble.'

Frank leans forward, his voice quiet. He wants Molly to know he's listening. 'That's cruel and horrible.'

'He came to her room once, when she was in bed. Melissa said she could smell alcohol on his breath, as he leaned forward and whispered. He said, *'I'd like to watch you die.'* And then he laughed at her, and said, *'Maybe one day I'll strangle you to death.'*

'Was that why Jocelyn found her somewhere far away to live, so she'd never have to see him again?'

Molly shakes her head. 'Melissa never left. Rupert killed her, just like he promised he would.'

'You can't know that, sweetheart.' Sandra holds her close. 'Jocelyn said she was living with relatives in Italy, and then they moved away, just to keep her safe. Nobody knows where she is now.'

'I know.'

'How do you know?' Templeton's voice is hushed; nothing in his experience in Grantley has prepared him for a testimony like this. Frank feels quite sorry for him. He remembers the first time he heard evidence from a minor. How does any child recover from experiences like that?

He's hardened to it now, but it still hurts, still shocks. He still can't understand. And this is something different. What the hell happened, deep in Rupert's background, to make him the man he's become? Something caused it. He wasn't born a monster. Nobody was. Someone had drawn on that clean sheet, someone had distorted that life into the twisted, broken form it now took.

'I know, because she told me.'

Molly glances towards her father, who holds his head in his hands.

'I know what you think. I know what you all think, but Melissa came back, and she told me.'

Frank raises a hand to silence Daniel, whose intervention is seconds away.

'What do you mean, *she came back?*'

'Her ghost came back. She told me she'd been murdered. She stood at the bottom of my bed, and she said, *I never left Leybury Grange. I was murdered by Rupert. He buried me in the grounds, near the summer house.*'

Daniel can hold back no further.

'You know that can't be true, Molly. There are no ghosts. Melissa is living safely with her new family.'

Sandra strokes her head. 'They daren't get in touch with us, in case Rupert finds out where she is. Jocelyn told us that.'

Molly's voice is low and subdued; her tears are falling now.

'She's dead. I know she is. Rupert killed her with poison. If you don't believe me, why don't you ask her?'

'What do you mean?' Templeton's eyes widen, and he glances at Frank.

'Ask her. She's there.' Molly points towards the door and then, in a voice which seemed to be drawn from the air, a voice not her own, a voice which draws gasps from her mother and father, she speaks.

Look for me by the summer house, where they buried me.

Chapter 63

'This is all crazy but I still think we should get a warrant and search the grounds. Better go through Sparks. I don't want to tread on any toes.'

Templeton changes down through the gears to negotiate the narrow corners of the village, then heads up the narrow road towards the Grantley bypass.

'He won't mind. He'll be pleased you took it off his plate.' He veers towards the hedge as a car rounds the corner ahead of him. 'Breathe in,' he says, 'there's only just room.'

The car slides past. A wave from a tourist face, two kids in the back, husband in the passenger seat, and a dog; pale brown poodle cross.

'But still, as a courtesy.'

'What about Fitzwilliam? Do we question him?'

'Get a car out to collect him. Arrest him if necessary. We've got enough circumstantial evidence to fill a moderately spacious potting shed. Melissa's words reported by Molly. The evidence about her fears, and Jocelyn's. The fact that Jocelyn has scarpered and we can't locate her, that nobody has seen or heard from her. It's enough to be going on with.'

The car pulls up at a junction; no slip-lane here, just a *Give Way* and a wait for something resembling a gap in the traffic.

'I hate this bloody road.' Templeton stares to his right. 'It's like a drain for cars and lorries. Vehicular effluent.'

'The city is easier. Everything goes slowly, or stops. Mainly, it stops. Quick, there's a gap. Go.'

Templeton accelerates into the inside lane.

'We need a bypass to bypass the bypass,' he says. 'On the subject of the city, when are you going back?'

'Janice and Jason are going back in a couple of days. I'm getting it in the neck from both of them. Janice wants to get home, and Jason wants to stay. Jason's already had a few extra days holiday. I had to phone up the school, and pretend he was ill. Janice has cabin fever. She's always the same. She spends months looking forward to a holiday and then after a couple of weeks she starts to miss all the routines of home. As for me, I'm here for a few more days. I like to see things through.'

A smile flickers across Templeton's face. 'Yeah, we heard that.'

'Oh? Been doing research?'

Templeton laughs. 'You know what it's like. Friend of a friend, quick phone call. What's he like, then, this Inspector Miller?'

'And?'

'*He's like a bloody crocodile. Once his teeth are into something, you couldn't prise him off with a crowbar. That would be the gist.*'

'Hmm.' Frank's grunt of disapproval is not uncontaminated by pride.

"You think Melissa is dead?' Templeton asks.

Frank turns and looks out of the window. A sloping grass embankment, saplings in protective sleeves, then open land and fields and trees. Templeton slows down to take the slip road to Grantley. Across the bypass to the right: dark brooding oaks, chestnuts and sycamores. Leybury Grange.

'Yes,' he says. 'She's been missing too long.'

'What do we do about Jocelyn?'

'Jocelyn knows something. She didn't suddenly decide to bugger off because she felt like a bit of continental sunshine. We need to find her. We need to find Dominic Sheedy, too. You can bet your last twenty pounds that he knows something. Why the hell would Rupert have him ferrying Melissa back and forth unless he was up to something? I don't get the feeling Rupert Fitzwilliam does anything by accident.'

They slow down and follow a motor home round the narrow streets, until they hit the gaudy centre, and the massed ranks of tourists. Eventually, Templeton steers the car to the left and then sharply right into the police station car park.

'Home, sweet home. I'll get to work.'

'Get Sparks up to date first.'

'What are you going to do?'

'I'm going to exercise a little executive discretion, and wander down to the harbour. I need some time to think.' He opens the car, and clambers out. 'And I need to find something nice for Janice and Jason.' He winks. 'Keep them sweet.'

Frank walks down the lane which leads to the harbour, passing a small café, tucked away between an estate agent and a gift shop, and set back from the roadside like something made more precious by isolation.

Janice would like that. Tasteful.

Only Janice isn't in the mood to enjoy anything much at the moment.

He reaches the harbour, and leans on the rail. It's not like Leybury. There's a sizeable marina, numerous tourist boats, lots of colour and noise, and nowhere to throw a recalcitrant yob like Dominic. He smiles, then frowns, then smiles again as he thinks of Jason. Things are going well.

Then his thoughts slip to Sammy, and anger flares like a gas jet.

Poor kid. How could anyone...?

His phone rings. It's Templeton and he sounds stressed.

'There's been another body washed ashore,' he says.

Frank swears under his breath. 'Another?' He feels a cold shiver pass through him.

'Some tourist out for a morning run stumbled on more than he bargained for. Wrapped in seaweed like a ghastly Christmas gift.'

'Any identification?'

'Yeah, that's the worst of it.' Frank listens and his heart beats faster. 'It was Harry Carver.'

'Carver? The guy I saw talking to Jocelyn outside the summer house? Are you sure? Jesus Christ.' Frank's brain is working hard to catch up. 'Murdered?' he asks.

'We'll need to wait for the autopsy but, from what I've been told, it looks like he was attacked with a bloody great hammer. Hell, Frank, this is getting out of control.'

Frank closes his phone and heads back towards the police station. He passes the little café, and glances in through the lace-curtained window.

Ghosts, ghosts.

Chapter 64

Castles like the one on the cliffs near Grantley have tales to tell; tales of power and intrigue, tales of the courts of local nobility. If you stand and listen closely, you can pretend you hear the clash of swords, and the cries of wounded men. From the high tower it is even possible to imagine the siege engines, the camps of soldiers, the rain of arrows tumbling from the sky.

There's a prison cell in the castle, several metres below ground; a dark and dreary hole viewed through an iron grille, with no more light than a cave. Imagine it full to its dripping roof with the groans of hopeless victims. Clench your eyes tight shut and imagine one such prisoner pacing three paces to the left, three paces to the right, on and on and on until exhaustion.

Yes, you can imagine all of this.

Some castles escape notoriety of course. They rumble and roll through history with no more than a few local narratives to break the monotony; their cells held no more than a few nameless miscreants for more than a few days.

Not Grantley.

Not the land of the Fitzwilliams.

Linger in the courtyard, your eyes closed, and hear the passing of day-to-day feet. Listen to voices, as they exchange news, complain, swear, bewail their lot or extol their good fortune, and talk about bread, ale, the shortage of fish, the tithes that bind them, the lord who controls them, and the age-old gossip of sex and lust.

Listen.

The air is full of them.

So many lives, lived. Ashes to ashes.

Dust.

Down by the wall, two men, long dead, talk in hushed voices. They talk of escape. Anywhere is better than here. Any risk is worth taking.

But they will not escape. Nobody ever does. Their cries will echo though the centuries.

They echo still.

And now, a new picture for you to see. Two boys play among the ruins. You can hear their laughter, and your heart surges like the tide as you watch them chase each other from wall to wall.

You cannot help but smile.

They are so engrossed with their game, they don't hear a car approach along the track, and pull into the small parking space. They don't hear the engine cut, and the door swing open. Nor do they see the young woman who climbs out and stands, as if scenting the air. She looks around.

Now she hears them, as they play within the castle, and she steps forward, her pale, pastel dress swaying as if caught in a breeze of its own making, brought into being simply to enhance her slender figure. It catches her hair, too; dark hair, which falls like satin down her back. She flicks a troublesome strand, and steps between the watchtowers.

She stops, and watches the boys at play. A wistful look flickers across her face, a moment of sadness; as if her mind is troubled, and the sight of the boys brings to mind memories of loss. They haven't seen her yet, but any moment now they will.

What then?

The woman glides rather than walks, as if her feet barely touch the ground. She carries in her hand a padded envelope; A4 size, you think. She holds it close against her side.

Now, the boys see her, and pause as she steps forward. The red-haired boy, Sammy, looks anxious, and takes a step back, his eyes fixed, watching her as if in fear of a sudden move, a threat. He recognises her. The other boy, Jason, is curious. Sammy mumbles a name.

'Jocelyn Fitzwilliam.'

Then Jason too steps back, and the two of them eye her like deer watch a cheetah lope among them. They prepare to run away. The young woman senses this, and raises a calming hand. She smiles, and speaks reassuringly. She knows they are anxious, and she understands why. Who wouldn't be scared to hear that name?

Move closer.

Listen.

'Your father is a detective, I believe.' She turns to Jason, a soft smile, and a voice like waves on a summer beach.

Jason nods, but doesn't risk words. He doesn't want to be drawn into the web she might be weaving.

'I have something for him,' she says. 'Will you give it to him for me?'

He glances at Sammy for reassurance, then nods quickly.

'Tell him I shall call, if I may. One night soon. I shall visit him at home. Will you tell him that?'

Again, he nods.

Jocelyn holds out the envelope, but neither boy moves, so she lays it on a low stone wall. Then she turns to Sammy.

'I am sorry for what has happened to you and your family,' she says, her eyes locking onto his. 'Do you believe me?'

Sammy nods quickly.

'If it were in my power, I would make things right.' Her mind seems to flit away for a moment, like a bird caught on a thermal, gliding somewhere beyond sight. 'I would put so many things right.' She sighs, as if speaking to herself. She turns back to Sammy, and again her eyes catch his. 'Tell your parents... tell them...' She turns away. 'Never mind. Perhaps one day soon I shall tell them myself.'

She walks away, gliding over the stony ground. At the gatehouse, she pauses.

'Don't forget the package, Jason. It will explain a great many things, but not everything. I shall call one evening very soon.'

She turns, and walks though the arch of the gateway, fading like mist from their sight. They stand still for a moment then run forward to the envelope. Jason picks it up first

'What's in it, do you think?' Sammy's voice is awed, like he's been offered a map showing the location of a buried treasure.

Jason turns the envelope over in his hands, and inspects it. 'There's no writing on it. It's just blank.' His fingers explore its contours. 'There's something inside,' he says. 'Feel it.'

Sammy presses and prods, then shakes the package. 'I can't feel what it is. Too well padded.' He hands it back to Jason. 'What shall we do?'

'Take it to Frank,' Jason says, with something like pride in his voice.

'Shall I come with you?'

Jason nods. 'You can help me remember the message.'

They move towards the gatehouse. Jason gives the envelope a final shake, then tucks it inside his jumper.

'Why does she want to meet your dad?' Sammy asks.

'Dunno.'

'Do you think he'll show you what's in the envelope?'

'Dunno,' Jason says again. 'Don't think so. It's police business. He doesn't talk about his work.'

'Maybe...' Sammy says.

'Yeah...' Jason replies.

And you watch them climb the rise to the cliff top and disappear from sight, and the air fills with their speculations, like insects in the summer air.

In the castle, the voices re-emerge. Ghosts of the long-dead step out from behind doorways, populate the walls, glide up and down the winding stairs, gossip in the sun. They have something new to talk about, and they make their speculations, too. That name—Fitzwilliam—stirs their thoughts, brings back their memories.

Nothing good.

Chapter 65

'**B** loody hell.'

Templeton looks at the tabletop where Frank has emptied the content of the padded envelope. They are in the lounge of the tiny cottage where Frank, Janice and Jason are in temporary residence.

'Bloody hell indeed,' Frank says.

'I don't understand. Why did she send them to you? And why choose the boys to bring them? Is this what Dominic was supposed to collect from the buoy? So, who collected it? And how did it end up in Jocelyn's possession and—'

'Templeton?'

'Yes?'

'Shut up, you're making my head hurt.'

A black pouch lies on the table, and beside it a square of velvet. On the velvet, two hundred or more diamonds. They're the real thing, Frank says, and, if he's right, not just your ordinary, everyday, smuggled diamonds. These are top quality.

'We'll need to call in the experts but I won't be surprised if these stones are worth a grand or more each.'

Templeton whistles through his teeth. 'I'd better call the gaffer, then. He won't like being kept out of this.'

Frank runs his fingers through the stones. He's thinking of the message Jason and Sammy relayed to him.

There's a long silence. Too many questions, too few answers.

'Do you think Harry Carver was on to this?' Templeton asks eventually. 'Or Zachary Blight?'

'If Zachary knew about this, he could have nailed Rupert Fitzwilliam ages ago. Same with Harry Carver.'

'Unless they were planning to follow the diamonds to their final destination.'

'Or there was something else going on.'

The lounge door opens, banging heavily against the cupboard set close behind it. Janice muscles into the room, carrying a tray. She kicks the door closed behind her but it strikes an obstruction, and bounces back. Sammy and Jason—the obstruction—peer into the room. Their eyes widen as they see the diamonds on their black velvet bed.

'Wow,' Sammy gasps. 'Are they real?'

Frank doesn't answer.

'They are real, aren't they? Is this what—'

'Go and fetch your dad, Sammy. This is as much to do with him as it is me.'

Janice drops the tray heavily on the table, swilling tea and coffee into saucers, and making the biscuits jump on the plates.

'Tell him to bring a crowbar. It's the only way he'll fit.'

Sammy disappears.

'Fetch your mum as well,' Janice shouts after him. 'I need someone who understands.'

A moment's silence, and a few glances exchanged, like a secret currency.

'When are you going back home, Janice?' Templeton asks, even though he knows the answer. 'You must be looking forward to getting back to normal.'

'I've forgotten what normal looks like.' Janice stands over the diamonds. 'Have you counted them?'

'Yes.' Templeton nods.

'Pity.' Janice turns away, and heads towards the kitchen. 'Send Maggie through when she arrives.'

Templeton fights back a smile.

'She can spit nails when she's in this mood,' Frank says. 'Can't she, Jason?'

Jason restricts himself to a big grin.

'What will you do with the diamonds?' he asks.

Frank looks at Templeton. 'I think we'll split them fifty-fifty, and then me and your mum will go and live in the South of France.'

'Ace. What about me?'

'Public school, with all the toffs. You can wear a funny uniform with a peaked cap.'

'No chance. I'd run away.' His eyes steal back to the diamonds. 'You'll have to give me and Sammy one each or we'll tell.'

'Blackmail, eh?'

'Yup.'

Five minutes later, the door opens. It's Richard. Behind him, Maggie's voice filters into the kitchen, calming Janice.

'Never mind, pet. You'll be home before you know it. Now, what can I help with?'

Richard closes the door behind him.

'Bloody hell.' He whistles as he too leans over the diamonds. 'It's true then, what Sammy told me. I thought it was another of his tales.' He looks up. 'So, that's what the bastards were up to. Dominic and Rupert. And in my bloody boat.'

His red hair seemed to flicker and flare, echoing a fire in his eyes.

'And Jocelyn Fitzwilliam handed them to you, just like that? What's she up to?'

'I don't know, but this isn't a family I'm inclined to trust any further than I could throw a sack of spuds.'

'What are you going to do?'

'I'll wait for her to arrive, and see what she has to say, and then I'll decide. But, one way or another, these diamonds must be locked away somewhere safe.' He looks around. Three pairs of eyes flicker, as if catching and trapping a reflected light from the precious stones. 'I don't trust any one of you,' he says, 'especially you two.' He turns a sharp look at Jason and Sammy. 'If I turn my back for one minute...'

There are cries of protest, but they are more subdued than Frank would like.

'They're so small,' Sammy says. 'I bet you wouldn't miss one or two, and then my dad wouldn't have to sell the boats, and we could stay here.'

'Sammy!' Richard feigns shock.

'I know,' Sammy says. 'It's better to be honest and poor.'

'Can we be here when Jocelyn comes to see you?' Jason sits down, and clings to Frank's arm. 'Please?'

'After all,' Sammy says, 'she brought them to us first of all. She probably *wants* us to be here.'

Frank laughs, but he shakes his head.

'There'll be nobody here but me. Not even you, Templeton.' He seems to think for a moment. 'Except maybe you, Richard. This affects you more than anyone else.'

The door opens. Maggie and Janice squeeze into the diminishing space.

'Take a deep breath, Maggie, or we'll not all fit.' Janice's voice is as sharp as an ice axe. 'Men!' she mutters, hands on hips, eyes glaring around the room.

'Have you been listening?'

Maggie looks at Richard with a gaze that could penetrate concrete. He wilts under the look.

'Perhaps Maggie should be here,' he says, 'instead of me. Jocelyn being a woman and all. If you think that would work, Frank.'

'I think that both of you would work fine, Richard. You too, Janice,' he adds, noting the look on her face. 'We could invite Aunt Jessica from Bermondsey, too.'

He stops. The warning lights are flashing red. Templeton takes the hint.

'I'll be off then,' he says.

Chapter 66

L isten to the voices in Leybury Grange.
    A man's voice rises first, as if from a foul swamp.

'Where's that boy? Where is he? What's he up to? He's always up to something.'

A woman's voice now, bitter perfume catching your throat.

'He's in the garden, killing things.'

The man laughs. 'He'd kill me and you if he could. He practises on rabbits, squirrels and cats.'

'He hates us.'

Picture a snake's tongue slip between her lips, as if to taste the air.

'I never took to him, you know. From the very first second I disliked him. When he slid from between my thighs, I took one look and knew he repelled me.'

'You tried hard, my love. The nannies you hired, the toys they bought on your behalf, the home you gave him. He never appreciated what you did for him.'

'Nobody ever stayed long with him. They made one excuse or another to get away. They were disgusted by him. Those cold, grey eyes. That pale, young flesh. The crying, shitting, the wailing. No wonder none of them stayed.'

'He was always a sickly child. Coughs, colds, vomiting, defecating. There was nothing for them, love. Even money couldn't keep them here.'

'You did all you could to keep them. Their own room in the tower, on the floor below his, so they could hear him when he screamed.'

'I should have punished him more severely. I was too soft, too kindly.'

'You never spared the rod when it was needed, my love. I recall his cries. I stood at the foot of the tower stairs, and listened to him when you beat him. It was strangely gratifying.'

'You were obliged to banish him from the dinner table, I recall.'

'I couldn't bear the sight of him eating.'

'Disgusting. Disgusting.'

'Dinner was better without him and he, I presume, was happier dribbling his food in his quarters, where nobody would chastise him.'

'Did you ever wonder what he did in there for all those hours?'

'Where is he now?'

'He's in the garden, my love, I told you.'

In the garden, a ten-year-old boy, sits on the grass outside the summer house. It is locked and there is no key. He has a small knife with which he stabs the ground, over and over. Stab, stab, stab. He glances at the summer house, and then stands up. He walks across to peer in the window, his hands cupped to block out the reflected light from the sun. He inserts the blade into the lock and turns it half-heartedly, then gives up, and walks lazily round the lawn, in and out of the shadows cast by the trees. Sometimes he jumps, leaping from light to light or shadow to shadow as the game demands, but mainly he walks. If you watch closely, you can see his lips move in silent conversations. Perhaps he imagines a friend playing with him.

Next week, he will go back to school.

He frowns as he thinks about it.

He hates them all: the bullies, the simpering kids, the teachers, the clever ones, the stupid ones. They hate him, too. Now, he smiles, as if in anticipation. He likes their hatred. It's easier to deal with than kindness. You just hate back twice as hard, and you never stop. Sooner or later, even the toughest of them slink away sobbing. Once you set your mind you can play all sorts of tricks. Shit in their beds. Shit in their food. Tear photographs of their mums, dads, kid sisters. Break their toys, tear their clothes, hide everything.

If you're careful, there are cleaning products you can steal, locked away in cupboards, and chemicals in the laboratories. Then lie back in the dormitory bed and hear them cry, and vomit.

He learns quickly.

'Call him! Call the boy! Send him to his room. Disgusting child.'

'He goes back to school tomorrow.'

'Good. Sooner the better.'

'There'll be complaints again.'

'There are always complaints. They can deal with him. What do we pay them for? Beat him! Make him cry! Make him howl! Nip him, pinch him, cut him! Lock him in his room and don't let him out. That'll stop him.'

'That'll stop him.'

'That'll stop him.'

Chapter 67

'How utterly fascinating.' In the interview room at Grantley Police Station, Rupert leans forward to inspect the contents of a padded envelope which DI Sparks has laid before him, the diamonds glistening like stars against a black velvet sky. 'Where did you say you found them?' A portly and ageing solicitor, Mr Grayling Senior, sits beside him. He casts a disparaging eye towards the display.

'We didn't. We hoped you might be able to cast some light.'

'Me? What on earth would make you think that I would have anything to contribute?'

'Certain allegations have been made against you.' Sparks is impassive, giving little away. He's on home turf, comfortable and at ease doing his job.

'Really? How intriguing. I assume it is fruitless to ask who made such a suggestion.'

'It is,' confirms Sparks. 'We're led to believe that you and ex-Detective Chief Inspector Zachary Blight were involved in smuggling these items.'

'Ah, poor Zachary. He's dead, isn't he? Poor man. Though never one I could relate to. I employed him for his professional knowledge of security issues. One can never be too careful.'

'You knew he was a Detective Chief Inspector?'

Rupert spreads his arms, and cocks his head to one side. 'Of course. I research my employees thoroughly.'

'Did you research Harry Carver?'

'Of course not. He was a menial. One of Jocelyn's waifs.'

'He was a police officer, working undercover. He was investigating you.'

For a moment, Rupert's overcoat of composure is penetrated as if by a chill wind. But not for long.

'Really? Did he discover anything of interest? Do tell.'

'He was investigating a smuggling ring.'

'And he thought I was involved? I can't imagine why. You must ask him.' He pauses, and raises a hand to his lips. 'But he's dead, too, isn't he? How very inconsiderate of him.'

'He was murdered, as you know.' Frank watches as a tick begins to pulse in Sparks' cheek. It has been a long day already, and Sparks probably has plans for the evening. Rupert Fitzwilliam is just pissing about, winding him up, grating on his nerves. He's doing it on purpose, as if he has all the time in the world.

'And you think I...?' Rupert raises his arms and eyes in dramatic disbelief, and looks, as if for support, towards Grayling Senior, who shakes his head at the affrontery, and looks down. 'These people seem to have a very high opinion of my criminal skills, Mr Grayling. Apparently, I have killed at least two policemen and a young girl, while smuggling thousands of pounds worth of diamonds. I do believe they think I'm Moriarty. Now...' He points at Frank and then at Sparks. 'Let me see if I can guess which of you is Holmes, and which Lestrade.'

Grayling interrupts. 'This is really becoming tiresome, Detective Inspector. We've been over and over this ground and, so far, you've shown not one shred of solid evidence. Do you have anything substantial with which to charge my client? This interview has consisted of nothing but vague suspicions and unsubstantiated accusations. If you have nothing more, I think we're finished here.'

Rupert shook his head. 'No, no, no.' He smiles, 'I'm enjoying myself. I get so little company at the Grange.'

'Where is Melissa?'

Frank ignores Grayling and tries to pin Rupert with a stare, but it would be easier to staple mist to a mountain.

Rupert yawns.

'I've told you already. Haven't you written it down somewhere? She's in Europe. With relatives. I don't know who, and I don't know where and, to be totally honest with you, I don't care. How many times?'

Frank ignores him.

'Where's Jocelyn?'

A shrug. 'She's a grown woman. She goes where she wants. She'll come back when she's ready.'

Frank leans forward, and pushes a piece of paper across the wooden table.

'I want a list of your European relatives,' he says.

'Rupert spreads his hands. 'All of them?'

'Every last one.'

Rupert sighs patiently. 'Have you any idea how many relations a family like mine has spawned. They're everywhere. They're a social infestation. I believe we have an Honourable Member, and the editor of a tabloid newspaper out there somewhere. Perhaps I should begin with them.'

'Begin where you like,' Sparks says, his patience clearly wearing thin.

Grayling is about to interrupt, but Sparks raised a peremptory hand.

'We have a missing girl, a child whom we need to locate as a matter of urgency. We have been unable to locate her, and your client has been far from helpful. One might even describe his attitude as obstructive.' He taps the table. 'Write!' he says to Rupert.

Frank looks at Sparks. The Detective Inspector is definitely good at his job; at least he is when he isn't checking the time to see if he can go home to Mrs Sparks and the little Sparklers.

'We've got as long as it takes. I don't care if we're here all night.'

True to form, he glances anxiously at the clock on the wall above Rupert's head, and grimaces as if affected by indigestion.

Frank smiles. 'We'll stick to Europe for the moment. Just to save time.'

Rupert shakes his head, and sighs theatrically.

'As you wish. Now, let me see...' He picks up the pencil, taps its end against the table, turns it in his fingers, makes as if to write, then stops. He sits back, turns it again, taps it again and then, with a smile, begins to write. Every action he takes, it seems to Frank, is designed to irritate. The tick in Sparks' cheek becomes a persistent throb. His fingers drum. Rupert notices, and his smile widens.

'Well,' he says, feigning deep thought, 'I'll approach the subject methodically, country by country. Italy first! There's Aunt Gwendoline. She's in Verona, I believe. But she's getting a bit old for the adoption game. She must be in her eighties now. She used to write for newspapers, about opera. She was quite the connoisseur, I'm told. Was it *The Times* or *The Daily Telegraph*? I can't remember. I was never interested. Opera bores me almost as much as Aunt Gwendoline.'

He pauses, glances at the two detectives and, noting no discernible difference in Frank's unperturbable expression, focuses on Sparks. Then he writes again.

'Cousin Gareth.' He continues the commentary as Spark's cheek tremors. 'Probably in prison by now. A dreadful con man, you know. Married elderly ladies, and fleeced them. Not the sort to indulge in acts of kindness. Then there's cousin Barty. He's in finance, very wealthy. He makes a speciality of betting on other people's losses. He's very good. I almost approve. As companies and funds sink into ruination, he rises like a phoenix from their ashes. Very rewarding, I should think, to profit on human misery, to create something from the detritus of other lives. He's married to some ghastly Italian with a shrivelled face, and wealthy parents. He's in Milan.'

He looks cautiously, and innocently, at Sparks.

'I wonder how many people have died to fertilise his gardens, how many suicides, how many broken hearts?'

Frank can see the warning signs. Sparks is approaching the edge. Rupert is goading him, nipping away at him, pushing him ever closer.

It's time to intervene.

'I think we'll leave you to your homework. Fascinating as these insights into your family relationships are, we have other business to attend to.' He turns to Grayling. 'Let the PC outside the door know when you're finished.'

Rupert pauses, and resumes tapping the end of the pencil against the desk.

'I do wish Jocelyn was here. This would be quickly settled. Can you not put out an APB or whatever it's called? I only know the term from television programmes. Can you not trace her, check the airports, view the passenger lists of outgoing flights, and other technological wheezes? I thought such things were easy nowadays, a mere click of a computer key and, like magic, you get a live-streamed picture of your target in a hotel bedroom.' He shakes his head, an indulgent smile on his lips. *Tap, tap, tap.* The pencil pursues its monotonous rhythm. 'Perhaps that's a little too James Bond for a crusty, rural policeman.'

His eyes search out cracks in Sparks' defences, but it's Frank who parries his attack.

'Jocelyn is back in the UK. I'm surprised you didn't know.' He opens the door and steps out. It's Sparks who pauses and turns.

'We've known for days,' he says. 'Now, get on with your fucking list.'

For once, Rupert Fitzwilliam is lost for words.

Chapter 68

Frank, sips from a cracked mug with a stained image of Homer Simpson. He grimaces. 'What *is* this stuff?'

Templeton pulls up a chair, takes a sip from his own cup. 'I don't look. I just press buttons at random. Treat it as a challenge.'

'I think you pressed two at once. This tea has a definite flavour of chocolate about it.' Frank turns back to Sparks. 'It's your call, of course. You're the gaffer here. But while he's busy concocting his list, he thinks he's in control. I suggest you give him half an hour and let him go and then, early tomorrow, while he's feeling smug and victorious, we can hit him with the search warrant. See how he reacts.'

Sparks nods. 'Anything to annoy the smug bastard. But we'd better find something. I can't take much more of that cynical, upper-class bullshit he's shovelling.'

'He's shovelling it straight at you. You can't let him see it's getting to you.'

'It *is* getting to me. I want the bastard locked away. No, more than that. I want to see the look on his face when we charge him, and he knows we've won. The trouble is, I can't see how we get him, not yet. Not unless we find something in the grounds.'

Frank hesitates. 'What if we had a secret weapon?'

'Go on, tell me. Make my day.'

'Jocelyn Fitzwilliam.' He raises a hand. 'It's all very tentative, all very hush-hush, but when she spoke to the kids up at the ruined castle, and gave them the diamonds, she sent a message.'

'Did you know about this?' Sparks fires a broadside straight at Templeton. 'When did you plan to tell me?'

'It's my fault,' Frank says. 'She wants to meet me alone. No other police. Just me and...'

He hesitates.

'And?'

'I want Richard Trevelyan there.'

'Hmm.'

'And his wife, Maggie.'

'What the f—'

'And Janice.'

Sparks groans, and sits down. 'I'll order a picnic basket, shall I? Take the kids, too. I'll chip in couple of bottles of that fizzy wine Mrs Sparks likes. What's it called? Prozac?'

'Prosecco.' A stifled laugh from Templeton receives a warning glare, like a slap across the face.

'So, when is this gathering of the clans to take place?'

'Tonight, tomorrow night or the night after. Soon, though.'

'I ought to be there.' Sparks says. 'Only... evening, you say? There's a concert at Lisa's school tomorrow. And tonight,' He glances at his watch. 'Mrs Sparks goes to a yoga class. Never misses.'

'It might be better if we agree to her terms. No other police. You can spend the evening with Mrs Sparks and the little... and the kids.'

Sparks wavers.

'Well. I suppose you're more than qualified. Okay, but give me a ring if there's anything to report. Only if it's before ten o'clock. Mrs Sparks, you know... early to bed, early to rise, *et cetera*. Emergencies only after ten.'

Frank nods. 'Of course.'

Sparks checks his watch and grimaces. 'Right, time to go back to our house guest. One more grilling and then we let the bastard go. Tomorrow, sharpish, we hit the house and grounds. I want to be there when we present him with the warrant. Thinking about that is the only thing that'll save him from a slap.'

Chapter 69

'And then I told your stepdad what Melissa said about Rupert, and he wrote it down in his notebook. He said he'd find out the truth about everything. The other detective looked like he was going to cry. They believed me. They knew I was telling the truth, about Melissa's ghost, and everything.'

Molly's eyes shine, and her dark hair swims in waves around her head, catching at last on her shoulder, and lying there. She brushes it away with a flick of her hand, and runs ahead up the cliff path. 'I like your stepdad,' she calls to Jason. 'He's the best.'

Pride bubbles like a warm soup inside Jason.

'Yeah, he's the best detective in the city. Everyone says so. He's caught hundreds and hundreds of bad people. Murderers, thieves, drug smugglers and...' He stops, having exhausted his repertoire of criminality. 'All sorts of nasty people.'

'Rupert Fitzwilliam will be the worst criminal he's ever caught,' Molly raises her arms sideways, and spins round and round, her face raised to the sky. 'Your dad will lock him away for ever and ever for killing Melissa.' She stops, and drops her arms to her side, swaying, dizzy. 'Poor Molly Toodle. I haven't told her yet.'

Jason is unsure what to say. 'She'll be pleased.'

'She may stop coming to see you,' said Sammy. 'You'll be able to go back to a proper school.'

'My school is a proper school. It's a kind of hospital school, that's all.'

'You should come to my school.' Jason steers the subject optimistically forward.

Sammy's thoughts drift towards his own concerns, and the memory of Dominic flashes like a lightning strike. 'The watchtower isn't far away now.' Was it only two weeks since their paths crossed, up here, near the tower?

'Will we see whales and dolphins?' Jason hurries to catch up with Molly, as Sammy follows behind them.

'We might.' Sammy sounds doubtful.

'We should have brought our binoculars,' Jason says.

Molly nods. 'Do you have binoculars at the cottage?'

Jason thinks for a moment. 'No. But still...'

Sammy strides past them. 'You don't half talk some rubbish sometimes, Jase,' he says, trying to sound like his dad. 'If you haven't got any, how could you bring them?'

'If I had, and if I brought them, we might see whales and dolphins.' Jason frowns. 'Just because I haven't, doesn't mean I couldn't have.'

He pauses and looks from Molly to Sammy, then he bursts out laughing, and runs on ahead.

'You're mad, you are,' Sammy shouts.

'That's what Frank says,' Jason shouts back, 'but he's madder than anyone. He pretends to be a gorilla, and chases me.'

'I'd like to see that,' Molly says. 'I'd laugh.'

The cliff path becomes less steep, and levels onto a heathery summit. A sudden wind rises, as if it has been hiding. The weather is changing. Clouds gather above them, and grow darker and deeper, and the sea trembles. Sammy looks out over the grey spine of the ocean towards the horizon. It's invisible now, buried below a mist which creeps towards them over the tremulous sea. Sammy checks the wind and sky with the authority of a born and bred fisherman. They have an hour, maybe less. The wind is already strong. Soon the rain will come, and will last for much of the day. The streets in Leybury will glisten as pools form. Then the pools will join together into rivulets, which will hurry towards the harbour and the sea, like they're going home. People will shut their doors, sit in their living rooms, and watch the television, read, or check their computers and phones. The streets will be empty.

His village.

His home.

The place he always wants to be, with his mum and dad, with *The Lovely Maggie* rocking and rolling against the harbour wall, humming and dancing to her own silent song.

A sharp gust of wind strikes him.

'Soon as we've been in the watchtower, we'd better get back,' he cries. 'We should make it before the rain. Maybe.'

He runs towards the door, and pulls at the catch. It won't open. He lifts the catch, and pulls again.

'Let me try,' Molly says. She takes hold of the catch, and pulls hard. 'It must be locked.'

Sammy frowns. 'It's never locked unless some of the older kids get in there, and damage things. Then my dad locks it up for a week or two until they get tired, and go somewhere else. My dad has the only key. It hangs on a nail in the pantry. We haven't used it for ages.'

'Maybe something has fallen, and jammed it inside,' Jason says, giving the door an extra hard tug, rattling it hard. He gives it a push for good measure.

'It opens outwards,' Sammy says. 'You can't jam it from the inside.' He stops and steps back, and back again. 'Come on,' he whispers, 'we've got to go.'

Molly presses her ear against the wood. 'I can hear something.'

'I can hear something, too,' Jason says. He giggles. 'Maybe someone's in there with their girlfriend.'

'Don't be gross,' Molly says. 'Shh! There it is again. Something's moving about.'

'Maybe it's rats.'

Molly shudders.

'I don't like rats.'

'Maybe it's snakes.'

'I don't like snakes either.'

Sammy stands a few steps away, transfixed. His voice is strangely urgent. 'We've got to go. We've got to go *now*. Come on.'

'We've only just got here,' Molly's words fade to a whisper as she turns towards him. 'What's the matter? You look scared.'

Sammy starts to run back along the path. 'Come on, we've got to go,' he calls back over his shoulder.

'What's the matter with him?' Jason looks at Molly.

'I don't know.'

They run to catch up.

'What's the matter?' Jason asks.

'There's a bolt on the inside.' Sammy stares beyond them, towards the watchtower. 'Someone has locked the door, from the inside.'

Molly's dark eyes widen. 'You mean...?'

Sammy nods.

'There really *is* someone inside.' Jason's voice shrinks to a tightly rolled whisper even though the watchtower is thirty metres away. The wind blows his words back over his head towards the village.

'And I know who it is,' Sammy says.

Chapter 70

At 7am three police cars draw up outside Leybury Grange. Sparks strides up the granite steps, and beats heavily on the door.

'Open up. We have a warrant to search these premises.'

There is something so triumphant in his tone that Frank can't resist a smile.

'I hope we wake the bastard up.' Sparks beats on the door with his palm. 'Come on, we haven't got all day.'

The door opens and Rupert invites them inside with an exaggerated flourish, and a sarcastic bow.

'If you expected to disturb me from my sleep or catch me unawares, I'm afraid you'll be disappointed.' His look holds Sparks like a velvet pin. 'I rarely sleep. An hour here or there.' He flicks back a shirt sleeve to expose an expensive watch. 'I was expecting you earlier. Father warned me you'd come bothering us with a warrant. Mother said you'd try to catch us unawares.' He glances over his shoulder towards the dead heart of the house. 'Mother and father are never wrong.'

Frank exchanges a look with Templeton.

'Mother? Father?' Sparks turns to Frank. 'I didn't know his parents were here.'

Rupert's laugh is slow and humourless.

'Ghosts,' he says. 'Just ghosts. Do come in.'

Sparks delivers a flurry of instructions to the group of officers gathered on the gravel drive. Some head away into the grounds, others disappear inside.

'Would you care for a coffee or tea while your minions do their work?' Rupert's calm seems unshakeable, but Frank knows just how thin that patina of confidence can be; it can crack and splinter at a touch. He watches as Rupert drifts towards the dining room. 'I'm about to take breakfast. A full English is the only way for a civilised man to begin the day. These modern people with their muesli and yoghurt have no idea how unpatriotic they are. Please, join me. I prepared enough for all of us.'

'Will your parents be joining us?' Sparks goads.

In the dining room, Sparks picks up a plate, and serves himself. He doesn't waste a glance on Rupert. Frank does. He sees a flash of something unpleasant as it passes across his eyes, like a carnivore eyeing its prey.

'My family don't like visitors. They'll stay hidden until you leave.'

'Ah well,' Sparks slides three rashers of bacon onto his plate beside scrambled eggs, tomatoes and toast. 'All the more for us.'

He draws back a chair and drops onto it, squatting, legs astride, an uncouth tableau designed to irritate his host.

Frank and Templeton join him and watch Rupert assume a proprietorial position at the head of the table, separated from his guests by several empty seats. A grandfather clock in the corner of the room chimes a languorous eight.

'Eight o'clock,' Rupert checks his watch to synchronise the time. 'I fear a change in the weather will soon be upon us. Your men searching the grounds will have a hard day of it. I do hope you provide them with suitable outdoor clothing. I could, perhaps, open the kitchen. Your men would be happy below stairs, I think. It's where my family housed our own minions. There's a kettle and some chipped mugs. There may even be some of that ghastly instant coffee which people of the lower orders drink nowadays. Sadly, I have no one-cup tea bags.'

He pauses to savour a bite of egg and bacon, sighing.

'Fresh, local produce. Not that it makes it any better of course. People are such fools, don't you think? This fresh, local produce could be grown by a drunken oaf with the hygiene standards of a homeless person. Who would know? Fresh, local produce! It means nothing, does it? It could be fresh, local, badly produced, poor quality, insanitary produce which has been vomited on by a drunken horticulturalist, could it not?'

Sparks stuffs a full mouth like an overflowing suitcase, and chews.

'Tastes good to me.'

Frank allows a subdued chuckle to travel the length of the table, where it raises an evil look from his host.

'Cafes which offer home-cooked meals are the same, I think.' He looks directly at Rupert, playing the game. 'They advertise it like a speciality. I've been in places where you wouldn't feed the home-cooked food to a starving dog.'

Rupert claps his hands excitedly. 'You understand,' he cries. 'How delightful to meet a policeman capable of noticing such things. I'd always believed you people were fish-and-chips, pie-and-cake types. I had never imagined discerning palates or fine judgement. You have taken me quite by surprise.'

He smiles sweetly.

'Oh, there are a lot of things about me that would surprise you.'

'Do tell. I'm intrigued.'

Rupert leans his elbows on the table, and props his chin with his hands. Frank leans back and rests an arm across the chair.

'We see all sorts of people in our profession, Rupert - victims, villains, the beaten and the beaters, those who thieve and those who have stuff taken from them, the violators and the violated. Yeah, we see them all. You get so you recognise them straight off. Do you ever watch crime films where the bad guys burst into a bank, waving guns about, shouting and threatening, their faces covered in masks so that only their eyes can be seen? Yeah? Well when we get them, when they're sitting opposite us, answering questions, they're still wearing a mask. Only now it's different. We get the outraged, innocent mask. *How could you think that I'd do something like that? I'm not like that. Ask anyone.* You get the silent, tough guy mask. *Fuck off, copper. I'm telling you nothing. You got nothing on me. No comment. No comment. Blah, blah.* Then there's the intellectual, the smug, superior mask. This guy thinks he's so smart he can outwit you at every turn. And there's the victim of course. *You stitched me up. It wasn't me. You've always had it in for me.*

'People like me and DI Sparks here, we get a feel for the truth, for what lies behind the masks. Sit someone in front of us for an hour or two and we can see right through them.'

'How utterly fascinating. I never imagined. Do you think I'm wearing a mask, right now?'

'Oh yes, Rupert. Yours is a particularly interesting mask. There are times when it's so convincing that it looks like it's tattooed to your skin. But it's a mask alright, isn't it, Sparks?'

Sparks nods. 'We see right through it. Like looking at an X-ray.'

Tell me what you see beneath it. I'm dying to know.'

Frank leans forward, and concentrates on the contours of Rupert's face. 'When I look really closely, I can see something oozing from the sides of the mask, something bubbling out, and trickling down the side of your neck. I can see the mask dissolving. It starts around the eyes and the mouth. That's where you see it first. Yeah.' He turns to Sparks. 'See that ooze, Sparks? What does that tell you?'

Sparks doesn't look up. He keeps eating and speaks full-mouthed. 'It tells me he's scared. He's just a little kid who's scared of the dark.'

'You see, Rupert? DI Sparks got it in one. An insecure, frightened child, locked in a room, in the dark. He's so scared, this child, because he carries that darkness with him wherever he goes. He's looking over his shoulder all the time, because the monsters that live in that darkness are always there, just behind him.'

'Is this me you're describing, Detective, or you?'

There is a brittle edge to Rupert's voice now, and a sneer on his lips. The mask is slipping, the patina revealing web-like fractures.

'Oh, I merely hypothesise.' Frank smiles. 'But behind your mask, I'd say there's an insecure, frightened kid. He's too frightened to love or care because he doesn't think it'll be returned. He thinks he'll be scorned or mocked or rejected. It's easier to hate, easier to feign indifference, easier not to care.'

Rupert rises to his feet and the chair falls away behind him.

'You don't know the first thing about me, Detective. If you did, you'd be very careful. I could rip your pathetic job away from under you without leaving my seat. You think you're safe, you think nobody can touch you because you've got a perch halfway up your professional tree. Well, let me tell you, even the tree isn't safe.'

He turns towards Sparks, spitting words like bullets.

'You think you're better than me because you've got a Mrs Sparks and two kids. Yeah, I know all about you. I know everything. Let me tell you, nobody is safe in this world. Nobody. The whole edifice can come crashing down around you.'

'Are you threatening me, Mr Fitzwilliam? Are you threatening my family?' Sparks is on his feet now, fists tight round the edge of the table, knuckles white.

Frank raises a calming hand. He hasn't moved, and only a slight tightening of his hands, and a tensing of the muscles in his neck, betrays him.

'As I said, Rupert. I merely hypothesise. If I've overstepped the mark, I'm sorry. Now, I must see how our police officers are faring.'

He walks towards the door. Sparks, whose eyes are still fixed angrily on Rupert, gradually relaxes, and strides after him. Frank hesitates and looks back.

'Thank you for the breakfast,' he says.

Sparks closes the door tight behind them.

From behind the closed door, plates and dishes crash and fracture against the wall. There's a howl, like the stifled cry of a wild beast. Frank pauses, glances back.

'I think I've just opened a cage door that was best left shut.'

'You'll have me feeling sorry for the bastard.' Sparks strides away.

Frank continues to look back at the dining room door. Everything is quiet now. The storm has passed.

'I think I already do,' he says, but the words are for nobody but himself.

Chapter 71

Molly, Sammy and Jason descend from the cliff path in time to surround Frank's car. They all speak at once.

'Woah! Steady on!' Frank forces a path between them, and closes the car door. 'One at a time. You first, Molly.'

'We went to the watchtower. We were going to look for whales and dolphins. But we couldn't get in. The door was locked.' She draws a hand across her hair, and flicks a curl back from her face, taking the opportunity to draw a rapid breath. 'There was someone inside.'

Frank sits on the harbour-side bench, and rests his hands on his knees. Molly sits next to him but the two boys remain impatiently standing. Sammy glances back towards the cliff path, as if expecting a figure to appear, following them to the village. Jason wipes away beads of sweat from his forehead.

'Maybe someone just wanted a bit of peace and quiet, without three noisy children. Did you knock to see if they'd answer?'

The children glance at each other. Molly shakes her head.

'How certain are you that there was someone inside? Maybe the door had stuck, and you just couldn't open it?'

'It was locked from the inside,' Sammy says. 'There's a bolt.'

'I heard someone moving about,' Molly says.

'Me, too.' Jason sits down beside Frank. 'You believe us, don't you?'

'Of course, I do, but it doesn't mean they're doing anything wrong. Like I said, it could just be—'

'It was Dominic.' Sammy stares beyond him, out over the harbour, to the sea. His eyes settle on the horizon, a thin glaze over his eyes. His voice is dull, as if the words belong to someone else. 'It's his secret place. I know it's him.'

Frank flicks open his phone. 'Templeton?' he asks. He covers the mouthpiece and speak to the children. 'If it is Dominic, we'll soon have him locked safely away. If not... well, no harm done. Better safe than sorry.'

'What if he knew it was us? What if he's got away?' Sammy's voice shakes, and there are tears in his eyes, despite his efforts to check them.

'He won't get far, Sammy, not this time. He's run out of places to hide. Now, don't worry. Go home, find something to play, watch TV, go on one of those interminable games you kids play nowadays.'

'Will you tell us if you catch him?' Sammy runs the back of his hand across his eyes and sniffs.

'Of course. But Sammy, I need you to do something for me. I'd do it myself, only I have to make a few phone calls so that the officers at the Grange can redeploy.'

It was a half-lie but Frank could see that Sammy needed something to do, some responsibility to take. Either he would ride those waves that threatened him, or they would overwhelm him, and he'd drown. He looks at their three pale faces, forces back the surging anger he feels, and draws a smile from somewhere.

'Sammy, I need you to find your mum and dad, and explain exactly what has happened. Tell them I'm at home if they want to speak to me. Tell them DS Templeton is on his way to the watchtower right now, with a couple of cars. Tell them what I've just told you. Can you do that for me?'

Sammy's lips tighten. He nods.

'Right, off you go. Molly and Jason, you two can come with me. Janice will phone Molly's mum and dad and we'll take things from there.'

It's late afternoon when Frank and DI Sparks are called back to Leybury Grange. Sparks is not in the best of humour.

'Whatever it is they've found,' he says, 'they should've found it earlier. Mrs Sparks will give me hell if I miss Lisa's concert, and Lisa will stomp about with a face like a wet sock. This is bloody inconvenient.' Sparks ploughs his own deep furrow. 'And what's this nonsense about a room he won't let them in? If he's playing silly buggers, I'll have him locked up as quick as you can say *sanctimonious bastard.*'

A police sergeant, down to shirt sleeves, and perspiring like a boxer despite the overcast sky, meets them on the drive.

"It's over there in the trees,' he says, drawing a hairy forearm over his brow. 'WPC Brownlow found it. You know, the young, keen one. We might have missed it.'

'Remind me to thank her,' Sparks says.

'There's some recently disturbed ground which was covered over in grass and branches and leaves. PC Brownlow felt the ground give a little under her feet, and stopped to check.'

'Bloody Sherlock Holmes,' says Sparks. 'Perhaps she can explain to Mrs Sparks.'

'We dug it up, right down to the heavier soil.'

'And?'

'The forensic team are taking samples. We won't get the results until tomorrow.'

Sparks' face brightens.

'Tomorrow, eh? Right. Show me what you've found, and then you can lead me to WPC Brownlow, so I can commend her enthusiasm and efficiency. Now, what's this about a room we can't access?'

The sergeant nods towards the house. 'It's locked, and his lordship is being awkward. I didn't want to kick the door down without your say-so.'

'Do you want to sort him out, Frank?' Sparks asks. 'Given a choice, I'd rather deal with a muddy grave.'

Frank braces himself, and walks across to the house.

'Where is he?'

Raised eyes indicate the stairs.

'He's perched up there on the top flight. Won't let anyone past. He's got a bottle of brandy for company.'

'The tower?'

A cursory nod.

By the time Frank reaches the narrow stairs leading to the Trophy Room, Rupert has slipped from the chair, and sits with his back against the wall. The bottle lies half empty beside him. When he sees Frank, he struggles to his feet.

'Thou shalt not pass,' he proclaims with a grand gesture. 'It is written, like the sign on the gates of hell. *Abandon Hope all ye who Enter Here.*' He drops down again onto the bottom step, and taps the space beside him. 'Sit,' he says, slurring. 'Take a drink with me.'

Frank sits down, but declines the drink.

Rupert studies the bottle, takes a drink, and sets it down beside him.

'I too am on duty,' he whispers, as if to a fellow conspirator, his face close to Frank's ear, brandied breath weaving around him like smoke. 'I am ordered to guard this room.' Another grand gesture with a raised arm. 'To the death.'

'We have to see what's in the room, Rupert. It's easier if you just let us in.'

Rupert struggles to his feet, and takes up a defensive position. He brandishes the bottle like a weapon. 'Never!' he slurs. 'I've seen the people you brought to my home. Insensitive brutes with piggy eyes and narrow mouths. They have no feeling, no compassion. They are coarse and ignorant. You cannot expect such people to respect the sanctity of my room.'

'Your room?'

'Mine.' Rupert sways forward and then, as he is about to fall, steadies himself. He angles his head towards Frank as if to gain a clear focus. 'And theirs.'

'Whose?'

'My ghosts,' Rupert whispers.

He pauses, concentrates, stares. He raises a hand to his lips.

'I'll show you.' He peers over Frank's shoulder. 'Not them. Just you. Shh! Follow me.'

At the top of the stairs, he fumbles in a deep pocket for a key. The door opens silently, as if it floats on oil. He ushers Frank inside, and closes the door, locking it after him. He returns the key to his pocket, and stands with his back to the door. 'They shall not pass,' he says, theatrically. 'I shall give my life. Oafs! Villains!' He reaches behind the shadow of the door and draws out a large blade, like a bayonet from a Great War rifle. He brandishes it.

'Put that down, will you?' Franks stands with his back to the window, braced to fight off an attack; taut, tense. 'Just put it down, eh? Before someone gets hurt.'

Rupert looks at the offending blade as if it has materialised just that moment in his palm. He rests it carefully behind the door.

'Shh!' He raises a finger to his lips.

Frank, without letting his eyes move too far from the bayonet, studies the room. Cold stone, a small arched window, a single bed frame in the corner, a soiled mattress above a tangle of metal springs, an iron headboard. In the corner, a small cupboard.

'May I?'

'Of course.'

As Frank kneels beside the cupboard, Rupert stands by the window and stares out, down into the garden below. In the distance the summer house lies against a background of trees, the lawns around it cut finely like a bowling green. Frank reaches across and removes the bayonet. He lays it beside the cupboard where he can see it. Then he opens the cupboard, and looks inside. Dust and damp, a shallow pile of children's books, and curled notebooks.

'I spent hours at this window,' Rupert says. 'When I wasn't allowed to join them, I watched Louise and Jocelyn, as they played in the garden. Hours and hours and hours and hours. Day after day.'

Frank brushes the dust from a cover, and opens a fragile book.

'Are these yours?'

Rupert glances over, nods, and returns to study the garden.

'Have your officers found anything in the grounds?' As if a switch has been thrown, the cold, indifferent mask is back on his face. 'Bodies, perhaps? My forebears had a penchant for unsavoury acts of violence. You never know what they may have buried among those trees. Or who.' He leans forward, suddenly animated. 'I do hope they stumble on buried treasure. Perhaps something left by my ancestors for bad times. How exciting that would be, and very helpful in times of austerity.'

But the effort is too much. He turns idly away.

'I almost wish...' he starts to say, then stops.

'You almost wish what?'

'Oh, nothing. Just idle thoughts. I find this room quickly fills with melancholy.' He gives an odd smile. 'And ghosts. So many ghosts. If you look at the stones long enough, you can see them. They creep out, and drop into the emptiness. I was scared at first, but it passed. It passed.'

Frank flicks through the pages of the notebook, and feels a chill spread through him. Childish scrawls; ugly, distorted faces emerging from walls and mirrors, heads mounted against the stony background like trophies on a wall.

Wide mouths, teeth dripping, eyes wide and staring. He shudders, and holds the book towards Rupert.

'Are these your ghosts?'

'The faces of those who came before. Those who shared my prison.'

Frank continues to leaf through the book.

'Jesus,' he says. 'What the hell happened here?'

Rupert looks once more towards the garden.

'Look, you see the clearing around the summer house.' Frank steps across, and stands beside him as Rupert leans forward and points. 'See the bushes and trees? We used to play there, when mother and father allowed me. Those were the happiest days of my life, you know. On other days, sadder days, days when the door was locked against me, I watched Louise and Maddy from here. They would stop and wave to me as they played. I think they felt sorry for me. Then Louise left, and the garden was empty. I blamed her at first for deserting me, for leaving me alone in my prison. I blamed her for a long time. But eventually I came to understand. The burden of responsibility was just too much. She fled.'

'And Jocelyn?' Frank's voice is low, awed by the sudden transformation in his host. A voice is reaching out to him, as if from an impenetrable depth. It is an echo, a barely comprehendible whisper, a murmur of waves, of wind, carrying with it a story he cannot grasp. Wasted days stretching back like Banquo's mirror, on and on into the past. But a past which, like that of another ghost, is linked at the ankles with a chain of interminable length, a chain from which no link can ever be removed. Such horror.

Frank raises a hand to lay it on Rupert's shoulder, one human being to another, but he pauses and lets the hand drop to his side. The spell is broken. As if a switch is thrown, Rupert is transformed.

'Oh, look,' he cries. 'There's that ghastly little sergeant of yours. I think he's given up for the day. Poor little man. All that effort and nothing to show for it except a sweaty skin, and a sore back. I'd feel sorry for him if he wasn't such a repulsive little squab. Oh, how lovely. There's your Detective Inspector. Mr Sparky or some such silly name. I don't know how you tolerate his presence. Imagine working with him all day. I'd rather have pins in my eyes. Imagine the conversation! Ugh! I shudder at the very thought. Poor Mr

Sparky, he wants to go home. He's looking at his watch. It'll be growing dark soon.'

He runs across to the door, like a child awaiting a gift, unlocks it, and flings it open.

'Come on!' he cries. 'Let's hear what they've got to tell us. Then they can go away, and you and I can share a glass of brandy, and laugh about them. What do you say? Wouldn't that be a jolly way to end the day?'

He doesn't wait for an answer, which is just as well because Frank doesn't have one. His head spins with a turmoil of thoughts and feelings; a maelstrom of churning impressions.

Sparks frowns as he sees Rupert's beaming face in the light of the doorway. He ignores him and speaks directly to Frank.

'I've closed it down for the night, Frank. We'll come back tomorrow. By then we'll have the forensic results on the soil samples.'

'Another day?' Rupert beams. 'Oh, how joyous! I rarely have company, and this has been so exciting.'

Sparks' cheek pulses in irritation.

'Anything up there?' he raises his head to indicate the tower, and the Trophy Room.

Frank hesitates. So much, and so little. Where to begin.

'No,' he says at last. 'Nothing.' He turns to Rupert. 'We'll be back tomorrow.'

'Good, that's good. You should stay for dinner. There's so much more we could talk about. Do say you'll come.'

Frank holds out a hand.

'We'll see you tomorrow, Mr Fitzwilliam.'

Frank's hand trembles as he opens the door of the car, but only when he sits down does he realise that his whole body is shaking as if he had been exposed to a fierce cold which has penetrated every limb.

'What the hell was that about?' Sparks drops heavily into the rear seat. He checks his watch. 'I've missed Lisa's performance. Deep shit is what I'm in now. Deep, deep shit.'

Frank starts the engine. 'We'll pick Templeton up, and head back. I'll drop you off at the school. Maybe you'll catch some of it. You can pretend you were there longer, tucked away at the back.'

'It's worth a try. Come on. Here's Templeton now. Put your foot down.'

As the car heads down the drive towards the road, Sparks leans back.

'Well, are you going to tell me? What the hell was all that about, back there on the step. You and your new mate, Rupert. Dinner invitations.'

Frank, who is still gripping the wheel to quell the tremor in his hands, shakes his head.

'I have no idea. But I'll tell you one thing. I'm not a man who scares easily, but Rupert Fitzwilliam scares the hell out of me. It's like standing on the edge of a volcano, looking down into a bubbling pool of magma, and feeling the ground crumbling at your feet. Everything about him is unstable, everything is moving, and I've no idea where it's leading.'

'Straight to a prison cell,' says Sparks.

Templeton, who notes the tension in Frank's hands and eyes, speaks more quietly.

'Or a padded one.'

Chapter 72

*I*t's nearly dark. *The water in Leybury harbour stirs, restless waves reaching up the sea wall, whispering secrets to the hushed village. What has it heard? Rumblings, strange sounds, warnings of dangers yet unfaced, of terrors yet unrealised.*

Everything is troubled tonight. The clouds flit fitfully, searching for cover, while the moon ducks behind them, and the stars peep down as if through charcoal curtains, or close their eyes and feign sleep.

The harbour is deserted. The rain has ceased for the moment. But you, from your seat by the window of The Harbour Inn, can see lights trapped in glistening pools, caught and pinned, shimmering on a trembling surface. You sip a rich, red wine and sit back. Your holiday is nearly over. Another day and then the weary journey back to the city, and the monotonous routine of work. Just memories and photographs to remind you.

This is a night for reflection, a night to submerge yourself in the fragile melancholy of life.

From the corner of your eye you see a movement as something, cat-like, emerges from the darkness. But this is no cat. It's a girl, a dark coat wrapped round her, a hood pulled over her head. She hurries, head down, towards the harbour, where she pauses.

Is she waiting for someone?

She looks left and right, rising on her toes as if to see even further into the shadows, where the lights cannot reach. She pulls her collar closer round her neck. As you watch, the rain returns and rivulets course down the window, partially obscuring your view.

Perhaps that's why you don't see the second figure until she is close to the girl, a figure clothed in a long, dark coat, with an equally dark scarf wrapped around

276

her head and neck. As she reaches the girl, she holds out two hands which the girl readily grasps. The girl starts talking at once, asking questions you presume, her movements animated.

Her hood falls back momentarily, and you sit forward, suddenly curious. Molly.

But who is the strange woman who now takes the child's cheeks in her hands, and talks to her, slowly, patiently?

Is it Jocelyn Fitzwilliam?

Who else could it be? For whom would Molly have so many questions, if not Jocelyn? Molly reaches in her pocket, and draws out a piece of paper, folded to a small square. She opens it, and gestures to its contents. What does it say? Is it an invitation from Jocelyn, secretly given, to meet here as the sun sets, and darkness fills the streets?

So many questions.

Jocelyn bends down, her knees almost touching the ground, and rests her hands on the girl's shoulders. She looks in her eyes and talks softly, slowly, raising a hand to quell the questions the young girl wants to ask. Talking. Talking. Explaining.

But explaining what?

After a few minutes, she rises, and takes Molly's hand. She turns towards the inn and, for a moment, you think she has seen you, and you draw back, fearful that you are caught in the light like an actor on a stage. You, the audience of this strange narrative, are now turned actor. You reach for your glass, look away, focus your eyes, if not your mind, elsewhere.

When you look back, Jocelyn is leading Molly towards the Trevelyan's house. They pause at the steps, and a second figure joins them. Another child. Sammy, perhaps, although you cannot be sure. You cannot see for the rain which gathers in strength and blurs the window. All you discern are the three of them, Jocelyn in the centre, her arms gathered around the young shoulders, as they walk along the harbour, and take another flight of steps to the first of the modern houses, perched above the old cottages.

They hesitate for a moment, and then Jocelyn knocks on the door.

In the light which illuminates this new stage you see Sandra, Molly's mother and, just behind her, Daniel. The figures disappear inside, and the door shuts.

Half an hour later, as you prepare to face the grim torrents of rain which pour ceaselessly now, dropping vertical curtains across the village, you see a light appear in the doorway and Jocelyn, glancing quickly left and right, flits like a shadow. She walks directly along the harbour to another cottage, a holiday cottage currently occupied by Frank Miller, Janice and Jason.

She waits for a moment until a light comes on in the hallway and the door opens. She disappears inside, and darkness descends.

Chapter 73

Jason sits on the third step of the narrow cottage staircase, his feet on the carpeted floor. An unfamiliar dark coat drips from the coat hook on the wall adjacent to the front door; above it a scarf. He listens closely trying to catch wisps of conversation as they slip from the lounge. His mum and Frank are in there, Richard and Maggie, too. They arrived, breathless and strangely anxious, shortly after the first visitor.

He knows the first visitor. They met her, him and Sammy, that day at the ruined castle. He carried a message from her to Frank. Now she's here, just like she promised. As she passed him in the narrow hallway, she smiled at him; a nice smile, warm and a little sad too, like she carried a burden which she needed to put down.

He flits to the top of the stairs, watching through the wooden rails, as his mum emerges from the lounge, and muffled words break momentarily free.

Cups of tea. Cake. Biscuits. His mum's solution to any crisis.

When she returns with a tray and cups and plates, and the door closes behind her, he slips down to the bottom step. The only sound is the letter box rattling, and an impatient voice outside.

'Let me in. I'm getting soaked.'

Sammy.

Jason opens the door enough for him to slip through. They sit, side by side, on the stair.

'Have they said anything?'

Jason puts a finger on his lips, and then to his ear. Be quiet and listen.

The voices are subdued but they hear Jocelyn, and, occasionally, staccato words from Frank as he asks questions. Once, they hear a cry from Maggie, quickly stifled, a gasp from Janice, but no words. Jocelyn talks and talks, her words as ceaseless as the rain.

'What's she saying?'

'I can't hear.'

'Shall we go closer?'

'They'll hear us.'

'I want to hear what they're saying.'

Sammy tiptoes to the lounge door, and kneels down beside it. Jason settles beside him, and the words trickle through.

'He has suffered so much,' they hear Jocelyn say, her voice hushed.

Her words are lost for a moment. Then they emerge, once again.

'I am all that he has left... I scarcely know what to do or where to turn...'

Another murmur, sounds lost in the darkness.

'...unbearable, cruel burden... murders...'

Then silence. The boys hold their breath, their eyes wide.

Murders.

They press closer to the door, aware of a heavy silence that has fallen within. Then the door bursts open, and Frank stands there, hands on hips, glaring down at them.

'How did you know we were here?' Jason says.

'I'm a detective, remember?' He points towards the stairs. 'And I used to be a ten-year-old boy who was more inquisitive than was good for him. Now go! And don't let me find you here again. You go with him, Sammy. We might as well have you both under one roof.'

'Is that our Sammy?' They hear Maggie's voice from the lounge. 'Well, the little blighter. Just wait...'

But by the time she reaches the door, the two boys have fled to the safety of Jason's bedroom.

'Boys,' says Maggie, as the door closes once again.

Up in the bedroom, Jason and Sammy sit on the bed's edge.

'Murder,' Sammy says.

Jason turns to him.

'She said "murders".'

Even the closed window cannot hold out the chill that slips round them; the breath of ghosts.

There is nothing to do but talk, then lie back in the silence and, finally, fall into an uneasy slumber.

Jason is awoken by the sound of the front door opening, and whispered voices. He hears Frank, urging, persuading, and Jocelyn's quiet tones, arguing, refusing. He creeps to the door, and opens it. The voices surge briefly on the cold air.

'If I can help him, if there is the slenderest chance,' Jocelyn is saying, 'I have to try. Promise me, you'll help. One day, that's all I ask.'

Jason peers between the banister rails and he sees Frank nod.

'You have no idea how he will react,' he hears him say.

Jocelyn smiles, as she had at him, in the castle.

'He's my brother. He won't harm me.'

'I'll be there, no matter what,' Frank says. 'That's the deal.'

The door closes, the air grows still, and silence grips the house.

Chapter 74

Frank doesn't go in to work until late the next day, long after lunch. Templeton is waiting for him.

'We've got him.' Templeton's voice is triumphant. 'Dominic Sheedy.'

'In the watchtower?'

'Him, a sleeping bag, a few packets of crisps and half a dozen cans of lager.'

'Has he said much?'

'Sparks got to work on him. I think he fancied a workout after dealing with Rupert Fitzwilliam. It didn't take him long to persuade Dominic that he was completely screwed. He left him to weigh up his lack of options for half an hour, and then started again.'

'What did he say about Sammy?'

'He admitted physical and sexual assault. Rambled on about how maybe it would go better for him if he confessed.'

'The Trevelyans will be relieved. Do they know?'

'I phoned them.'

What about the smuggling racket?'

'That took a bit longer but, given the testimony of the Trevelyans, and what Carver and Zachary Blight gathered, his resistance didn't last long.'

'So, we've got him for both?'

'Yes.'

'Did he implicate anyone else further up the line?'

'He's too scared to point the finger. He said all his dealings were through Zachary Blight. There's no way he's going to turn on Rupert Fitzwilliam. He had the same solicitor too. The old guy. I think their private conversations laid clear parameters. His knees were shaking when they finished.'

Templeton leans back on his chair, and yawns.

'When this is over, I'm going to sleep for a week.'

'What about Melissa?'

A shake of the head from Templeton.

'Nothing. He kept saying, "ask Jocelyn Fitzwilliam", over and over. Every question, the same. "*Ask Jocelyn*". I thought Sparks was going to swing for him.'

'Where is Sparks?'

'He left about an hour ago, saying something about making up for missing most of the little Sparkler's concert.'

'I guess he didn't get away with it then.'

'I think he's taking her to the zoo.'

'Poor Sparks. The doghouse is an uncomfortable place to live. I guess we can cover for him. A bit of male solidarity. He pauses to check his watch. 'Besides, it may be better he doesn't know what I've got planned.'

'Oh?'

'I'll explain on the way to the Grange. Only...'

Templeton gathers his coat, and slings it over his shoulder. 'Only what?'

Frank sidesteps the question. 'How's the forensic work going?'

'The team was back out at the Grange this morning, but apparently it's like a swamp out there. They've called it a day.'

'Good,' Frank says. 'That'll help.'

'Help what? What are you up to, Frank?'

Again, no answer. 'What about the soil samples?'

Templeton's smile carries a heavy burden of irony. 'They pulled the stops out, worked overnight.'

'That was good of them.'

'Yeah, but they've got faces like a bulldog's arse this morning. I daren't tell you what they had to say.'

'I already know.'

'I doubt it. Apparently, those samples they collected and worked on, as a matter of extreme urgency, produced nothing. At least, nothing except—'

'Like I said, I know. We've got to get moving. We can't be late.'

'Late for what?'

'I'll explain in the car. You'd better let me drive. I've one hell of a story to tell. We can't have you veering off the road before we can arrest him.'

The swing door closes behind them. Frank and Templeton, still talking, head for the car park.

In the village, Richard, Maggie and Sammy sit at the kitchen table. In the corner, cardboard boxes collected from the Grantley supermarket, are stacked carelessly, ready to be packed. Maggie keeps busy, her mind occupied, avoiding thinking.

'So, it's all over?' she says. 'He's confessed.'

'I hope they lock him up, and throw away the bloody key. I hope the others gang upon him, and give him a hard time. I hope they...' Richard sees Sammy's anxious face looking at him. 'I hope they tie his shoe laces together so he falls flat on his ugly face. I hope they spit in his porridge. What do you say, our Sammy?'

'I hope they put vinegar in his custard and that it's lumpy custard and that the lumps aren't custard at all. I hope the lumps are big lumps of—'

'Enough!' For a moment, Maggie looks stern, then her face breaks into a smile. 'I hope they pull all his teeth out, and give him nothing but tough meat to chew,' she whispers in Sammy's ear.

'Will I still have to go to court?'

'I don't know, pet.' Maggie strokes his cheek. 'Maybe not. But whatever happens now, there'll be people to help you, and everyone will make it very easy for you. You've nothing to worry about. He's confessed. It's all over.'

'Do we still have to move?'

Maggie glances at Richard. 'I'm afraid so. We just don't have the money to stay. We've got to sell the boats, and the house to pay what we owe.'

Richard leans forward. 'But we'll be alright, you, me and your mum. We're together, aren't we? We're as tough as a navvies' boots, we are.'

'As a fisherman's boots,' Sammy corrects him.

'Aye, as a fisherman's boots.' He whispers conspiratorially. 'Especially mum. Her boots have six-inch nails.'

'Cheeky sod.' Maggie slips her arm around Sammy's shoulder, and hugs him close. 'But your dad's right. We're tough, we are. We're tough because we're a family, and because we love each other, and there's nothing and nobody can break that. Not Dominic, not Rupert, not anyone in the whole wide world. You remember that, Sammy. Don't ever forget it. We could live in a wet, slimy cave, and still be happy. We could live in a cage at the zoo with everyone watching us.'

'No, we couldn't. Don't be daft.' Sammy laughs.

'Well, we can certainly live in a nice little house somewhere else. We'll have some money coming in, we can keep warm and we'll have enough food to eat, and you can go to school, and grow up clever and kind...'

'And so long as I have a computer,' Sammy says, 'and a phone, and a bike...'

'And good friends.'

'And a fishing rod.' He pauses. 'Can Jason and Molly come and visit me?'

Maggie looks at Richard. A question darts like electricity between them. Strange smiles work across their lips, and find refuge behind the tears in their eyes.

Sammy looks alarmed. 'What's the matter? You're crying, both of you.'

'Go on, Richard,' Maggie says. 'You tell him.'

Richard sniffs and runs a hand across his eyes. 'There's something else, something we have to tell you.'

At Leybury Grange, Rupert Fitzwilliam leans on the sill of the Trophy Room window, and looks out over his realm. Emptiness everywhere. The old house, the expanse of grass, the mask of trees, the orb of sky, the clouds. Just a solitary crow winging from nothingness to dreary nothingness.

'I hope she comes home soon,' he says. 'She promised she would.'

The timbers of the old building creak and groan an aching resonance. He sits on the edge of the bed and pulls the soiled sheet onto his knee. He turns it round in his fingers, forming a loose knot.

From the corner of the room, darting from the shadows: a woman's voice like a nail on stone.

They all promise. Promises are easy, boy. Words, just words. Louise promised, and then she left. And then she died. Now Jocelyn.

'Jocelyn loves me. She'll come back to me. She promised never to leave me, not ever. And I believe her.'

A man's voice now, twisted and bitter, like a rope drawn around his throat.

You're a fool, boy. You always were a fool. We despised you.

The woman strikes again.

Everyone leaves. You drive them away. You disgust them. They hate you. Jocelyn will hate you too, just as we did. Evil child!

Rupert's voice is hard and cold. 'Jocelyn can't leave. There's nowhere else for her to go.'

You're a murderer. The woman's words cut like a dagger.

The man twists the blade. *You have blood on your hands.*

Poison in your heart.

Everything you touch.

Everything you love.

Dead. Dying. Killed by you.

Rupert grips the sill and focuses on the empty garden, and the summer house.

'Jocelyn won't desert me.'

The sound of a car on the driveway fractures his thoughts. He stands up, weary, and dusts himself down.

'I must play my part again,' he says. 'Every day it gets harder.'

From the wall, he sees the ghosts watch him through bitter eyes.

'And yet I must.'

He pauses only once, at the bottom of the stone steps. He can hear his ghosts cackling and whispering beyond the oak door.

Frank walks up the steps of the balustrade to the front entrance, takes a deep breath and walks inside.

In the distance, unseen to anyone, Templeton enters the summer house.

All is still.

Chapter 75

Rupert bounds down the final flight of carpeted stairs and flings back the door.

He reaches a hand out to Frank, and greets him gleefully. 'I believe you searched the family vault?'

'Yes, we did.'

'How terrifyingly ghoulish.'

'It would be an appropriate place to hide a body.'

'Rather cliched, I would have thought. Very gothic. Did you find anything?'

'You know I didn't. There was nothing to find.'

He pats Frank's arm. 'Well, it's best to be thorough.' For a moment, fleetingly, a look of anger courses like coloured dye through the veins of Rupert's face, burning him, and twisting his lips into a bare-toothed sneer. 'They are all there, give or take a few unfortunates who died abroad or were executed for one crime or another. The entire crew of HMS Leybury. Except mother and father, of course.'

'Oh?'

The sneer widens into a snarl.

'It was their dearest wish to be interred with their family. They were sticklers for tradition, my dear parents. Such a shame I couldn't accommodate.' He waits for a response from Frank but, finding none forthcoming, he continues. 'I had them cremated, and I dumped their ashes in the slurry pit at Grantley Home Farm. It was a touching ceremony. Ashes to ashes, shit to shit.'

Frank tries to look unconcerned. 'I believe they died in tragic circumstances. A joint suicide. Carbon monoxide, wasn't it?'

Rupert's brow creases as if struck by an unexpected thought. 'Tragic? Do you think so? I considered it most appropriate, and timely. They had lived far too long, and achieved so little. What was there to live for?'

'Their family, perhaps?'

Rupert's head falls back in affected laughter.

'My dear Detective, they didn't give a damn about us. They hated us as much as we hated them. The only difference was that they had all the power.' The laughter dries like a stain in the sun. 'Until they died, of course. My little *coup d'état*.'

He rests his eyes on Frank, adding weight to his words, then he walks towards the lounge.

Frank leans against the closed door.

'Jesus Christ,' he mutters to himself.

He follows Rupert to the lounge where he finds him staring out of the French windows.

'We arrested Dominic Sheedy last night.' Rupert continues to stare but his shoulders tense. He relaxes, and passes a casual hand through his hair. 'His testimony implicates you.'

'Ah.'

Rupert turns and holds out his wrists.

'I'll come peacefully, guv.' He feigns a cockney accent. 'You'll get no trouble from me. It's a fair cop.' When Frank doesn't move, he allows his hands to drop to his side. 'Are you going to charge me?'

'I'd prefer to charge you with murder,' Frank says. 'The murder of Harry Carver.'

Rupert spins round, a look of contempt wheeling like a bird across his face.

'He was a minion, a treacherous toad, a worthless speck on the spectacles of the world.'

'Treacherous?'

'He would have taken her from me. He was conspiring.'

'So, you follow him, club him to death, and dump him in the sea like so much garbage?'

'He was garbage, treacherous garbage. He would have betrayed her. He would have betrayed me.'

'So, you admit you killed him.'

'It's possible I did.' Rupert shrugs. 'I have difficulty keeping track of my actions, these days. I will, of course, deny everything. Diamonds, murders, everything. Dominic is a most untrustworthy fellow, with some decidedly sordid habits. I doubt anyone will listen to him, and you have no proof of my involvement in the death of the toad. If you had, you'd arrest me.'

Frank smiles. 'Perhaps later.'

Rupert opens the door and looks up at the sky. Charcoal clouds threaten the treetops.

'There's a storm coming,' he says. 'It's been building for a long time. All my life, I think. I'm relieved it's here at last.' Frank feels a tremor of alarm. Outside, caught in a gathering gloom, even the trees look as if they're about to retreat into the shadows, drawn into a different time, a different place. 'I thought it would come with flashes of lightning and thunder but it hasn't. It is just the same rolling darkness it's always been. Just deeper, more intense, like it is coiling into a knot, shrinking under the weight of its own gravity.' He turns, his eyes suddenly wild, and beats his chest with a clenched fist. 'It will settle here,' he cries, 'where my heart should be, a knot of infinite weight, infinite density.' His voice falls away into a groan. 'Where is Jocelyn? Why isn't she here?'

Rain speckles the glass; a mist gathers near the trees.

'Tell me about Melissa.'

The groan grows into a cry of pain and spreads around the lounge. Rupert drops his head between his arms and beats it once, twice against the glass of the open door, while his voice forces its way from some deep, secret prison inside him.

He slams the door shut, pushes past Frank, and stumbles down the corridor towards the stairs. 'I need Jocelyn!'

He stumbles up the staircase, up and up.

The Trophy Room.

'I've something to show you,' he says, like a child with a secret. At the foot of the final, narrow stair, he stops, and holds a finger to his lips. His eyes shine wildly, unnaturally bright, like there's a fire burning out of control in his mind. 'You can't tell anyone, though. The child you're looking for, Melissa, she's here, in the Trophy Room, where I keep my prizes. Come and meet her. I'll tell you everything.'

The steps seem to grow narrower and darker, and the door more distant. The air itself seems to gather round Frank like a pillow pressed against his face.

Rupert fumbles at the lock, and flings the door open. He steps inside, and disappears from sight. Then another wail emerges, even deeper and more pained, more savage and unreal than before. It spins and spirals through the air.

Frank leaps up the last few steps into the room.

In Grantley Police Station, a lonely figure sits on a narrow bed, his back resting against the wall. He looks up at a clock above the steel door with its viewing hatch, and tucks his knees. He watches the second hand move slowly towards the end of another minute. Never has he been so aware of the relentless, laboured passage of time.

Thirty minutes. He allows his eyes a few moments to slip their leash, and take in his surroundings again. He has signed his statement, been charged, photographed, had his fingerprints taken, and been led to his current location. There was something so very final about the door closing behind him, even though he knew his stay would be temporary. They told him he'd be taken from this cell to another, where he'd await trial.

Then there'll be another cell, another clock, another life.

Time to reflect on what has brought him here, perhaps.

Who to blame?

Himself, he mutters, nobody but himself. And no sooner have the words escaped than he draws them back, locks their door, imprisons them. He's never had a chance, not with his background, not with his family, his school, his teachers, the bastard kids who picked on him, bullied him. Then there's Sammy and his happy fucking family. It was only once, just once, for God's sake, and the kid bleats about it. It's his fault, too. All of this. Besides, he wasn't attacking Sammy. No, not that scrawny little ginger brat. He was attacking all of them, every last one of them with their clean clothes, their smiling faces, their happy families. He was taking away the things that were taken from him. He was stealing their assurance, their optimism, their hope.

Why should they... when he...

He sits up suddenly, his feet on the bare floor, his head in his hands.

I hate them. I hate them all.

If I'd been like them...

If I'd...

If...

'I hate them.' He swears and beats his clenched fist on the thin mattress. He beats it again and again, and tears sprang to his eyes. 'I hate them. If it wasn't for them...'

Above the door, the clock is relentless, advancing second by second. He sees another minute pass.

Sammy and Jason are in Sammy's bedroom. They sit on the bed, facing a screen, guiding race cars round a track. They are silent, and concentrate intensely. Their bodies move with the cars and their fingers jab and dart at the console. Outside, the rain falls heavily, beating at the window, carried on the first winds of a growing storm. Grey sky, grey sea, grey houses. Everything dark and grey.

Sammy drops the console and clambers to his feet. He switches on a light, and stands by the window, his hands on the curtains, ready to close them.

'There are ships out there,' he says. 'Always. Some are so big they hardly notice the storms. They slice through the sea, like it's hot butter. But there are small ones, too. Fishing boats. They'll try to outrun the storm or circle around it.'

'Scary,' Jason says. He drops the console on the floor, and swings his legs onto the bed. 'I wouldn't like to be out in a storm. I'm not a good swimmer.'

Sammy laughs. 'It wouldn't help you. Imagine swimming with thirty-foot waves.'

'I can't even swim in a pool.'

'I'll teach you, if you like.'

'Yeah, that'd be cool,' Jason says, then he remembers he's going home tomorrow, and back to school on Monday. Sammy will be going to school, too. No more plans. Time has run out.

'Friends forever,' he says.

'Yeah.' Sammy turns and nods.

'Blood brothers,' Jason says.

'Only without the blood.'

'Yeah.'

Sammy closes the curtains, and lamplight fills the room. Brightness and shadows. His duvet, blue and grey. His bookshelves, his posters on the wall, his lamp, his dresser, his bathrobe hanging behind the door, his clothes in drawers and cupboards. The rain can beat as hard as it wants. In here he's safe, warm, loved.

He lies on the bed beside Jason, and they both stare at the ceiling.

'Maybe...' Jason says. Then he stops. There can be no more maybes. In a month this house will be empty, and Sammy's bedroom will belong to someone else.

Only the rain will be the same.

Downstairs, Maggie and Janice share a glass of wine.

'Here's to friends, old and new,' Maggie says.

'And to the future, whatever it may hold.' Janice holds her glass to Maggie's.

'Sounds like there's a big storm brewing.' Janice looks towards the window. 'That rain is beating a fair old rhythm out there. It's nice to be in here, all nice and warm.'

'With a glass of wine in front of you.'

Maggie studies the clock on the fireplace: brass inside a glass dome, a pendulum ticking away the seconds.

'What do you think is happening up at Leybury Grange?' she asks, her voice only just audible above the rain and wind.

Janice doesn't answer.

For a moment they are alone with their thoughts.

'Storms pass,' Maggie says at last. 'Then you pick up the pieces, repair the damage, and move on.'

Janice leans forward and takes her wine glass from the table.

'Here's to getting on,' she says.

'And to better weather.'

They clink glasses.

Molly paces the lounge. She walks to the window where she looks out on the gloomy streets, then back to the sofa. She picks up a book, then drops it again, sighs, and picks up the television remote. She switches the TV on, flicks through channels. Bursts of random sounds, incoherent, irritating.

Her mother's exasperated voice.

'For goodness sake, Molly, settle down to something. They'll be alright, I've told you. DI Miller is there.'

'I hate waiting.'

Molly flicks from channel to channel.

'Choose something to watch or put that damned thing down, will you?'

'There's nothing to watch.'

'Then watch nothing. Read a book, draw something.'

'I don't want to. I can't.'

She flops back on the sofa, her arms crossed across her chest, her foot kicking the edge of the rug.

Her mother folds her magazine, and lays it on the chair arm. She slips across to the sofa, and settles beside Molly, her arm curling round her shoulders.

'Everything will be alright, you know. Jocelyn is there, and the police, too.'

'Why couldn't I go? Molly Toodle needs me.'

Her mother strokes her hair, slowly, repetitively, as if the movements alone will calm her.

'But we have to trust Jocelyn now. We have to believe she knows best.'

'But Rupert is a monster. He wanted to kill Molly Toodle. He told her he wanted to kill her.'

Sandra continues to stroke her hair. 'He wasn't born a monster,' she whispers, her mouth close to her daughter's ear. 'He was a little, cuddly baby and a little toddling boy taking his first steps, and falling over.'

'I bet he was a monster baby, and a monster toddler.'

'But that's still what he was.'

'So, why's he a monster now?'

Sandra pulls her daughter close.

'That, Molly, is a very good question.'

Molly pulls away and sits forward. She stares at the clock. 'They'll be there now, in the summer house, waiting, won't they?'

'Yes, it's started.'

They are silent for a moment, listening to the rain as the growing wind rattles and whistles round the windows and doors.

'Where's Dad? Why's he not here?'

Sandra suppresses a look which slips unwillingly across her face. 'He had to go to work this afternoon. He'll be back later.'

'He should be here with us, waiting to hear. What if something happens?'

'He'll come back as soon as he can. Your dad has never been good at waiting. He likes to keep busy. He likes to bury his head in the sand.'

A flicker of bitterness creeps into her voice. A moment passes.

'Are you still cross with Dad?'

'A little, but I'll get over it.'

Another moment of silence as the rain whispers at the window.

'You and Dad won't get divorced, will you?' A nervous voice, quiet, asking a question whose answer it fears.

'Of course not. Whatever made you think that?' Sandra laughs softly, reassuring.

Molly shrugs. 'Someone in my class.'

'Mums and dads sometimes fall out. It happens. Just like you fall out with your friends. It doesn't mean you stop being friends.'

'It does sometimes. Sasha isn't my friend anymore, and I don't want to be her friend, either.'

'Well, that's not going to happen to your dad and me. We've got you to think about.'

'Will Melissa come to live with us again?'

'I hope so. That's what we all want.'

Another silence. Fears rising like bubbles through hot mud.

'What if Rupert says no?'

'DI Miller says he's probably going to prison.'

'But what if he doesn't? What if he makes Melissa stay at the Grange? Just to be horrid to her.'

'Jocelyn and DI Miller will make sure she's safe. Now, let's go up to your room, and look out at the storm. The waves will be crashing over the harbour wall soon. It's nice watching a storm when you're inside in the warm.'

She takes Molly's hand, and leads her up the narrow stairs.

And outside, the wind growls, and the rain falls as if it will never stop.

Chapter 76

Jocelyn steps out into the rain, an umbrella held tightly against the breeze which pulls towards the treetops as if urging her to fly. She turns back to the doorway, and holds out a hand.

'Don't worry, you are quite safe.'

A little girl, shrouded in a pale, red coat with a hood, takes her hand, and steps under the security of the umbrella. Templeton emerges and kneels beside her.

'I'll be here all the time, watching, and DI Miller is with Rupert. You have nothing to be scared of.'

Jocelyn shakes her head. 'Rupert won't hurt her.'

'I hope you're right.'

Jocelyn's eyes fix on his. 'Rupert has been unhappy for a long, long time. It makes him do foolish and evil things. We have a chance now, to help him.'

Melissa turns to Jocelyn, and then to Templeton, her look an echo of her aunt's, her words equal in strength and determination.

'He loved my mummy,' she says.

'He did, and she loved him.'

It is Melissa who takes the first step, as she and Jocelyn bow their heads against the rain and walk across the lawn.

Chapter 77

Rupert looks out of the Trophy Room window, his arms propped against the stone frame, his head hanging down on his chest. There's something about the scene that penetrates you like ice. You shudder. Backlit by a single bulb which hangs on a cord from the ceiling, he stands like a grotesque parody of a crucifixion.

He relaxes, and raises his head to stare through the rain which falls onto the garden, and is carried in waves across the lawns. He stirs, and his eyes focus on something moving towards him, growing gradually clearer, as if emerging from a mist. He shields his eyes from the reflections of the window glass, presses his forehead to the pane, and looks out.

Two figures walk across the lawn, their heads hidden beneath an arching umbrella: one tall, one small. An adult and a child. A woman and a girl. They pause, and look up to see him looking down. Jocelyn draws back her hood so that he can recognise her and then, with words of assurance, slips the red hood of the child's coat back.

You cannot hear it, but you know he gasps, and a strangled cry breaks from his lips. You see him step back, and then back again. He turns and cries out to someone in the room behind. Two men move to the centre of the floodlit stage.

You step forward to stand in the wings, unable to draw your eyes from the scene, compelled to watch.

The final act.

Chapter 78

The main door opens, and a blast of light overflows from within, breaching the dam of darkness. Rupert appears and stumbles forward, oblivious, it seems, to the relentless rain. The audience of trees howl and throw their heads angrily back, and roll and sway.

He staggers over the grass, pauses, and stumbles forward again. Jocelyn bends down to the child beside her and cushions her cheeks in her hand. She says something, and points back towards the summer house. The child nods and flits over the lawns. Templeton emerges from the darkness, and holds out a hand which she takes. They disappear inside.

Jocelyn stands alone, and watches Rupert approach. He slows, then stops some yards short of her. Behind him, thirty metres back, a second figure pauses and waits. Frank.

'The child?' Rupert asks.

Jocelyn, beneath the protective shield of her umbrella, nods. 'Melissa,' you hear her say.

'Then you're dead.' Rupert's voice is tremulous. 'You're both dead.' He looks sharply to his left and waves a dismissive hand. 'Be silent!' he snaps into the darkness. 'Let her speak.'

Jocelyn offers her hand but he does not take it. When she speaks, her voice is soft, emerging like a snowdrop from the earth. 'I'm alive. Melissa is alive. There are acts that even Dominic Sheedy cannot perform. Contemptible as he is, he wouldn't risk his freedom by killing a child.'

Rupert swats a hand against the falling rain, once, twice, and calls towards the house. 'Leave me alone! Why can you never leave me alone?'

Jocelyn proffers her hand again but still he ignores it. He wipes the back of his sleeve against his eyes. 'Too many tears,' he says. 'I cannot wipe them all away. You are dead.'

In the distance, Frank moves a few yards forward, watching, ready to act.

'He buried her,' Rupert cries, 'and just this week I drew her from the earth again. Dominic knows. Ask Dominic.'

'A bag of bones and flesh, a young deer, caught in one of your traps, broken to shape.' Her voice softens. 'You never saw the body. You weren't there that night. Do you remember, Rupert? Only Dominic, he alone.'

Rupert beats his fists at the rain, and screams into the darkness. Then he falls silent and when he speaks, you gasp and draw back. Something crueller by far than the endless rain, and the driving cold, pierces you.

'Look, Maddie.' The voice is the voice of a child, a child freed for an hour from his solitary prison, to stand in a sunlit garden. He holds out his hands. 'I got it for you. It's a buzzard. It was dead in my trap.'

Jocelyn's eyes flow with tears.

'My poor brother,' she cries.

He runs to her, and now he takes her outstretched hands. 'Shall I put it with the others?' he asks. 'I have a space between the fox and the hare. Will you come and see it there?'

'You know I can't.'

He smiles. 'They're my trophies. Do you think Mama and Papa will be pleased with me?'

The tears flow down her cheeks. Even the swollen clouds cannot compete.

Rupert drops his hands slowly. He stands tall. 'Of course not,' he says, his adult voice restored. 'Why would they? Listen to them now, cackling and laughing, just as they always did. But they're trophies too now. I hunted them down, and drowned them in the noxious fumes of their car. How clever I was!'

'And poor Mr Carver?'

'He would have taken you from me.'

'Nobody could do that. I'm here because you are my brother and I want to help you. You know you need help, don't you?'

'It's too late. You're dead. Everyone is dead. Only ghosts and nightmares. A scream which stretches out to the stars.'

Jocelyn's voice is patient but there is an urgency about it which scares you. You want to step forward and step forward again. There is danger everywhere.

'I came back,' she says. 'I didn't have to, because you have no hold over me. Melissa is alive. I didn't harm her. I came back because I want to help you. I want you to give yourself up and get the help and the care that you need, and that you deserve. Because you do *deserve it. No matter what you have done. You were driven to it by the cruelty and abuse of others. You are broken, Rupert, but you can be mended.'*

Frank takes a couple more steps forward, ready. The rain has soaked him to the skin, but he barely feels it. His eyes are fixed on the couple just ten metres away. From the darkness of the summer house, Templeton too steps forward. A tiny, pale face appears in the window behind him. Melissa raises her hand to brush away the mist of condensation, and she watches. Rupert looks around, and gestures hopelessly to the rain.

'It will never stop,' he cries. 'Never, never, never...'

He raises a hand, and in it a pistol.

'Jesus Christ!' You hear Frank's words splinter the darkness, and you see him lurch forward. He throws himself at Rupert, and wrestles him to the ground. A struggle, a gunshot, and then another, and a figure limping over the grass towards the house.

Jocelyn is rooted and cannot move. The umbrella swirls on the ground beside her. Caught in a flurry of wind, it rolls and bounces until it lies trembling beneath an old sycamore. Her eyes are wide, her face white with shock.

Templeton brushes past her.

'Go to Melissa,' he says, and when she doesn't move, he yells at her. 'NOW!' As he leans over Frank, and draws his body back, she turns and stumbles across the grass. In the doorway of the summer house, Melissa stands motionless. Jocelyn sweeps her into her arms, and draws her inside. The door shuts.

'Frank?' Templeton asks. 'Frank?'

Frank opens his eyes, grabs his arm. 'Get after him!' he mutters. 'The Trophy Room.' He drops his hand, and picks something from next to him. 'I have the gun. Now go!'

'Let me get help,' Templeton says.

Frank pushes him away. 'There's no time. You've got to stop him.'

And then he remembers.

'He has a sword up there. An old bayonet. Go now, go quickly. Go!'

He rolls back, and groans.

Templeton sets off at a run. Ahead of him, Rupert reaches the steps of the house and drags himself towards the door. He staggers inside, leaning against the frame before stumbling on.

By the time Templeton reaches the door, the blood from Rupert's wound is spreading with the rainwater, and overflowing the steps. He leaps up the steps, splashing through it. Blood everywhere, like it's going on and on forever, until it fills the earth.

You are compelled to follow, repelled, appalled, but unable to resist. A bloody trail weaves from step to carpeted step. Templeton, gasping now from the exertion, turns at the top, follows a wide corridor, throws back a door and circles on and up towards the tower. Ahead of him, the final flight. You follow him.

You watch Rupert crawl the last few steps, and raise himself at the door. It opens, as if to welcome him. Templeton reaches out a hand, grasps a coat sleeve, only to find it wrenched from his grasp. The door slams shut. The lock is turned.

Templeton beats his fists on the door, shouts, pleads.

To no avail.

There comes a cry, carried on a final breath. You draw your hands to your cheeks, you cover your ears, close your eyes, but nothing can shut out the sound. Nothing will ever shut it out again.

A child's desolate cry reaches out.

'Mama! Papa!'

And there is nothing you can do.

'Lou-Lou! Maddy!'

And then nothing.

Outside, the sky sobs and the trees shake with grief.

Templeton sits on the top step, his hands around his head. In the garden, Frank lies still on the grass. In the summer house, Jocelyn holds Melissa close to her as she fumbles with her phone.

And still the rain falls.

Chapter 79

Dear Janice and Frank,

Excuse the handwriting. I don't write much nowadays, just shopping lists and the like. The folk we know all live within a mile or two so we just call round or pick up the phone. Sammy says I should get a computer and use He-Mail but I've never been much for technology. I leave that to Richard. He can just about manage, what with needing it for work and everything. So here I am, with an old-fashioned piece of paper and a pen.

Do you know how much a first-class stamp is nowadays? I nearly fainted. I said to the man, I told him, *I don't want to buy the post office. I just want to send a letter to my friends. I could send it cheaper by taxi.* He just shrugged. They're not polite in Grantley. There are too many tourists so they don't care about local folk any more.

Anyway, I do hope you are well, and that Jason has settled better at school. I'm glad to say Sammy is doing well. He gets a bit of teasing from the other boys because his two best friends are Molly and Melissa, but he takes it well. He says he just laughs at them and watches while Molly tells them what she'll do if they don't shut up. As for us, I've got some news for you.

Last night, about eight o'clock, the doorbell rang. Well, nobody ever calls that late, so I said to Richard, *What do you make of that? Who could be knocking on our door at this time of night?* He says, *You'll not find out sitting there,* and since he doesn't make a move, I mutter a few things at him about being murdered on my own doorstep, and then go and see.

You'll never guess. Jocelyn Fitzwilliam, large as life, standing there. We haven't seen hide nor hair of her since... well, you know since when. She looked a bit pale and those sad eyes were doing overtime, but she was much the same.

I'm sorry to call so late, she says, with a shy smile that looks like it's hiding something special *Could I come in for a minute?*

Well, you can't say no, can you? So, in she comes and, to cut a long story short, she says she feels responsible for everything that's happened to us, what with Rupert and the boats and the house, and everything. I tell her it's nought to do with her and it was our own silly fault. But she won't listen. She shakes her head. She tells us the courts have finished with her at last, and she's got control of the estate, which means she's in charge of the money and Leybury Grange.

Then she hits us with it. She raises a hand to tell me and Richard not to interrupt, and then she tells us. *I'm not having you driven out of your home and away from your roots because of something my family did. No, she says, I won't have it.* And then, right then and there, while me and Richard look on with our mouths open like a couple of village idiots, she takes out a cheque, and starts to write. Then she tears the cheque out, and hands it to Richard. You'll never guess. More than the house and the boats added together. *There's a bit of compensation, too, she says, for all the trouble we've caused.*

Well, Richard is the first to gather his wits from the corners of the room, where they fled at the first sight of all that money. He says no, of course. We don't want charity, no matter what. We're used to looking out for ourselves. No disrespect, he says, and he thanks her for her kindness, but no.

I'm torn between wanting to kick him, and wanting to kiss him. But he's right. I know he's right, so I do nothing.

Have you got a buyer for the house? She asks.

Not yet, I tell her.

Then I'll buy it, she says. *You can't argue with that. What about the boats?*

Richard explains about Frederick.

Well, she says, *I'm sure he'll be willing to let me buy them when I explain.*

Richard is about to object but she gives him a look that would melt a harder heart than his.

You want to sell, and I want to buy. It's business, she says, and it's a no messing kind of voice.

Richard can't cope with tough women. Never could. He just nods, and I stay quiet.

Right, says Jocelyn, *so the house and the boats are mine, and that means I can do anything I want with them. That's right, isn't it?*

Richard's mouth looks a bit silly, half-open like that, but I don't think I'm any better. We both nod like a couple of those daft toys people have in the backs of their cars. The things that just nod and nod. Silly things, I always think. Why would anyone want one? Nod, nod, nod.

Then I'm giving them to you, she says, just like that, *and before you start saying I can't, you just agreed I could. Besides, if you don't, I'll just give them to Sammy. I'll put them in trust until he's older with the condition you live in them until you pass on.*

She turns, and walks to the door. Then she stops and she looks back, and she has the sweetest smile you could imagine, and the saddest eyes. It's like the sadness goes right down into her soul. *Please, she says, it would make me happy. I'm selling the Grange, and moving away. Not too far. I want to be able to see Melissa occasionally. Just far enough to try to forget. I really need you to do this for me.*

She wipes away a tear that's misted her eyes. It takes all Richard's self-control not to run forward and put his arm round her, soft sod that he is. Then she says, *I know you don't owe me anything,* so softly my heart melts, *but please, do it for me.*

Well, there was no more arguing after that. I had to have words with Richard though, the way he looked at her, like he was her pet puppy. I was waiting for him to roll over to have his tummy tickled. Pathetic!

Men!

So, there you are, a happy ending for the Trevelyans.

I do hope we see you again soon. Do write, if you get the chance, or use that He-Mail thing. I'm sure Frank knows all about that, in his job.

Love to Jason, but no hugs because he's a big boy now, and wouldn't appreciate them.

Sammy says hi. So do Molly and Melissa, and their mum and dad, although I can't rightly say I've taken to them. Nice enough but not really my sort. Not homely, like you and Frank.

Maggie.

Dear Maggie,

How nice to hear from you and what wonderful news you had to tell. I couldn't be more pleased, and nobody deserves a bit of luck more than you and Richard, and especially Sammy. Who'd have thought it? A good Fitzwilliam. They must be as rare as dodo's eggs. Still, it was a very kind thing to do.

Poor girl, she's had her share of suffering. I didn't have much time for Rupert, no matter what he'd been through, but I felt heart-sorry for her, I really did. Frank said he felt sorry for Rupert by the end, but he's just a big soft sod, too, for all he's a Detective Inspector. He said he felt like he'd been walking in Rupert's soul for the last few days. He said it was a sad, cruel place to be, and he was glad to be out of it.

I can't say I'm that forgiving.

Did I say Detective Inspector? Well, that's where I have some news of my own. It's Detective *Chief* Inspector now. He came home, wearing a suit, carrying flowers and a bottle of sparkling wine, grinning like a Cheshire Cat. He's so important I hardly dare talk to him anymore, and Jason's walking about with his chest stuck out like a prize pigeon, he's that proud. The job's here in the city, too, so no moving away for us either. I'm pleased about that, because Jason is doing ever so much better at school. Mr Caine says he'll be football captain if he carries on the good work, so that's a big incentive. And there's been NO MORE FIGHTING! Fingers crossed, I think things are going to work out.

Happy endings all round.

I said Frank was a big, soft sod, didn't I? Well, you'll never guess what he's gone and done? Not in a million years. I couldn't believe it when he told me, and as for Jason, well... I'd better tell you or you'll be wondering what I'm going on about. Wait for it! He's only gone and bought us a brand-new caravan on the site at Leybury.

I didn't know what to think. I mean, you know how expensive those things are! But he says we can afford it, and besides, he says, it'll be good for Jason, and now we can come any time we want. Weekends, holidays, whenever Frank isn't working at any rate. You'd have thought we'd won the lottery when we told Jason. He wanted to tell Sammy straight away but I told him he'd have to wait until I told you about it. He said I should email because it's quicker, but a letter deserves a letter back, I always think, and I can't remember the last time I got one.

Frank says we're so well-off now, he might buy another caravan, just so he can go and hide when I get one of my moods.

Cheek!

I can't wait to see you again, but Frank says it'll be a few weeks before everything's straight. I'll have to be patient. Perhaps we can book a table at The Harbour Inn, and celebrate.

He's better, by the way, and the wound is healing nicely though he'll not be playing rugby for a while, and I doubt he'll try throwing anyone off a harbour wall again. He got a reprimand, an award for gallantry, and a promotion all at once. He said he didn't know if he was coming or going.

A happy ending! Who'd have thought it?

Love,

Janice

SAMMY'S POST

TOP SECRET! TELL NOBODY!

I'm going to marry Molly when I'm older. I thought about marrying Melissa because Dad says she's going to have lots of money, but Melissa is moody sometimes. I think it's everything that happened. Sometimes she's sad, and sometimes she's angry. Mostly she's okay, though.

Maybe you could marry Melissa??

I'm going to buy a boat and call it *The Lovely Molly*. What do you think?

A COMMENT ON SAMMY'S POST

Gross!!

ANOTHER COMMENT ON SAMMY'S POST

Can I be best man??

Don't miss out!

Visit the website below and you can sign up to receive emails whenever Barry Litherland publishes a new book. There's no charge and no obligation.

https://books2read.com/r/B-A-QBLI-ISYMB

BOOKS 2 READ

Connecting independent readers to independent writers.

Also by Barry Litherland

The Hand of Ronan Hawke
Waves Break (on Unknown Shores)
Shifting Sands
Breakers
The Trophy Room

Watch for more at www.bleaknorth.net.

About the Author

Barry Litherland is an author of crime and paranormal crime mystery thrillers. He lives and works in the far North of Scotland where he lives with his wife and two energetic springer spaniels.

Read more at https://www.bleaknorth.net.

Printed in Great Britain
by Amazon

49232485R00178